St. Martin's Paperbacks Titles
By Tamara Sneed

All the Man I Need

You've Got a Hold on Me

The Way
He Makes
Me Feel

TAMARA SNEED

St. Martin's Paperbacks

ISBN: 0-312-98731-5
EAN: 9780312-98731-2

Printed in the United States of America

St. Martin's Paperbacks edition / June 2005

St. Martin's Paperbacks are published by St. Martin's Press, 175 Fifth Avenue, New York, NY 10010.

10 9 8 7 6 5 4 3 2 1

For all those who experienced
the "crush" of unrequited puppy love and survived

Acknowledgments

I would like to thank the creators of the *MacGyver* fan sites on the internet, who have meticulously and lovingly summarized every "MacGyverism" from the television show.

The Way
He Makes
Me Feel

Chapter One

". . . Then she took me to her hotel room and . . . I don't need to draw you boys a picture, do I?" Duncan Hillston finished his story, with a smug grin.

He gulped down the last of his beer, then slammed the bottle on the table just as his friends burst into loud, incredulous laughter. Not exactly the reaction that Duncan was looking for. He pretended not to notice the laughter and scanned the crowded restaurant for any beautiful women. His friends would have to stop laughing once Duncan invited a beautiful woman to their booth. He caught the eye of an ebony-skinned honey standing in the bar area, but she immediately turned her back when she noticed Duncan staring. He quickly shifted his gaze but got similar receptions from two other women. Great.

After it became obvious that Hawk Morrissey and Patrick Morley were going to keep laughing and poking each other in the sides, Duncan turned his attention back to them. He should have been used to it. Hawk and Patrick had been doubting Duncan's conquests since the ninth grade.

"You and Janette Baxter . . . *the* Janette Baxter?" Patrick said, recovering from his attack of laughter before Hawk did from his. "The most beautiful actress in the world? The woman who makes Halle look like a citizen of the Planet Ugly?"

"What can I say?" Duncan replied with a casual shrug. "The Hillston magic extends to all women, regardless of age, religion, or occupation."

"You're lying," Hawk said flatly.

"You're jealous," Duncan shot back.

Hawk snorted in disbelief, then said, "You expect us to believe that you, a mere electrician, picked up the most beautiful black woman in the world in a bar last weekend and that she dragged you back to her hotel room for a marathon sex session?"

"Have I ever been proven wrong before?" Duncan asked, because he knew the answer. Although Hawk never believed anything Duncan said, and Patrick only believed half of what Duncan said, neither man could ever prove that Duncan lied. And Hawk had been trying to prove exactly that since ninth grade.

Hawk abruptly laughed bitterly, then shook his head. "You've told some whoppers in the past, Duncan, but come on . . . Janette Baxter? For once in your life, just tell the truth. You didn't meet her in a bar last weekend? Have you even met her?"

"Hawk," Patrick warned in a quiet voice.

"I'm sick of his lies," Hawk snapped, glaring at Patrick. "Since ninth grade, we've had to listen to this crap. I'm surprised he has time to ever hang out with us, since he apparently spends all his time fighting off women who supposedly throw themselves at him all day long. I need him to admit the truth for once, Patty. I need him to say that he's just like everyone else, and that he has to work just as hard as everyone else."

Duncan smiled coolly and said to Hawk, "This is about Kathryn Wilcott, isn't it?"

"Duncan," Patrick gasped, as if Duncan had questioned the existence of the universe itself.

Even after sixteen years, Duncan could not speak Kathryn Wilcott's name in Hawk's presence without his looking like he was seconds away from strangling Duncan. So, maybe he had slept with Hawk's Venus in high school, but Duncan had been sixteen years old and Kathryn had seduced him. Sort of.

Hawk's dark skin had taken on a strange tint of red as he hissed through clenched teeth, "How dare you bring her up?"

"I heard that the desserts here are excellent," Patrick chimed in nervously. Duncan and Hawk both ignored him.

"If you need verification that I'm not a liar when it comes to my stories about women, you can ask Kathryn. Oh, wait, you did that sixteen years ago and she told you that—"

Hawk's hands on the table clenched into fists as he snarled, "You smug son of a—"

"Stop it," Patrick interrupted, glaring from Duncan to Hawk. "I feel like I'm having dinner with my two nephews."

"If you would just follow my three simple rules, you could have the same success I have," Duncan said, taking pity on Hawk because it had been almost six months since he had gone on a date.

Hawk's eyes narrowed in anger while Patrick asked curiously, "What three rules?"

"Soothe. Entice. Seduce," Duncan said simply. Hawk audibly groaned while Duncan explained to the intrigued Patrick, "First, you have to soothe a woman. Since childhood, their mothers have taught women that men are the enemy, that all we want from them is sex—"

"They're right," Patrick said with a laugh.

"Of course they're right," Duncan agreed. "But your first step in conquering them is to pretend that sex is the furthest thing from your mind. You have to soothe them. Pacify them. Make them think that your only interest is getting to know them."

"This is a load of crap," Hawk snorted.

Duncan ignored him and continued, "This step is the most dangerous because one wrong move and you can fall into the land-mine area known as 'he's just a friend.'" Patrick gasped in horror at the offending *f*-word, and Duncan nodded in sympathy. He didn't have to explain the horrors of being known as a woman's friend to Patrick because that was his specialty.

Patrick's last girlfriend had dumped him on the basis that

she had more fun shopping with him than sleeping with him. Duncan and Hawk had cringed themselves when Patrick relayed the conversation in the same dull tone used by tornado survivors on the evening news.

Duncan added, "That's why, even while in the soothing stage, you have to make certain that the woman always knows that you still find her desirable, that if she says one word, she can have a night of ecstasy."

"How do you do that?" Patrick asked.

"A look. An accidental caress. A borderline inappropriate comment about the short length of her skirt or the amount of cleavage displayed in a blouse. It works every time."

"This is such bullsh—"

Duncan interrupted the fuming Hawk and told Patrick, "Next, you entice. This is where flowers, candlelight dinners, walks on the beach, and all that crap come into play. You want them to think that maybe—just maybe—you're not like the others. And then you come in for the kill—seduction.

"One night where you fulfill her every fantasy. It doesn't have to be sex—although that's the ideal. It could be whatever she thinks is romantic—like taking her horseback riding, in a hot-air balloon . . . something she's dreamed about doing but can't or won't do for herself. If you follow these rules, my friends, you'll have any woman you want. And, most important, she'll do anything you want. I haven't done my taxes in about ten years. I just find an accountant and soothe, entice, seduce until the government is paying me money."

"Prove it," Patrick challenged.

Duncan's confident smile froze on his face as he met Patrick's intense dark gaze. He was the teddy bear of the three, but once he became focused on a goal, he was like a bulldog with a bone.

"Prove what?" Duncan asked blankly.

"Hawk is right. Since we were fourteen years old, you've always bragged about your player status," Patrick said, a trace of bitterness in his voice. "I want you to prove it."

"What do you want me to do, Patty? Videotape my next

sexual encounter?" Duncan asked drily. "I'm not getting arrested for you morons."

Patrick's vanilla cheeks instantly filled with color as he stared at the table, embarrassed, but Hawk grinned and nodded excitedly.

"No, Duncan, this is perfect," Hawk said, laughing maniacally. "You claim that you can get any woman you set your sights on, right? All you have to do is lie, beg, and annoy?"

"It's soothe, entice, and seduce," Duncan said through clenched teeth.

"Whatever," Hawk dismissed, then said, "We pick the girl. I don't care if you use your three idiotic rules or if you hypnotize her, but you have to prove that she's in love with you, that she'll do whatever you want her to do."

"Even when Kellie said that she loved me, she didn't do whatever I said," Patrick said weakly.

Hawk sighed loudly and muttered, "And here I thought we would actually go the whole night without any mention of the *K*-word."

Duncan silently agreed while Patrick looked wounded. "Kellie and I were together for two years."

"Two years too long if you ask me," Hawk retorted.

"It's been six months since she dumped you, Patty," Duncan said gently. "It's time to move on."

"I still love her," Patrick insisted.

Hawk rolled his eyes and groaned in frustration. "Judging from the wedding invitation she sent you last month, she doesn't love you." Patrick cringed as if he had been physically hit. Hawk added, "Besides, you've never claimed to take away a woman's ability to think after one date. You've never claimed that a woman will do anything for you at any time. For Duncan here, making a woman his obedient toy should be an easy feat since he does it all the time. Right, Duncan?"

Duncan knew that Hawk was throwing his own words back at him and inwardly cringed. He had a big mouth and maybe every once in a while, on rare occasions that warranted it, he could admit that he overexaggerated his prowess with women. But so did every other man in the free world.

OK . . . maybe he and Janette Baxter didn't have a wild night of passion last weekend. But he had bought her a drink and they had flirted for an hour before Duncan left to pick up one of his nieces from a Girl Scout meeting. That had to count for something. Duncan had only told the revised version of his Janette Baxter experience because he had wanted to spice up the evening.

Patrick still pined over Kellie, who obviously had moved on, judging by the wedding invitation, and Hawk was too bitter and wrapped up in being a "screenwriter," when he wasn't writing tickets in the city's traffic enforcement department, to ever attract his own woman. That left Duncan to liven things up. He dated a respectable amount and, maybe, he doubled the number now and then, but he did it for them. Duncan had a feeling that neither Patrick nor Hawk would appreciate that explanation.

Hawk eyed Duncan and continued, "If you can do this, I'll take back every bad thing I've said about you and I'll never doubt another one of your lame, over-the-top, unbelievable stories."

Duncan cleared his throat and said uneasily, "Wait a second—"

"How is he supposed to prove it?" Patrick asked curiously, ignoring Duncan's attempt at a protest.

"The Westfield annual block party in two weeks," Hawk said. "He can bring her there."

Duncan tried not to show his rapidly rising panic. Every year, Westfield, their tight-knit community, which was officially considered part of the city of Los Angeles, held a block party. Although no local residents in the area, separated from the borders of Los Angeles by about twenty miles considered themselves Los Angelenos, Los Angeles claimed the small area of about thirty thousand residents because it sat on the harbor and accounted for the starting point of the majority of commercial marine shipping to Los Angeles County. One way the neighborhood showed local pride was the famous annual block party.

It wasn't just a block cordoned off, but basically the entire area became closed to all motor traffic and one could stroll from one street to the next, sample homemade pies, different barbecue recipes, live music, and enough goodwill to cause the event to garner local media attention. Obviously, the media couldn't believe that a blue-collar multiethnic neighborhood in Los Angeles could hold such a peaceful event. But since the creation of Los Angeles, Westfield had managed to retain that small-town feel that baffled all those who had not been born and raised there.

"Two weeks is not enough time . . . not even for Duncan," Patrick said as if he were Duncan's agent negotiating a deal. Duncan watched the two men, momentarily fascinated, even as he wondered how he could stop this speeding train.

"Have confidence, Patty," Hawk said with a careless shrug. "Duncan has enough confidence in himself for all of us."

Duncan ignored the dig and said, with a convincing amount of boredom, "So, you want me to date some woman for two weeks just to prove to you jokers that I'm the player extraordinaire? That's not enough of an incentive for me."

"What would qualify as enough of an incentive?" Patrick asked.

"I don't know," Duncan said with an apathetic shrug.

"How about enough money to pay for that European trip you've been talking about for the last year?" Patrick said with a hint of a knowing smile.

Duncan stared wide-eyed at Patrick. Last year, Duncan had seen an advertisement for a fourteen-day six-city tour of Europe. He had told his friends that the booty a black man could get in Europe would be astronomical. Not to mention the mileage of saying "when I was in Rome" to a woman. And, of course, there was the whole experiencing-European-culture thing. But neither Patrick nor Hawk had jumped at the idea, and Duncan hadn't liked the idea of spending all that money to go by himself and maybe not have fun, so he had given up. Until now.

Duncan asked doubtfully, "And where are you two going to come up with five thousand dollars? Hawk can barely afford to pay his light bill every month."

"The Bachelor Party Fund," Patrick stated simply.

Duncan gaped in disbelief; even Hawk's smile disappeared as he stared at Patrick. The three had started the Bachelor Party Fund after high school. The three contributed separately at least once a year to a joint bank account in order to throw "the bachelor party to end all bachelor parties" for the first "victim" to walk down the aisle. Since none of them had any plans—or possibilities—to get married soon, Duncan had joked that they could relabel it the Retirement Party Fund.

"Wait," Hawk said uneasily. "Are we sure about this?"

"Yes," Patrick said firmly.

Duncan suddenly grinned as he thought of the number of senoritas he could buy drinks for with a wad of money in his pocket. And there were the nice souvenirs he could buy for his nieces and nephews, his mother, and his sisters-in-law. Suddenly the bet didn't seem nearly as stupid as it had seemed a few minutes ago. How hard could it be to get a woman to fall in serious-like with him? He had two weeks to work his magic. He had had women eating out of the palm of his hand after one night . . . or, maybe, he had just told Patrick and Hawk that. He couldn't really remember anymore.

"That happens to be a very good incentive," Duncan said, grinning. "If you boys are serious, I'm more than happy to open the classroom for a little schooling."

Hawk's smug grin scared Duncan a little. He suddenly realized why when Hawk said, "I already have the woman picked out. In fact, she's a Westfield girl, although she hasn't lived in the neighborhood in years. She's standing at the bar right now."

Duncan told himself that he would not give Hawk the satisfaction of a reaction no matter what Creature from the Black Lagoon stood at the bar. But then Duncan turned around. Although he managed to clamp down his own gasp of shock and disgust, Patrick didn't.

Patrick groaned. "At least give him a fighting chance."

Duncan swallowed the sudden lump in his throat as he

stared across the restaurant at Claire Scott. She was now Dr. Claire Scott. Even if he had managed to miss the occasional mention of her in national magazines and newspapers, he couldn't stop his parents from constantly talking about his former high school classmate who made the neighborhood proud with all of her accomplishments.

While Duncan and his friends had been barely able to handle switching classes every period in their first year of high school, eleven-year-old Claire Scott could have taught the classes. Even though three years younger than most of her classmates, she had been at the top of every academic list, the star of the math and science clubs, and the one guaranteed to raise her hand and correctly answer the teacher's question while everyone else was slinking behind their desks to avoid being called on.

Claire's intelligence and age had been more than enough to make her a pariah, but she also had been able to reduce a high school boy to tears with just a few multisyllabic words. She would question his heritage, his manhood, and the most awful part was that the guy wouldn't know it until he got his hands on a dictionary. She was an elementary school brat with a Ph.D. vocabulary, and the boys couldn't fight back. No one respected a man who outwitted an eleven-year-old, but everyone laughed when the eleven-year-old made him look like an idiot.

As a result of their collective wounded pride and their inability to fight back, the boys at Westfield High School had fought back the only way they knew how. Since Claire had usually tied her thick hair in three or four ponytails and had been in the middle of that prepuberty physical weirdness, the boys had christened her Medusa.

Duncan shook his head as he laid his eyes on Medusa for the first time in the fifteen years since high school graduation. It was Friday night in a popular downtown LA bar and Medusa looked like . . . like a normal woman. Gone was the eleven-year-old baby face and pudginess. Her face was more oval, her cheekbones more refined, and her honey brown skin unblemished from her attack of pimples during their junior and senior years. Her thick dark hair was gathered in an impeccable ponytail at the nape of her neck, but she was no Medusa. She looked sophisticated and—Duncan could admit it—a little intimidating. Almost as intimidating as she had been as an eleven-year-old kid.

She had sprouted in various places that Duncan would have never imagined Claire Scott sprouting. She was taller than he remembered, which was not a big surprise, since the last time he had seen her, she had barely reached his chest and had been fifteen years old. Now she probably stood over five-eight. He couldn't tell much about what was going on between her knees and long, graceful neck because most of that area was hidden beneath a dark suit. But, her skirt did stop at her knees, and Duncan was not disappointed by the miles of shapely leg he saw.

Of course, she wasn't smiling. Medusa didn't smile, except when she was laughing at the remains of her latest victim.

"Medusa," Patrick gasped, with a sorrowful glance in Duncan's direction. "I didn't know it would be that hard, man."

"Two weeks," Hawk reminded Duncan, glee dancing in his eyes. "Are you up to the challenge, or are you ready to admit right now that you're just as clueless as Patrick when it comes to women?"

"Hey," Patrick protested.

Hawk laughed, and even Duncan cracked a smile.

"Wait, wait, wait," Patrick said, suddenly awed. "Who is the woman standing next to Medusa?"

"A woman like that would not be friends with Medusa," Hawk said after he and Duncan both looked in the direction that Patrick indicated.

The woman was a dark chocolate beauty with long black hair and the boom-boom shape that caused a grown man to reconsider his priorities in life. In the gold sparkling minidress with a neckline that stopped somewhere around her belly button and a hemline that stopped somewhere just below the treasure chest, she made Claire look more like a nun than the most feared woman of Westfield High.

"Coworkers?" Duncan suggested, focusing on the serious eye candy standing next to Claire.

"My mom goes to church with Medusa's father. He told Mom that Medusa does research work at some big pharmaceutical research firm," Patrick said. "I've never seen a researcher look like that."

"Whoever she is doesn't matter. She's not a part of the bet," Hawk said, facing Duncan. The fact that Hawk would willingly turn his back on a woman like that told Duncan how serious Hawk was about this. "You have two weeks to train Medusa, Duncan. Get her to the block party and have her convince Patrick and me that she's head over heels for you, and you'll get that European vacation. Do we have a deal?"

"What if he loses?" Patrick asked.

Hawk's smile grew wider as he said, "If Duncan loses, at the block party he has to admit that half of his stories are exaggerations and the other half are outright lies. In front of all the guys who have suffered through his tales over the past three decades. I don't need anything but that."

"Maybe we shouldn't do this," Patrick said hesitantly. "Isn't it a little cruel?"

"Claire won't get hurt," Hawk said with a dismissive shrug. "She'll get a few nice dinners—if Duncan can convince her to go to dinner—and some stories to tell her other nerd friends when they're standing around the lab sniffing chemicals. This will probably be the most exciting thing to happen to her since she won the high school science fair."

Patrick glared at Hawk and muttered, "You're a real bastard sometimes, Hawk."

"It's called being a man," Hawk shot back. "You should get your balls back from Kellie and maybe you'll remember what it feels like."

Duncan stood before Patrick could retort. He had had enough. Claire Scott would be a tough sale, but she was still a woman and Duncan had no doubt that she could not resist his patented standard operating procedure. Soothe. Entice. Seduce. If it worked on other women, it would work on Claire.

He straightened the lapels of his suit jacket and said confidently, "Watch and learn, boys."

Chapter Two

Claire Scott signaled the bartender for another drink, then forced herself to focus on Annabelle Richards—or Belle, as Annabelle insisted on calling herself now. She hadn't stopped talking since the two women had met at the bar an hour ago. Annabelle and Claire had been best friends through the hell that other people called high school, even though they had been as different as night and day.

Claire had been eleven years old—scared, bratty, and arrogant. Annabelle had been the same age as everyone else but had worn all-black clothes and heavy black eyeliner—the only "goth" kid in a high school that had considered Prince too alternative—and couldn't be bothered to attend classes. Claire wouldn't have survived high school without Annabelle. The first month of her high school career, Claire had eaten in the bathroom stall, scared to face her "peers." Then one day, Annabelle had thrown open the stall door and just motioned for Claire to follow her. She had led Claire to a corner of the quad where other kids like them—the outcasts—congregated during lunch. From that day on, Claire had begun to feel like a true member of Westfield High School.

After high school graduation, the two women had lost touch. Claire had heard through the grapevine that Annabelle had moved to Paris and become a model or an actress. Claire had thought she would never see Annabelle again until Annabelle called her, out of the blue, two days ago.

". . . Isn't that the funniest thing you've ever heard?" Annabelle finished another long-winded story.

Claire forced a smile and murmured noncommittally. Annabelle definitely had changed since high school. She had lost the all-black clothes and the extra seventy-five pounds that Claire had always suspected was the reason for the all-black clothes. Gone was the bird's-nest hair that Annabelle said she refused to attempt to tame based on principle, although Claire had suspected it was based more on laziness.

Annabelle now looked like the model or actress that she was. Long, shapely legs and large cantaloupe breasts were showcased in all their glory by the dangerous-looking dress. Her brown hair with blond highlights streamed to her shoulders in smooth waves that hinted at some enhancement, along with other parts of her protruding body.

Next to Annabelle, Claire felt . . . frumpy. Even though she tested in the ninety-ninth percentile of every major intelligence test and could have thought of a more appropriate word, she could only think of one word—*frumpy*. Maybe *professional* was a better word. Whatever the word, this feeling was the exact reason Claire rarely went to bars. One didn't care about frumpiness in a lab, which was why the lab made more sense to Claire, not places where she felt like a piece of meat hanging from a hook for a man to examine and test.

"So, Claire, tell me about you," Annabelle said, actually showing interest in something other than herself for the first time in an hour. "You did everything you said that you were going to do. You went to Harvard and then to MIT. You got your Ph.D. You're working at a lab, attempting to find the cure to cancer. Tell me all about it. College, the lab, everything."

"I went—"

"Oh, I almost forgot!" Annabelle exclaimed, interrupting Claire. "There is a fabulous party at Club Sunset next week and you have to come with me. It is *the* hottest place in the city, rich men falling off the trees. I'm trying to get back to Europe without buying a ticket, and—trust me—after one night in Club Sunset, I'll have several offers. Maybe we can even find you a man, too."

"Maybe," Claire said noncommittally. She dug her fingernails into the palms of her hands to resist from commenting on Annabelle's tone, as if finding Claire a man was a task only suitable for Hercules.

"How long has it been for you, Claire?" Annabelle asked with a look of pity.

"How long has it been since what?" Claire asked blankly.

Annabelle shook her head with a sympathetic sigh. "You can't even remember it, can you?"

"What are you talking about?"

"Sex, Claire," Annabelle said loudly enough to cause several people near them to stare in amusement. "*S-e-x*. You do remember it, don't you?"

Claire glared at Annabelle, even as embarrassment heated her face to the near-boiling point. She said sharply, "I have other things on my mind, like trying to find a cure to a life-threatening disease . . . you know, unimportant things like that."

"Of course," Annabelle said, nodding, but her eyes told another story. She thought Claire was insane.

Claire wanted to laugh out loud in disbelief. Maybe she didn't "have a man," but she considered it a blessing that she didn't have to deal with the insecurities of the male sex. Claire was smarter than most of the world's population, and she had discovered in high school that most men could not handle that. It didn't particularly bother Claire. When she needed a husband for childbearing purposes, she would conduct systematic research that would yield a suitable mate. Until then, Claire would focus on her work.

"I think Club Sunset will be perfect for you," Annabelle said, completely oblivious to Claire's growing irritation. "The competition is fierce in a place like that, but some of the men there will appreciate a woman like you. Really smart women. . . . It could be a fetish, like breast men. We get you the right dress and makeup, and you could get lucky."

Claire stared at Annabelle in disbelief, then finally laughed. It was either laugh or strangle her. Claire was a world-renowned scientist, and Annabelle's only concern was her love life.

Annabelle's eyes widened as she looked over Claire's left shoulder. She gasped, then said, "Don't look now, Claire, but I think the most perfect specimen of manhood that I've ever seen is coming over here to talk to me."

"Where—"

"Don't look," Annabelle shrilly ordered, then began smoothing her tresses. "How do I look?"

"Great," Claire said automatically as she scanned the bar for "the most perfect specimen of manhood." She didn't see such a creature and turned back to the replenished drink that the bartender had placed in front of her. Claire had a feeling that she would need all of the drink if she had to endure one more awkward conversation between Belle and an admirer. There had already been two such conversations since they had sat at the bar. Annabelle had happily flirted with the guy who had flashed a Rolex, and had attempted to pawn off the Timex man on Claire.

Annabelle abruptly clutched Claire's arm, causing her to gasp in protest as her drink sloshed onto her jacket.

"Claire, I think that's . . . It can't be. . . . I think it is. That's Duncan Hillston," Annabelle gasped, and actually sounded like the girl Claire had known. "Didn't you have a huge crush on him in high school?"

Claire bristled even as she resisted the urge to frantically search the bar. She had not had much in common with the other girls in high school except their unanimous crush on Duncan Hillston. Although Claire actually thought that she was in love with him, while most of the other girls just thought he was fine.

By high school graduation, Duncan had stood well over six feet, and had begun to develop an impressive physique that included long legs, broad shoulders, and arms that rippled with muscles. And then there had been his mouth. It had been wide and sinful, plush lips and even, white teeth.

The whole package had been topped with dark brown bedroom eyes, a regal nose, and a perfectly round head that he had kept almost bald. Over the years, Duncan Hillston had become the man Claire had compared every other man to, even though she logically knew it wasn't fair, since no flesh-and-blood man could compete with a fantasy.

Since Claire's family still lived in Westfield and she often was in the neighborhood, she had thought she would run into Duncan, but in the five years since Claire had returned from MIT, she had never seen him.

"I did not have a crush on Duncan Hillston," Claire whispered to Annabelle, then clutched the edge of the bar so she wouldn't bolt from the stool. She couldn't be certain if she would try to find Duncan or run from him. It wasn't every day that a woman had the chance to come face-to-face with her fantasy man. What if she spoke to him and he was a disappointment? Claire had never spoken to Duncan in high school, and that had been part of his allure. He had been unattainable. Perfect.

"Yes, you did," Annabelle insisted, laughing. "You followed him around like a puppy. When he joined the football team sophomore year, you watched practice every day from the bleachers. And, at lunchtime, you made me sit near him and his brain-dead friends in the cafeteria—"

"I did not," Claire hissed, then froze when she suddenly found herself staring at Duncan Hillston.

He stood a few feet from her, casually leaning against the bar, oblivious to their presence. Claire gulped. Everything about him as a high school boy had been amplified and expanded and changed to almond brown chocolate Technicolor. He lived up to her fantasy billing. If anything, he surpassed it. He had grown several more inches, become broader and more defined. His face had lost the boyish innocence to blossom into full-fledged manhood, chiseled perfection. Claire felt something that she hadn't felt in a long time—nerves.

As if Duncan felt someone staring at him, he turned until his gaze locked with hers. For a few seconds their eyes held; then he nodded slightly in greeting. Claire gasped and instantly averted her gaze. Her palms were damp and her stomach rumbled like an approaching storm. She felt like she was back in high school—trapped like the proverbial deer in headlights.

Annabelle's voice dropped to a low whisper as she asked, "Since you didn't like him in high school, you won't mind if I take him back to the hotel tonight, will you?"

Claire's voice was several octaves higher than normal as she replied, "He's all yours."

Annabelle shook out her mane and turned to Duncan with a 60-watt smile, just as he glanced in their direction again. Duncan, however, wasn't staring at Annabelle. He was the only man that night who looked straight past her impressive cleavage to notice that Claire was there. Her heart thumped against her chest like a ticking bomb when she saw recognition and something else flitter across his dark gaze.

Duncan smiled at her and Claire once more looked somewhere—anywhere—else. She was a world-famous scientist, and she couldn't have remembered her name at that moment if her life depended on it. She glanced back at him and nearly lost her balance on the stool when he walked around the couple separating him from her and Annabelle.

He stepped around Annabelle, whose expectant smile froze in place, and stopped in front of Claire.

"Claire Scott." His voice was caramel smooth, deeper and richer than in high school. Her entire body shivered in one single mass of highly charged energy. "I thought it was you. I haven't seen you since high school. How are you?"

She stared at him, unable to speak. She had three advanced degrees, operated her own lab, and was in charge of a project that could potentially save millions of lives and make the lab billions of dollars, but she couldn't think of one word to say to this man.

Duncan took her confused silence for lack of recognition and said with a smile, "I'm Duncan Hillston. We went to Westfield High together."

Her ears burned as she managed, "Hi."

Annabelle loudly cleared her throat and leaned between the two, her cleavage framed by her two arms resting on the empty stool in front of Duncan. She said in a husky voice, "I definitely remember you, Duncan, but I bet you don't remember me. I hope you don't remember me or I might be insulted."

Duncan studied Annabelle, then shrugged and said politely, "I'm sorry. You're going to have to give me a hint."

"Annabelle Richards, but everyone calls me Belle now. That means 'beautiful' in French," she cooed as she held out a hand, with the expectation of a kiss.

Duncan shook her hand instead, and Claire tried hard not to smile but didn't succeed.

"Annabelle Richards," he repeated, as if mulling the name over in his mind. He abruptly smiled as he glanced at Claire for confirmation. "You and Claire were friends, right?"

"Best friends," Annabelle said with a throaty laugh. "I'm a model now. Paris, Milan, New York . . . I've been all over the world at least twice. Tyra Banks is one of my best friends."

Duncan murmured noncommittally at Annabelle, then turned to Claire. He just looked at her, and Claire could feel her hands trembling. She didn't think this physical reaction was normal. He was just a man. She worked around men all day long at the lab, but her face didn't heat up and her breasts didn't throb from the men in the lab looking at her.

"Claire Scott. I can't believe it," he murmured, then smiled and asked, "What do you do now—doctor, professor . . . astronaut?"

"I work at BioTech Laboratories," Claire responded while Annabelle giggled too loudly at his joke.

Duncan said with a questioning shrug, "BioTech?"

"BioTech is the top pharmaceutical research firm in the world. I run my own lab, where we're developing a form of gene therapy that will cure ovarian cancer. I also am a frequent guest lecturer at universities and other institutions around the world. I've written two books and I've published numerous articles on various subjects." Claire squared her shoulders even as, *Good going, Scott,* sarcastically blared through her head. She had just given Duncan Hillston her résumé.

Annabelle said, amused, "Modesty has never been one of Claire's weaknesses."

Duncan didn't take his eyes off Claire as he murmured, "She obviously has nothing to be modest about."

Claire gulped down the ball of nerves blocking her throat and finished her drink. Was he just flirting with her? It hadn't been what he had said but the tone he had said it with. Claire mentally shook her head. She was overanalyzing the situation, creating false positives, the absolute one thing no good scientist ever did.

Annabelle asked brightly, "What do you do now, Duncan?"

"I'm an electrician. I own a construction business with my brothers. Our office is in Westfield at McCormick's old travel agency."

"You still live in Westfield?" Annabelle squeaked in horror.

Claire glared at Her Royal Rudeness, but Duncan smiled and said, "I can't seem to escape."

"Whatever happened to your friends?" Annabelle continued. Claire had a feeling that if Annabelle could have stepped in front of her to make Duncan exclusively concentrate on her and her dark brown breasts without seeming too obvious, she would have. "There were three of you. You never went anywhere without each other. You, Hawk Morrissey, and . . . I can't remember the other one."

"Patrick Morley. We keep in touch. In fact, they're sitting in that booth right over there," Duncan said, waving to a table across the restaurant. The two men instantly turned toward each other, apparently pretending that they hadn't been watching them.

Duncan shook his head as he laughed. "They obviously don't recognize you two from high school and are trying to pretend that they're not watching me fly solo."

"Fly solo?" Claire repeated, confused.

He looked at her, and something twinkled in his eyes that made that warm feeling in her stomach spread farther south.

He smiled—almost bashfully—as he said to Claire, "I was coming over here to talk to you. I didn't realize that we knew each other until I got closer. But, at least, high school gave me an opening line."

For a woman with a world-class intellect, it took her several moments to understand what he meant.

She asked, "You came over here to talk to me?" When he nodded, she asked, perplexed, "Why?"

"Why not?" he shot back instantly.

He wasn't supposed to answer that way. He wasn't supposed to force her to point out the obvious differences between them—like the fact that a man like him wasn't supposed to be interested in a woman like her. He was supposed to act offended that she wasn't playing into his strange flirting ritual. A ritual that Claire had never mastered.

"We could meet for coffee tomorrow and I could try out the other opening line I was thinking of using on you," he suggested with a grin. "I think it went something like 'come here often?' "

Claire frowned at him as she realized that he was flirting with her. "Coffee?" she repeated.

"Yeah, coffee. It's a liquid. You should try it; it's a new craze."

"I know what coffee is. At MIT, I was on the team that invented a chemical to keep coffee beans fresher during shipping," she said defensively.

"Really?" he asked, leaning closer to her, suddenly making her feel like she was the only woman in the bar. In the whole damn world. "How does it work?"

"Don't ask her that, Duncan. She may actually tell us," Annabelle instantly chimed in, ruining Claire's feeling.

"You can tell me later," Duncan said to Claire. "Like over coffee on Monday?"

For the first time in a long while Claire felt uncertain, and she didn't like that feeling. In fact, it was dangerous in her line of work. She needed to get away from this bar as far as possible, regain her equilibrium. The gene therapy that she and her team were developing was only two weeks away from preclinical trials. Now was not the time for her to be distracted by hopeless dreams of Duncan Hillston.

"I don't think that's a good idea," she told him, not truly certain how to turn down a date, since she had never done it before.

He looked momentarily surprised before he asked hesitantly, "Why not? Are you involved with someone?"

"Of course not," Annabelle said before Claire could answer.

Claire glared at her, and Annabelle shrugged innocently. Claire turned back to Duncan, who looked relieved now that her dating status was clear. Another surreal moment. No man had ever asked her or acted relieved that she was single.

"I'm just really busy at work," she said, desperately clinging to her excuse for refusing all social engagements.

"They don't let you out for coffee?" he asked with mock disbelief. "You need to report that to the union."

"Yes, but I . . . I don't think it's a good idea," she repeated lamely. She ignored his confused expression and pulled several dollar bills from her purse and placed them on the bar near her drink. She turned to Annabelle, who looked just as surprised as Duncan. "I really should leave. I have to be in the lab early tomorrow morning."

"You're leaving?" Annabelle asked, surprised. "Tomorrow is Saturday."

"Cancer research is a twenty-four-hour, seven-days-a-week occupation," Claire informed her. She impulsively hugged Annabelle, who felt even skinnier than she looked. Claire glanced briefly at Duncan, who continued to watch her, with a half smile that made her feel uncomfortable, as if he had known about her high school fantasies that made her blush even as a twenty-nine-year-old woman. She said politely, "It was nice seeing you again, Duncan."

"I'll walk you out," he said.

"That's not necessary—"

"Of course it is," he said, then waited expectantly as she grabbed her purse and heavy briefcase that contained her laptop, which she hadn't wanted to leave in the car. Duncan smiled at Annabelle, who looked annoyed. "Annabelle, it was nice to see you again."

"You, too," Annabelle said dully, her gaze already sweeping the bar for someone more interesting.

Claire ran through her options for a moment, then decided she had no recourse but to walk out of the bar. Maybe Duncan would get the hint that she didn't want him around and leave her alone. Except she wasn't fooling anyone. Claire did want him around. She wasn't done drooling over him.

The two stepped out of the staid atmosphere into the clean, crisp night. The skyscrapers glowed a few blocks away, but the streets were quiet and deserted. It was much later than Claire had intended to leave the bar. She had parked a few blocks away, refusing to pay the exorbitant garage fees, having planned to leave with the late office workers, but there was no one on the street now. Claire knew the statistics about violent crimes in the LA area, and she was suddenly glad for Duncan's presence.

Duncan broke the silence between them, asking casually, "I'm curious. . . . Why isn't it a good idea for you to date me?"

She sighed heavily. She didn't want to have this conversation with him. Claire logically knew that the difference between her intellect and that of an average man would mean that a relationship would never work, but she had never had to tell an average man that—mainly because no average man had ever asked her out.

She said haltingly, "You're very attractive, Duncan, and I'm sure you're very kind, but . . . Because I'm smart and you're . . ." Her voice trailed off as she tried to think of a nice way to explain it.

"And I'm not so smart," Duncan supplied helpfully, seeming unoffended.

Claire smiled in relief, grateful that she didn't have to be the one to point out the obvious.

"Smart women can only date smart men. Any other man is a waste of time because competition or insecurity inevitably arises and ruins the relationship."

He rubbed his jaw, as if deep in thought. Finally, he said, with total seriousness, "And I'm assuming you have scientific data to back this up?"

"Don't be ridiculous," she said, frowning.

"Then you must have dated a random sampling of this city's heterosexual male population to come to this preliminary conclusion?" he asked, just as serious.

Claire's frown grew deeper. She hadn't dated anyone in Los Angeles. The last man she had dated seriously had been a fellow student at MIT. That relationship had ended disastrously after she won a coveted teaching assistant position with the top faculty member in the chemistry department and Gilbert had not. That had been over five years ago. Besides a few blind dates, who had run—not walked—at her first mention of microscopes, Claire hadn't had much success or experience in the LA dating scene.

Duncan abruptly laughed and said, "I watch a lot of *CSI.*" When she continued to stare at him blankly, he smiled and said, "Look, Claire, I just want to buy you a cup of coffee, not challenge you to a game of *Jeopardy.*"

Claire shook her head in regret and felt compelled to remind him, "I'm not just smart, Duncan; I'm *really* smart."

"I know. You're really smart and very humble about it."

She allowed herself a small smile at his amused sarcasm, then said, "Trust me, I'm saving us a lot of grief and time. It won't work, so there's no use trying. We'll go on a date, I'll mention something about a proton or hydrogen bond over dinner, and your eyes will glaze over and you'll start staring at the waitress's behind. By the time dessert rolls around, you'll be drooling in your tiramisu, and I'll be annoyed that I'm wasting the evening with you when I should have been in the lab."

Instead of becoming offended, he said with a regretful sigh, "You're wrong about one thing, Claire. I would never order tiramisu. I hate tiramisu." She actually found herself relaxing. Now her body just felt like it was on simmer, instead of boiling. He said, "How about this? No expectations. No promises. And no restaurants that employ waitresses with nice asses. Just two friends grabbing a cup of coffee one night in the not-too-distant future?"

She laughed, then narrowed her eyes and asked doubtfully, "Friends?"

"I'm sure I don't have to tell you what *friends* means. You probably wrote the definition for Webster's dictionary."

Claire's surprised laughter was interrupted when someone bumped into her from behind. She was on the verge of looking over her shoulder to see who the offender was, but then she felt something hard and metal digging into her back.

"I have a gun. If you scream, I will kill you both," a man's harsh voice said from behind Claire.

Claire almost screamed when she saw Duncan's gaze move over her head to the man behind her. A flash of panic flew into Duncan's eyes before they went completely blank. Claire just barely managed to clamp down on her fear.

"Do not scream, and do not turn around. Just remain calm," the man said.

Duncan nodded at Claire in some attempt at reassurance as she frantically glanced up and down the deserted sidewalk.

"We don't want any trouble, man," Duncan said calmly.

"Then shut up. Give me your wallet, and have your girlfriend hand over her briefcase," he ordered gruffly.

For the first time, Claire caught the trace of an accent in his voice that she couldn't quite identify. It was a strange thing for her brain to focus on, but she needed something, besides the fear that completely paralyzed her. Even if she wanted to, she couldn't have moved at that moment.

Duncan sounded as if he were sitting in front of his television, watching one of his favorite programs, as he said, "No problem." He held Claire's gaze as he murmured reassuringly, "We're OK, right, sweetheart?"

Duncan waited for her short nod in response, then reached into his suit jacket pocket and held up his wallet over Claire's head. The man snatched it from Duncan, then dug the gun deeper into Claire's back, causing her to gasp in pain.

Duncan's expression hardened as he protested, "Hey, give her a break. She's scared."

"Give me your briefcase," the man demanded.

Claire's stomach lurched as she subconsciously tightened her grip on the strap of her briefcase. A different fear grew in her belly. She said weakly, "I can't. . . . My laptop—"

"Claire, give the man the briefcase," Duncan said, no longer looking calm and in control.

"My work," she whispered, knowing it was stupid but still clutching her briefcase.

She had months' worth of research and notes on the laptop—information that her team would need for the pre-clinical trials, data for the next article she was writing for a prestigious science quarterly. She cursed herself for not listening to her best friend and lab partner, Vino Ricardo, who had warned her for months to take the information off her laptop hard drive. Claire would rather deal with the gunman than listen to Vino's smug I-told-you-so.

"Your work . . ." the man said, sounding suspiciously frustrated. "Do you realize that I am pointing a loaded gun at you?"

"I can't," Claire cried, picturing herself like every other great scientist who risked his life for his work. Just like Aristotle. Of course, Aristotle probably would have taken the information off his laptop hard drive.

"Claire," Duncan warned.

"I have credit cards and eighty dollars cash in my purse," she blurted out. "You can have it all. I'll wait a full day to call the credit card companies. You could buy anything you want with no trouble. But I can't give you my—"

The man's flat tone sent a chill down her spine as he asked, "Do you really want to die over a stupid laptop?"

"No one has to get hurt here," Duncan said anxiously.

"Shut up with the *Cops* talk," the man snapped.

"I just can't—" Claire's protest ended in a scream as Duncan suddenly pushed her aside and launched himself at the man. The gun flew into the street as the two men tumbled to the ground, accompanied by grunts and the sound of flesh meeting flesh. Claire got her first look at the assailant and realized, with a sinking heart, that he was tall and big—much taller and bigger than Duncan—and wore a dark ski mask.

Claire thought about joining the fray and helping Duncan, but when she saw the flying fists and legs, she reached into her purse and fumbled for her cell phone. Her hand shook as she punched 911. The gunman swung a fist at Duncan, but he ducked. He didn't duck the next fist in time and Claire cringed as it plowed into his face.

Claire vaguely heard a voice answer the emergency assistance line.

"We're being mugged on Figueroa and Seventh . . . ," Claire croaked, then watched in horror as the gunman landed several power-packed punches in Duncan's midsection.

If Claire continued giving directions, she would have to face the gunman on her own, because Duncan would be unconscious. He already looked unsteady on his feet. She dropped the phone and swung her heavy briefcase at the gunman's head. There was a resounding crack, which she identified as the precious laptop that she had been trying to protect, as the bag crashed into the gunman's head. He dropped to one knee, rubbing his head and cursing.

She took several steps back and prepared to release a scream worthy of a vixen in a King Kong movie, but then Duncan launched himself at the man again. At least Claire had given Duncan recovery time, and she heard the welcoming song of police sirens around the corner.

With a move worthy of The Rock, the man lifted a struggling Duncan by his arms and threw him onto the hood of a nearby parked car, which set off the alarm. The gunman glanced at Claire for one heart-stopping moment, then sprinted down the street just as a police car rounded the corner.

Duncan fell off the parked car and rolled onto the ground on all fours, coughing and wheezing in pain. Claire ran to his side.

"Are you all right?" she asked, panicked.

"I just got the crap beat out of me by King Kong. No, I'm not all right," Duncan said in between strangled gasps. Claire couldn't believe it, but she actually laughed. And, most surprising of all, Duncan laughed, too, before he winced in pain and grabbed his side.

Chapter Three

"When you think about it, the mugging actually helped me. It gave us a connection. Don't you agree?"

Duncan looked back at Patrick for an answer as the two men ran around the Pan Pacific Park trail on Sunday morning. Or Duncan ran while Patrick half-limped and half-stumbled after him on the trail that wound around a few miles of prime real estate in the center of Los Angeles.

Patrick lived in the luxury apartments across the street from the park. From his apartment window Duncan had noted the number of women in brightly colored and very tight running outfits who tackled the trail, so he had moved his runs from a community college near Westfield to the park. He had already raked up two dates from the trail.

Patrick managed to say in between heavy gasps of air, "Only you would twist being held at gunpoint into an aphrodisiac."

Duncan ignored Patrick's sarcasm and said smugly, "What better way to soothe a woman than to save her life? I'm thinking about taking her to La Bella Cucina on our first date. No woman can resist that place."

Patrick grunted in frustration—or fatigue—and asked, surprised, "She actually agreed to go out with you?"

"Not yet, but that's just a mere technicality," Duncan said with a casual shrug.

"Well, once you take her to an expensive place like La

Bella Cucina, won't she suspect that you want more than friendship?"

"Probably, but by then I'll be on step two—entice—and she won't care," Duncan responded.

"I still cannot believe that you're seriously going through with this," Patrick muttered.

Duncan wiped the dripping sweat from his face with the back of his hand, careful to avoid the painful bruise on his chin. His body still protested in pain from the old-fashioned butt whipping he had received on Friday night. He had even canceled a date on Saturday because he couldn't picture getting out of bed, let alone trying to explain his bruises. But every ache was just a reminder that step one—soothe—had been accomplished and Duncan was that much closer to his dream vacation. Claire felt safe around him. Although Duncan wasn't certain if he felt safe around her if she made it a regular habit to argue with muggers.

"Are you listening to me?" Patrick demanded in between his deep gasps for air.

"I've been listening to you for the last four miles," Duncan muttered.

"You've been staring at women for the last four miles," Patrick shot back. "How you can run, listen to me, and still manage to flirt with every woman you see is truly a miracle."

Duncan laughed and felt a small surge of sympathy for Patrick and his flushed face. He had always been overweight, but Duncan had thought it gave Patrick an advantage with the opposite sex because they instantly felt comfortable around him. And as far as Duncan was concerned, getting past a woman's first instinctual mistrust was a man's hardest job. But after Kellie had dumped Patrick, he had demanded that Duncan help him lose the extra seventy-five pounds. Patrick didn't want women's trust; he wanted their unadulterated lust.

The two men reached their agreed-upon finish line. Duncan stepped off the path onto the grass to stretch out his legs and arms while Patrick fell onto the grass with a sigh of exhaustion.

"Water," he gasped.

Duncan laughed and tossed Patrick one of the water bottles that he had been carrying during the run.

Patrick took several long gulps of water, then seemed better able to speak. "Duncan, you know this isn't right."

"What?" Duncan asked blankly.

"Claire. This bet. It's wrong."

"Friday night you were all for the bet, remember? It was your idea."

Patrick looked momentarily uncomfortable as he said, "I never thought that I'd know the woman. I thought she'd be . . . That's no excuse. I don't know why I encouraged you and Hawk. I guess that I was just feeling down on myself, down on you. Everything seems so easy for you."

"I've had my share of rejections, too," Duncan said truthfully. Patrick stared at him, surprised, and Duncan quickly added, "Not that many, but enough where I can sympathize with you."

Patrick grimaced, then said, "I still think of Claire Scott as that eleven-year-old kid in biology class."

"Claire is definitely not an eleven-year-old kid anymore," Duncan said, and for a moment thought about her long honey brown legs that had haunted him all day yesterday. He shut down that uncomfortable thought and said to Patrick, "And, if it helps, I think she's going to be a bigger challenge than I had anticipated."

"So, she really is as smart as she tells everyone she is."

"Very funny," Duncan said drily as Patrick sent him a teasing smile. "She claims that it won't work between us because she's this world-class genius and I've just mastered the concept of walking upright."

"She always was confident," Patrick muttered, then laughed and poked Duncan's arm as he said, "Actually, maybe you two are perfect for each other."

Duncan ignored his sarcasm and said, "She's suspicious of me. Suspicion is always hard to overcome in the soothe stage."

"I wonder why," Patrick said with fake surprise. "Even

she knows it's weird that you risked your life to save her laptop."

"Was I supposed to just leave her to fend for herself?" Duncan grumbled, annoyed for some reason.

"No, but you should have taken the laptop from her and given it to the mugger. She could have gotten you both killed."

Duncan glared at Patrick. "Her life's work was on that laptop."

Duncan didn't like the bewildered expression that crossed Patrick's face. In fact, Duncan was bewildered by his own ardent defense of Claire. But there had been something in her pleading tone, in the way she had looked at him as if he were her personal bodyguard and he could make everything right, that had made him act uncharacteristically . . . unselfish.

Duncan quickly clamped down that thought as well and said, "Besides, that little stunt won me major points. If a woman won't fall in love with you after you risk your life for her, then she won't ever fall in love with you."

Duncan continued his routine series of stretches while Patrick continued to sprawl on the grass.

A few moments of companionable silence passed before Patrick whispered, "I drove by Kellie's apartment last night."

"Patty," Duncan sighed, disappointed.

"She's really getting married," Patrick said in an even softer voice that made Duncan stop in midstretch and stare at his friend. Patrick looked ravaged. There was no other word for the wounded look on his face. A part of Duncan wanted to slowly creep away and leave Patrick to his private misery. Guys didn't talk about these things. If a woman had dumped Duncan, his automatic response would be to find another woman. But no woman had ever dumped Duncan because he never stuck around long enough to be dumped. It was easier that way.

"It wasn't meant to be, Patty," Duncan said with an awkward, too-hard pat on Patrick's arm. "You have to move on."

"I'm just not like you, Duncan," Patrick said, looking on

the verge of tears. Duncan quickly scanned the area to make certain that no one was witnessing this. "You make fun of your brothers for having the wives, the kids, and the mini-vans. To you, that's a fate worse than death. But I want all of that."

"No, you don't," Duncan sputtered in disbelief. "Trust me. Spend a day with one of my brothers and their kids. You'll be begging to get your life back."

Patrick shook his head and said, "You've never been in love, so you don't know what it's like. I loved Kellie. I wanted a life with her, children with her."

Duncan groaned and fell back on the grass. He stared at the blue cloudless sky for a moment and tried to contemplate love. He really tried, but he got distracted by the sound of women's voices and propped himself up to watch two women in very little clothing jog by. He smiled when one glanced at him.

"Can you at least pretend to listen while I'm spilling out my guts?" Patrick snapped, irritated.

"I don't believe in love," Duncan said simply, then began his repetition of sit-ups. "I believe that a man has sex with as many women as he can, then when he gets sick of the uncertainty of when and where he'll have sex next, he gets married and accepts that he'll never have sex again."

"You're so closed off from your emotions, Duncan," Patrick said matter-of-factly.

"Can we stop with the *Oprah* now?" Duncan muttered.

At Patrick's wounded silence Duncan instantly felt guilty. As Hawk had said on numerous occasions, Patrick couldn't help it that he was a wuss.

"Let's go out tonight, Patty," Duncan said excitedly. "I canceled a date last night, but I could call and see if she wants to go out tonight. And I'll ask her if she has a friend for you."

Patrick quickly shook his head while laughing bitterly. "A double date with you? No thanks."

"What's that supposed to mean?" Duncan asked, insulted by Patrick's instant refusal.

"It means that I've been on double dates with you before. I know what's going to happen, and I'd rather stay home and watch the Lakers play the Spurs."

"What are you talking about?" Duncan demanded in between sit-ups.

Patrick visibly hesitated before he blurted out, "You can't stand the idea of a woman within five feet of you not falling in love with you. You take over."

Duncan stopped his sit-ups to glare at Patrick. He said through clenched teeth, "That is not true."

Patrick snorted in disbelief. "Why do you think I took Hawk's side last night, Duncan? It's not because I care whether you're in the Player Hall of Fame. It's because I'm so damn sick of you trying to prove it all the time. I know exactly what would happen if we went on a double date. You'd monopolize both of the women's attention, flirt with them both, and then act wounded when I say I want to go home early. I'd rather not spend another night watching you work overtime to impress your date and every other man's date close enough to listen."

Duncan jumped to his feet, his chest heaving with anger and maybe a spurt of guilt. He grabbed his water bottle and the shirt he had previously discarded.

He said stiffly, "Forget I said anything. Stay home alone and wallow in your Kellie memories. See if I give a damn again."

"Duncan," Patrick said tiredly. "Don't leave. I'm sorry—"

Duncan shook his head, annoyed at Patrick's protests, and kept walking. A small part of him wondered if he was so angry because Patrick was right.

"Be careful with that knife, Claire," Joan warned, worried, obviously not caring that Claire regularly handled sharper tools than a kitchen cutting knife at the lab. She could have had the cutting precision and experience of Emeril Lagasse and Joan still would have felt the need to warn her about sharp knives.

Claire shook her head in amusement, then—carefully—
began slicing the stack of carrots that Joan had placed in
front of her for the dinner salad. Claire had tried to tell Joan
years ago that she was no longer a child, but it was like talking to a street pole. Joan had never stopped thinking of
Claire as her child. Even though the two sisters were six
years apart in age, Joan had been the only mother Claire had
ever known. Their own mother had disappeared after Claire
turned three years old and began reading at an elementary
school level.

It had been Joan who watched Claire after school, made
her snacks, kissed her scrapes and bruises, and took her to
the library before she entered preschool. Al Scott had tried
to keep up with his younger daughter, but he had barely
made it through high school himself and had gladly accepted
his role as a chauffeur when Joan took over. She had found
the after-school programs for gifted children, the academic
summer camps, and the precollege-level courses that would
accept eight-year-olds.

On the eve of Joan's high school graduation, she had
found out that she was pregnant. She married her high
school sweetheart, Elgin, who worked at the same sanitation company as their father, and became a housewife.
Joan had miscarried that baby, but eventually she and Elgin had Kira, who was a replica of her aunt Claire, and
Joan found herself once more calling Mensa for help with
a gifted child.

"Did you have fun with Annabelle the other night?" Joan
asked after nodding in approval at Claire's slicing technique.

"It was interesting to see her, but after the mugging—"

"Mugging?" Joan squeaked, her eyes round with fear and
outrage. "You were mugged?!"

Claire inwardly winced. She had meant to keep that bit of
information from Joan until she could break it to her in a
calm setting after reciting a few statistics about the com-
monplace nature of nonviolent crimes.

"I may have exaggerated. *Mugging* is too strong of a
word," Claire said hastily.

"You don't exaggerate," Joan snapped, then demanded, "What happened? Are you all right? Where were you?"

"I'm fine, Joan," Claire soothed, pausing in chopping to pin her sister with a firm look. Joan looked doubtful. "I am fine. Duncan, on the other hand, had a few injuries—"

"Duncan? Who's Duncan?" Joan demanded, naturally latching on to the mention of the opposite sex.

Claire cleared her throat and said as casually as she could manage, "Duncan Hillston."

Joan's wide smile made Claire frown at her. "*Your* Duncan Hillston?"

"He's not *my* Duncan Hillston."

"You had a huge crush on him in high school."

"I did not," Claire protested as she dumped the sliced carrots into a large salad bowl.

"Yes, you did. Remember when I caught you in front of your mirror practicing saying 'hi' to him," Joan said, in between loud bursts of laughter. "You couldn't decide on 'Hey, Duncan,' 'Hello, Duncan,' or—my personal favorite—'What's up, Duncan?'"

"I have no idea what you're talking about."

"Selective memory. I read about it in *Redbook* last month. It's when your husband can remember who won the pennant in 1972 but claims that he can't remember when it's his turn to wash the dishes."

"I thought Duncan was attractive in a rather obvious way, just like every other female at Westfield High School, but I didn't have a crush on him."

"Of *course* you didn't. You were too mature for a crush in high school," Joan said, her wide grin contradicting her statement. Claire glared at Joan and she laughed, then asked, "So, how does he look?"

"The same as in high school," Claire responded stiffly.

"Still fine?" Joan asked with a saucy grin that made Claire laugh because she didn't think Joan was capable of that.

"He's handsome," Claire admitted begrudgingly.

Joan grinned, then stuck her hand inside a colorful oven

mitt. "Does he still have that smile that could melt ice on a cold day?"

Claire gasped in surprise and mock betrayal. "You told me that you had no idea who he was when I asked you about him in high school."

"Of course I noticed him," Joan said as she opened the oven door and removed the casserole dish. "Even though I was a big, bad senior when you started high school, my friends and I still noticed a guy like Duncan. He was the cutest guy in the freshman class."

"You slut," Claire teased. "You were dating Elgin in high school and still looking at other men?"

Joan laughed, then took out four plates from the cabinet. "I would have told you, but I didn't want you to think that I was scoping out your man."

"He was not my man." Before Joan could refute her, Claire said, "Anyway, Duncan happened to be with me during the mugging and he and the mugger got in a fight—"

Joan gasped, "Is Duncan all right?"

"He's fine. He . . . He saved my laptop."

Claire barely held in her sigh of longing. As in high school, Claire had spent all night dreaming about Duncan. No man had ever risked his life for her. No man had ever risked getting a paper cut for her. Whether she wanted to admit it or not, Duncan's almost mythical image in her mind had grown even bigger, which meant that she was even more determined to stay away from him. Duncan was just a flesh-and-blood man, and the sooner she realized that, the sooner she could get back to her research, which she had neglected for most of the weekend because she had been fantasizing about him.

"He saved your laptop?" Joan asked with a frown. "That's what you're so excited about?"

"I'm not excited," Claire lied. "Can we change the subject?"

"I like this subject. This is a first-time subject for us. You and a man."

"I date," Claire said defensively.

"You're young, single, and you spend most of your weekends with your married sister and your eight-year-old niece. That is, when you're not in a lab."

"I'm having a dry spell," Claire conceded begrudgingly. At Joan's amused expression she quickly added, "All right, maybe it's more like a drought."

Joan laughed, then murmured, amazed, "Duncan Hillston . . . After all these years. I see him and his brothers around the neighborhood sometimes. If I had known he was into you, I would have reintroduced myself to him years ago."

"He's not *into* me, Joan, and you're making more out of this than it is," Claire warned. "Duncan is a born flirt. He can't help but flirt with every woman he comes into contact with. In fact, the probability is staggering that I'll never see him again—"

"Whatever you say, Claire," Joan said with a quiet smile, then turned back to the steaming pots on the stove as she demanded in a firm tone, "Now, tell me about this mugging and what we're going to do to make certain that it never happens again."

Claire groaned in response.

Chapter Four

"For your reading pleasure . . . the latest printouts," Vino Ricardo announced as he walked into Claire's private office at BioTech Laboratories with a stack of papers.

Claire's office was in the back of the lab she had been given at BioTech straight out of MIT, with the mandate that she continue the gene therapy research that she had started during her freshman year at Harvard. Claire had immediately called her trusted friend and fellow MIT alumnus Vino Ricardo.

Claire and Vino had met in the Ph.D. program at MIT. Like Claire, who had been the youngest female and the only African-American in the program, Vino had been an outcast at the prestigious university. He rode a Harley, lifted weights, which led to an impressive physique that had scared most of the other students, and regularly dyed his hair alarming shades of neon colors, courtesy of his longtime girlfriend, Fiona, who worked as a stripper part-time. The fact that Vino had a girlfriend was another thing that separated him from the other students.

Furthermore, Vino would rather discuss soccer than ionic bonds and would rather sit in front of a television than attend a lecture by a world-famous scientist. He had been as different from the other MIT doctoral candidates as Claire. Inside the lab, however, he and Claire were a team that could anticipate each other's thoughts and see the solutions to problems that no one else could. It hadn't taken much convincing for

Claire to get Vino to reject his original job offer and follow her to BioTech.

Claire immediately set aside the stack of ready-to-be-mailed packages that she had just pulled from her battered briefcase and began to skim through the computer printouts.

"Is something wrong?" Vino asked carefully. "Usually when printouts come in, you hop on them like some women hop on a new pair of Manolos."

Claire lifted an eyebrow and asked, amused, "Been watching Fiona's *Sex and the City* DVDs again?"

"I have no idea what you're talking about," he growled, obviously lying through his teeth. He pointed at the papers and said, "It looks like your guess about the hydrogen bond was dead-on, as usual. We need to calibrate . . ."

Claire looked up when Vino's voice trailed off in confused amazement. He was no longer looking at the readouts but now stared toward the entrance of their lab, visible through Claire's office windows. She followed his gaze and nearly choked when she saw Annabelle standing at the secured entrance. Actually, Annabelle didn't stand; she posed, as if waiting for a gaggle of paparazzi to show up and snap her picture.

Claire had seen a lot of strange things while working in a lab—explosions that had enough force to level a city block contained in a small beaker, miracles on petri dishes—but she had never seen a sight like Annabelle Richards. The lab by nature was white and sterile. All of the team—which consisted of Claire, Vino, two junior researchers, and a few graduate school interns—wore white lab coats. And most of the team, besides Claire, who wore suits, and Vino, who wore jeans and black leather, wore whatever rumpled clothes had been within reach and clean that morning. But as Claire stared at Annabelle, Claire decided that she had never seen so much naked skin in the lab before. Or so much jiggling.

"Who is that?" Vino whispered, awed.

Claire stood when she realized that not only Vino but also the other team members—who were male—had stopped working to gape at Annabelle. Of course, she made certain to smile at each and every one of them.

"I'll be back," Claire told Vino, which was unnecessary, because he had obviously forgotten her existence.

"What are you doing here, Annabelle?" Claire asked quietly with a forced smile as she walked through the lab and tried to block the sight of Annabelle from her team.

"I need to talk to you," Annabelle said, then stepped around Claire to boldly stare back at the men.

Claire said impatiently, "You should have called. . . . How did you get past lab security?"

Annabelle looked at her with wide, innocent eyes. "I just told the nice security guards that I wanted to see my friend."

Claire had been working at BioTech for five years and still had to show the guards her lab identification card every time she walked into the supposedly secured building.

Annabelle once more glanced at the various men in the lab. "Some of these geeks are actually decent looking. I could make a killing in here."

Claire grabbed Annabelle's arm and ordered, "Cafeteria. Now."

Annabelle giggled but didn't protest as Claire led her out of the lab. The two walked down the bland hallway and took the elevator to the ground level, where Claire led Annabelle to the large cafeteria. Claire bought herself a cup of coffee from the vending machine, then followed Annabelle to a small table in the corner of the room. The cafeteria was empty, except for the busy cafeteria workers preparing for the lunch rush. Claire shuddered to think what would happen if all five hundred of BioTech's sex-starved male scientists got a look at Annabelle.

Annabelle rested her chin in her hands and asked innocently, "So, how much exactly does one of those lab geeks make in a year?" Claire glared at Annabelle in response and she shrugged innocently. "What?"

Claire struggled for patience as she said, "I have to get back to work. What did you want to talk about?"

Annabelle's now-blue-tinted eyes gleamed with excitement as she said, "What happened with Duncan after you two left the bar?"

"This is what you wanted to talk about?" Claire asked, annoyed.

"I've been waiting for you to call me for two days to tell me what happened," she admonished Claire.

"Nothing happened, Annabelle," Claire said, leaving out the part about the mugging. Judging from Joan's reaction last night, Claire decided to keep that information to herself from now on. She hadn't even told Vino. Her team needed to maintain their focus on the gene therapy when they were this close to preclinical trials.

"I don't believe you," Annabelle said flatly. "Duncan wasn't exactly being subtle in the bar. He wants you. And from what I remember, what Duncan Hillston wants, he gets."

Claire instantly stiffened and demanded, "What exactly do you know about Duncan, Annabelle?"

Annabelle laughed as she held up her hands in self-defense. "Easy, Claire. I don't know anything about Duncan, except the rumors you and I both heard in the locker room after gym class."

"That was almost fifteen years ago."

"He hasn't changed one bit," Annabelle said firmly. "Did you see him? Any man who looks like that . . . He probably just has to breathe and a woman falls in his lap. I know the effect he has on women. I have that same effect on men."

Claire tried not to roll her eyes but didn't succeed. Annabelle ignored her reaction and asked excitedly, "Did he ask you out again?"

"Yes. He was actually very persistent about it," she admitted, then added hesitantly, "He claims that he wants to be friends—nothing more."

"He is good," Annabelle said with a sigh of admiration. "And what did you say?"

"I told him 'no,' of course."

Surprise crossed Annabelle's face. "Why?"

"Why would I go out with Duncan Hillston? We have absolutely nothing in common. I told him exactly that."

"You told him that?" Annabelle squeaked in disbelief. "Claire, you've been in love with him since high school—"

"That is not true—"

Annabelle held up one hand, effectively cutting off Claire's protests. "Don't bother denying it. I was there, remember? Now the universe has decided to reward you. You have the chance to right a wrong, to make the man you wanted in high school more than you wanted to win the academic decathlon want you."

Claire laughed nervously. "I have no idea what you're talking about—"

"You're in the position that every woman dreams about when she thinks of that one unattainable guy from high school," Annabelle continued excitedly. "You've already piqued Duncan's interest by doing something probably no woman has done in a while—you said no. He'll be thinking about that and just for reputation's sake, he'll have to pursue you. In fact, I would be surprised if he doesn't call you tonight."

"You make it sound like a game," Claire said, frowning.

"The man–woman thing *is* a game, Claire. The sooner you realize that, the better off you'll be, especially if you're going to be tangling with the likes of Duncan Hillston."

"I didn't say I would *tangle* with him," she snapped, annoyed. "Besides, Duncan is . . . He swaggers, Annabelle. He actually swaggers down the street. A man who swaggers could never handle dating a woman who's smarter than him. Not to mention the fact that I may have had strong affection for the Duncan Hillston I knew in high school, but the adult Duncan Hillston is an unknown quantity—"

"I'm not saying you have to marry him, Claire," Annabelle said, frustrated. "You have the chance to fulfill a high school fantasy. Use him, abuse him, and then when you're done with him, throw him away. Men have been doing it to women for years. Now it's our turn."

"That seems cruel," Claire said weakly, even as her traitorous brain thought of all the ways she'd like to abuse Duncan's big, strong body.

"It's called having fun. Not every man you sleep with has to be husband material. Besides, Duncan will just find another woman to help him mend his broken heart, that is, if a man like Duncan can get hurt. Men like him know the game too well to allow that to happen."

Claire stared at her coffee for a moment, appalled that she was actually considering Annabelle's advice. Could she really casually enter into an affair with Duncan for fun's sake? In high school, all of her Duncan-centered dreams had involved the two of them living in a big old house in Westfield with kids, a dog, and her own private state-of-the-art lab in the garage. Of course, she had been a child then and had known logically how children were created, but hadn't been able to imagine her and Duncan doing that. She just imagined her and Duncan kissing and hugging a lot, and that had been enough for her eleven-year-old mind.

But Claire was older now. She had long ago stopped dreaming about having kids and a dog with a man, and especially not with Duncan Hillston. After the initial attraction wore off and Claire realized that Duncan was just a man, she was certain that she would tire of him—assuming he didn't tire of her first. But, until that happened, didn't she deserve to have a little fun? In particular, a little fun with a man she had drooled over in high school. Maybe Annabelle was right. Maybe a casual affair was the answer.

"Think about it, Claire," Annabelle coaxed. "Don't tell me that you haven't dreamed of this exact scenario."

Claire couldn't prevent the smile that crossed her face. "Maybe," she admitted.

Annabelle laughed and said, "I knew it."

Claire shook her head suddenly. "I can't believe I'm even contemplating this."

"Why not? You're single and over the legal age of consent. You're allowed to have some fun. And I have a feeling that Duncan is just the man to show you how much fun you can have," she said with a laugh.

"How do you know Duncan will want to . . . to show me how much fun I can have?" Claire asked doubtfully.

"Because I have two eyes, and I saw the way he was checking you out at the bar. I mean, he barely looked at me. What other proof do you need?"

Claire laughed as she shook her head at Annabelle's confidence. "Assuming I want to do this, how would I tell Duncan?"

"You won't have to tell him anything. The harder you resist him, the more he'll want you. Don't give in until you're sure that you have him wrapped around your little finger. Got it?"

Claire studied Annabelle for a moment suspiciously. "Why do you care so much whether I go out with Duncan?"

Annabelle's smile faded as she said, "Because I'm still Annabelle Richards, and no matter how many men have told me I'm beautiful, I remember high school. I remember feeling unwanted and unloved. I want you to feel that power that comes with bringing a man to his knees. Every woman should experience it at least once, even reformed child geniuses like you."

Claire smiled, catching a small glimpse of her old friend. Annabelle giggled, grinned, and said excitedly, "Now remember, when he calls tonight, keep the conversation as short as possible. Don't let him pin you down to a date yet."

"How do you know he'll call tonight?"

"Trust me, he'll call," Annabelle said with a smug grin.

Claire shrugged in confusion and wondered what she had allowed herself to be talked into. Except she knew that Annabelle had not talked her into anything. Claire had wanted Duncan Hillston since she was eleven years old, and if Annabelle was right, Claire finally had her chance to have him.

Chapter Five

Claire stared at the telephone that sat in the middle of her king-size bed. She shifted her position to cross her legs but continued to stare at the receiver, as if she could will the phone to ring. Annabelle had been confident that Duncan would call, and since Claire didn't really have any experience to contradict Annabelle's mandates, Claire had assumed that Duncan would call.

Claire glanced at the neon bright lights of her alarm clock. It was ten o'clock at night. Claire had been waiting for the phone to ring since she had walked into her small cottage in Santa Monica after work, but the phone had stubbornly remained silent. Duncan obviously wasn't going to call. Annabelle was wrong, and Claire—as usual—was right. The whole idea of her "tangling" with Duncan had been preposterous. At least in high school, Claire had been realistic about her chances with Duncan. She had known that he would never give her a second look.

Claire had just convinced herself to return the phone to the nightstand and catch the ten o'clock news when the phone rang, causing her to scream like a silly college student with perky breasts in a scary movie. Claire stared at the telephone in shock for a few seconds, then flinched as it rang once more. She licked her suddenly dry lips and grabbed the receiver.

"Dr. Scott," she answered hesitantly.

"Dr. Scott, this is Electrician Hillston," came Duncan's smooth voice.

Her body instantly shimmered to life. "Colleagues from around the world call me at home, so I answer the phone with my title," she said defensively.

He still sounded amused as he said, "If I was a doctor, I would always answer the phone 'Dr. Hillston.' I would also talk about myself in the third person all the time just so I could say 'Dr. Hillston.'"

Duncan's rich laughter spilled over the telephone and Claire actually found herself smiling, although she couldn't think of an appropriate response.

Duncan said easily, "I hope I'm not calling too late."

"No . . . No, I was just sitting here and . . . I wasn't doing anything." She had a feeling that Annabelle would not be happy with that response.

Claire remembered Annabelle's orders and grabbed the stopwatch that she had placed on her nightstand in preparation for Duncan's telephone call. She fumbled with the small object, then managed to press the start button. Annabelle had decreed that the first conversation could last no longer than five minutes—something about Claire leaving him wanting more. She wished that someone had told her these rules years ago. It would have made everything so much easier.

Duncan's voice became somber as he asked, concerned, "How are you doing?"

"Fine."

"Have you heard from the police? Have they caught the mugger?"

"No, and studies have shown that the perpetrators of street crimes are rarely ever caught."

"Then I'm glad that you kept your laptop."

Claire licked her lips nervously, then said, "I never thanked you. I risked both of our lives for something that could have been replaced. It's rare that I lose perspective like that."

He protested, "Your work was on that laptop."

"But work can be replicated . . . even if it would take months or years to replicate it, but our lives can't. I apologize for endangering—"

"You don't have to apologize to me, Claire," he interrupted her. "I'll put my hard head on the line any day to protect you and what you do. Your work saves lives."

"In theory," Claire mumbled, then grimaced as she realized that she had spoken out loud.

"What do you mean?" Duncan asked, confused.

"It's not important," she quickly said. "You were very chivalrous the other night, and I still must apologize for placing you in that situation."

He groaned. "I accept your apology. Now can we talk about something else? I'm starting to blush. Grown black men don't blush. I could lose my membership card."

Claire laughed, then immediately straightened when she remembered the stopwatch that she had dropped on the bed. Only two minutes left.

"Tell me about your work. You mentioned something about cancer research earlier," Duncan said, and he actually sounded interested. Claire had to give him credit. He was good.

"You don't want to hear about it," she said flatly.

"If I didn't want to hear about it, I wouldn't have asked," he responded simply. "Besides, my motives aren't entirely pure. I get turned on every time I hear you say 'hydrogen bond.'"

Claire laughed nervously and resisted the urge to ask him if that was true. If so, she planned to make the phrase "hydrogen bond" the most oft-repeated words in her vocabulary. Claire once more felt that warm, squishy feeling settling in her stomach and soaking lower through her body. If only she could re-create that feeling in the lab, bottle it, and sell it. She would be rich. She would call it *Feeling Duncan* or something equally romantic and silly.

"My research focuses on ovarian cancer," she finally said stiffly.

"What about ovarian cancer?" he prodded.

Claire hesitated, then took a deep breath. If she was going to bore him to death, at least she could claim that he asked for it. "Normal cells in our body grow at a steady, contained rate. Cancer cells, on the other hand, represent out-of-control cell growth. There are certain genes in the human body that suppress the growth of these defective cells, the cancer killer genes. In cancer victims, this gene is inactive or defective. We're developing a gene therapy that restores the function of this tumor suppressor gene in the ovaries. It usually takes fifteen to twenty years for a new drug to hit the market, but my team and I have gone further than anyone else in half that time. Our IND application was cleared by the proper government channels and we're only a few weeks away from starting preclinical trials, where we administer the drug to animal subjects. If the drug proves effective, we can start clinical trials—testing on human subjects."

"You would have made a good teacher. I actually understood that."

"Of course, it's more complicated than that," she quickly added.

His laugh was low and warm across the telephone, causing her toes to tingle before he said, "I bet it is. I'm proud of you, Claire. You're doing what we all dream of doing—you're leaving this world a better place than how you found it. In high school, I always knew that you would do something important."

Claire had the sudden urge to tell Duncan about her doubts and fears—that the new gene therapy would not work, that she would be the laughingstock of the research community, that she had spent the last six years of her life working on a failure, and that all of the success predicted for her since she was four years old had never been fulfilled. As a child, Claire had thought by thirty years old she would be on her second Nobel Peace Prize or, at least, would have more degrees. But she had none of that. She just had a procedure that may or may not work. Only time would tell.

Claire silently gasped as she grabbed the stopwatch again. She had gone way over the allotted five minutes.

"I have to go," she said abruptly.

"You have to go?" Duncan repeated, confused. "But—"

"No, I really have to go. It's been great talking to you. Maybe we can do it again."

Duncan sounded concerned as he asked, "Claire, is some-thing wrong? Did I say something?"

Claire's excuse was interrupted by the sudden blaring of her car alarm from her driveway.

She cursed and jumped from the bed to run to her bed-room window that overlooked the driveway. All the lights on the sedan were switching on and off and the horn was blar-ing, disturbing the stillness in the quiet neighborhood. There was nothing around the car to explain the sudden alarm, but Claire was not surprised. Wind blowing in the wrong direc-tion could get her car to throw a fit.

Claire glanced up and down the quiet, dark street. The majority of houses were dark, meaning that the occupants were asleep or close to sleep. But the street wouldn't be dark for long if her alarm continued.

"What is that noise?" Duncan demanded, suddenly sounding alert.

"My car alarm," Claire said, distracted. "I'm going to go turn it off."

"Don't go outside," he ordered. "Stay inside the house and use the key remote."

"If I'm not standing close enough to my car to unlock it myself, the key remote doesn't work."

"What's the point of a remote if you have to unlock the car by hand?" he asked blankly.

Claire muttered, "Exactly."

"What if someone is out there?"

"No one is out there, Duncan. Maybe my neighbor's cat landed on the hood or a caterpillar accidentally stumbled against one of the wheels. Who knows? My car has gone off for less," Claire mumbled as she snatched her robe off the edge of the bed and started down the hallway toward the front door. "I'll call you back—"

"Do not hang up this phone," he said, sounding angry for some reason.

Claire rolled her eyes but obeyed. She juggled the phone in between her hands as she slipped into her faded and com-fortable purple terry-cloth robe and hastily tied the sash.

Only because Duncan was making her paranoid, Claire glanced out the windowpane that ran along the length of the door. She didn't see anything but her car. There were a few shadows in the driveway, but there were always shadows in the driveway.

"What's going on?" Duncan demanded.

Claire gritted her teeth in irritation at his tone. Where was the smooth-talking flirt from five minutes ago?

"I'm unlocking the door. Is that all right with you or should I send out a flare first?" she muttered sarcastically as she flipped the locks on the door.

"You should be taking this more seriously, Claire," he said, not sounding amused.

Claire grabbed her car keys from the small dish that she kept on a table near the front door and walked out of the house. The instant she left the warm brightness of her house, a chill ran down her spine. Claire knew the chemistry. It was a typical cool Santa Monica night. Santa Monica was always slightly cooler than the inland parts of Los Angeles due to the ocean breeze, and her body was simply reacting to the change in temperature from the interior of her warm house.

Except a small part of Claire that suddenly gripped the phone didn't believe that. Her breathing became heavier as she hesitantly studied the dark shadows that crept across the front lawn and threw half of her car in darkness. Suddenly the shadows didn't seem so ordinary. Now they looked downright sinister.

Claire hesitated on the threshold of the door and glanced around the yard. Nothing. She was being illogical. If only the car weren't making such a racket, she could listen, feel . . . She stopped herself. She was acting like a frightened small animal in the woods, sniffing the air for predators before leaving the nest. She was in the middle of her safe neighborhood that she had lived in for five years, that hadn't had so much as a shoplifting incident since she moved there. She had nothing to fear. Still, Claire remained on the porch. The hairs on the backs of her arms seemed to stand at attention—not from cold but from fear.

Claire swallowed the sudden lump in her throat as she stuck one bare foot out the front door.

"What's going on?" Duncan asked, sounding frustrated that he wasn't there to boss her around in person.

"Nothing," Claire said, in a whisper for some reason.

"Something's going on. I can tell," he said.

"Be quiet," she hissed into the receiver. She held out her arm from the safety of the porch and pressed the key remote. Nothing happened. The car continued to blare.

Claire silently cursed whoever invented car alarms, then took another step onto the porch. Then another. She carefully walked down the wooden steps and her feet touched smooth, cool pavement. She forced herself to square her shoulders. She was being not only illogical but also a scaredy-cat. She had been out to her car in the middle of the night several times this month alone to turn off the alarm or to grab forgotten reading material, and she had never felt such . . . such fear. Claire gripped the telephone as she moved closer to the car, her palm suddenly clammy.

She pressed the key remote again, and this time the car shut off instantly. Silence filled the neighborhood, but for some reason it felt more disturbing than the noise had been.

"There," Claire said into the receiver, sounding more confident than she felt. "Happy?"

"I won't be happy until you're in the house with all the doors and windows locked," he responded. "As soon as possible, I'm checking your remote."

Claire felt another wave of warmth wash over her. No one had ever worried about her remote before. No one had ever worried about her before. Claire was on the verge of smiling when the glint of glass on the ground next to the rear car tire caught her attention.

Confused, she walked to the other side of the car and saw more glass sparkling under the moonlight. Then she saw the cause. The back window of her car had been smashed in and a large, violent hole opened into the backseat window on the passenger side.

"Oh no," she whispered, shaking her head in disbelief.

"What is it, Claire?" Duncan asked, alarmed. "Do you see something?"

Her body tensed in fear as she frantically glanced around the yard. It was too dark. She couldn't see anything, but she felt creepy; she felt like she was being watched. She could feel the eyes on her back, pinning her to her spot, unable to move. She wanted to pretend that it was just her imagination, but Claire didn't have much of an imagination when it came to scaring the hell out of herself.

"It's nothing." She forced herself to sound calm. "A back window was smashed. Probably kids."

"Get inside the house," Duncan ordered, his voice loud and firm over the phone and calming her a little bit. "I'm coming over right now."

"It's just a broken window," she said in an unsteady whisper as she forced herself to take one step toward the house. She could take another and another. She could do anything when she put her mind to it, including walk, despite her suddenly trembling legs. It was just a broken window. It was just a broken window only two days after she had been mugged. "It's nothing," she said again for her own benefit, more than for Duncan, as she remembered the feel of the gun in her back.

"Then why do you sound so scared?"

"I'm not. . . ." She glanced around the backyard once more, then answered truthfully, "I feel like I'm being watched."

That was apparently all Duncan needed to hear. "I'm on my way."

Claire told herself to run into the house and slam the door, but her gaze flew to the front of the car, completely hidden in shadows. Every instinct in her body told her to run, screamed at her to run. Still, Claire gingerly walked toward the front of the car, not certain what she would find but unable to stop her driving obsession to prove that no bogeyman hid beneath the fender of the car.

Claire heard the sound of glass breaking behind her. She gasped in fear and whirled around. She briefly closed her eyes, relieved when she saw that fragments of dangling glass had merely fallen from the window to the ground. She forced herself to breathe. She was being ridiculous. There was no bogeyman or eyes watching her. And did Duncan just say that he was coming over?

She turned back to the front of the car, determined to march past it and straight into her house, and ran straight into a solid male chest. Claire's eyes traveled up the dark sweater, the hulking shoulders, and stared directly into the faceless black void of the same mugger wearing the same ski mask from Friday night.

No sound came out of her throat as she stared in speechless shock at the man. Fear rendered her immobile and mute. She didn't realize that she still clung to the telephone until Duncan's voice calling her name cracked through her fear and sent the world spinning into motion again. Claire looked at the man again and screamed in sheer terror.

The man abruptly sprang into action, moving toward her. Claire's scream was cut off as one of his shoulders drove into her chest, knocking her to the ground with enough force that the air whooshed from her lungs. The phone flew from her hand and she skidded across the driveway, banging into the car. She shook the bright white spots from her vision and turned onto her stomach just in time to see the man sprinting down the middle of the street until he blended into the dark night.

Chapter Six

Duncan and the first Santa Monica police car screeched to a stop in front of Claire's house at the same time—fifteen minutes after Claire managed to drag herself back into her house to change out of her gown and robe. Strangely enough, she had felt more relieved when she saw Duncan charging across her lawn than she had been to see the police officer. Claire had originally thought she would wait inside the house when the other officers and investigators began to arrive, but with Duncan outside, Claire felt safe enough to stand in the driveway and watch, intrigued, as the crime scene investigators searched her car for fingerprints or microscopic evidence. Duncan had joined the officers, who searched the neighborhood for the escaped man.

Claire looked up from her car as she felt Duncan. She hadn't seen him walking toward her, which he was doing, but she had felt him. Very peculiar. Claire frowned when she saw the detective in charge of the investigation, Victoria Hansen, walking next to him. The two appeared to be in deep conversation. Very peculiar indeed. Claire had been able to tell with one glance at the six-foot blonde, who looked like she should have been spiking volleyballs on the beach instead of investigating crimes, that Victoria Hansen would know what to do to "tangle" with Duncan.

"Did you find anything?" Claire asked, pushing aside her irrational and immature feelings of jealousy as Duncan and Detective Hansen shared a laugh before stopping in front of

her. Duncan could laugh with other women. He could do
whatever he wanted with other women. Claire didn't care.
Yeah, right.

"He's long gone. He probably had a car parked in the
vicinity that he hightailed it to when you caught him snoop-
ing around," the detective answered gravely. "There were no
signs that he tried to enter your house, so this looks like a
simple attempted car burglary."

Claire glanced at Duncan, who appeared a little too focused on Detective Hansen, and clenched her hands together. So much for Annabelle's big theory about Duncan
going crazy with lust over Claire.

Detective Hansen, apparently oblivious to her hold over
Duncan, glanced at a small notepad she held, then asked, "You
said that you were mugged in Los Angeles two nights ago?"

"Yes. The mugger wanted Claire's laptop," Duncan
snapped impatiently. Claire glanced at him, surprised. Maybe
the intensity on his face wasn't about plotting ways to ask
Detective Hansen out. A man didn't use that tone with a
woman he planned to ask out. Claire almost smiled.

"Dr. Scott, you told the responding officer that a duffel
bag you keep in the backseat of your car is missing. Is that
correct?"

Claire forced herself to pay attention and to stop playing
junior high he-likes-me, he-likes-me-not games. She had
been attacked in her front yard. This was important. It was
not important whether Duncan thought Detective Hansen
was beautiful, especially since it was obvious that he could
have cared less.

"*Yes*," Claire answered, more emphatic than necessary in
her newfound attempt to focus on the reason Detective
Hansen was there.

"What was in the duffel bag?" the detective asked.

Claire's face burned with embarrassment as she mumbled, "Gym clothes."

Claire hoped the detective didn't investigate her story.
Powerhouse Gym would probably be glad to hear that member Claire Scott was still alive and well.

"Gym clothes?" Detective Hansen repeated, sounding disbelieving.

Claire defensively crossed her arms over her chest. Maybe she had an extra fifteen or twenty pounds around her hips and thighs and she wasn't in the best shape, but the potential benefits of developing a cancer gene therapy took priority over everything else in her life. Of course, before Claire began working on the gene therapy, she hadn't been a big exerciser either.

"This isn't about her gym clothes," Duncan said, glaring at the detective. Claire had never wanted to kiss him more than at that moment. "This car break-in is obviously related to the attempted mugging."

"Is that so?" Detective Hansen asked drolly.

Duncan rolled his eyes impatiently, looking nothing like the smooth-talking playboy from the bar. He hadn't even looked this upset when he lay groaning in pain in the middle of the street after the mugging. Not for the first time, Claire noticed how good he looked in his jeans. Good enough to make a woman like Claire invent ways to take out a woman carrying a loaded gun, because it was obvious that Detective Hansen thought Duncan looked good in his jeans, too.

"Tell her what you do for a living, Claire," Duncan ordered, looking at Claire and making her feel instantly guilty about her thoughts. She should be focusing. Not fantasizing.

"I work at a pharmaceutical research firm," she responded automatically.

"See?" Duncan said to the detective.

Detective Hansen shook her head with a slight smile. "You're going to have to make it a little more plain for a tired cop, Mr. Hillston."

He sighed heavily, almost like Claire did when she was asked to explain something. He said with exaggerated patience, "Claire is on the verge of finding a cure for ovarian cancer—"

Claire quickly clarified, "We haven't gotten past preclinical trials."

"You will, Claire," Duncan said firmly, staring at her. She

swallowed over the sudden ball of emotions in her throat at his dark gaze. Duncan turned back to the detective and continued, "I did a little research on the pharmaceutical industry last night. Competition is very fierce. Corporate espionage, blackmail, sabotage. You name it, it's been done in that industry."

"You researched my industry?" Claire asked breathlessly. Annabelle would have a field day with that information.

Duncan glanced at her and hastily muttered, "Just for a few minutes." He focused on the detective again. "Two times in four days, someone has tried to take something from Claire. They're looking for information, probably information on her drug. It explains why the mugger didn't leave when he had my wallet. Claire even offered him money, but he didn't care about that stuff. He wanted the laptop."

"I don't believe that," Claire said while shaking her head. "No other company could use our results. All of our research is under patent protection."

"So what?" Duncan said, frustrated. "If I was a competitor, I would take my chances. Your drug has the potential to bring in billions of dollars."

"There could be a connection there," Detective Hansen begrudgingly admitted, then added wryly, "or Dr. Scott just has bad luck."

"Not this bad," Duncan said, then asked, "What are you going to do?"

Detective Hansen took a deep breath, obviously struggling for patience. Claire had the feeling that if Duncan hadn't looked so good in his jeans, the detective would have lost patience a long time ago.

"We'll pursue all lines of inquiry, Mr. Hillston, and if this is some attempt at corporate theft, we'll find that out, too. I can't overestimate our need to proceed carefully here. This could have been the work of bored and drunk teenagers and the mugging was just a coincidence. I don't want to accuse anyone of something they didn't do." She turned to Claire and smiled in sympathy. "I would normally tell you to make certain to lock all doors and to take extra precautions over the next few days, until we establish what happened, but I have a feeling that you'll be hearing that and a lot more from Mr. Hillston."

Duncan instantly frowned while Claire smiled. He asked the detective, "How about a patrol around the house?"

"Is that necessary?" Claire said, alarmed.

"Yes," he answered, then glared at her, as if daring her to contradict him. Claire didn't.

"I'll make certain that an officer patrols the area every half hour for the next two nights." The detective handed Claire a business card. "If we find out anything, I'll contact you immediately."

"Thank you," Claire said.

The crime scene technicians gathered their tools and equipment and waved to Claire before they followed the detective to their respective sedans parked in front of her house. Claire watched the uniformed officers leave next until suddenly she was alone with Duncan. She turned to him uncertainly.

Duncan held her gaze for a moment, then said simply, "I'm hungry."

He walked into her house, leaving her standing in the middle of the driveway alone. Claire quickly ran into the house after him and closed the door.

Duncan carefully watched Claire as she picked at the cereal in the bowl that Duncan had plopped in front of her at the breakfast nook in her kitchen. He had finished his own bowl in less than five bites. As far as he was concerned, there was no occasion that cereal wasn't good for. Except maybe he had found one: sitting across from Claire in her home after she had scared ten years off his life. Even over two hours later, Duncan could remember hearing her piercing scream over the telephone. He had broken every speeding record he knew by driving from his house to hers—a trip that normally took about thirty minutes with no freeway traffic had taken him fifteen minutes.

Good grief. His hands still shook. He didn't normally play Dale Earnhardt Jr. on the freeway just because a woman thought someone was watching her. Duncan had had his cell phone attached to his ear and was in his pickup doing nearly 90 before Claire screeched like the best horror movie victim. Then the phone had gone dead, and Duncan had racheted the speed up to 100 miles per hour—a speed that his five-year-old Ford truck had not been happy with.

Duncan didn't know what was wrong with him. Playing the German Autobahn on the 405 was a little much for this stage in his seduction, even for him. And staying here with her after the police left was definitely going above and beyond the call of duty. But he couldn't force himself to leave. He wasn't done reassuring himself that she was all right.

"You want some more cereal?" he asked abruptly when Claire looked up from her bowl to find Duncan staring at her for the third time since they sat down.

"No, thank you," she murmured. She pushed away her bowl. Duncan immediately grabbed it and dug in.

"Rice Krispies, my favorite," he announced. When she stared at him quizzically, he said defensively, "I like cereal. It's simple. Uncomplicated."

"I wasn't aware that some foods were considered complicated."

"When you're a single guy, anything seems complicated. I've mastered cereal and milk and, of course, peanut-butter-and-jelly, but if I had my pick, I'd take cereal. I have Cereal Day with my nieces and nephews. We buy different brands of cereal; then we go home and try them all."

Claire smiled, and Duncan realized how much he liked seeing her do that. Her whole face lit up. Her eyes twinkled. She looked much younger. If she hadn't been wearing a suit and had her hair in a ponytail, Duncan would have thought they were back in high school. Although Medusa hadn't really smiled in high school. She had squinted and glowered.

"How many nieces and nephews do you have?" she asked curiously.

"Eleven and counting," he replied easily, attempting to hide the pride in his voice. Maybe he was a little wild about his nieces and nephews, but Claire didn't need to know that.

Once a woman knew a man had a soft spot for kids, he didn't stand a chance in the Player Hall of Fame. "I think a couple of my brothers' wives are pregnant right now. They've stopped telling me. They just wait nine months, then pop another kid into my arms."

Claire laughed, then murmured, "It must be nice to have such a big family."

"It has its moments," he admitted begrudgingly.

After the two spent several seconds grinning at each other, Claire shifted her gaze, then stood and carried his empty bowl to the sink. Even though Duncan reminded himself that this was still the soothe stage, he wanted to touch her. He had to touch her. When he had first arrived at her house that night, he hadn't known whether to take her in his arms or punch a tree out of anger that some bastard had scared her again. Duncan had done neither. Now that the anger had passed, he needed to feel her. Be reassured. Strictly for soothing purposes, of course.

Duncan grabbed the other half-full bowl of cereal and milk and followed close on her heels to the sink. She set the bowl down and turned. Her eyes slightly widened and she gasped when she realized that Duncan stood behind her. Duncan held her gaze as he moved closer, effectively trapping her in between the sink counter and his body. He leaned even closer and caught the scent of clean, pure old-fashioned soap before he averted his gaze and set the other bowl in the sink.

He moved his hands on top of the sink, trapping her on either side with his arms. Their bodies hadn't touched, but they may as well have. Duncan was aroused to the point of it being almost painful. That had never happened this early in the soothe stage. That had never happened just from eating cereal and milk in a woman's kitchen. *What the hell,* he decided, *straight on to the entice stage.*

He lightly touched the lapel of her suit jacket, and Claire sharply inhaled. Duncan smiled at her, and her eyes darkened in response. He had her. He could tell.

"Why the suit? Do you have some midnight meeting with

lawyers or politicians that I should know about?" he asked in a husky whisper.

Claire shook her head, but Duncan saw the nerves dancing around the edges of her mouth. Her big brain hadn't predicted this, and she was thrown off-balance. Duncan liked that. He also liked that her gaze kept dropping to his mouth and lingering, almost hypnotized. If there were a more blatant sign that a woman wanted to be kissed, Duncan didn't know what it was.

"I like to be taken seriously. And by wearing a suit I can guarantee that," she finally stuttered in response.

"I take you very seriously, Claire, no matter what you're wearing," he murmured, his own gaze fixed on her mouth.

He would never admit it to anyone in a million years, but he had noticed her mouth in high school. He had considered her a child then, so he had felt almost illegal even glancing at her plush, naturally pink lips, but now she was grown-up. And there wasn't a hall monitor in sight.

Duncan stepped closer until the tips of her soft breasts touched his chest. He withheld a groan. Barely. He tore his gaze from her mouth to meet her wide, dark eyes.

"I was scared shitless when I heard your scream on the phone," he admitted in a quiet voice. "I've never driven that fast in my life."

"I was wondering how you got here so quickly," she whispered in a shaky voice.

"I probably hit Mach ten at some point."

Claire regarded him steadily for a few moments; then she asked, "You were worried about me? I guess that explains your behavior when you first arrived at the house. Studies have shown that men generally react with aggression when faced with worry or fear."

Whatever had been making her eyes darken with arousal suddenly had given way to intellect. She no longer looked at his mouth but now cast frequent looks at the table. She wanted to escape. Too damn bad. Now that he had finally gotten close enough to touch her, neither one of them was going anywhere for a while.

"When someone threatens me and mine, I feel real damn aggressive," he said tightly.

His hand trailed from the suit jacket lapel to the expanse of honey brown skin at the V of the jacket, above the hem of the dress. Her soft gasp fanned the back of his hand as he touched the impossibly soft skin, as if that patch of skin had never known a day of the sun's rays in her life. Duncan withheld another groan as his penis hardened even more. Things were getting out of control. He was no longer soothing or enticing or whatever the hell he was supposed to be doing. Now he was moving on pure instinct, and every instinct told him to lift her on the counter, throw up and down whatever material was in his way, and plunge into her to the hilt.

"I'm not yours, Duncan," Claire reminded him, her eyes holding his.

"Not yet," he said with a slight smile.

Claire actually grinned as she murmured, "I would tell you that you're ridiculous, but I think you'd take it as a compliment."

"And you'd be right." Duncan grinned, then removed his hand from her soft skin. This was a dangerous game he was playing. He was rushing things. That wasn't good for the bet. The bet . . . He had almost forgotten.

"I'll sleep on the sofa," he said abruptly, friendly Duncan again. "I'll be out of your hair by eight, since I have to be at a site in Gardena by nine."

She looked panicked as she protested, "Duncan, you don't have to stay here tonight—"

"Losing battle, Claire," he said simply. "I sleep either on your sofa or in my truck in front of your house. Do you really want me to wake up tomorrow morning walking like the Hunchback of Notre Dame?"

Claire sighed in exasperation, then muttered, "You really are a Westfield man, you know that? Stubborn, opinionated, and bossy."

"Thanks," he said simply.

"I'll get you some blankets and pillows."

Duncan planted a soft kiss on her forehead. He meant to

keep the kiss light—gratitude, thankfulness that she was alive, soothing—but then he felt her tremble and he remembered her scream. He briefly closed his eyes and placed another kiss on her right cheek. The feel of her skin reminded Duncan that he still hadn't held her in his arms and that had been his one driving thought as he had sped across Los Angeles. So he allowed himself to do that. Duncan wrapped his arms around her waist and pulled her against his body, and when he felt her soft body melt against his, his arms clenched around her tighter, as if he really cared and this wasn't for a bet.

Claire took several deep breaths to calm the rising tide of desire growing in her belly as Duncan held her in his strong arms. Just held her, as if that were enough. And it almost was enough. No one had ever held her like that. No one had ever shown such tenderness and care. Claire hesitantly wrapped her arms around his waist and clung to him, allowed herself to—for once—lean on someone else. Duncan could take it.

But after a few moments of feeling his hard chest against hers, Claire realized that it wasn't enough. She wanted to taste him, needed to taste him.

"Duncan," she whispered, almost in awe.

She heard his gulp and that emboldened her a little. Claire pulled back from him slightly and carefully traced the outline of his beautiful mouth. His lips were soft and moist. He made a strange noise in the back of his throat but made no attempt to move. Her gaze moved from his mouth to his eyes, and she almost jumped from his arms at the pure desire she saw in the dark depths.

Duncan shifted closer to her, and for the first time Claire felt the hard bulge in the front of his pants as his penis nudged into her stomach. She felt a little bolder and she leaned toward him. Claire had never made the first move in her life, but now it seemed right.

Claire hesitantly swiped her tongue over his full top lip. Duncan groaned louder this time and his hands tightened at her waist and pressed her even closer. Being this close to Duncan overwhelmed her senses. Smelling him, feeling him, tasting him. She made another hesitant foray across his lips with her tongue. He tasted like sugar that he had sprinkled onto his cereal and fresh milk. She suddenly agreed with him—she would take cereal and milk over anything else, too.

Duncan appeared content to let her lead the kiss, so Claire kissed him again, this time holding on to his bottom lip a fraction longer before she pulled away. She searched his expression, wanting to know if she was pleasing him, but his eyes were closed and his nostrils were flared. Claire smiled. Even she knew the signs of arousal.

She kissed him again—and this time there was nothing sweet or hesitant about it. She traced the small gap between his lips and he instantly opened his mouth to her silent entreaty. She plunged her tongue into his mouth and began to play with his long, sleek tongue. He crushed her to him, his mouth suddenly alive, as he began to take control of the kiss. Claire clenched her thighs together as a wave of something hot and sweet poured through her body and landed directly in her core.

His tongue plunged into hers over and over, eating her, devouring her. His hands moved from her waist to her behind, squeezing the globes and molding them through the thick material of her suit. Her hips dug into the kitchen counter behind her as he moved even closer, but Claire didn't notice any discomfort. She gasped into his mouth at the power of the feelings running through her body, which gave him more of an opportunity to abuse her mouth in a sensual frenzy. Her hands dug into his biceps, holding on to him so he wouldn't go away and anchoring herself to earth.

Duncan abruptly pulled from her. He stumbled back and looked at her like she was a witch who had cast a spell over him. Claire placed a trembling hand over her abused and swollen lips as their combined ragged breathing filled the silent kitchen.

His gaze dropped to her breasts and Claire thought that he would come to her again, but instead he dragged a hand down his face like a man on the verge of torture.

His voice was deep and rough as he said, "Go to sleep, Claire."

"I'll get the blankets—"

"Forget the blankets," he said harshly as his gaze zeroed in on her mouth again. Claire had never felt so desired in her life. She wanted to smile like the sexy seductress he made her feel like and order him to keep kissing her.

Instead, she mumbled, "Good night," and hurried from the kitchen. Annabelle would be very disappointed. Claire's first phone call with Duncan had lasted a lot longer than five minutes.

Chapter Seven

Duncan woke up the next morning hard as a rod and annoyed at the insistent ringing doorbell. The ringing was soon followed by an impatient knocking that made him grimace. He wished it was the bastard who had attacked Claire last night in her driveway, because Duncan felt about as angry as a black bear aroused from hibernation and willing to take on just about anyone or anything that moment. But with a depressing sigh he realized that no mugger/car vandal would knock on the door at six o'clock in the morning.

Duncan slowly staggered from the sofa, groaning at the tension that tightened his neck and shoulders, not to mention the ache in his groin. He wasn't surprised. The tension came from trying to fit his long body on a small, narrow space, and the ache came from restraining the urge to walk the few feet to Claire's bedroom after those amazing kisses in the kitchen. He had been a gentleman for once in his life and he had learned his lesson—being a gentleman sucked.

Somewhere in the middle of the night, his need to have Claire had become an obsession. And it was very disturbing. He had a bet to win, not just so he could finally have his player status undisputed but also because the penalties for losing would be nothing short of disaster. If Duncan had to stand in front of his hometown crew and admit to being a punk . . . He shuddered to think of what would happen. After all the years of his waving his exploits in the faces of his friends at the local pubs, picnics, parties, baptisms . . . Duncan should just buy his one-way ticket to Siberia now.

This bet was becoming a pain in his ass, taking much more time than he had anticipated. But, then again, no man barreled down a freeway at 90 miles an hour in the middle of the night just for a bet. And sure as hell no man spent the entire night on a lumpy, too-short sofa for a damn bet. Duncan had never done anything that stupid for a woman while in the soothe stage.

Duncan ran a hand down his face, including the light morning stubble that he needed to shave before work, and decided to think about this later. Right now, he had a paperboy to strangle. Duncan didn't bother with pulling on his shirt before he stumbled across the living room and squinted through the peephole. He groaned and banged his head hard against the front door. Annabelle. The tight leopard-print minidress she wore hurt his eyes.

"Did I hear the doorbell ring?" Claire asked from behind him.

Duncan turned and his heart tripped. She had obviously been awake for a while, because she had showered, judging from the gentle soap smell that drifted across the living room to wrap around him, and wore another dark suit. Duncan momentarily pictured her closet and smiled at the image of one dark boring suit after another. Her hair was in that immaculately maintained ponytail low at the nape of her neck. A touch of lipstick, mascara, and a hint of academic smugness completed the picture of Dr. Claire Scott, first thing in the morning.

His breath caught in his chest. He had never reacted to a woman in a suit like this before. Maybe to a woman in one of those suits onstage in a "gentleman's club," but a woman wearing a regular suit with a regular knee-length skirt and a regular jacket and regular three-inch . . . He nearly choked. She was wearing open-toed black high heels. Bare toes this early in the morning. How much more could he take? He was only human. At least, her toenails weren't painted. Then Duncan would have lost all control.

As the silence in the room lengthened, Claire's gaze dropped to his bare chest, and Duncan actually felt goose bumps rise on his skin. Duncan always had a smooth word, a compliment to make a woman feel good, for every situation. But he found himself absolutely speechless at that moment. Maybe the Medusa rumors about Claire were true and she *could* turn a man to stone, because Duncan could not move.

"Is something wrong?" Claire asked softly.

Duncan took a few defensive steps away from her and forced air into his lungs. She was just a woman. He didn't even like her . . . that much. This was all for a bet. Some good times. Nothing more, nothing less.

Duncan cleared his throat and remembered English. "Annabelle is at the door."

"Annabelle," she murmured, surprised. She walked past him, and Duncan curled his hands into fists to resist the urge to grab her. Before he did something really stupid, he began to frantically search for his shirt. He had to get out of her sweet-smelling, entirely too-comfortable house. He needed to rethink his entire strategy.

Claire opened the door, and Annabelle breezed in while cheerfully chattering, "I tried to wait to a decent hour, but I had to come over as soon as I woke up because I have to hear about your phone call. Did you stick to the time limit—"

"Annabelle," Claire gasped in horror.

Duncan didn't bother to hide his smile as Annabelle finally spotted him. Claire was obviously embarrassed as she placed one hand on her forehead and shook her head. Annabelle obviously felt no such reservations, because she grinned at Duncan, then began to saunter toward him like a real-live Catwoman. Duncan frantically scanned the room for an escape but found none.

"Well, well, well . . . Good morning, Duncan," Annabelle purred, pointedly staring at his bare chest. "Very, very nice. Just the trace of a six-pack, just enough hair, nicely colored nipples. I'm impressed."

Duncan frowned at her, ignoring her comments, then spied his shirt under a pillow on the easy chair and quickly slipped it on. He missed a few buttons but got the job complete in record time with Annabelle closely watching to spur him on.

When his chest was completely covered, she sighed in disappointment, then turned to Claire and said, "You slut."

Duncan opened his mouth to defend Claire's honor, but then Annabelle laughed in obvious glee. She said to Claire, "And I thought I would have to give you diagrams."

Claire said evenly, "You're jumping to conclusions that aren't warranted—"

"I'm not your father, Claire," Annabelle interrupted with a huge grin. "I think it's great that you and the stud obviously had a full night of horizontal mambo. I don't think it's healthy for a woman to go as long without sex as you have—"

Claire's gasp was loud enough to snap Duncan from fantasies that had instantly started at the word *horizontal*. Personally, the idea made Duncan grin, but judging from Claire's dismay, she didn't feel the same.

Duncan felt the need to tell Annabelle, with as much sincerity as he could muster, "Nothing happened. I spent the night on the sofa."

Annabelle gaped at him in disbelief. "You expect me to believe that two consenting adults, one of whom is Duncan Hillston, spent the night alone in this house and didn't get jiggy? Come on, Duncan. You'd sleep with Claire just on principle. There's no need to protect little Claire's reputation. I'm her friend. I'm happy for her."

The longer Annabelle spoke, the more Duncan's amusement faded and the angrier he became. Whether it was because Annabelle characterized him as a rutting animal or because she characterized Claire as lonely and desperate, Duncan didn't know. Either way, this woman was getting the hell on his nerves.

Claire obviously could see Duncan's mounting annoyance and said quickly, "I have an early-morning meeting, Annabelle, so I can't talk. I'll call you later today."

"And I'll be waiting," Annabelle sang. She cast another glance at Duncan and shook her head in wonder. "You stud."

Before Duncan could respond, Annabelle walked out the still-open front door. Duncan looked at Claire, and she returned his gaze, her mouth twitching with obvious amusement, which she tried to hide as she closed the door.

Duncan faked a glower in her direction and muttered, "Don't even say it."

Claire shrugged and said sweetly, "I was only going to ask if you would like some coffee . . . stud?"

Duncan groaned but found himself smiling. "Now I know how a Chippendale dancer feels."

"Annabelle has never been shy," Claire said with an amused shrug. "In high school, I always knew where I stood with her."

"And that's a good thing?" he asked doubtfully. Claire burst into laughter and Duncan couldn't help but grin. Something warm curled in his stomach and every self-preservation instinct in his body screamed at him to get out of that house that moment.

"How about that coffee?" Claire asked.

"That sounds good," Duncan responded instantly, as if his mind weren't battling his body for supremacy.

Duncan followed her into the kitchen, and without the excitement and drama from last night he took the opportunity to scope out the place. Not an item was out of place, from the cheerful flowers on the windowsill above the sink to the gleaming pots and pans hanging over the island in the middle of the room. Everything in the kitchen shouted order and neatness. He could only imagine what her lab looked like.

"Would you like Costa Rican or Greek?" she asked while holding up two coffee bags from the pantry closet.

"It doesn't matter to me. Coffee is coffee."

Claire gasped in horror and held one bag against her chest, as if to shield herself from his ignorance. "Duncan, please do not allow me to hear those words from your mouth again. All coffees are not created equal. Just like all cereals are not created equal."

"You have a point there," he conceded.

"What kind of coffee do you normally drink?"

"Instant, mainly."

Claire gasped again and this time Duncan laughed, because she looked more distraught at the possibility of him drinking instant coffee than she did about someone attempting to steal her research.

Claire shook her head, then said, "I'll go easy on you this time. Initiate you with a nice, gentle Costa Rican blend."

Duncan smiled because, whether she knew it or not, she had implied there would be other times. He leaned against the island in the middle of the kitchen and watched her efficient movements as she scooped the finely ground coffee beans into the coffee machine. She had a gracefulness and economy of movement that he figured must have come from years of moving in the confined space of laboratories. Then his eyes drifted to her breasts beneath the snug-fitting jacket. He remembered the feel of her breasts pillowed against his chest last night in this exact room. If he had held one of her breasts in his hand, it would have flowed over and kept him real happy for a long time.

To keep his mind off his drifting thoughts, Duncan said, "In high school, Annabelle wore thick black eyeliner and a lot of black clothes. She was kind of scary, but I don't remember her being so . . . so . . ." He scratched his head, searching for the right word.

"Clueless," Claire supplied helpfully. Duncan nodded in agreement. She smiled as she finished the coffee preparations and the machine began gurgling and spurting. "I don't know what caused her drastic change. She and I lost touch after high school. She told me that she's been in Europe, modeling."

"You sound like you don't believe her?"

"Of course I believe her," Claire said, but Duncan caught the hint of hesitation in her voice.

"What else could she have been doing?" he asked curiously.

Claire appeared on the verge of saying something; then apparently changed her mind and said, "She and I have just led very different lives since high school. We probably led very different lives in high school, but she understood me. We both felt so out of place."

"Everyone felt out of place in high school," Duncan said with a simple shrug.

"Not you," she said.

She pulled out two coffee mugs with the names of her respective prestigious universities emblazoned on the sides and set them on the counter. For the first time, Duncan realized that the only time he had ever set foot on a college campus was for Tavis's graduation a few years ago. That fact had never bothered Duncan before, but now for some reason it did.

Duncan enjoyed being an electrician, and he loved working with his brothers more than he would ever admit to the blockheads, but what if he had gone to college? Done the whole coed thing. Read a bunch of books by a bunch of dead white men, joined a fraternity, played the guitar . . . Duncan silently cursed. He was musing about college? Duncan had never regretted not going to college in his life. The rational part of his brain reminded him to get the hell out of this house as soon as possible.

"You couldn't have felt out of place in high school if you had tried," Claire told him matter-of-factly. "You were the most popular, the most gor—the most everything."

"I was just as screwed up as every other kid in high school," Duncan assured her. "My two older brothers had been superjocks, and their legends were still fresh on-campus when I started at Westfield High. Kobie, my younger brother, started two years after me, and then my senior year, my baby brother, Tavis, started high school, and those two put my older brothers to shame with all of their athletic achievements. So, my parents had the starting lineup for the NBA, NFL, and Major League Baseball . . . and then there was me. I got cut from the basketball team freshman year, my one football season was subpar, at best, and I almost flunked freshman algebra."

Duncan nervously cleared his throat when he realized that he had put into words for the first time what he had thought his entire life. And to his surprised relief, Claire didn't look disgusted. She looked . . . She looked like she understood.

"You should have come to me," she said simply. "I could have helped you with the algebra, at least."

"I was more concerned about the basketball than the math," he said with a laugh, remembering how simple life had been to him then. "I thank whoever invented accounting software every day when I turn on my computer."

"Your football playing was not subpar," she pointed out. "You were very good, if I remember correctly."

Duncan grinned, proud for some reason, as he said, "You remember?"

He wasn't certain if Claire blushed, because she abruptly turned from him and began to wipe the already-clean counters with a dishcloth.

"Football players were treated like Roman gladiators in Westfield," she said. "Of course I remember that you were on the team. I remember the day of games Mr. Monier didn't make you turn in homework because he said you were probably too anxious about the upcoming game to concentrate on homework the night before."

"The good ole days," Duncan sighed.

She shot a look at him over her shoulder, then asked, "Why didn't you play junior or senior year?"

"I didn't want to waste my summers training for the upcoming season," he said with another nonchalant shrug.

Claire turned to him with a quizzical expression. "Is that really the reason?"

He nodded with a shrug. "I'm a pretty lazy guy. Hawk played through senior year, but Patty and I preferred to sit in the bleachers and scam on the cute girls rather than be on the field away from the real action."

"You're not lazy," she said seriously. "You're a classic middle child. You're afraid of your own success, so you don't even try. You were scared that you would be the one family failure, so instead of failing, you didn't try."

He forced a dry laugh when he realized that Claire was

watching him closely. "What? In the middle of all that school-ing did you find time to become a psychiatrist, too?"

"Technically, no, but I could get a Ph.D. in psychology with two more classes," she answered, then began to pour steaming coffee into the two mugs.

Duncan shook his head in amazement. "Have you slept in the last fifteen years?"

Claire smiled in his direction, then asked, "How do you like your coffee?"

"Black."

She handed him the mug, then poured a small shot of cream into hers. The scent of freshly brewed coffee soaked through Duncan's brain. Instant coffee never smelled like this. Duncan took a hesitant sip and found the liquid went down smooth.

"How is it?" she asked, watching him closely.

Duncan shrugged casually, and when her eyes narrowed, he laughed and admitted, "It's great, Claire. Where can I buy this?"

"I go to a shop on La Brea that has this coffee shipped in once a week. The next time I go, I'll pick you up a bag."

Duncan felt a strange fuzziness in his stomach. She was treating him like a friend, concerned about his coffee educa-tion. And he was technically only here because of the bet. He suddenly felt too much guilt to continue standing in her kitchen, drinking her delicious coffee. Taking her to dinner, showering her with a few insincere compliments, was one thing. Playing her knight in shining armor and having her buy him coffee beans was something entirely different.

"I should go," he said abruptly. Her eyes widened in mo-mentary surprise before she nodded and set down her coffee cup. He felt the need to explain himself to a woman for the first time in his life and said, "I have that early meeting in Gardena."

"That's right. You mentioned it last night."

Duncan held her gaze for a moment, not certain how to answer the questions swirling in her eyes; then he quickly turned and walked out of the kitchen. He grabbed his car keys and wallet off the coffee table, aware of Claire behind him. He opened the front door, prepared to gain some much-needed distance and to muddle through his next plan of attack, but then he found himself turning to face her. She watched him warily from across the room, and Duncan once more felt that twisting in his gut. He'd never had a physical reaction to lying . . . er, exaggerating before. It was his trademark. With his reputation and a trip to Europe on the line, now was not the time to get a guilty conscience.

"How about dinner tonight?" he asked, a tad too eager.

Claire studied him for a moment, then averted her gaze as she said, "I still haven't changed my mind about us, despite the . . . the, uh, events of last night. A relationship between us would be futile—"

"It's just dinner, Claire," he cooed, feeling on more familiar ground as he tried to talk a resisting female into something. "Besides, I'll just spend all night worrying about you, and I may get aggressive and hurt someone if I can't see for myself that you're all right."

"So, this is all about you?" Claire asked with a laugh.

"Yes, but you'll get a good meal out of it," he promised. Claire laughed, but Duncan could see that she was still hesitant. He had to get her on a real date for any real progress on the bet.

"I can't tonight," she said, avoiding his eyes.

To hell with not sounding eager. "How about Friday night?" he pressed.

She smiled and said simply, "All right."

"I'll pick you up at eight?" Duncan had the strange urge to hug her again. Not kiss her—although he wanted to do that, too—but just hold her against him and feel her breathing in and out, feel her heart beating in her beautiful chest. Instead he cleared his throat and said, "Be careful today."

"I will," she promised.

He didn't leave. He continued worriedly, "Don't take any chances. Until the police get to the bottom of this, you should be extra careful about who's around, who's watching you, where you park your car at work. Maybe have lab security meet you—"

"I'll be careful, Duncan," she groaned with a long-suffering sigh.

For some reason, he became more worried at her casual response. He decided to ignore it, for now. "Do you remember Elton Chambers from high school? He has an auto repair shop in Westfield now, does decent work. He can fix that window—"

"I already have an appointment at my regular repair shop," she said, then laughed. "Stop worrying about me. You're going to be late for your meeting."

Before he found himself warning her about the dangers of staying too long in the sun, Duncan nodded, then hurried out the door.

Chapter Eight

"Either you have the worst luck of anyone I've known or your life is becoming a *CSI* episode," Vino announced, then bit into a chicken salad sandwich.

"Has anyone ever told you that you watch too much television?" Claire replied as she peered through one of the high-powered microscopes mounted on the lab counters.

After a hectic morning spent at the auto repair shop and then in a series of meetings regarding the upcoming preclinical trials, around one o'clock Claire had finally been able to step into her lab. Whenever she donned that lab coat and her comfortable but distinctly unsophisticated Adidas running shoes that she had never run in before, Claire could relax. In the sterile confines of the lab, the world finally made sense again.

Claire would have much preferred to deal with exploding beakers than be subject to a Vino inquisition, but he had finally heard about the mugging and there was no escape. In the fifteen minutes she had been in the lab, he had dragged out of her the events from last night as well.

"You have to admit it sounds like a cop show," Vino continued excitedly. "First a mugging, then a fake car alarm to lure you out of the house—"

"There was no luring," she said. "I shouldn't have kept my duffel bag—"

Vino continued, oblivious to her interruption, "What if it's a case of mistaken identity? That happened on *Law and*

Order: Criminal Intent the other night." Claire laughed at him, then jotted down observations on the clipboard next to her. "But *Law and Order* doesn't really focus on romance . . . so it's more like an episode of *NYPD Blue*."

"You have a television sickness; admit it."

Vino grinned as he asked coyly, "So, you're admitting there is a romance with your high school crush?"

"I did not have a crush on Duncan in high school," Claire cried, frustration causing her voice to rise. Across the large lab, several of the postdocs who were hovered around a computer screen, oohing over the latest pictures from Mars on NASA's Web site, stared at Claire in surprise. She nodded stiffly, turned back to the microscope. It wasn't every day the postdocs heard her wail like a teenager.

"I did not have a crush on Duncan in high school," she repeated more calmly. "He was a handsome young man, and I, along with ninety-five percent of the female population at Westfield High School, noticed that. Furthermore, there is not a romance. A few kisses does not mean romance. It means lust or desire or some other quantifiable emotion."

Vino's mouth dropped open, and Claire cringed because his mouth was full of half-chewed sandwich. He quickly swallowed the mass, then said, "You were kissed?!"

"I have been kissed before, Vino."

"I've known you for over ten years, and I can count on one hand the number of dates you've been on in that time. So, unless you had a swinging social life which you hid from me, and which you managed to squeeze around sixty hours a week in school and lab work . . . it didn't happen that much."

Claire narrowed her eyes at Vino, but she couldn't contradict him. In fact, he was probably the one person she couldn't correct.

Vino suddenly frowned, then wiped his mouth with a napkin and said, "Now that I know you've actually been kissed, it makes me look at you in a whole new light. A whole new very weird light. You're not supposed to be kissing men. Aren't you like ten years old?"

Claire rolled her eyes, annoyed, but she laughed at his

stricken expression. "I'm very proud of you for being able to handle this talk. The last time I told you I went on a date, you grunted and told me to pass a calculator."

"I'm turning over a new leaf, trying to show more interest in others. . . . And Fiona has been forcing me to watch *Girlfriends,*" he admitted.

Claire wondered exactly how much "forcing" Fiona had to do. "Annabelle convinced me to have an affair with Duncan," she blurted out.

Vino frowned in confusion. "An affair? Do people even still use that word? What exactly is an affair?"

Claire suddenly wished that she had never started this subject with Vino, but she also had no one else to talk to about this unusual development in her life. Vino, wearing dark jeans and a sleeveless, torn T-shirt under his lab jacket, with hair strands dyed neon blue today, would have to qualify.

"It's a step below a relationship."

Vino nodded in understanding. "So, you're just sleeping with him?"

"I did not sleep with Duncan," she gasped, shocked, although last night she would have done exactly that if he had seemed interested.

"So, you're planning to just sleep with him? Not let your emotions get involved?" Vino scratched his scraggly beard, then shook his head and said seriously, "Carrie tried that with Aleksandr Petrovsky. It didn't work."

"What in the world are you talking about? . . . Forget it. The truth is I could use a break from worrying about the preclinical trials every waking hour. Duncan takes my mind off all the stress and pressure. He's fun, and he doesn't expect anything."

"Contrary to popular belief, men have feelings, too," Vino shot back.

"You know what it's like being as smart as we are," she said with a heavy sigh. "Maybe its easier for men because society tells us that men are the smart ones, but women . . . Trust me, a smart woman may as well have leprosy, because no man will come near her once he finds out that she's smarter than him. And I'm not just a little smarter; I'm a lot smarter. Duncan didn't even attend college."

"So, he deserves to have his feelings hurt?" Vino asked, annoyed.

"There is nothing I could do to hurt Duncan's feelings," she snorted, ignoring the flash of guilt.

Duncan had been caring, kind, and sweet last night. Not to mention that morning when he had looked ready to attach himself to her hip and follow her to work because he was so concerned for her safety. That morning he hadn't seemed like a no-strings-attached, affair guy; he had seemed like a guy a woman could depend on and fall in love with. And maybe last night when he had hopped out of his truck, she hadn't been thinking about the difference in their intelligence.

Claire shook her head at her thoughts and told Vino, "Don't worry about Duncan. Women are a game to him."

"He fought off the mugger for you, he was prepared to come to your house late at night just because your car alarm went off, without even knowing that some psycho was outside, and then he spent the night on the sofa. He definitely sounds like a man out for one thing to me." Vino shook his head, then walked across the lab to his station.

Claire glared after him. She would have to tell Vino's girlfriend to cut down on his TV intake, because he was actually starting to make sense.

Duncan frowned at the endless ringing, then cursed and slammed the telephone back down on his desk. No answer. That was the third time he had tried Claire at BioTech in the last two hours. It was two o'clock in the afternoon; she should have still been at work. He cursed himself for not asking for her direct line at work or for her cell phone number, but he hadn't wanted to seem too eager. Being eager was not how a player played a game. Except now he couldn't get in touch with Claire, and it was driving him crazy.

Duncan turned back to the construction site, where three part-time workers were finishing laying concrete. Hillston

Brothers Construction had been hired to expand a landmark in Westfield, Estefan's Bookstore. They were running slightly behind schedule, and to add an extra jolt of stress, Kobie had misstepped and fallen off a ladder earlier that morning. Duncan had had to rush him to the hospital, then drive him home with a sprained ankle and a bruised ego. Since Estefan had already sent out thousands of flyers promoting the grand reopening in a month, Duncan knew that the rest of the brothers—and their part-time help—would have to work round-the-clock to make certain that construction was finished on time, under budget, and fault-free.

Grand reopening or not, Duncan was debating leaving one of the new hires in charge and driving to Claire's lab. Every time Duncan told himself that he was being stupid, he thought of the sound of Claire's voice last night when she had found the broken window on her car. She had specifically told him that she couldn't see him tonight, but Duncan didn't care. Maybe she had another date and couldn't . . . Duncan gulped. He had thought she needed to work tonight, but maybe she did have a date. Duncan was almost to his truck when his older brother's dusty truck rumbled to a stop next to Duncan.

Alex, the second-born and most annoying, as far as Duncan was concerned, stepped from the truck, still looking like a football hero at thirty-four years old. Broad-shouldered, with not a hint of fat on his sturdy, tall athletic frame, he wore a dark suit, which meant he had attended another meeting with prospective clients. Since Alex was the only Hillston brother who could stomach wearing a suit and tie for hours at a time, he handled most of the clients.

"I got here as fast as I could. I was at a meeting in the San Pedro," Alex said, concern marring his features. "How's Kobie?"

"Feeling stupid. The doctor said that he has to stay off his foot for, at least, the rest of the week. Lee is pleased. She has a whole list of projects that she wants him to do—like fold laundry, iron clothes, fix the kids' broken toys. . . . Kobie is already begging to come back to work," Duncan answered with a laugh.

Alex grinned as he shrugged out of his suit jacket. "Remember when I got sick last year and stayed home for about a week? A day on-site was nothing compared to Kathleen's list of chores."

"Another reason I'm still single," Duncan said simply, then asked, "How'd the meeting with the Jacksons go?"

"Very well. They're going to make their decision by tomorrow, but I feel good about it." Alex watched the workers for a moment, then nodded, satisfied. "Even with Kobie out, we should be able to finish this job in time for Mr. Estefan's grand reopening. I'm going to change in the trailer and help with the cement."

"Good, because I have to leave," Duncan said hurriedly.

"Where are you going?" Alex asked as annoyance flashed across his face. "We need to finish this project on time, Duncan, and every second counts. We only have a few more hours of sunlight. Can't it wait a few hours?"

Duncan glared at his older brother. Since they had been children, Alex had felt it was his personal responsibility to boss around his younger brothers as much as possible.

"No, it can't wait," Duncan replied stiffly.

Alex's eyes narrowed as he spit out, "This better not be about some woman."

"What the hell is that supposed to mean?"

"Kobie said the whole time you were sitting with him in the waiting room at the hospital, you were trying to reach someone on your cell phone. I think the word he used to describe your behavior was *frantic*. Who is she?"

Duncan silently cursed Kobie and his big mouth. Sometimes Duncan felt like his brothers were worse than the gossiping senior citizens at the community center where his grandmother went to play poker in the afternoons.

Embarrassment heated Duncan's cheeks. Alex would kill him if he knew about the bet. Then Alex would tell their parents, and Vincent and Dorrie Hillston would kill Duncan all over again. But Duncan didn't mention Claire's name. For the first time in his life, Duncan had no desire to brag.

Duncan ignored Alex's question and muttered, "I didn't know I needed your permission to see a woman."

"When it interferes with work you do," Alex shot back, his voice rising.

Duncan didn't normally blow up. He left that to Alex and their volatile youngest brother, Tavis, who could explode over someone looking at him the wrong way. Duncan was a lover, not a fighter, despite what Claire had witnessed. But Duncan suddenly found his blood boiling to the danger point.

"I'm interfering with work? Are you actually suggesting that my leaving early for once will interfere with our work?" Duncan demanded angrily. "What about you, Alex? What about Kobie or Tavis? Do I complain that you guys interfere with work when one of you has to take off early to pick up the kids from school, or go to a soccer game or a Brownie meeting, or—hell—to fix Jell-O snacks because you miss the kids? You three have missed more work in the last two months alone than I have in the last five years."

Rage shone in Alex's brown eyes and he advanced toward Duncan. "Do not compare our wives and children to one of your hos—"

Duncan didn't think about hitting his brother; his fist just flew reflexively. A jolt of excruciating pain raced through Duncan's hand to his shoulder as his fist collided with Alex's chin. That hurt. Apparently, Duncan hurt Alex more, as he flew to the ground and landed on his behind with a cry of pain. Duncan stood over him, his hand throbbing, his heart racing, but he was prepared to continue fighting if Alex tried to call Claire another name.

"You hit me," Alex whispered in amazement, then experimentally moved his jaw. "I cannot believe you just hit me."

Duncan shook his head in confusion because he couldn't believe it, either. The last time he had struck one of his brothers, he had been in junior high school and all five brothers had gotten into a fistfight on the front lawn that had their father threatening to send them all to military school, no matter how old they were. Duncan shook his throbbing hand to ease the pain.

Alex moved his jaw again from side to side, then actually laughed as he repeated, "You hit me."

"Yeah, well . . . You deserved it. You shouldn't call women hos. Kathleen would tear you a new hole if she heard you talking like that," Duncan muttered, then noticed that the sounds of machines running had stopped. He glanced toward the workers, who were gaping at the two brothers. The workers instantly returned to work at Duncan's stare, and once more the comforting sounds filled the air.

Duncan stared down at his brother, who remained reclining on the ground, as if he was still too shocked to stand. Duncan held out his uninjured hand and Alex took it. He hauled Alex to his feet and dusted off his shirt while Alex continued to shake his head.

"You know I'm telling Mom and Dad," Alex announced with a smug smirk.

"I'm a little too old to be grounded for fighting," Duncan muttered while trying not to laugh. He had right-hooked his brother. As many times as Duncan had wanted to do that over the years, he had never done it. He had never lost control, especially over a woman. Players didn't roll like that.

"I'm not telling them that you hit me, you idiot, although I should," Alex said, smiling. "I'm telling Mom and Dad that you're in love."

"What are you talking about?" Duncan growled, advancing on Alex.

Alex laughed and held up his hands across his face. "Don't hit me again," he said with a feigned shudder of fear.

"Stop acting stupid," Duncan snapped. "Why would you tell Mom and Dad that I'm in love?"

"Because you are, little brother. Whoever this woman is, she has you wrapped around her little finger. You nearly broke my jaw because you thought I was calling her a ho. You've got to tell me who she is. I want to shake her hand." When Duncan only glared at Alex, he abruptly laughed and patted Duncan on the shoulder. "Good luck, Romeo. This whole deal is not as easy as it looks."

Alex walked past Duncan and began shouting orders at the workers. Duncan glared after him and flexed his aching right hand. He should hit the idiot again. He was not in love with Claire. Duncan gulped over the sudden lump in his throat. Alex had said worse things about some of the women whom Duncan had brought around, and half of the time, Alex had been right. Duncan wasn't known for being too selective. He loved women. He could find something beautiful in every one of them, which was part of the reason for his success. Of course, he made the women sound like Halles and Tyras in the stories he told his friends, but Duncan had never been choosy.

But Alex saying something insulting about Claire hadn't felt right. Hell, it had felt like Alex deserved to be hit. Duncan suddenly cursed. He could not be in love with Claire Scott. He had only seen her twice, and she thought he had the intelligence level of a gnat. Duncan cursed again because he suddenly had the urge to try to call Claire again. He needed to hear her voice.

Chapter Nine

"I'll get it, Dad," Claire called to her father as she hurried from the kitchen to the front door of her father's house.

She doubted that her father would move to answer the ringing doorbell anyway. When Claire had been a child, her father had been taciturn, but now she was lucky to hear more than a sentence from him during Sunday dinner at her sister's house. Al Scott rarely spoke; he rarely smiled. He had attended every one of Claire's piano recitals, math competitions, and graduations, but Claire had never been able to tell if he had been happy about it. Since she had arrived at his house in Westfield after work that evening, Al had barely said more than five words to her.

Despite his quiet nature, Claire couldn't have asked for a better father. Whether driving her to college campuses for summer chemistry classes, while other children were taking swimming lessons, or flying with her to visit various college campuses before she decided on Harvard, Al Scott had been there.

Claire stopped in her tracks when she saw who stood on the other side of the security screen, ringing the doorbell. Even through the black ornate metal, Claire was rendered speechless by Duncan's smile.

"What are you doing here?" Claire asked, surprise making her voice faint.

"We're renovating the bookstore around the corner. I was

driving by on my way home and saw your car in the front," he said with a casual shrug.

Claire forced herself to move to the door and open it. She sucked in air at the full, unencumbered sight of him. Every kiss and every touch from the night before slammed into her like a tidal wave. In his baggy carpenter pants and stained T-shirt, he looked sweaty and dirty and . . . good enough for her to lick.

"Is this why you couldn't go out tonight? You had plans with your father?" Duncan asked while leaning against the door frame.

"Kira is in the summer league spelling bee. The championships are tonight at Westfield Elementary."

He grinned, and her thighs clenched, as if prepared to accept his weight. "That sounds like something you would have done when you were her age," he mused.

"I did."

"Finished first, no doubt?"

She smiled. "Of course."

"Of course," he murmured; then his gaze dropped to her mouth. She knew it wasn't her imagination that his gaze darkened or that his breathing grew heavy. Claire's own breathing suddenly became labored as she remembered the feel of his mouth on hers, his tongue plundering through her mouth as if on a search-and-conquer mission. He broke the spell by abruptly shifting his weight and clearing his throat.

"Did you hear anything from the police today?" he asked.

"Detective Hansen called and told me that she had interviewed a few of BioTech's competitors who are also working on ovarian cancer gene therapy treatments. None aroused her suspicion."

Duncan grunted in disagreement, then asked, "What about the fingerprints from the car?"

"Nothing conclusive."

"Nothing conclusive," he repeated, annoyed. "Some man is stalking you."

Claire quickly glanced over her shoulder toward the hall, where her father would appear at any moment. She turned back to Duncan and whispered urgently, "I would appreciate it if you would keep quiet the unusual . . . what happened between us."

"Why?" he demanded, his voice still loud and rough.

"Because I haven't told my father and I don't plan on telling him. I don't want to worry him."

"Why?" Duncan growled again.

She sighed heavily when she saw his clenched jaw and narrowed eyes. "Duncan, I know you're worried again because you're behaving aggressively, but there's nothing to worry about. When you think about it logically, you'll realize that I'm not in any danger. Whoever is behind this can't harm me or it would raise too many questions. Their only hope is to steal my research—"

"Damn it, Claire, I spent all afternoon worrying about you," he interrupted her angrily, but at least he was whispering. "I called your home and I called the lab, but the switchboard wouldn't put me through. Do you know what that made me think—"

"You called?" she asked softly, her brain congealing into nebulous mush in a petri dish. "I didn't know you wanted to . . . I would have called you—"

"You're still not taking this seriously," he hissed, stepping toward her in a way that made her heart pound against her chest. This level of aggression was beyond what the studies had described. Maybe there was something else going on besides worry for her safety. "What if we hadn't been on the phone last night when your car alarm went off? What if you had been walking by yourself when the mugger attacked? The more I think about this, the more I'm convinced that those two attacks weren't a coincidence. You are being purposely targeted, and we have no idea why. You should be in protective custody, or maybe we should hire a bodyguard—"

"A bodyguard," she said, shocked.

Duncan continued, ignoring her outburst, "I could barely concentrate at work thinking about you. I hit my brother—I actually hit my brother—and you're . . . This is stupid." He cursed, then stalked to the porch railing, his shoulders hunched.

Claire didn't know whether to yell back at him or soothe him. She had seen a mixture of worry and anger in his eyes. It was more than worry; it was fear. But Duncan wasn't afraid for himself. He was afraid for her. It didn't make sense. It didn't make sense that she hadn't seen this man in fifteen years and after a few nights she felt the same overwhelming sensation around him that she had felt in high school.

Claire hesitantly walked onto the porch and placed her hands on his solid, strong back. For a few minutes she gently massaged the tense muscles, attempting to find an appropriate response to his anger. No one at MIT or Harvard had taught her how to respond to such strong emotion.

She said softly, "I'm all right, Duncan. Nothing happened today. No muggings, no car alarms, not even a dirty look from this cafeteria worker that hates me because I said her meat loaf looked like chemical waste."

Duncan turned to her, his eyes still flashing, but his voice was soft—almost confused—as he said, "I was really worried about you today, Claire, and I've never felt that way for . . . The more I called and didn't reach you, the more my imagination began to run wild. To be honest, I drove to your father's house from the site because I was planning to ask him if he knew how I could get in touch with you."

"Really?" she squeaked, the concern in his voice making her feel all soft and squishy again. She stepped closer to him, enjoying the feel of all his maleness around her. "I should have given you the number to the phone in my lab."

"You should have," he agreed, the muscles under her hands relaxing as he smiled slightly.

The smile did it. It had always been his smile. Claire found herself leaning toward him, unable to resist the temptation his lips offered, unable to resist the comfort he offered.

"We need to leave if we're going to . . ." Al Scott's voice trailed off as he walked out of the house and spotted his daughter near lip-lock with Duncan.

Claire jumped from anywhere near Duncan and forced a smile at her father, who looked confused. She didn't blame him. It was confusing to see his younger daughter in a position he had never seen her in before. The only other man Claire had brought around Al was Vino, and Al had just stared at Vino like he would have at an animal in the wild. Al had spent forty years working for the local sanitation company. He occasionally took some of the divorcées in the neighborhood to dinner, but that was the extent of his social interaction outside of his family, even thought Claire thought her father was handsome, with latte-colored skin, wavy salt-and-pepper hair, and hazel eyes that would twinkle around Kira. He was too thin but very strong from years of hauling garbage around the city. And obviously finding his daughter with Duncan Hillston was not a scene that Al was prepared to deal with.

"Mr. Scott," Duncan said, recovering before either Scott. Duncan stepped forward, offering his hand. Al hesitantly shook Duncan's hand, and Claire hoped that her father would recover from his shock soon, or Duncan would begin to realize how rare it was for her to be with a man. "It's nice to see you again, sir. How have you been?"

Al glanced from Duncan to Claire, then back again. Claire sighed, relieved, when Al finally mumbled, "Good."

"This is Duncan Hillston, Dad. Remember him? He and I went to high school together."

Recognition flashed in Al's hazel eyes as he nodded. "Your parents lived on Maple Street."

"Yes, sir. They still do. I live a few blocks from here on Oak Street."

There was an awkward pause as Al studied Duncan, who continued to smile politely, and Claire tried not to run from the porch. She wondered how any woman survived the first meeting of a parent with a . . . Claire stopped herself. What was Duncan to her? She definitely didn't want to deal with that question while her father watched her.

Claire pointedly glanced at her watch, then said, too

brightly, "Dad, we should leave if we want to get a good seat for the spelling bee."

She almost thought her father hadn't heard her, since he continued to stare at Duncan. Then Al asked Duncan, "Are you coming with us?"

"Dad," Claire warned.

Duncan looked uncomfortably at his clothes, then said, "I haven't had a chance to shower—"

"The spelling bee doesn't start for another forty-five minutes. You still have time to head home, shower and change, and meet us there," Al said.

Claire gaped at Al. Her father would choose to suddenly become a warm and affable version of Bill Cosby in front of Duncan.

Duncan glanced at Claire, and she instantly shook her head in response to his unspoken question. As if that was what Duncan had been waiting for, he grinned and said to Al, "That's a good idea, sir. I'll meet you two there."

"We'll save you a seat," Al said, then turned to Claire and waved a disposable camera at her. "I got the camera. Let's go."

He walked off the porch toward Claire's car. She stared after Al, speechless, then turned to Duncan with the same amazed disbelief.

"I'll see you there," Duncan said lightly, then ambled off the porch as if he didn't have a care in the world.

Claire briefly closed her eyes and resisted the urge to bang her forehead against the door.

Duncan hadn't realized how much he had gotten into an elementary school spelling bee until he and Elgin did a very quiet and barely concealed high five below seat level when Kira correctly spelled *smorgasbord*. Duncan and Elgin had been doing much louder high fives earlier in the competition, until Claire and Joan and a few other parents in the crammed school auditorium had glared at them. If Duncan's family or friends had seen him, they would have thought he was watching the Super Bowl or the baseball world championship, not a spelling bee involving a child he had never met before.

Through seven rounds of spelling words and fifty fourth and fifth graders, third-grade Kira had survived. After an hour, the spelling bee had come down to Kira and Ben Osbourne. And Duncan did not want Ben Osbourne, or the kid's loud and obnoxious father in the front row of the auditorium, to win.

Duncan twisted his surprisingly damp hands together as the Osbourne kid walked to the microphone that stood in the center of the stage. In the seat next to Duncan, Elgin glared at the redheaded little kid as if he were a serial murderer. On Duncan's other side, Claire sat ramrod-straight, her expression impassive, almost an exact replica of Al Scott, who sat in between Elgin and Joan.

Duncan remembered Al. The tall, thin, quiet man had scared Duncan when he was a kid and, truthfully, scared Duncan now. Throughout the night, he'd caught Al staring at him, and he clearly didn't care that Duncan had caught him, because he would continue to stare at him. That wasn't the scary part; the scary part was that Al seemed to know that Duncan shouldn't have been there. Duncan tore his gaze from Al's and turned back to the stage.

The teacher, Mrs. Hunt, who looked like every fifth-grade teacher Duncan could remember, stepped to the microphone at the edge of the stage. She gave the Osbourne kid an encouraging smile. Kira sat in the lone chair at the center of the stage next to the microphone, her huge brown eyes alert. The alertness made Duncan smile because it looked so familiar. So like Claire.

"Mayonnaise," the teacher said to Ben.

Duncan felt Claire tense slightly when the Osbourne kid's eyes flew to his own contingent who sat in the front row of the auditorium. It was the first sign of a chink in his fifth-grade spelling armor.

"He doesn't know how to spell it," Elgin whispered gleefully to Duncan, who promptly gave him another quiet high five. Joan leaned across Al to glare at them.

The Osbourne kid's gulp was picked up by the microphone and broadcast throughout the auditorium as he stepped closer. Sweat beaded on his porcelain forehead before he said in a squeaky voice, *"Mayonnaise. M-a-y-o-n-a-y-s-e. Mayonnaise."*

"Damn it," Elgin hissed softly, which caused Duncan to laugh, because Elgin obviously thought that the Osbourne kid had spelled it correctly.

Mrs. Hunt smiled sadly and said, "I'm sorry, Ben. Please remain onstage, because if Kira misses her word, you will have another chance."

The Osbourne kid instantly looked at his family, and Duncan, along with the rest of the auditorium, heard the father's deep voice mumble something about "damn it." Duncan restrained the urge to jump from his seat and pummel the man. Even Elgin shot a glare at the father over the heads of the other parents and children in the auditorium.

"She looks so small," Claire whispered to Duncan, her gaze on Kira.

"She'll be fine," he said, then took Claire's hand in his. Duncan had never been a hand-holder. Hand-holding was nowhere in his rules for getting women, but he realized that he had been missing out when the warmth of her hand permeated his. Her hands were rough from years of dealing with chemicals in the lab, but compared to his callused palms, hers were softer than a baby's bottom. Still, there was something soft and seductive about her touch that made him imagine her wrapping them around his— Duncan quickly shut off his thoughts as Elgin's nervously tapping leg bumped his thigh. Duncan silently cursed. He was getting a hard-on in the middle of an elementary school spelling bee.

Kira stood and, in her shiny black patent-leather shoes and blue cotton dress, covered the distance to the microphone. Elgin momentarily stood to snap his probably hundredth picture of the night.

Mrs. Hunt spoke slowly to Kira, as if she hadn't spelled words that Duncan wouldn't even begin to know how to pronounce. "Kira, if you spell the next word correctly, you will win the Westfield Elementary School Summer Spelling Bee and go to Glendale next month to represent the school in the county summer championships. Your word is *sarcophagus.*"

Claire exhaled in relief, but Elgin muttered, "This thing is rigged. They don't want my baby to win."

"Kira knows this," Al whispered confidently. "She spent all last summer reading every book she could find on ancient Egypt. Claire and I took her to lectures and exhibitions at the museum. . . . She knows this word."

"So, *sarcophagus* has something to do with Egypt?" Elgin quietly asked Duncan. He shrugged in response, then turned back to the stage.

Duncan, the Scotts, and Elgin took a collective breath. For the first time since the competition started, Kira didn't promptly spell her word. She paused and looked over her shoulder at Ben Osbourne, who was staring at his hands and obviously trying hard not to cry as he sat in the seat she had vacated. Kira then directed her huge eyes to his family, including his still-mumbling father.

Kira took a deep breath, then raised her gaze to her aunt. Duncan glanced at Claire, who returned her niece's gaze. Duncan didn't believe in mental telepathy like *Star Trek* geek Patty, but Duncan could almost swear that Claire and Kira were communicating. Then Claire smiled, with a heavy sigh, and nodded.

Kira firmly said into the microphone, *"Sarcophagus. S-a-r-k-a-f-a-g-u-s. Sarcophagus."*

Mrs. Hunt said quietly, "I'm sorry, Kira."

Elgin released a disappointed breath but still clapped. The rest of the family smiled at Kira and gave her various thumbs-up signs. The Osbourne kid walked to the microphone and spelled his next word correctly, causing his family to jump up and down, as if they had just won the lottery. Kira remained in her seat, swinging her legs as if she were at the park, and not losing a spelling bee. Elgin looked more upset by the loss than she did.

"There's nothing worse than a poor winner," Elgin muttered, annoyed, glaring at the Osbournes.

Joan looked at him in disbelief, then grabbed his arm and dragged him toward the stage. Al melded in with the throng heading toward the exit.

Duncan waited until the people around them had cleared out the aisles, then he turned to Claire, who was gathering her sweater and purse.

"Kira threw the spelling bee, didn't she?" he asked. Claire stood and met his gaze squarely before she nodded stiffly. He shook his head in confusion. "Why?"

Claire's response was interrupted as Duncan was nearly bowled over by a brown blur that barely reached his waist. Kira ran past him and threw her arms around Claire. He had never seen such delight on her face as she wrapped her arms around Kira and squeezed. A longing like Duncan had never known rammed into him, causing him to grab the back of a folding chair. The truth, a concept he admittedly didn't have much experience with, hit him with a force that stunned him.

He wanted Claire. Not because of the bet but because he wanted her. He wanted her mouth on him, around him, on places that he shouldn't be thinking about in an elementary school auditorium. He wanted her all night and into the morning. He wanted to make her smile, he wanted to make her sweat, and he wanted to make her feel all the confusing things that he was feeling. Duncan instantly tried to cool down his suddenly raging libido when he realized that Kira was giving him curious looks.

"You were remarkable," Claire told her niece, oblivious to the sudden danger she was in from Duncan, who had begun to sweat.

Kira beamed at her aunt, then turned to Duncan. She stuck out her hand, like a pint-size adult, and said solemnly, "I'm Kira Brown."

Duncan gently shook her small hand, afraid he would crush her delicate bones if he squeezed too hard. "Duncan Hillston."

"It's a pleasure to meet you, Mr. Hillston. Did you enjoy yourself?"

He smiled at her precise, exact way of speaking. Claire

had spoken like that in high school. Big words in a high-pitched, small voice. In fact, Kira could have been Claire's child, even down to the dark mole next to her right eye.

"Very much," he said solemnly. "You did a great job up there."

"I lost," she said, but didn't sound very upset about it.

At that moment, the Osbournes walked down the aisle. The father held Ben in his arms, lavishing praise and beaming. Three other small children and a woman walked behind him, their eyes downcast, their shoulders slumped. Ben looked more miserable being the center of his father's attention.

The family disappeared out the auditorium doors and Duncan suddenly understood why Kira had lost and his admiration for her grew even more. He squatted to her height and hugged her, as he would have done one of his own nieces, hard and full of love. After a brief hesitation, Kira's thin arms wrapped around his neck.

"You did a great job up there," Duncan repeated firmly when he released her. She sent him a shy smile, then looked up at Claire, who squeezed Kira's small shoulder.

Elgin and Joan approached in a noisy mass, hugging and kissing Kira and acting as if she had just won the Olympics, instead of losing a spelling bee. Kira began to giggle under the attention and picture-taking, and Duncan finally saw the eight-year-old girl she was supposed to be.

"Are you ready for ice cream?" Elgin sang like a demented ice-cream man, any disappointment he had felt earlier wiped from his expression.

"When am I not ready for ice cream, Daddy?" Kira said with a giggle.

Elgin glanced at his wife and said, "She has a point."

The family walked out of the auditorium, and Duncan followed.

Chapter Ten

Claire's heart pounded against her chest loud enough for Duncan to hear as he followed her into her house. The alarm beeped in the background, and she quickly ran to the panel next to the door to disarm it. She heard Duncan close the door, and she took a deep breath. It took her a few tries, but she finally managed to punch in the correct code. The beeping instantly stopped, leaving them in quiet darkness.

Claire remained at the panel, uncertain how to proceed. She learned very quickly, but she had no previous experience to learn from. She had never been alone in her home with a gorgeous man who with just one look rendered her unable to string together a coherent sentence. Maybe it was seeing him be so gentle with Kira after the spelling bee, how he managed to nudge Claire's father a little out of his shell at the ice-cream parlor, or how he had been like a steady port in the storm during the last few crazy days. Whatever had happened tonight, Claire felt like her skin was on fire, too sensitive to endure the touch of her clothes, and the only person who could give her relief was Duncan. She wanted him tonight.

Duncan turned on the floor lamp next to the sofa, then glanced around the living room. "Everything appears to be in place," he said gravely.

Wringing her hands, she forced herself to turn toward him. Claire had never initiated sex. She had barely thought about sex before Duncan, outside the context of Shemar

Moore in a hot tub with no bubbles. Claire had always been ahead of her classmates in all areas except one. Relationships. Most of the men she had gone to school with had considered her either too young or too smart to even ask out. And the ones who had asked her out had lost interest after Claire began talking about her latest advanced physics class. Besides a few fumbling experiences in dark dorm rooms with a physics Ph.D. student she'd called her boyfriend for six months in graduate school, Claire didn't have much experience in the whole area, and she had absolutely no experience close to a man like Duncan Hillston.

"Thanks for following me home. That was very sweet of you," she said, barely able to meet his eyes, for fear that he would see her unmitigated lust. She didn't want to scare him away. Not yet, at least.

"It was sweet of you to invite me to Kira's spelling bee," he said, his voice coming closer as he moved across the living room toward her.

Claire finally forced herself to meet his eyes and her breath caught in her throat at how close he was. She tried to sound unaffected by his nearness as she said, "I didn't invite you. My father did."

Duncan smiled and murmured, "That's right. Well, it was sweet of your father to invite me."

Claire smiled in return, then stared at the ground. The house was silent as a library, but Claire had never felt anything like this while standing in a library. She forced herself to look at him again and flinched when she realized that he was watching her. The look in his eyes made her heart pound, because she realized that she wouldn't have to initiate anything. The aching need inside of her began to build.

His gaze slowly drifted over her body, branding her skin and making it tingle everywhere that his gaze touched. His eyes finally stopped at the point of her V-neck suit jacket. There was no cleavage, not even a hint of skin, due to the high-neck blouse that she wore, but Claire felt like she was laid out nude in front of him. She flexed her hands at her sides, eager to touch him.

"She reminds me of you when you were a kid."

"Who?" she asked blankly.

He flashed that predatory smile again, then said, "Kira."

Claire laughed and shook her head. "I never would have allowed anyone to beat me in a spelling bee. And I definitely would not have given anyone the opportunity to beat me. I was a hard kid."

"You had to be competitive to get as far as you did as quickly as you did. It took a lot of guts. Walking into high school on the first day of school is petrifying for anybody, let alone an eleven-year-old."

"It was challenging," she said haltingly. When Duncan continued to stare at her, she said quietly, "When Kira first showed signs of being . . ."

"Special," he supplied helpfully.

Claire smiled at the understatement, then continued, "I was worried. I didn't want her to be different, like I was. I wanted her to have a normal childhood."

"I never thought of you as abnormal."

"I was," she said with a bitter laugh. "The only thing that kept me going was the fact that one day I would be as successful as everyone always predicted."

"And you are," he soothed.

"No, I'm not," she confessed. When Duncan stared at her in surprise, Claire shook her head in disbelief that she was on the verge of telling him her dark secrets. But, she was, because he wanted to hear them. Her voice dropped to a whisper as she asked, "What if it's not enough? What if the tests fail and my research is just another one of the thousands of failures? This is my last shot, Duncan. I've had my whole life to prove to myself that I was worth all the accolades and predictions, and I haven't proved anything, except I can get a few degrees."

"Are you serious?" he asked in disbelief. "You've accomplished more in your short twenty-nine years than some people accomplish in a lifetime."

"Why? Because I have a few degrees?"

"No," he said, stepping closer to her. "Because you've

devoted your professional life to creating something that will save millions of people. That's admirable. It's amazing."

"But I'm doing it for my own gain," she confessed almost desperately. "You don't get it, Duncan. If my eleven-year-old self saw the failure I had become today, she would be so ashamed. So dejected. Other gifted children from my age group are winning Nobel Prizes, developing cleaner energy sources, developing foreign policy. What have I done? I have a theory that may or may not cure ovarian cancer."

"Claire, you're not a failure," he said firmly. His eyes burned like two black diamonds as he said softly, "You're an incredible, beautiful woman. And even if your drug fails, you'll go back to the lab and you'll try again because that's how you are. You're brave and, yes, you're smart, but being smart is only a small part of who you are."

Claire swiped at the sudden moisture in her eyes. She hadn't been fishing for compliments when she made her confession, but she was glad to get them even if she had ruined things. She had a distinct feeling that women who entered affairs with men like Duncan did not confess the deep, dark secrets that kept them awake at night.

She asked suddenly, "Would you like a cup of coffee? I bought a new Russian blend that's supposed to be delicious."

His eyes never left her face as he murmured, "No, I don't want any coffee."

"A glass of wine?" she tried again, her heart beating fast at his strange tone. He was going to leave. She had scared him away. "Beer? Water?"

"No. No. And no."

She took a deep breath for courage, then asked hesitantly, "Do you want to leave?"

There was that smile again before he took a step closer to her and whispered, "No."

A soft sigh escaped her lips as he stared down at her, his expression intense. Claire felt her neck falling back as she stared up to meet his gaze. She wanted to touch him. She wanted him to touch her even more.

His voice was as soft as the moonlight as he asked, "Don't you want to know what I do want?"

"What?" she whispered dumbly.

He took both of her hands in his, his hard calluses causing friction along the palms of her hands. He held her gaze as he said, "I want to make you realize how special you are. I want you to stop letting your eleven-year-old self browbeat your twenty-nine-year-old self for being human. I want to do all of that eventually, but right now, at this moment, I want you to show me what you like."

"Show you what I like?" she repeated, barely able to breathe.

His gaze never wavered from hers as he moved both of their hands to rest on top of her breasts, her erect nipples beaded against the palms of his hands through the suit jacket and blouse. His nostrils flared at the contact.

"Yes, Claire, show me what you like. Show me what you want me to do to you," he said softly, stepping closer to her.

Claire licked her suddenly dry lips as she unconsciously pressed his hands against her breasts, flattening them, arousing them, torturing them. Her eyes slid closed as she exerted slight control on his hands to mold her breasts. Even through all her clothes, she felt his touch as if he touched her bare skin. Fire leaped from her center to spread throughout her body.

He lowered his head and kissed her neck. A soft kiss. Then his tongue swept to her ear and to the point where her neck met her shoulder. His mouth opened and his mouth owned that spot, caressing, sucking, and pulling.

Claire heard her own heavy breathing and the rustle of clothes as he continued to knead her breasts like an erotic form of clay molding. Her own hands dropped to her sides uselessly. She felt like she had no more bones, no more muscles, no more brainpower. She was just a mass of nerve endings. And that was fine with her.

Duncan's tongue lazily moved across her neck to pay erotic homage to the other side, leaving a trail of screaming nerve endings in its wake. She stood on her tiptoes to give him better access. His hands remained on her breasts, becoming almost rough, moving in motion to the rhythm of her slowly undulating hips that she hadn't noticed until then. At some point, he took off her suit jacket and unbuttoned the first few buttons of her blouse. Her bra was exposed to the cool air, but he didn't reach inside to give relief to her fiery skin. All he did was concentrate on her neck, her ears, the sensitive area behind her ears, her hairline. It was making her practically vibrate with need.

The more she pressed her hips against him in an instinctive invitation, the more focused he seemed on massaging her breasts, on nipping her ear and sucking the lobe. She whimpered in pleasure and frustration, her hands moving around his neck to cling to him. He was the center and the cause of the maelstrom around her.

"Show me what you want, baby," he whispered right before his tongue swirled in her right ear.

The ticklish sensation turned into a brief view of ecstasy and she moaned. Then his words penetrated the fog. He wanted her to show him. Claire was too aroused not to take his invitation. She clutched one of his big hands in hers, then slowly moved it down her chest, down her stomach. Duncan became as still as a statue as she led his hand past the waistband of her skirt. She gulped as their hands went down her thigh and then past the just-above-the-knee hem of her skirt.

Then his hot hand was on the inside of her stockinged knee, scalding her. Duncan's jaw clenched and he imprisoned her gaze as she moved his hand up the inside of her bare thigh and to the damp cotton in between her legs. She pressed his hand there and sighed in relief when she felt his long, strong fingers, felt how strong he was, so close to where she needed him. Her own hand dropped away, but Duncan continued to hold her there. He didn't move a muscle in his body; he just pressed against her, as if holding a small dam in place.

Claire hadn't realized that she had closed her eyes at the intense feelings coursing through her body until she opened them to find Duncan watching her, strain and desire evident in his clenched features. He removed his hands and she tried not to cry out in protest or regret.

Before she could wonder what that meant, he growled in a low voice, "Your bedroom. Now."

Claire stared at him for a moment, scared of moving, scared of breaking the spell. Then Duncan reached for her and she quickly turned and walked to the bedroom. He followed her, his footsteps heavy on the floor. They entered the dark bedroom, and she quickly walked into the room. Duncan flipped on the ceiling lamp, and she cringed, suddenly feeling self-conscious under the too-bright light.

"Duncan, I—"

He didn't allow her to finish her protest because he was on her, kissing her, plunging his tongue into her mouth. He was ruthless in his invasion of her mouth. He kissed her like she was his, as if he had never kissed another woman and he had waited his whole life just to kiss her. Claire responded, attempting to match his kisses, but she didn't have the strength to keep up with his questing, searching tongue. She finally sighed into his mouth and released herself, allowed herself to be conquered and controlled by his delicious mouth.

Claire suddenly felt the warm softness of her bed beneath her, and Duncan quickly moved on top of her, his mouth never leaving hers. His tongue bathed her bottom lip, then nipped her top one, pulling and releasing with a flick of his teeth. His kisses suddenly turned more languid, more thorough, almost lazy, as he settled over her, her legs in between his. She tensed when she felt how hard and long he was resting on her stomach. Her center began a new urgent call, begging her to do something to stop the need.

Claire couldn't do much of anything but feel, and the sensations were everywhere. His mouth on hers, the brush of his knuckles against her chest as he worked through the buttons of her blouse, and his groin ever so slightly rubbing against her in the most delicious way.

Duncan nipped her lips, then whispered, "You have an

incredible mouth. Simpson Cole always said you did, but the guys just made fun of him for looking at you. Not only were you Medusa, but you were a baby. I always agreed with him but never told anyone."

"Simpson Cole. Bastard," she murmured, unable to form a more coherent thought at the moment as her hands moved slowly up and down Duncan's back. He had changed into a long-sleeve dark blue shirt that had a silk feel to the material, and she loved running her hands over it, enjoyed feeling his strength and hardness underneath.

Duncan's laughter rumbled deep in his chest and transferred to their joined mouths.

"He was right about your mouth, though," he said as he traced her bottom lip with a finger. The intensity of his gaze on her mouth made her still for a moment. "I could spend all night just kissing you, but . . . You wanted me to do something else, didn't you?"

She murmured incomprehensibly, the pressure building in her like an impending tornado. She licked the corners of his mouth, then pulled his bottom lip into her mouth, attempting to gain entrance to the sweet saltiness inside. She loved the taste of his mouth; he tasted like the chocolate ice cream he had eaten at the ice-cream parlor, and Claire knew that she would forever associate dairy products with him. He abruptly moved away from her mouth, making her moan in protest. He planted a kiss in at the start of her cleavage, then slowly and deftly removed her bra with the flick of his hands.

Cool air rushed around her breasts, and Claire realized that with the bright ceiling lamp she was more bare for Duncan than she had been for any other man in her life. She forced herself to refrain from covering her breasts, but she couldn't stop herself from tensing. Duncan's eyes were trained on her breasts, looking like Tarzan given his first glimpse of a woman; then he slowly leaned over. Claire couldn't contain her scream as he took her left breast into his mouth. He pulled and the breast popped out of his mouth, jiggling softly into place.

Claire reared off the bed, but his weight kept her in place as he began to suckle the now-damp nipple. Spikes of painful pleasure ripped through her, destroying her. His hands moved around her stomach, pulling down her skirt as he continued to torture her breast with his tongue, licking and teasing the nipple with a mastery that left her body trembling. Claire was so focused on the sinful things he did to her breasts that she didn't realize he had divested her of her skirt, stockings, and panties until she felt the rush of cool air against her curls. His hand once more pressed against her, but this time without the barrier of clothes. Claire felt every ridge of his hand, every old scratch and scrape. She shivered.

His mouth transferred to her left breast, lavishing it with the same single-minded obsession and detail. His hand pressed against her, rubbing gently; then one finger began to dawdle at the entrance. The brush of that single digit sent sparks ricocheting through her body like a set of chemical reactions. Claire moaned his name, her head thrashing from side to side. No woman could handle all of these feelings at once and survive. Could she? Then that finger paused and pushed inside of her. Claire screamed and would have come off the bed if his chest hadn't been lying on top of her stomach, holding her down.

"Beautiful," he whispered, his breath hot on her damp breast. His finger worked inside of her. Slowly. "And very tight."

Claire's face was already hot, but it became hotter at his hoarse words. She forced herself to open her eyes, but she could only stare at the ceiling as her entire being focused on the finger being pumped carefully and slowly in and out of her, making her wetter and slicker than she had ever been in her life. His finger continued its rhythm as his thumb gently touched the bundle of nerves above her nest of curls. Claire screamed his name again, her head falling back in ecstasy. This couldn't be happening to her. Things like this didn't happen to her. But her writhing and combustible body told a different story.

Duncan moved down her body as his various digits continued their magic, the pressure inside of her body increasing to the point where she thought her ears would pop. She heard an almost crying sound in the bedroom and realized it was her. Then his hot breath touched her curls, and she froze. She liked to think that she was cool about it, but Duncan noticed, because he looked up at her.

"Uh-oh, you're thinking," he said, holding her dark gaze. "That can't be good."

She tried to close her legs, but she couldn't because there was big Duncan. His big body in between her legs. His head at the center of her. She felt herself rapidly cooling off as she thought about him being there. Right there. In a space so private and uncluttered by big men with big bodies.

"Talk to me, Claire. What's going on in that big brain of yours?" he asked while gently biting the soft mound of her stomach. She gulped as she thought about her less-than-perfect J. Lo abs. She tensed a little more and glanced around the room for her clothes, but there was the Duncan problem. His body rested over hers, and he didn't look like he was going anywhere for a while.

She said nervously, "You don't have to do that."

When Duncan heard the nerves in her voice, he became very still. He had to, or else he would be plunging into her welcoming wetness without a second thought. He had a feeling that this conversation was very important, and he tried to focus.

"I don't have to do what?" he asked carefully.

She was silent as she stared at the ceiling. Her body was now about as relaxed as an Olympic athlete at the starting block, and he felt like a pervert because he still could only think about licking her like an ice-cream cone.

"I like what you're doing now," she said, finally meeting his gaze with a pleading look that begged him to understand.

Duncan would have laughed in frustration if he weren't so close to bursting out of his pants. "I like what I'm doing now, too, but give me a few minutes and you'll love what I'm going to do to you."

"Are you sure?" she asked, narrowing her eyes.

Duncan gently moved her legs farther apart, or more like battled to open her tense legs; then he stared. He shook his head in wonder at the beauty he saw before him.

"I'm not one to brag—OK, maybe I am—but I'm pretty good at this," he said, and for the first time in his life, he was actually underestimating his skills so as not to scare a woman. He wasn't just pretty good. He was damn near legendary.

His hands massaged her thighs and slowly they began to relax and she began to breathe again, but he made no move toward her. Not yet. She still seemed too ready to close shop for business. Duncan said softly, "Relax your brain for a minute, and just breathe. OK?"

"Is that how long you can last?" she asked seriously.

He smiled, then licked his lips before he said, with a raised eyebrow, "Is that a challenge?"

Whatever she had been about to say died on her lips as he slipped a finger into her again. She hadn't cooled off that much and was still wet enough that he met no resistance. Her eyes slid closed and she moved against his finger, making a valiant effort to get back into it.

Duncan muttered a curse. She felt like a wet, luxurious glove. He wanted to pound into her until he passed out; instead he moved his finger, and she said his name. Duncan knew a lot of women worried about what they smelled like or looked like, but like most men, Duncan thought the main difference between a man and a woman was full of mystery and the most intriguing and sexy part on a woman's body.

He waited until she naturally began to open to him more, when she was no longer pretending, and then he added a second finger. He pumped his fingers into her, tight and hot, and his own body began to move unconsciously, in longing. Her eyes were closed and her breasts bobbed like a delicious Jell-O snack. She was all real. No silicone in sight. Duncan tried to breathe. She presented an erotic early Christmas present, and he was the lucky damn bastard who got to unwrap it. And then he bent forward and licked her. Slow and gentle, like an ice-cream cone.

She screamed his name and her heels dug into the bed. He smiled to himself, then licked her again. And again.

"Do you want me to stop?" he whispered over her harsh breaths.

Claire moved her head from side to side, but more from pleasure than as a response. "Duncan, please," she rasped. "Whatever you do, don't stop. I order you not to stop."

He wanted to say, "I told you," but it didn't seem like the right time, so he slowly and luxuriously lapped her from one end to the next. She screamed in pleasure and curled her nails into his shoulders. He didn't mind the pain; it grounded him a little. Only a little, because she was the sweetest-tasting, hottest woman in the world. He reached the bud of nerves and pulled it into his mouth, suckling and licking. She almost threw him from the bed when her hips reared.

Duncan tasted her again and again, occasionally sticking his tongue inside of her like he longed to do with another harder part of his body. She grew louder and more frantic in her struggles. And then Duncan kissed her. And she blew apart in his hands and mouth. And that was enough for Duncan.

Fifteen minutes later, Claire didn't trust her raw throat to speak. She could barely move as she opened her eyes and registered the sound of running water from the bathroom across the hall. She groggily glanced around the bedroom, embarrassing heat filling her cheeks as she saw her clothes strewn across the floor. She couldn't believe that she had instantly fallen asleep like a . . . like a man after such an incredible experience. She had been out for, at least, fifteen minutes. And she had passed out without helping Duncan get where he wanted to go?

A smile played on her lips as she performed one full body stretch for her supple, loose muscles. If she had known that she could feel like this after oral play, she would have given this affair business a closer look a long time ago. She felt more relaxed than she had in ages. She didn't even think she had been this relaxed in elementary school.

Claire heard Duncan's footsteps in the hall and she instantly pulled the sheet up to cover her breasts, although, considering what Duncan had just seen, it was a pointless exercise in propriety. Her eyes darted toward the nightstand where she kept a box of condoms. Until that moment, the box had been sitting in the back of a drawer, gathering dust, but now . . . She cleared her throat, uncertain of exactly how to bring up the condoms. They definitely hadn't covered this in her public-speaking courses at Harvard.

Duncan entered the bedroom, fully dressed. He smiled as he sat on the bed, staring down at her with such a gentle, caring expression that she almost lost her death grip on the sheet and kissed him. She wanted to start all over again.

"I should go," he said softly.

"You're leaving?" she croaked, the box of condoms going back into her mental drawer. "What about your . . ." Her voice trailed off as she looked at the front of his pants, which had been tented with his arousal moments before.

She swallowed the sudden lump in her throat when she realized the bulge wasn't so big anymore. He had obviously been busy in the bathroom. She quickly returned her gaze to his amused expression.

"Are we still on for dinner Friday night?" he asked, sounding as if he thought there was a possibility she would say no. Claire couldn't have said no to anything at that moment. Even if someone from BioTech's main competitor, Eternalife, had walked into the bedroom at that moment and asked for all of her research from the last ten years, Claire would have handed it over.

"Yes," she said, nodding, then added hesitantly, "You don't have to leave. . . . I wouldn't mind it—"

"No, I should go. I have an early morning tomorrow. One of my brothers injured himself on-site and the rest of us have to pitch in to pick up the slack."

"Is your brother going to be all right?"

"He'll be fine," Duncan reassured her, then leaned over

and kissed her on the mouth. A chaste kiss after everything he had done to her, after everything her body had gone through. He moved back and ordered gently, "Don't ignore your phone tomorrow. I'll be calling."

"I'll answer."

He kissed her once more; this time the kiss lasted longer, became heated. Just as she reached for him, he groaned, then moved from the bed. Then he was gone. Claire told herself that she should get out of the bed, make certain the alarm was on, finish some work from the lab, but instead she turned on her side and went to sleep with a satisfied smile on her face.

Chapter Eleven

"Has she seen through your corny ass yet?" Hawk asked as soon as Duncan slid into the booth at their local bar Friday night.

Duncan rolled his eyes and muttered, "Can I at least get a beer before you start?"

"He's in a bad mood," Hawk teased while nudging Patrick, who was already seated in the booth, his tie loosened and his shirt partially unbuttoned. "I guess that answers my question."

Duncan ignored Hawk and signaled the waitress for a beer, which was easy to do since it was barely five o'clock and much too early for any kind of rush at Woody's Bar. The only people in the dark and dingy bar that sat on the border of Westfield and San Pedro were Woody, his one waitress, and the three friends.

Duncan had suggested the bar when he agreed to meet Hawk and Patrick after work because he wanted to be close to home, so he could rush home and shower and change for his date with Claire. Duncan had spent all week thinking about the date—what he would say, what she would say, how he could get a hand inside her panties. Duncan couldn't believe that after everything that had happened between them after the spelling bee, after talking to her on the phone every night that week, he still hadn't taken Claire for the patented Duncan Hillston first date. Nice restaurant, candle-light, live music. It was time to get back on-track with soothe, entice, seduce. He didn't know what the hell had happened after the spelling bee, but he had purposely stayed away for the rest of the week so it wouldn't happen again. Not that he didn't want it to. God, how he wanted it to, but things were getting out of control, and the rules had been thrown out the window.

After that first taste of her mouth that night, he had gone a little insane. She had been so hot and had felt so lush against him. There was only so much temptation a man could take. And then when he had gotten her into the bedroom, she had turned into a little firecracker. She had been so tight gripping his fingers that he had nearly come in his pants. He had had to run from her house before he had driven into her sweet wetness like a crazed, rutting animal. Another first for the former self-proclaimed player king. Claire had been more than willing. Even after her full-body orgasm, her body had been shuddering with need. But Duncan, who could lie to the pope on Easter Sunday, could not sleep with her. Not when the bet hung over his head like a mythical hangman's noose. Only a few more weeks, and Duncan could win the bet and stay far away from Claire and her red-hot forever kisses.

"I can't stay long," Duncan said. "I have somewhere to be by eight o'clock."

"Here ya go, sweetie," the waitress said while setting a glass of beer on the table. Duncan ignored her suggestive wink and she walked away with a disappointed frown.

"You have your beer," Hawk said eagerly. "How's it going with Medusa?" Duncan glared at Hawk in response, his jaw clenched. Hawk laughed in disbelief, then said, "You can't do it, can you? Your stupid rules don't mean anything because she's not fooled by you."

Patrick shifted uneasily in his chair as Duncan continued to stare at Hawk. Patrick said suddenly, "He was at her niece's spelling bee earlier this week."

Duncan glanced at Patrick, surprised. Duncan hadn't told anyone about that, not even his brothers. It didn't seem very playerlike.

"You were where?" Hawk asked with wide eyes.

"How did you know that?" Duncan asked Patrick.

"My great-aunt was there watching her neighbor's kid," Patrick explained, then turned to Hawk and said, "This is all obviously a part of his grand plan. Remember step one? Soothing. How much more trustworthy could a guy seem after spending hours at an elementary school spelling bee?"

Hawk rolled his eyes and said drily, "And I used to think you were the smart one, Patty." Patrick bristled while Hawk stared down Duncan. "Come on, player," Hawk said in a nasty tone. "Tell the truth. You can't get past 'hi' and 'good-bye' with her. She's smart; more than smart, she's one of those bona fide eggheads. It's going to take more than a few recycled corny lines to get her to give you the time of day."

Duncan had the urge to tell Hawk about all the talking he and Claire had done last night, but he didn't. It may have been the first time in his life he deliberately withheld facts from his friend about a woman. Duncan didn't want to figure out why he had; he could think about that later. But right now a man did have his pride, so he had to say something.

"Claire and I are going on a date tonight, Hawk. La Bella Cucina. Eight-thirty reservations," Duncan said calmly, then prodded with one arched eyebrow, "You were saying?"

"You think one dinner at that overpriced place is going to make her fall in love with you in time for the block party?" Hawk asked with a loud laugh that didn't sound nearly as confident as Duncan knew Hawk would have liked it to sound.

Duncan sagged against the booth, suddenly feeling in his element. "Did I ever tell you about the time I met that woman on the freeway? All I did was pull over to help her change a flat tire and the next thing I know—"

"We know, we know, you were swinging from some harness she had strapped to the ceiling of her loft," Hawk interrupted impatiently. "So you claim. But Claire is not one of your fantasy women. She's real, and you're going to look like an idiot at the block party when she puts your ass in place."

Duncan shrugged and said, "The freeway girl was real, Hawk. Don't hate the player; hate the game."

"You know who I hate. I hate whoever came up with that stupid saying," Hawk snapped viciously.

Duncan laughed gleefully, because Hawk was obviously pissed. Duncan told Patrick, "I still have more than enough time, and everything is going according to plan."

Patrick looked worried as he asked, "There haven't been any more muggings, have there?"

"Muggings?" Hawk said, surprised. "You were mugged?"

"Some guy tried to take Claire's laptop that night we left the bar together, but I handled him," Duncan responded, without mentioning that he had "handled" the guy by being a human punching bag.

"Is Medusa all right?" Hawk asked, actually looking concerned.

Whatever good mood Duncan had been in instantly vanished. He said through clenched teeth, "Her name is Claire, Hawk."

Patrick sent Duncan a strange look, and even Hawk looked confused. Duncan silently cursed. He was behaving like a first-rate punk. First he'd punched his brother, and now he was ready to wipe the floor with Hawk's face for calling Claire by an old nickname.

Duncan abruptly threw a few dollars on the table and stood. "I have to go. I'll see you two later." He ignored the quizzical looks they both shot him and walked out of the bar, his head hung low.

Duncan stopped at his truck in the half-empty parking lot, then released a growl of frustration and kicked the rear tire. He was angry with himself, angry with Hawk, angry with the situation. All Duncan had to do to get Hawk to shut up was tell him that he and Claire had done a lot more than say "hi" and "good-bye" together. Hawk probably wouldn't have believed him, though Patrick would have. But Duncan hadn't told Hawk that. In fact, Duncan hadn't mentioned anything about his growing closeness with Claire or the fact that he had been in her bed, making her moan, last night. What the hell was wrong with him?

"Duncan, are you all right?" Patrick asked hesitantly, having hurried from the bar to stand next to him.

"I'm fine," Duncan muttered, rubbing his face. "I'm just tired."

"I heard about Kobie's ankle. Is he all right?"

"He'll be fine."

Patrick nodded, then said hesitantly, "The other night at the spelling bee, I heard . . . Never mind."

"What did you hear?" Duncan demanded, directing his frustration and anger at Patrick.

Patrick looked distinctly uncomfortable before he said, "My aunt Linda said that you and Claire looked . . . looked like a couple. She said that you looked at Claire how Uncle Rufus used to look at her. And she was happy for you because you had finally found someone."

"We just sat next to each other," he muttered, avoiding Patrick's eyes. "We're not a couple."

"Aunt Linda also said that you and Claire were holding hands?"

Patrick's question landed between them like a nuclear bomb. Duncan was still feeling the repercussions when he forced a laugh and said, "It's all a part of the three steps, man. You know that. Soothe, entice, seduce. I do what I can."

"You weren't going to tell Hawk about the spelling bee, though, were you?"

"I don't have to tell him everything," Duncan said defensively, then added with a fake laugh, "I can't give away all my secrets."

Patrick nodded in apparent agreement, then said, with a pat on Duncan's back, "Have a good time tonight, man."

Duncan winked and replied, "I always do."

The doorbell chimed through Claire's house at precisely eight o'clock. Duncan was right on time, as Claire expected. Claire stared at her reflection in the bathroom mirror one last time and wondered if she should have bought something to wear for the date. Claire didn't have many date clothes—actually, she had zero date clothes—but by the time she had gotten home from the lab, she had barely had time to shower, shave her legs, and throw on a black suit and a pair of matching heels. The skirt was flared and the jacket was tighter than she normally would wear, mainly due to the fact that it was a size too small. Maybe that counted for something.

The doorbell rang again, and Claire stumbled in the black three-inch-high sandals she rarely wore, and hurried into the living room. She grabbed her purse off the sofa, then straightened her outfit before she opened the door. Claire knew it was a scientific improbability, but as she gazed at Duncan, who looked better than he had that night in her bedroom, she would have testified before a congressional committee that time could stop.

Even though Duncan had called her every night since Tuesday, this was the first time that Claire had actually laid eyes on him. And, besides being flushed and aroused, Claire also realized that she was embarrassed. Not only because he had seen her in a position no one else had—as a complete hedonist—but because their phone conversations had been so intimate. She had told him her hopes and dreams about her cancer research; he had shared with her his desire to travel, and the position of being an unmarried, childless uncle in a big family. Claire didn't know if she was more embarrassed about the things she had told him or about that night.

Duncan sent her a slow, sensuous smile, as if he was remembering that night in her bedroom, too. His smile abruptly disappeared when his gaze dropped to her feet. He looked on the verge of choking, but then he met her eyes again and said, "You are breathtaking."

"I'm not breathtaking. I'm wearing a suit," she felt the need to point out.

"I happen to like women in suits," he said matter-of-factly. "It's a new addiction."

Claire couldn't help but smile, and Duncan reached toward her, then gently smoothed her hair back to her low ponytail. Claire felt the touch to the soles of her feet.

Duncan sent her another smile, then presented her with a dozen deep red roses that she hadn't noticed bunched in green foil paper in his other hand. Claire took the flowers and suddenly realized that she was smiling. She had received flowers before—from universities that were courting her for teaching positions, from labs that wanted to poach her from BioTech—but she had never received flowers from a man who had a look of such heat and promise in his eyes. Such X-rated memories of her.

"Thank you," Claire said softly as she inhaled their rich fragrance. "They're beautiful."

"They don't compare to you."

Claire shot him a suspicious look because he was being too perfect, too right, and she didn't trust that. But he only smiled at her in return.

"I'll put these in water," she told him, then hurried into the kitchen.

She found a vase under the kitchen counter and partially filled it with water before adding the flowers. She arranged the bunch for a moment, refusing to feel a little melty just because Duncan had brought her flowers. Roses were so cliché. Then she smiled. Who was she kidding? Red roses and a tall, dark, and handsome man wearing the hell out of his suit. This was already the best date she had ever been on. She couldn't wait to see what the rest of the night held.

Chapter Twelve

After a twenty-minute drive into the cramped hills above Hollywood, Duncan led Claire into a cozy restaurant. She had thought Duncan was lost as he wound his way through the dark streets of Hollywood, far from the lights and bustle of Sunset Strip, until he had turned into a parking lot of a small restaurant covered by ivy. Claire shook her head in disbelief, because Duncan had found the most romantic, most perfect restaurant in the county. She shouldn't have expected anything less.

The valet opened the passenger side door, but it was Duncan who raced around the car to hold her hand to help her out of the gleaming dark BMW. Claire didn't know where his truck was, but she had loved riding through the streets in the sleek luxury car. Claire stared at the restaurant, feeling a shimmer of excitement. Everyone in Los Angeles had heard about La Belle Cucina. The food was rumored to be excellent, the service impeccable, and the views of the city actually outshone the celebrities who regularly dined there.

"You didn't have to do all of this," Claire said, turning to Duncan.

"Of course I did," he said with a small smile, then opened the door and motioned for her to enter.

Claire smiled when they walked into the reception area of the building. The model-beautiful hostess stood near the door, behind a waist-high table. Beyond her stand was the intimate dining room, where tables of people—a few with faces Claire had seen on movie and TV screens—sat. The whole back wall of the restaurant consisted of glass, giving a view of the LA skyline. With glowing candles, fresh flowers, and white tablecloths on every table and tuxedo-clad waiters efficiently moving around the floor, Claire could admit that she was sufficiently impressed. La Bella Cucina's reputation was obviously well deserved.

"Good evening," the smiling hostess said. "May I help you?"

"We have a reservation under 'Duncan Hillston' for two," Duncan said, his hand coming to rest at the juncture of Claire's hip and thigh with a subtle possessiveness that made her face feel hot again. It was amazing how her body instantly reacted to his touch—humming, sparkling.

The hostess nodded, then touched the computer monitor. After several seconds, the woman's smile faltered and she glanced at Duncan. "What was the name again?"

"Hillston," Duncan replied, then spelled out his name for good measure.

The hostess slowly shook her mane of carefully blown-out blond hair as she stared at the computer screen. "I'm sorry, sir, but we don't have a reservation under that name."

Claire noticed the flash of alarm that crossed Duncan's face before he said smoothly, "There must be a mistake. I made a reservation this morning—"

"Tonight's dinner seating has been booked for more than four days, sir—"

Duncan's eyes narrowed and he said tightly, "I made reservations this morning with Connie. I always make my reservations with Connie—"

The hostess grimaced, looking almost as pained as Duncan did. "Connie was fired this morning, sir, for granting too many special favors. The owners decided that she was abusing her position. As you well know, La Bella Cucina is one of the most astounding dining experiences in the Los Angeles area that one can have, and it wasn't fair—"

"Fair," Duncan repeated in disbelief. "Since when does a place like La Bella Cucina care about fair?"

Claire placed a restraining hand on Duncan's arm as she said to the hostess, "Regardless of whether we have reservations or not, is it possible for us to be seated?"

"Not until Monday . . . at ten thirty p.m.," the hostess replied automatically.

Duncan cursed and his hand dropped from Claire's hip. Claire smiled at the hostess, who suddenly looked nervous, as Duncan's frown turned into a full-blown glower. Claire took Duncan's arm and nodded at the hostess, then dragged him out of the restaurant.

"I'm not leaving," Duncan said angrily while glaring at the entrance to the restaurant. "Did you see all those empty tables? They just didn't want to seat us—"

Claire couldn't stop the laugh from escaping her mouth. When Duncan directed his glare at her, she clamped a hand over her mouth, but she couldn't prevent the laughter that bubbled through.

"What the hell is so funny?" Duncan demanded while crossing his arms over his chest.

"You," she said. "I've never seen you look so . . . so human, even when you were getting your butt kicked by that mugger—"

"I was a few seconds away from getting out of that headlock," he muttered.

"Right," she said for the sake of his ego, then suggested, "Let's go somewhere else to eat."

"Where?" he asked, annoyed. "It's eight thirty. The only restaurant where we won't find a two-hour wait without reservations is McDonald's. And I'm not sure that one qualifies as a restaurant."

"Of course it does," she said simply. "I saw the golden arches on the way up the hill. I love those McFlurries."

Duncan stared at her as if she had suddenly started speaking another language. He sputtered in disbelief, "You want to go to McDonald's? On our first date?"

"Is there a problem with that?"

"Yes, there's a problem with that. I'm not taking you to McDonald's. We're going to La Bella Cucina. I always take my first dates to . . ." His voice trailed off and he actually looked embarrassed.

Claire crossed her arms over her chest and tried to hide her amusement. "You bring all of your dates here, don't you?"

"Just the first date," he muttered defensively.

"The patented Duncan Hillston first date," she guessed, and judging from the guilt in his eyes, she had hit the nail on the head.

He studied her for a moment, then said with a heavy sigh, "I'm not taking you to McDonald's, but I will take you somewhere that I've never taken another date in my life." She stared at him with a doubtful expression and he frowned, then said, "Just remember that you asked for this."

To say that the night was not going as Duncan had planned would have been a gross understatement. Instead of sitting across from Claire in one of the most romantic restaurants in the city, with a bottle of wine, candlelight, and a jazz trio, Duncan was sitting in a bright red vinyl booth in his brother's all-American "Nate's Grill" in the middle of Westfield.

Duncan ate at his brother's restaurant at least three times a week and could become a living and breathing commercial for Nate's Grill on cue, but this was the last place Duncan wanted Claire for the foray into the entice stage. The diner was loud, crowded, and there was always guaranteed to be a screaming baby or two. Then there were the pool tables in the rear of the restaurant, where the young dads gathered to act macho before being signaled by the wife to change the baby's diapers. How the hell was a man supposed to be romantic in a place like this?

Duncan's mood grew darker when his gaze drifted to the back of the restaurant, where Claire stood at one of the cursed pool tables, laughing with Patrick. Duncan should have known that it would be love-at-first-sight for the two science geeks. In high school, Patrick had gone out of his way to avoid the appearance of being smart. He had dropped that shtick in college and become an astronomer. Apparently, Patrick—the traitor—and Claire had a lot to talk about.

Duncan had escorted Claire into the diner an hour ago and hadn't spoken to her since. Half of the people who had been sitting in the restaurant had gone to high school with her and wanted to ask her about her life, convinced she was discovering the cure to cancer by now . . . which she was. Then Patrick had coincidentally arrived at the grill for dinner, and he and Claire had struck up a conversation about subatomic particles and black holes—which apparently were real—and disappeared to one of the pool tables. Duncan had been stuck guarding their booth and glowering at them.

Duncan would never admit it, but he was jealous. Claire seemed to be having a better time with Patrick than she had been with him. Duncan's eyes narrowed as Patrick and Claire burst into laughter that drifted across the restaurant even over the other din.

"One beer and one iced tea," Duncan's oldest brother, Nate, announced as he set two full glasses on the table.

Duncan directed his glare at his oldest brother. Nate had been the only Hillston brother who hadn't joined the construction company. Nate's dream had always been to open his own restaurant. He had declined a football scholarship to UCLA, gone to culinary school, and when he finally saved enough money after years of working in five-star restaurants, opened the grill. Hillston Brothers Construction had built the restaurant at half-cost in exchange for a lifetime supply of cheeseburgers. Duncan had to stop accepting payment, due to his doctor's stern warning about eating so much beef.

"You should take Claire's iced tea to the pool table, since she's obviously planning to stay at Patrick's side for the rest of the evening," Duncan mumbled.

For some reason, Nate smiled as he said, "Maybe you should join them, instead of glaring at them."

"I'm not glaring at anyone," Duncan growled. He was supposed to be on a romantic date, enticing Claire to want him, not taking love advice from his brother.

Nate's smile faded, and he abruptly slid into the booth across the table from Duncan. He looked worried as he asked, "What are you doing, Duncan?"

"I'm not doing anything, except being ignored by my supposed date and my supposed best friend—"

"Claire Scott," Nate interrupted impatiently. "What is she doing here?"

Duncan shifted uncomfortably in the booth, then met his brother's intense gaze. "I'm on a date."

Nate's gaze didn't waver as he said, "You don't date women like Claire."

"What's a woman like Claire?" Duncan asked, annoyed.

Nate visibly grappled for the right words; then he said quietly, "She's the type of woman a man marries. You don't date women like that, or at least the way you use the word *date*."

"Relax, Nate. Claire is not some virgin sacrifice. She's a very, very, very smart grown woman."

"Alex told me what happened the other day at the Estefan site," Nate said.

Duncan rolled his eyes, exasperated. He should have known that Alex would tell someone about their scuffle. Duncan had been surprised that his mother hadn't called him yesterday.

"Claire is an attractive woman, and I like attractive women. That's all that's going on."

"You better not be doing something stupid, Duncan, or I swear—"

Nate's hoarse warning turned into a beaming fake grin as Claire and Patrick stopped at the table, matching smiles on their faces.

"How was the game?" Nate asked cheerfully as he slid out of the booth.

Patrick immediately took Nate's abandoned seat, and, figuratively slapping Duncan in the face, Claire glanced at him, then slid in next to Patrick. Duncan bit the inside of his bottom lip to refrain from grabbing her arm and dragging her across the table to sit beside him. Did he smell?

Did his breath stink? Duncan wanted to slam Patrick in his face.

"Claire claims she's never played pool before, but she just beat me out of ten dollars," Patrick said with a feigned pout.

Claire giggled, and Duncan clenched his hands into fists under the table as desire shot directly to his suddenly raging hard-on. She was near. That was all he needed. Duncan had never fought over a woman in his life. He figured there were too many women in the world to deal with the potential bloodshed, but he would take Patrick outside and tear him into tiny pieces if he thought he was taking Claire from Duncan.

Claire waved a ten-dollar bill in front of Duncan and said with a teasing smile, "I'm buying dinner tonight."

Duncan's response caught in his throat at the sight of her unrestrained grin. Maybe he had stepped into the Twilight Zone. Patrick was getting the girl, and Duncan was sitting tongue-tied and alone on one side of the booth.

"You've played before, haven't you, Claire?" Patrick teased while nudging her in the arm. Duncan's eyes narrowed, and he could have sworn that he heard Nate actually smother a laugh with a cough. "Just admit it. You're a pool shark."

"I haven't played before," Claire insisted, laughing. "Pool is a game of angles. Geometry was one of my favorite subjects in school."

"Geometry was my favorite subject, too," Patrick said excitedly.

Duncan rolled his eyes in annoyance. He had barely passed geometry in high school. Then Claire looked at Duncan and smiled. A secret smile just for him. Whatever anger and rejection Duncan had been feeling disappeared. His hands itched to touch her, and he realized that he was straining against his pants, too hard to stand, too hard to sit. He needed relief, and he didn't think his brother would appreciate it if Duncan threw Claire on the table and sought the relief he needed in the middle of the dinner rush.

Duncan tore his gaze from Claire and glanced at Nate for

support or to put him out of his misery, he wasn't certain which.

Nate winked at Duncan, then said to Claire and Patrick, "How about a pitcher of beer on the house?"

"Sounds good," Patrick said, clapping his hands together. "A man needs a beer after being swindled by a pool shark."

Claire turned from Duncan to playfully hit Patrick's arm. "I am not a pool shark."

"Oh, is the politically correct word *hustler* now?" Patrick teased. Claire laughed while Duncan clenched his jaw.

Nate disappeared just as a waitress walked over carrying three orders of burgers and fries. Duncan sighed heavily. It looked like Patrick was staying. He sure as hell wasn't catching any of Duncan's pointed looks telling him to leave.

"Who ordered the California burger?" the waitress asked in a chipper voice that Duncan knew must have driven Nate crazy.

"I did," Claire said, raising her hand.

The waitress set down Claire's plate, then handed Patrick and Duncan their regular old-fashioned cheeseburgers. She sent Patrick an extra smile, then twirled on her heel and left their table.

"Doesn't she remind you of Kellie, Duncan?" Patrick asked, his smile fading, as he watched the waitress walk across the restaurant to another table.

Duncan inwardly groaned and tried to catch Claire's eye, but she was looking at Patrick with that concerned expression that women always got when they heard hints of a heartbreak. Apparently, not even super-duper intelligent Claire could see past that trap.

"Who's Kellie?" Claire asked.

"My ex-girlfriend," Patrick said with a dramatic sigh that made Duncan shoot him a warning look, which Patrick ignored.

Before Patrick could get started, Duncan quickly said, "Patty, this isn't the time—"

The dagger-filled look that Claire shot Duncan immediately made him shut up. She admonished, "Duncan, Patrick is in obvious pain. Let him talk. Studies have shown that being able to talk about severe emotional trauma with trusted friends and acquaintances is more effective than professional counseling."

Duncan snorted in disbelief, then threw up his hands in surrender. "I tried," he muttered to no one in particular, since no one was paying attention to him anyway.

Claire had already turned back to Patrick. She said soothingly, "Go on, Patrick."

"I met Kellie my freshman year at USC. I thought we were going to be together forever. . . ."

Duncan focused on eating his burger, because once Patrick got going on Kellie, there was no telling when anyone else would be able to get a word in. It was official. This was the worst date of Duncan's relatively long dating life. Although a date required two people participating in the misery, so Duncan didn't even know if this qualified. Patrick had stolen his date, and the most annoying fact of it all was that the date didn't seem to mind.

Chapter Thirteen

From across the pool table, Duncan watched Claire lean over the table to line up her shot. He quickly averted his gaze when he realized that he was staring at her breasts, the honey brown tops of which were visible as the suit jacket gaped open. He saw a hint of cream-colored lace against her skin, and he discreetly adjusted his pants around the painful erection he had carted around for the past few hours. Duncan drained the last of his beer bottle and tried to think about anything but Claire's brown breasts.

He glanced around the empty restaurant. Patrick had finally left an hour ago, taking his tales of Kellie and their endless love—on Patrick's part, at least—with him. The tired parents with their screaming toddlers were also long gone. Duncan and Claire had even outlasted the cleaning crew. Only Nate remained, and he had disappeared into his upstairs office. Duncan and Claire were effectively alone, and all Duncan could think about was tasting Claire's lips, peeling off her suit, and wrapping those long, thick honey-colored legs around him, grabbing those hips and behind that were prominently outlined when she bent over the table. . . . Duncan gulped. It suddenly felt very hot in the usually cool restaurant. He hadn't accomplished any of his goals of enticement tonight, and with the appearance of Patrick, winning the bet seemed further and further away.

Duncan didn't realize that she had won the game until Claire looked up at him with a grin. He forced a smile in return, hoping that she hadn't noticed where his attention had been.

"That's three in a row, Duncan. Do you give up?" she asked with a smug smile.

"You're a sore winner," he told her, laughing.

"There is no such thing as a sore winner. There's just a winner and a loser. In this particular instance, I'm the winner and you're the loser . . . again." She stuck her tongue out at him, then began to pull balls from the pockets.

Duncan laughed, because she obviously enjoyed beating him. She enjoyed winning. And Duncan enjoyed watching her win, especially if it meant that she had to bend over the table a few more times.

"Have you always been such a brat?" he asked as he went behind the counter and twisted open two additional beer bottles.

"Probably." She set her pool stick on the table and followed him to the counter.

Duncan studied her from under his eyelashes, then asked casually, "So, did you enjoy yourself tonight with Patrick?"

Claire nodded excitedly, oblivious to the undercurrents of his question. "He's such a sweet guy. I'm surprised our paths didn't cross in high school. I remember that he came to a couple of the science club meetings freshman year, but then we never saw him again. I can't believe he's working at the observatory now. That is so admirable. Positions at the observatory are harder to come by than Pulitzers."

Duncan told himself to remain calm. He took a swig from his beer, then said dully, "Yeah, Patrick is great."

"He's still so in love with Kellie," Claire continued sadly. "I hope he finds a woman who'll appreciate his dedication."

"Yeah," Duncan muttered, taking another long draw on the beer. His chest hurt.

Claire abruptly smiled as she stared at Duncan. "Duncan, you're not jealous of Patrick, are you?"

Duncan snorted a little too loudly and practically shouted, "Of course not."

"Because you've been showing signs of jealousy all night.

Studies show that certain emotions, like jealousy, manifest physically. Flared nostrils, narrowed eyes, exaggerated disinterest coupled with random belligerence. You have all the signs."

"You know, it's really not fair that you can tell all this stuff from just looking at me. What the hell books and magazines do you read anyway?" he muttered grumpily.

Claire laughed. "You don't have to be jealous of Patrick, Duncan. You could be an astronomer if you wanted to. I have to admit that I may have underestimated you. You're much smarter than—"

"I'm not jealous because Patrick works at some observatory; I'm jealous because it seemed like you and he had a real fun date tonight," Duncan blurted out.

When Claire's eyes widened in surprise and the amusement left her expression, Duncan inwardly cursed. If he could go back in time, he would definitely do it and make certain he didn't say that last sentence. His lack of finesse around this woman was mortifying.

When Claire averted her gaze and stared at the counter, as if uncertain how to respond, Duncan cleared his throat and tried to save some player points by saying, "I just wanted tonight to be special for a special woman. Nothing turned out like I planned."

She looked at him, her gaze unreadable, before she said softly, "It was a special night, Duncan."

"We're at my brother's diner in Westfield," he pointed out in case she had forgotten.

"I'm at a diner in Westfield with you, and that's why it was special," she said, then ducked her head in obvious embarrassment.

Duncan grinned as he actually felt a blush cover his cheeks. That should have been his line, and Claire should have been the one blushing. He couldn't take the separation anymore. He set the beer bottle down and walked around the counter to stand in front of her. For the first time since Duncan had met her, she didn't immediately tense at his closeness. He should have felt a small thrill of triumph that he had officially passed the soothe stage, but instead he only felt that breathless feeling he got when he stood too close to her.

"So, you don't wish that you were on a date with Patrick, instead of me?" he said, even though he hated himself for asking. "You two do have a lot more in common than you and I—"

Claire placed one finger against his lips, and Duncan stopped talking. Her eyes had grown dark, swirling with the intensity he remembered from that night right before she had blown apart on her bed under his tongue.

"Patrick is lonely. I know what that looks like and feels like," she said softly. "I just wanted him to know that he's not alone. But you're my date, Duncan, and I wouldn't want it any other way."

Duncan liked to think he was embarrassed for needing reassurance from a woman, but he was too busy being relieved. He suddenly had to touch her, to confirm that his memory hadn't been tricking him last night and that her skin really was as soft and satiny as he had dreamed about. He caressed her right cheek, and her skin lived up to his memories. His other hand moved to her neck, sliding down the graceful column to gently wrap around her width.

His gaze dropped to her full lips and he whispered, "And to think all I had to do to make you smile was bring you to a hamburger joint in the old neighborhood and buy you a few beers."

She smiled, even as she leaned closer to him. She wanted to kiss him. Duncan's hand tightened around her neck as he stepped closer to her, pressing his hips against hers. Her eyes momentarily widened at the feel of his hardness, but she made no move to get away from him. In fact, she moved closer, pressing her breasts against his chest. Duncan groaned in pain because he literally ached to have her, to be inside her, and to feel her moving beneath him. Bet or not, Duncan needed this woman.

Duncan was drawn from his lust-induced fog when he heard the sound of a man clearing his throat. Claire squeaked and quickly stepped out of his grip. Duncan's hands fell empty to his sides and he turned to glare at his brother, who stood at the other end of the bar, near the kitchen entrance.

"I was going to lock up for the night, unless you guys want something else," Nate said, the large grin on his face indicating that he had seen the heated moment between Claire and Duncan. Nate also looked relieved, as if he no longer thought Duncan would ravish Claire, even though that was exactly what Duncan was planning to do.

"I'm sorry we kept you this long," Claire apologized as she grabbed her purse off one of the pool tables.

"I enjoyed the company," Nate said, dismissing her apology. "It takes me about an hour every night to close. Usually my wife is here with me, but she's at home tonight. We're expecting, and she's due any day."

"Your wife is pregnant?"

Duncan teased, "The real question is, when is Toya not pregnant?"

Duncan smiled innocently when Nate shot him a hard glare. Nate laughed, then told Claire, "Listening to this joker, you would think we all have enough kids to staff the Lakers."

"How many children do you have?" Claire asked, amused.

"I have three, soon to be four. Alex has four. Kobie has two and Tavis has two," Nate said, exasperated.

Claire glanced at Duncan, surprised. "That's only twelve children, Duncan."

"Only twelve?" Duncan said, pretending to be shocked. Truthfully, he loved every one of his brothers' crumb snatchers and would have given a limb to save any of them from a day of sadness or pain, but no one needed to know that. "Only a couple more and we could have a whole baseball team."

Claire laughed while Nate shook his head. Nate said to Claire, "Don't worry. His day is coming. My mother predicts that when Duncan finally settles down, his herd is going to put the rest of us to shame."

Claire stared at Duncan long enough to make him uncomfortable, then murmured, "I can't picture Duncan as a father."

"You haven't seen Duncan around kids, have you? Kids automatically love him, and he loves them. He always complains about his nieces and nephews, but guess who all the kids in the family go running to as soon as he enters the room? Uncle Duncan. And guess who takes the whole lot of them, including the ones in strollers, to pizza and to the park once a month? Uncle Duncan—"

"All right, Nate," Duncan interrupted, embarrassed. He glared at Nate, who sent him his own version of an innocent smile. Not even Patrick or Hawk knew about Duncan's monthly outings with his nieces and nephews. Children were natural women magnets, but Duncan was usually too busy enjoying the time with his nieces and nephews to notice any women.

"Do you really do that?" Claire asked, surprised, turning to face Duncan.

Duncan shrugged, then mumbled, "The older ones help me out a lot. . . . Nate, don't you have to get home? Toya is probably waiting up for you."

"I guess I've tortured Duncan enough for one night," Nate said as Duncan emptied their near-full beer bottles in the counter sink and then threw them in a nearby recycling can. Nate, meanwhile, threw an arm around Claire's shoulders and led her toward the exit. Duncan glared at his brother's back, for the first time in his life jealous of one of his brothers. "Claire, you have to come over for Sunday dinner. I'll have my mom pull out Duncan's baby pictures."

Duncan heard Claire's laughter echo throughout the empty restaurant, and he felt himself smiling before he realized that Claire would not be coming to his parents' house, because this was all for a bet. Duncan's gaze drifted to the material stretched across Claire's behind, and not for the first time that night, he wondered just who was seducing whom.

Claire didn't know why she was so nervous as Duncan glided the BMW to a stop in front of her house. She hadn't lied to Duncan. It had been a special night, more special than the night she had won the prestigious grant to fund her college research project.

The two walked to her front door in silence. Duncan didn't bother to hide the fact that he stared at her. Even if she hadn't seen him watching her, she could feel his gaze all the way to the pit of her suddenly nervous stomach. Claire reached into her purse and fumbled with the keys before she managed to insert the key in the lock. She felt Duncan move closer behind her, his heat washing over her. Claire forced herself to turn around and face him. Bad move. She gulped when she realized how close he stood to her.

"Thank you for a lovely evening, Duncan," she said, forcing herself to meet his gaze.

"I would bet that I had more fun than you," he said.

Claire smiled in response and he took that as an invitation to close the small distance between them. Claire was convinced that they were an electron and a proton. It was absolutely impossible for them not to touch each other when they were this close.

Duncan was quiet as he trailed a thumb down her right cheek. She would never get used to the feel of his callused hands on her skin. His hand dropped to his side as he leaned toward her, slowly, giving her time to move away, to protest, but she did neither. Finally, his mouth pressed against hers.

His hands didn't touch her, he didn't pull her close, but she was as glued to him as if he had imprisoned her there. Claire sighed in pleasure and Duncan took the opportunity to slip his tongue into her mouth. She moaned this time as his tongue began to lazily stroke through every inch of her mouth with long, sweeping, torturous strokes that promised much more.

His hands wrapped around her waist—carefully and hesitantly, as if he was afraid to touch her. As if she was fragile. Desire screamed through her body like a tornado, uprooting any resistance in its path. Claire's own hands skimmed over his rock-hard arms to wrap around his neck. She stepped into his embrace, pressing herself against his body, against the hard planes and surfaces. She suckled his lower lip, pulling it into her mouth, and this time he groaned.

Duncan abruptly wrenched his mouth from hers, his breathing ragged, as his hands gripped her waist almost painfully. "This is insane," he said in a harsh whisper. "I can't even think straight. I can't want you this much."

"Why not?" she asked, a challenge in her voice.

Duncan focused on her, surprise across his features at her sensual challenge as she boldly met his gaze.

He searched for an answer, then stuttered, "We haven't known each other long enough for—"

"We've known each other for almost twenty years," she interrupted him, smiling. He was scared. The physical signs were there, but she wouldn't tell him that.

He grimaced, then said through clenched teeth, "I don't want to take advantage of you, Claire."

"I'm not that eleven-year-old kid anymore, Duncan. I make my own choices, and I choose you."

He stared at her dumbfounded; then lust crossed his features with enough force to make Claire blink. She thought he would pounce on her at that moment. Her body tensed in anticipation.

Then Duncan seemed to collect himself and shook his head and said, "There are a lot of things you don't know about me."

"I know you've been with a lot of women. It's all right."

"I'm not talking about . . ." His voice trailed off as he looked at her suspiciously, then he asked, "What exactly have you heard?"

"It doesn't matter, Duncan," she said, grabbing one of his hands. His hand was hot in hers. Strong. She squeezed it. "Maybe I was initially envious at the thought of you with other women, but that's the past. I want to feel you inside of me. Since that night, I've dreamed about . . . I can't go another night without having you—all of you—inside of me."

"You don't understand, Claire. . . ." His voice trailed off and he laughed drily, then muttered, "I can't believe that I'm trying to talk *you* out of making love."

She grabbed his shirtfront and tugged him against her. She whispered against his mouth, "Then stop it."

He sighed tiredly and his breath fanned her lips, making her skin tingle with need. He closed his eyes briefly, his dark eyelashes fanning his cheeks, before he whispered, sounding tortured, "You have no idea how much I want you, do you?"

Claire tried to respond to his heated words, a multisyllabic word that would summarize her feelings. For once, words failed her. So, contrary to everything that ever had happened in her life, she resorted to action. She pulled him into the house, closed the door, then kissed him.

Chapter Fourteen

Claire dipped her tongue into Duncan's mouth and devoured his thick lips. He tasted so delicious, so intoxicating. She placed her hands on his chest, gently squeezing the pectoral muscles through his shirt and suit jacket, eating his mouth, sinking into his body. He made no move until she felt his hand in her hair. He pulled off the holder that held her hair in a ponytail and dug his hands into the strands that fell around her shoulders.

The more calm he remained under her kiss, the more Claire forgot all restraint and dignity. She clung to his kisses, clung to him. He was driving her insane, because she knew relief was within him. One of her legs brushed against his length. . . . She groaned into his mouth when she felt how hard he was. Like steel. He wasn't as cool as he wanted her to believe.

"Claire," he murmured, seconds before he turned into a madman. Whatever internal battle he had been waging was over, because he began to gulp her up like she was his oxygen. She didn't even have time to think, which was becoming a regular occurrence around Duncan, before the strength and force of his kisses took over.

She curled her hands around his neck and tried to keep up as his tongue fed her mouth, plunging, taking, and destroying whatever sanity she had left. His tongue, his lips, and his teeth all played a part in destroying whatever objectivity she could have retained around him. The wet feel of his tongue inside her mouth, the slow undulation of his hips as he moved slightly, could have qualified as excruciating torture. Claire's entire world became waiting for the next swipe of his tongue, the next brush of his hands.

His hands were rough as they moved down her body, fondling her breasts and then coming to a stop on her behind. He squeezed her body through the suit; then without warning he ripped open her suit jacket. His mouth disengaged from hers as the jacket fell open. His gaze raked over her body, and she could have found completion right there with just that look in his eyes. He whispered a curse as his eyes lingered on the cream-colored lace camisole she wore. She hadn't worn a bra, and the silk material outlined her erect nipples and large breasts.

"I like this," he told her in a barely intelligible murmur, fingering the strap of the camisole. "Wear it all the time."

It was silly request, but it made Claire smile. "Every day," she replied.

Duncan froze for a moment; then he pulled the camisole up and over her head. Claire held her arms up for the camisole to come off fully, and when it did he threw it to the floor. Her entire body reacted and tensed as her bare breasts bobbed into view. Duncan grimaced, as if in pain; then he tweaked one nipple, then raised his gaze to stare at her. Claire gasped from the sheer need and want in his gaze.

His hands gently moved to her shoulders, then dug in, holding her to the ground before she floated into space. Then he reached around her and unzipped her skirt. It slithered to the ground, and Claire stepped out of it, clad only in her cotton, not-very-sexy but serviceable underwear. Duncan didn't appear to mind as he simply stared at her. She didn't feel any cold or any heat; she just felt the intensity from his gaze.

"I'm going to need the bed for this," he said as if speaking to himself.

He took her hand and led her to the bedroom. Claire felt a small brush of nerves while Duncan shucked off his clothes until he only wore a pair of dark blue briefs, which clearly exhibited the impressive erection that Claire had felt, but then he was on her in an instant. Hard and fast. He laid her on the bed at the same time that his mouth fastened to one breast. Claire groaned his name as her eyes slid closed. She had once more been reduced to moans by this man.

Claire whimpered as his mouth settled over her other breast while his hands stroked and possessed every other part of her body, his hands moving high on her thighs and briefly covering her mound. He was moving so fast that her body didn't have time to react to his touch until he was somewhere else. It didn't matter where he touched her, though, because her whole body burned.

Duncan growled and continued his oral worship. She continued to lie on the bed like a weightless mass, but the need to touch him gave her the strength to move her hands down his bare, muscled back. He felt like silk wrapped in granite. She continued her journey and finally her hands rested on his behind. The muscles tensed and she heard and felt his groan as his tongue circled her nipple.

Duncan moved back to her mouth with another soul-wrenching kiss that kept her on the edge of completion. His body was on top of hers, his skin touching every inch of her skin, his chest against her breasts. He was heavy, but she didn't want him to move even if dynamite was involved. His groin settled against hers and she almost thought he would enter her at that moment, despite their underwear, and she mumbled her pleasure into his mouth. Then she felt his hands on the waistband of her panties. She clung to him, keeping his mouth on hers, as he removed her underwear, then his. For a moment she felt all of that wet, silken hardness on her thigh, but then he shifted.

His mouth continued to devour her before his finger dipped into her, fast. It went in smoothly and without much resistance. She reared up from the unexpected invasion but closed her eyes against the heat of clenching his finger, feeling him inside her.

Duncan released a string of guttural curses and closed his eyes. He cursed, then added a second finger. She screamed and almost bucked from the bed, but he held her down with his weight. She began to rock to the rhythm of his plunging fingers as her head fell back in mindless wonder. This felt too . . . too perfect. This couldn't be real. He leaned down for another kiss. His rough kiss telling her how real it all was.

The kiss ended and his mouth stayed inches from her lips as he stared at her. It was the first time he had stopped moving since they walked into the bedroom.

He asked gently, "Are you sure about this, Claire?"

Claire nodded, then bit her bottom lip and closed her eyes because his fingers had stopped but were still inside of her. She pulsated around him.

"There are condoms in the nightstand," she said in a shaky voice.

He ignored her statement and asked, in a voice so deep that it made another wave of nerves rumble through her body, "You haven't done this in a while, have you?"

Her hands dug into his shoulders as she whispered, "Does that mean you want to stop?"

He smiled and her body clenched his finger again. "I couldn't stop right now if I wanted to, but I was trying to be nice about it."

"Good," she responded, smiling.

He smiled, then slowly withdrew his fingers, much to her disappointment, before he disappeared from over her for a moment. She closed her eyes as she heard the drawer open.

He sounded amused as he asked, "How long have you had these?"

"Awhile," she said defensively, glaring at him as he blew dust off the top of the box. "I like to be prepared."

"Good thing I like to be prepared too," he said, then reached for his pants on the floor. Claire quickly looked at the ceiling. If she watched him put on the condom, she would start to think about this too much. She was starting an affair with Duncan. A passionate, erotic affair that felt nothing like an affair to her but more like what she had always hoped love would be when she'd still believed in love.

Duncan shifted in between her legs, warming the area that had grown cold without him.

"Ah, Claire," he whispered before he moved into her with an exquisite slowness that made her mouth drop open in a soundless gasp.

He moved slowly, giving her time to adjust. He was bigger than she had thought, making things a tad uncomfortable. Claire groaned at the feel of him inside her—full and thick, almost to the point of bursting. He was still for a few moments; then he slowly pushed more inside her. There was more. She dug her nails into his back, her eyes flew open, and she debated whether to make him stop.

Duncan whispered her name, then kissed her, distracting her, right as he drove his full length home. Claire moaned in discomfort, but his tongue continued to bathe her mouth with a ferocity that belied the gentleness of his strokes. The intensity and pressure eased in direct proportion as the buildup of glorious pleasure increased. Pleasure that made Claire's toes curl and that made her forget she was debating stopping. She tore her mouth from his, unable to concentrate on more than one thing at the moment, and she wanted to strictly concentrate on the feel of his thickness inside of her. She began to meet each of his strokes in a rhythm that was as timeless and pure as the ocean's tide. The pace increased, and Duncan gripped the sheet on either side of her.

Claire didn't know how long it lasted: it felt like forever; it felt like seconds. The rhythm became even faster and then she heard Duncan curse and she felt the tension grow in his body. He was on the edge with her. He caressed her bud of nerves seconds before he shuddered and groaned her name. She instantly followed him into the stars, the rainbows, and every other miracle.

"Are you all right?" Duncan asked, moments later, as he tucked the sheet around their still-entwined bodies.

Claire nodded and snuggled against his chest. The world felt different. Her body felt different. She was suddenly aware of nerve endings that she hadn't known existed. Or she had known they existed because a textbook told her so, but she hadn't *really* known. Claire didn't know if she could ever look at two cells duplicating and see the same thing again. It was as if her entire view of the world had been altered with a Duncan lens, and she knew without a doubt that this was anything but an affair to her.

"May I confess something to you?" she asked abruptly.

"Anything," he murmured, sounding close to sleep.

"I had a crush on you in high school," she admitted, then buried her face in her hands at his suddenly wide-awake, stunned expression. Seconds passed and she sneaked a peek at him. She laughed because he still looked like a man who had learned that the earth was really flat.

"You did?" he finally managed.

"It was a severe, for lack of a better word, crush," she said, giggling. A smile tugged at the corners of his mouth and Claire wondered if she had created a monster.

"On a scale of one to ten, how severe was this crush?"

She pretended to seriously consider his question before she answered, firmly, "Fifteen."

"No," he said in disbelief.

"Sophomore year when you were on the football team, I would sit in the bleachers and watch you during football practice."

"What?" he gaped, sitting up in the bed to stare at her. "I never noticed you in the bleachers."

"Why would you notice me when half of the cheerleading team were jumping up and down to get your attention? Not to mention the other girls in the bleachers who were also pretending not to watch you."

"You had a crush on me?" he asked, as if to be certain; then he smiled and murmured, "You had a crush on me."

She frowned at the arrogance playing across his face. "It was a long time ago, Duncan, before my brain was fully developed."

"You were in love with me," he insisted, a smile playing across his lips.

"I shouldn't have told you," she murmured, shaking her head.

"Did you write my name all over your notebooks? Did you write 'Mrs. Duncan Hillston'? 'Mrs. Claire Hillston'? 'Mrs. Claire Scott Hillston'?"

"I would have never done anything so immature," she said, then laughed because she had.

"I never would have thought that Medusa was in love with me. You never gave me the time of day."

"I couldn't believe it, either. I chalk it up to early adolescence," she teased.

"How did this obsession with me begin?"

"I wouldn't call it an obsession, Duncan," she corrected him. "We were in art class together freshman year, and I sat one person over from you."

He squinted his eyes in concentration; then he murmured, "I sat next to Tara Jackson in art class freshman year. I don't remember you."

"You remember Tara, but you don't remember me?" she asked, sitting up in the bed to glare at him, the sheet tucked firmly under her armpits. He smiled guiltily and she muttered, "That doesn't have anything to do with Tara Jackson's penchant for wearing short skirts even in the dead of winter?"

Duncan grinned before he said, with feigned innocence, "Tara wore short skirts. . . . I don't remember that. I remember that she liked to draw rainbows."

Claire shook her head in amusement. "You're full of crap."

"You just said 'crap.' One week with me and you're already losing your vocabulary." He laughed, then placed a kiss on her bare shoulder. That easily, Claire was pacified. He asked curiously, "Did we ever talk?"

"Only once. On the first day of school, I was late to class. Everyone was already seated behind their easels, and the whispering began as soon as I entered the classroom. Even the teacher looked at me like I was a freak. I guess I should have expected it, but I didn't. At my junior high school, I had known most of the children since I was five years old, so they and the teachers were used to me. Westfield High School was a different story. I didn't know anyone.

"I finally found an empty easel, next to Tara, who looked at me like I might throw smart beams at her or something. After the whispering and staring had stopped, Mrs. Fannigan told us to pick out our color boxes. She said that she only had twenty, but since there were twenty-five students, some of us would have to share. All of the students ran to the counter like a pack of wild animals. I was horrified and about to run out of the classroom, find Joan, and beg her to put me back in junior high school. Then you walked over to my easel and handed me a color box. You said, 'Don't make us look too bad.' Then you winked at me. You were the only student who spoke to me that day. I guess I . . . I remembered you after that."

She forced a laugh when she saw the amusement fade from his face with her story. Now he just looked confused.

He asked hesitantly, "That's why you were obsessed with me? Because I was nice to you? Not because of my looks or my athletic ability?"

"I was not obsessed with you," she said with a slight laugh. Then she pressed a soft kiss against his mouth, clinging to his bottom lip for a moment longer than she should have. His eyes darkened with desire when she finally released his mouth. She said quietly, "People liked you because were nice, not because you were handsome or were on the football team. You were nice to a lot of people, the people no one else was nice to, and that's why the girls were in love with you."

He shook his head in confusion as he protested, "But I didn't go out of my way to—"

"I know, and that's why I liked you so much," she said.

Suddenly his hand on her hip turned from a comforting pressure to a sensual caress. Duncan abruptly moved on top of her, his legs over hers, pressing her against the mattress, trapping the sheet between them. Just like that, the amusement, the friendship that Claire felt, faded in lieu of something richer and more colorful. Her body reached for him, prepared for him, as if he had pressed a secret button that caused her body to respond like Pavlov's dogs.

Duncan lowered close enough to kiss her but didn't. His expression was serious as he said, "I wish I had known how lonely you were."

"I was an eleven-year-old know-it-all," she said with a soft smile. "You were a fourteen-year-old boy. I didn't expect to be your friend."

"If I had known, I still would have tried."

"You would have been friends with Medusa?" she asked in disbelief.

"Yeah, I would have, especially if I had known that you would grow up to look like this," he whispered, then smiled before he kissed her. She moaned as he dragged his tongue through her mouth.

Claire clung to him, her hips undulating against his. She felt his hardness slowly take shape against her thigh, the heaviness hot through the cotton sheet. This time she was active, running her hands over his body, any place she could touch, loving the contours of his muscles and smooth skin. She disengaged from his hands and moved to straddle him, forgetting the sheet. She wasn't self-conscious anymore, not when she was moments away from pleasure that she had never known existed.

"Claire, baby," he whispered, strained, as she planted a kiss in the middle of his chest.

She rained kisses across the sparse curly hair decorating his chest; then she journeyed down to his stomach, paying particular attention to the ridges of his barely there six-pack. She heard his curse as his muscles played under her tongue. He was shaking. She felt powerful and in control, realizing for the first time that she had control over his body, too. She gently raked her nails down his chest, digging lightly in the skin that had become her addiction.

"Claire?" he choked out as she moved lower.

"Hmm?"

In response to her distracted answer, Duncan swung her back around and plunged into her. She would have protested if she had been able to speak, but she could only arch her back under the feel of him so deep inside her.

"I'm really, really glad you're legal now," he said in a tortured voice.

Claire wrapped her legs around his waist and held on for the ride. She was glad, too, because having a child's fixation on him was nothing compared to loving him as an adult.

Chapter Fifteen

"We have to get out of bed at some point, Duncan," Claire groaned in that deep, throaty voice that Duncan had come to love over the last twenty-four hours. It meant he was doing something right.

"Why?" he murmured, then placed another kiss on the back of her silky neck.

The two had finally slept a few hours around dawn. Then Duncan had woken up to the sight of honey next to him, and he couldn't help but coax her into waking up so that he could take her again. The morning had drifted into the afternoon, which had turned into early evening, but they hadn't left Claire's house. In fact, they hadn't left Claire's bedroom, besides to answer nature calls and to take a shower that gave Duncan an opportunity to examine her body up close and personal while he washed her. But then she had wanted the same opportunity, and they had made love in the shower. Since Duncan's supply hadn't lasted, her dust-covered box of condoms did not have a speck of dust on it anymore and was damn near empty.

At some point, Claire had gone to the kitchen and come back with delicious-smelling coffee, and cereal and milk. The proud smile on her face had made Duncan take her again, without touching the cereal and milk. It was now almost eight o'clock at night, and the two were still tangled in each other and the sheets, too weak to move. Or, at least, Duncan thought he couldn't move until Claire, who had been lying on her stomach poring over a Chinese take-out menu, had looked over her shoulder and smiled at him while he had told her a story about one of his nieces. And Duncan had of course gotten hard—because her smiles did that to him—and now he was lying on top of her, nibbling on her neck like she was dessert.

Duncan had stopped marveling over the insanity of his insatiability for Claire. He had stopped marveling over the dread he felt every time he thought about leaving her. He had even forgotten his damn three-step plan. What was it again anyway? Encourage. Persuade. And attack. He had never felt this way about another woman. He had never lain in bed all damn day and half the night with another woman. Duncan had stopped thinking about all of that around six o'clock that morning and had just accepted it. This was how things were with Claire. And now Duncan finally understood why his brothers didn't find the idea of mortgages and minivans as claustrophobic as Duncan did. Because as long as Claire was thrown into the mix, the rest didn't seem so bad.

She laughed, then turned over, pushing him off her. Duncan frowned, then leaned in for a kiss. She met his mouth with an eager tongue. She always met him with the same eagerness and passion that he felt. Whether he wanted to go slow or fast, she was right there with him, perfectly in sync. He grinned against her mouth, because apparently she wasn't that ready to get out of bed, but then Claire abruptly moaned, and pushed him away.

"Duncan," she groaned, shaking her head. "It can't be healthy for two people to spend this much time in a horizontal position. Our muscles are going to deteriorate from nonuse."

"I know one muscle that won't," he teased before kissing her again.

She laughed and pushed him away again. "We have to get up. You have to feed me. And I have to check in at the lab."

Duncan frowned and felt every one of those protective instincts that were buried come back to life. He didn't have to worry about her when she was squirming underneath him. "The lab? Why do we have to go there?"

"I told you that my team and I are starting preclinical trials next month, which means that there's a lot of work to be done before then. Most of my team have been working seven days a week for the past three months, and I have to do the same, regardless of my extracurricular activities."

"So, other people will be there?" he pressed.

"Probably not this late on a Saturday night," she said lightly. She smiled, clearly exasperated, when she noticed that he stared at her. "Duncan, you can stop worrying. Detective Hansen was right. The mugging and the car theft were just coincidences. It's been almost a week, and there haven't been any attempts on my life so far."

"That's not funny," he growled, then muttered, "but maybe you're right. I'm still going with you to the lab."

For some reason, she looked troubled. Worried. Duncan wondered if she was using work as an excuse to get away from him. Well, that was too damn bad. He wasn't going anywhere. He wasn't nearly done kissing her swollen lips and touching all the places that made her sigh in abandon. A part of him wondered if he would ever be done.

She protested weakly, "I may be there for hours—"

"We have to stop by my house so I can shave and clean up anyway, so I'll pick up some paperwork from the office. I'll work on that while you make the world a better place," he said simply.

Claire opened her mouth as if to speak, but then she moved to the edge of the bed. Duncan allowed her to climb out of the bed. His frown turned into a smile as he got an eyeful of the honey brown curves and valleys that he had been worshipping for the last twenty-four hours. He thanked the angel on his shoulder for getting him into this room, into this bed. Claire narrowed her eyes at him, then quickly pulled on an oversize purple robe that covered her from neck to ankle. He frowned in disappointment.

"After I leave the lab, I was also planning to stop by Annabelle's hotel," she said, obviously still trying to get him to stay home. She walked to her dresser and began to brush out the long tangles in her hair that Duncan had had fun putting there. "I haven't seen her since she came over Monday. I've left two messages."

"I guess the thrill is gone if you're worrying about Annabelle while I'm laying in your bed," Duncan mumbled, reluctantly getting up.

He pulled on his wrinkled pants that had been crumpled on the floor since last night, then glanced up to find Claire staring at his behind. He had seen that spark of interest in her eyes enough over the last few hours to know what that meant.

He grinned and murmured, "Unless . . ."

"No," she said firmly, but there was a hint of a smile on her lips. "I'm going to take a shower—"

"I like that idea—"

"While you wait in the living room," she finished pointedly. Duncan looked downcast, and Claire laughed, then pointed toward the door. "Give me twenty minutes."

"All right," he said reluctantly. "Have you figured out what you want to eat? I'll call while you're in the shower and then we can pick it up on the way to my house before we head to the lab."

Claire studied him for a moment before she squared her shoulders and said, "Duncan, you don't have to . . ." Her voice trailed off and she suddenly looked uncertain.

"What?" he prodded.

"I know you're worried about me, but . . . but you don't have to do this—"

"Hey," he whispered, interrupting her before she said something that they would both regret. He instantly was at her side, his hands framing her face. Her eyes were huge as she held his gaze. "I'm here because I want to be. If you want some space, just tell me. I can follow you to the lab in my truck and I'll wait in the parking lot until you finish working."

Claire smiled, like he wanted her to. "That wasn't exactly what I had in mind."

A new possibility for her attitude made him take a deep breath and ask, "You sick of me? You want me to leave you alone for a while—"

"No, I'm not sick of you," she said softly, avoiding his eyes. "I just . . . You overwhelm me. I can't think clearly when you're around, and I need to think."

"About the upcoming preclinical trials?"

She finally looked at him as she said softly, "No, about us."

"Ah," he said, then felt the beginning of a smile cross his face. He ran one thumb down her cheek, then murmured, "In that case, I'm definitely not letting you out of my sight now."

Claire smiled and turned into his touch. A little piece of Duncan's heart came alive at that exact moment. It was that small sign of trust that did it. No other woman had responded to him like that. Maybe that was why everything was so different with Claire. She trusted him. Or she trusted the Duncan she thought she knew.

He told himself to shut up, but then he found himself saying, "Since I met you—again—when I'm not with you I'm worrying about you. As long as I know you're at that lab by yourself I'm not going to be able to sleep, so the best solution would be for me to come with you."

"You can't worry about me forever," she said with a slight smile.

For the first time, the word *forever* coming from a woman's mouth did not make Duncan cringe. In fact, he kind of liked hearing Claire say it. He said, "It's not for forever, just until the police have some idea about what's going on."

She groaned. "Nothing is going on. They were random acts—"

He ignored her protest and said, "Not to mention I like spending time with you. You're the only woman I know who's probably read and memorized every scientific study published in the free world."

"I like spending time with you, too," she said softly.

He grinned, then continued reluctantly, "Now, if you really just don't want me around, because we've been together for the last twenty-four hours—"

"I want you around too much," she said, placing her hands over his to press them against her face.

Duncan smiled in relief, then brought her hands to his mouth. He kissed each palm, then said, "Take your shower."

She looked down at his growing hardness regretfully, then walked out of the room. Duncan sighed heavily and ran a hand over his face. Claire had had the right idea. They probably did need time apart after the past intense twenty-four hours, but he just couldn't bring himself to leave her.

"This is fancy," Duncan said, followed by a whistle as he and Claire walked into the ornately decorated lobby of the Beverly Hills Hotel.

Since he continued to stand in the entrance, gawking at the plush furniture and expensive decorations, Claire grabbed his hand to lead him to the front desk. Normally, she would have been just as awestruck by the interior of the expensive hotel as Duncan was, but she was too busy studying the reactions of people around her, wondering if they could tell what she and Duncan had been doing since last night. Even after dinner, a shower, and putting on a fresh suit, Claire still felt her body aching for Duncan as if she hadn't just spent the last twenty-four hours screwing his brains out.

Waiting in his living room while he showered and changed into dark jeans and a button-down shirt that emphasized his broad shoulders had been a test of her self-control. She had sat there imagining the water running down all of his beautiful dark skin, caressing the parts of his body that Claire had caressed and kissed over and over again. But she had forced herself to remain on his leather sofa. They had to stop. Claire had been raised by a father who would have been right at home in Puritan New England, where she and Duncan would have been burned at the stake for what they had been doing, because anything that felt that good had to be wrong.

"May I help you?" the desk clerk asked cheerfully upon Claire and Duncan's approach.

"I need to speak with a guest staying in the hotel. Annabelle Richards," Claire said.

"Of course," the young girl said excitedly, as if contacting a hotel guest was the most exciting task of her life. She tapped on the computer keyboard, then suddenly frowned and peered closer at the computer screen.

"Uh-oh, I'm having a flashback to La Bella Cucina," Duncan mumbled.

"Annabelle Richards?" the clerk asked, looking at Claire.

"It may be under 'Belle Richards,'" Claire said uncertainly.

The clerk pressed a few more buttons, then became stone-faced. She sent Claire and Duncan a nervous smile before she said, "Excuse me for a moment."

Before Claire could respond, the woman turned and practically ran through a door behind the desk.

"What in the world is going on?" Duncan asked, perplexed.

"With Annabelle involved, there's no telling," Claire responded just as a short older man with a gleaming bald head and pencil mustache walked out the door. The cheerful girl was nowhere to be seen, which seemed a bad sign to Claire.

The man didn't smile as he said, "I'm the manager, Wendell Ashcroft. I understand you're looking for Belle Richards."

"Yes, she told me that she was staying here. Is there a problem?"

"You could say that," the man said flatly. "Ms. Richards is gone. Disappeared. When we ran the credit card number she gave us, it was declined. Ms. Richards owes this hotel twenty thousand dollars and three Beverly Hills Hotel robes."

"Twenty thousand dollars?" Duncan repeated in disbelief. "How much do the robes cost?"

Claire barely restrained a laugh as the man's head almost did a 360-degree turn. She felt Duncan's arms shaking with restrained laughter next to her, which caused one of her giggles to escape before she clamped her mouth closed. Wendell Ashcroft's eyes narrowed into tiny slits as he glared from Claire to Duncan.

To avert the impending tantrum, Duncan quickly asked, "When was the last time Annabelle was here?"

"Two nights ago," Wendell answered stiffly. "We had complaints from her neighbors the next morning, in fact. She created a ruckus in her room."

"What kind of ruckus?" Claire asked.

He pursed his lips and said, "I wasn't there, so I can't say for certain, but I will tell you that several guests saw her escorting two gentlemen to her room. I can only imagine, since our rooms are virtually soundproof, that for her neighbors to complain, it must have been quite an evening."

Duncan pulled a business card from his wallet and handed it to Wendell. "If you hear from her, have her call me. Tell her that her friends Duncan and Claire are concerned about her."

Wendell glanced at Duncan's card as if it were a lower life-form before he stiffly nodded.

"Thank you," Claire said, for lack of anything better to say.

"What about her bills?" Wendell demanded when Claire and Duncan turned to leave. "Someone owes this hotel twenty thousand dollars."

"And three Beverly Hills Hotel robes," Duncan added.

The look in Wendell's glacial blue eyes scared Claire. She had a feeling that the Beverly Hills Hotel took the theft of its robes more seriously than the room charges. Before Wendell called hotel security, she grabbed Duncan's arm.

Wendell glared after them until the two walked out of the hotel. Claire quickly handed the waiting valet their claim ticket.

"We'll find her," Duncan reassured Claire, obviously misinterpreting her concern about the evil hotel manager as concern for Annabelle.

"I wasn't worried about Annabelle; I was worried about hotel security. Did you know that hotel guests suffer more physical injuries on hotel premises from overzealous guards than from—"

She didn't get the rest of her sentence out because Duncan grabbed her waist, slammed her against him, and claimed her mouth with a ferocity that made Claire's body turn boneless. She clung to his arms and moaned in pleasure against the sweet invasion. He released her as abruptly as he had grabbed her.

She took deep breaths as her head spun from the onslaught of raw desire. "I love it when you talk sexy," he growled in explanation.

Claire shook her head in disbelief, then grinned in return.

Chapter Sixteen

Claire glanced across the lab at Duncan as he sat at one of the empty workstations, poring over a stack of bills. Logically, the simple act of looking at him should not have made her stomach quiver with desire, but apparently desire didn't care about logic. She had spent the past hour at the lab, fighting the urge to cross the room, coax him into a kiss, and lead him to the cot in the back room.

She seemed to be the only one having problems with her attention span. True to his word earlier that evening, Duncan had gone straight to an empty corner of the lab, and he hadn't said a word to her in the last hour. He hadn't been a distraction at all, except that he simply existed. That was all Claire needed to be distracted. Knowing that Duncan Hillston existed, how could any woman not be distracted? And Claire faced the truth that had been staring her in the face for the last twenty-four hours: she was in love with Duncan Hillston all over again.

Claire shook her head and pushed away from the counter. She and Duncan had been together for two consecutive days and Claire needed a break from his magnetic pull. She felt distracted, out-of-sorts. Maybe once she got a little distance from him, she could think clearly, because while she was in love with him, she had no idea about the extent of his feelings. He obviously cared about her, but Duncan cared about everyone he came into contact with. It was one of the reasons she loved him.

"I'm going to the restroom," she announced, standing.

Duncan looked up from his papers and smiled at her, making her heart double pump in salute. Claire quickly left the lab before she attacked him. Attacking Duncan in the lab was not a good idea.

Claire's heels echoed in the quiet, empty hallway as she walked toward the restroom. During the day BioTech halls teemed with people who busily scurried from one lab to the next. The barely controlled chaos of a laboratory was exactly what Claire thrived on. But she had to admit that at night the lab could be downright creepy.

The dark shadows in the corners of the gargantuan halls, the mechanical hum of the air-conditioning. She glanced at the cameras mounted at regular intervals on the ceilings. Twenty-four-hour security. She was only one wave at the camera away from having immediate help. Of course, Claire knew the statistics on cameras providing any form of security. The cameras couldn't help if no one watched them, and most guards did not watch the cameras.

Claire entered the restroom and flipped on the light. Bright, cheerful light filled the industrial restroom, showing four empty stalls. She quickly entered one, slamming the stall door behind her. Just as Claire locked the stall door, she heard the restroom door open and swing closed. For some reason, she held her breath as the silence in the room grew heavier. One moment passed before heavy footsteps walked across the room to stand at the sink.

Claire forced herself to breathe, slowly relaxing. She had nothing to be afraid of. She wasn't the only scientist who worked late on Saturday nights. In fact, Claire knew of a few of her colleagues who hadn't left their labs in days—sleeping in their cot rooms, showering and changing in the gym facilities in the building's basement. She would feel silly when she walked out of the stall and came face-to-face with one of her colleagues.

The stall door next to Claire's closed with a heavy thud, shaking the adjoining wall. Claire placed a hand on the wall that separated her from the other stall, as if that would help her see through it. The longer the silence grew in the rest-room, the more downright scared Claire became. She waited for some sign that the woman next to her was in the bathroom for a legitimate reason, but there was nothing.

Claire quickly pulled up her stockings and pulled down her skirt. She knew it was not rational to be afraid just because another woman had entered the bathroom, but Claire suddenly didn't care about rational. She wanted to get back to her brightly lit lab and back to Duncan.

She cautiously opened the stall door. There was no one at the sinks. Claire walked to the sink, telling herself that nothing was wrong. She washed her hands as quickly as possible. Against her will, her gaze was drawn to the mirror over the sink that reflected the four stalls behind her. Only one door was closed. Her gaze lowered and she froze in speechless fear when she saw long men's shoes under the stall door.

Claire bit off a scream and didn't bother to turn off the faucet before she ran toward the door. She had one hand wrapped around the door handle when she felt two strong hands grab her shoulders. She screamed as the hands dug into her and whirled her around to slam her face-first against the linoleum wall. Only Claire's outstretched hands kept her face from slamming into the wall. She was momentarily dizzy as her palms stung from the force of contact.

A man, strong and big, leaned against her, pressing her against the wall. She was suffocating under his heavy weight. She tried to push back, to get him off her, but that only made him press harder against her. She turned her head as her cheek pressed against the cold wall. Tears of fear filled her eyes, blurring her vision.

"Where is it?" a raspy male voice demanded in her ear. His hot breath on her ear, which strangely smelled of mint, sent shivers of disgust down her spine. And then there was the fear because she recognized his strangely accented voice. The mugger. The man from her house.

Claire tried to speak, but her mouth wouldn't cooperate, not with the thick, metallic taste of fear clogging it. The man's hands dug painfully into her shoulders as he repeated more forcefully, "Where is it?"

Claire felt another chill wrack her body. She suddenly felt like every stupid woman in every horror movie she had ever seen. She shouldn't have gone to the bathroom alone in a dark, abandoned lab. That was a recipe for an attack. Anyone who watched a movie on the Lifetime channel knew that.

Claire tried to look at him over her shoulder, but she only got the impression of a black sweater and large man.

She finally managed to speak in a low, trembling voice: "Even if you take the research, what good will that do? It's been patented by BioTech. We'll just prove that—"

"What the hell are you talking about?" he demanded, abruptly whirling her around to face him.

It was her first look at the man, and the fear ran cold in Claire's body because he wasn't wearing a mask this time. He was allowing her to see his face. That couldn't be a good thing.

He was tall, built like a tank, with olive-colored skin, dark hair slicked back, and piercing brown eyes that showed no emotion. He didn't look like a killer-for-hire. He looked normal.

His voice was surprisingly nonthreatening, in direct contradiction to his hands digging painfully into her shoulders, as he said, "I don't care about any damn research. I just want the account code."

It took her a few moments to realize what he had just said. "Account code?" she repeated uncertainly. "You're not trying to steal my research?"

"I'm not trying to steal anything from you," he said, sounding almost offended. "I just want my employer's property."

Anger caused her back to stiffen and the tears to stop. "My team and I created this gene therapy procedure. It's the property of BioTech. Just because your boss thinks that he should get the benefit—"

"Wait a second, lady," he said, confusion crossing his compact features. "I don't know what you're talking about, and I don't care. Stop trying to stall for time and give me the account code."

"I have no idea what account code you're talking about," she shot back.

His hands loosened a fraction on her shoulders as he asked uncertainly, "You don't?"

"No," she said firmly. "I am a scientist. I do cancer research—"

"You're trying to trick me," he said suspiciously.

"No, I'm not."

"He said that you were smart. . . ." His voice trailed off, and Claire almost thought he would call it a case of mistaken identity and walk out of the room. But then his eyes narrowed and he said, "I'll give you three days to bring me the account code. Midnight Tuesday at the Santa Monica Airport, hangar thirty-one."

Claire was now getting annoyed. "I don't have—"

His voice was low and serious as he warned, "If I even smell the police, you and your boyfriend will think our encounter on the street last week was just a little tango. Henri Vittels has eyes and ears everywhere, and we'll know. You're a smart lady; don't be stupid. Bring me the code, and you and your boyfriend will never see me again. Understand?"

Claire's fear returned like a fist in her stomach at the man's mention of Duncan. She whispered urgently, "I have no idea what you're talking about—"

"Then you better ask your friend where it is, because your life and your boyfriend's life depend on it."

"What friend?" she asked, confused.

"Belle," he said flatly.

He no longer had to hold Claire against the wall, because she couldn't move. She was too angry to move. Annabelle. Claire was going to kill her before the Hulk could ever get his hands on her.

"Annabelle," Claire growled.

The man actually sounded amused as he said, "You know her."

"Unfortunately. What did she do?"

"Your friend was stupid enough to take an account code from my employer. That account contains a lot of money, but without the account number, Mr. Vittels cannot access any of it. Mr. Vittels was . . . holding that money for some very important friends. And those friends will not be friends any longer if he doesn't have that money by the end of the week."

"Why don't you just ask Annabella about the account code?"

"Gee, I wonder why I didn't think of that," he replied with feigned surprise. He rolled his eyes, then snapped, "I can't find Belle. Last week at Zanzibar's I saw her slip the code into your briefcase. I had just planned to steal your briefcase, but your boyfriend got involved. Then I searched your car, but I got nothing but a pair of never-been-used gym clothes—"

"I've used them," Claire interrupted defensively, momentarily distracted from his story and her mounting anger at Annabelle.

"I was prepared to have this little talk with you earlier, but then Belle showed up at your house. My associate and I followed her to her hotel room and had a nice long talk with her. She said that you still had the account code, but that she would get it from you. We were stupid enough to believe her. In the middle of the night, she slipped out of the room somehow. I've spent the last few days looking for her. Time is running out and Mr. Vittels needs that account code, which leads me back to you and your boyfriend."

Claire didn't know whether to be hurt or angry. Annabelle had used her. That night at Zanzibar's, the visit to the lab, and then the visit to Claire's house hadn't been about reestablishing a friendship; it had been about using Claire to get rid of some gangster's property. Claire finally settled on anger. It was an easier emotion to deal with.

Still, as the Incredible Hulk continued to tower over her, Claire realized that she had no choice in the matter. She was involved now. Her mind raced through the endless possibilities of how this scenario could end, and she didn't like any of them.

"I don't know where Annabelle is, and I don't know where the account code is," she finally told him.

"But you can find her, or more likely she'll find you, because she needs that code." He clenched his jaw, then abruptly nodded. "You and Rambo have three days."

Suddenly the sound of the internal lab alarm blasted through the building. The man cursed, then gritted his teeth and muttered, "They must have found that guard. Tuesday night, Dr. Scott."

He ran out of the bathroom. Claire heard the sound of the security guards yelling at him to stop and then shoes slapping against the floor. Claire didn't move from her position on the wall because she didn't care about the man. She had bigger fish to fry. Or more accurately, she had bigger, silicone fish to fry: Annabelle Richards.

Chapter Seventeen

At close to one o' clock in the morning, Claire and Duncan stumbled into her house. The security guards hadn't been able to catch the man, but they had called the police. Claire had spent the last hour being grilled by Detective Hansen. For the first time in her life, Claire was facing the humiliating realization that someone else was smarter than her. Namely, Detective Hansen. The woman obviously could spot a lie from a mile away, and she hadn't believed anything that Claire had told her about a masked man accosting her in the bathroom but immediately leaving as the alarm sounded.

Claire believed every word the man had said in the restroom. Henri Vittels was a dangerous man, Annabelle was a traitor, and Claire and Duncan were in a lot of trouble. Claire knew the statistics on the number of witnesses who survived in the protective custody of law enforcement, and she didn't like the odds. Besides, how could she be on the cover of *Time* or *Newsweek* if she was holed away in witness protection, unable to continue her work?

"How are you feeling?" Duncan asked softly, coming behind her to place his hands on her shoulders.

And just like that, Claire's brain and body turned into mush. She just needed his touch, and all the worries, pressure, and stress disappeared. Her body and her brain were betraying her, and Claire didn't like it. But, she had read a study that identified the complete lack of self-control as the prime indicator of love.

Duncan guided her to face him. His expression was so gentle and caring that tears stung Claire's eyes. She blinked them back as one of his hands moved to caress her cheek.

"A lot of good I did tonight," he said, sounding defeated. "I should have stayed home."

"No, Duncan, I was glad you were there," she said fiercely, shaking her head. She hadn't had the chance to tell him about Annabelle's treachery because the two hadn't been alone since the attack, but now she wished she had told him sooner. He obviously felt guilty.

Duncan snorted in disbelief, then dropped his hands from her face and walked across the living room. He stared at the candles littering her bookshelf.

"Claire, I've been thinking. . . ." His voice trailed off; then he stared at her. His tortured expression made her flinch. He was hurting because he thought she was in danger. If Claire hadn't loved him before that moment, she did now. She knew exactly how he felt because when the man had threatened Duncan, she had felt the same sheer hopelessness, the rage, and the drive to do anything to make him safe.

Duncan cleared his throat and said, "I mentioned this before and you didn't seem thrilled at the idea, but I really think it's time to hire a professional bodyguard."

"Duncan—"

"Alex was in the marines. When a few of his buddies left the marines, they formed a security agency. I could ask—"

"I don't need a bodyguard," she said, shaking her head, with a slight smile.

Duncan didn't smile. In fact, he looked pissed as hell. His voice was rough as he said, "Whoever this bastard is, he has proven that he can get to you anywhere and anytime. The bodyguard is the best option we have right now. Do you want to know what my first plan was? To take all of your damn research and hand it to your competitors myself, so they'll leave you the hell alone."

Claire couldn't stop from smiling. "Duncan—"

He stalked across the room to glare down at her, interrupting her. "I know you're doing noble and important work, but it's not worth your life. As far as I'm concerned, nothing is worth your life."

She grinned and blurted out, "I love you, Duncan, and if your aggression and anger is any indication—as studies show it is—you love me, too, but it's all right if you're not quite ready to admit it."

Duncan's eyes widened and Claire thought that he'd stopped breathing for a few seconds. Maybe he wasn't ready to hear the truth about his feelings. Maybe he wasn't ready to accept it, but Claire could accept the truth for the both of them. She loved him. It felt like a relief to say it out loud.

"I love you?" he asked uncertainly.

Claire grimaced. The first time those words came from his mouth, she hadn't pictured them in question form.

"We've only known each other one week," he said, confused.

"We've known each other almost twenty years," she corrected.

Duncan took several defensive steps from her, as if she were on the verge of pounding his face in. Claire had the urge to do exactly that, since he still looked at her as if she were an alien, but she decided to give him a little more time to get accustomed to the idea. It had taken her twenty years. She could give him a couple of minutes.

Duncan finally sighed heavily, then said, "I'm not sure what I'm feeling. I just know that I've never felt like this for anyone else in my life, that you make me want to do things and say things that I've never wanted to do and say in my life. Is that love?"

"Close enough," she murmured, then wrapped her arms around his neck and kissed him.

Duncan slipped his tongue between her lips to lazily dance in her mouth. Women had told him that they loved him, but none had told him that he loved them and been damn near right. Too bad he couldn't admit it to her. Duncan could barely admit it to himself. Just last week, he had told Patrick that he didn't believe in love; now here he was with the words on the tip of his tongue.

Claire loved him. She had told him in her matter-of-fact manner, with no fear or uncertainty. Duncan had won the bet and knew immediately that he had to lose it. He gathered her in his arms and took a little more of the honey that she offered before he forced himself to release her. He grinned at the reddish tint that splayed across her cheeks. He loved that flush that was the telltale sign that she was all hot and bothered. Duncan felt that sharp jab in his chest again. Lust sure as hell didn't feel like this.

"I love you, too," he finally admitted.

He hadn't expected to say it that night, but saying it lifted a pressure on his chest that he hadn't noticed. In fact, it almost felt like the truth, not the typical Duncan Hillston reaction to a woman's feelings—pretend to reciprocate and then get the hell out of Dodge. It felt right.

"I know," she said matter-of-factly, but she was beaming.

Duncan laughed as he shook his head. He had always said that he liked a confident woman. "Now that we got that out of the way, explain why you're trying to distract me from this bodyguard issue."

Claire's smile faded and she suddenly looked nervous as she sat on the sofa, tucking her skirt around her knees. "I wasn't exactly truthful with Detective Hansen earlier tonight."

"What do you mean?" he asked warily, sitting next to her.

Duncan's gaze was instantly drawn to her mouth as she licked her lips. Her taste lingered in his mouth. He shifted uncomfortably. Instead of taking her immediately to the bedroom, he had to ask about Detective Hansen. No wonder Claire thought he was an idiot.

"I actually spoke to the man who broke into the lab."

Duncan's hands tightened into fists, but he was proud of how calm he sounded as he asked hoarsely, "You spoke to him?"

Claire nodded and said, "For approximately five minutes."

The flash of anger was so brief and intense that Duncan was nearly blinded by the force of it. His voice was low as he said through clenched teeth, "Did he hurt you?"

"No," she said defensively, but Duncan knew she lied.

"Did he hurt you, Claire?"

"Not really," she said, not sounding very concerned about it. Duncan was very concerned. But before he could work himself into a suitable lather of rage, she continued, "If he wanted to kill me, Duncan, he would have done it by now. Both times that I've encountered him, he has had the ability to seriously hurt me, but he hasn't. I don't think he's violent, Duncan. In fact, I think that once he gets what he's looking for, I'll never hear from him again—"

Duncan shook his head, annoyed, and snapped, "Are you really psychoanalyzing this creep?"

"He would make an interesting case study. I have colleagues from MIT who study men in the mercenary field of employment and—"

Duncan tried to be patient, but his head was spinning. Did he really just admit that he loved Claire? And did she really just decide that the man trying to kill her should be part of an experiment? He cut her off impatiently, "Did you see his face?"

"Yes. It was the same man from the mugging, and from the night my car was broken into. I know it was him."

Duncan tried to remain calm, he really did, but the idea of someone hurting Claire made his skin crawl. Duncan did not consider himself a violent person, but maybe that was because his woman had never been threatened. He had never had a woman whom he considered "his" before.

He said calmly, "We'll call Detective Hansen and tell her that you can identify your attacker. I'm sure we'll have to go down to the station to look at photographs or something, but it should only take a few hours. Or maybe you can talk to a sketch artist—"

"I can't tell the police," she said simply.

"Why not?"

A hint of fear flashed in her eyes before her expression

went blank. "This isn't about my research. That man could care less about cancer or cancer research."

"Then what does he want?"

"Annabelle," she said with a grimace of distaste. "When Annabelle left Paris, she took an account code from a very dangerous man named Henri Vittels. Apparently, this account has a lot of money in it, and Mr. Vittels can't access it without the code. He needs the money by the end of this week for God knows what."

"Poor Annabelle," Duncan said dully, then demanded, "but what the hell does this have to do with you?"

Claire's eyes hardened as she said through clenched teeth, "Mr. Vittels's man saw Annabelle slip the code into my laptop briefcase that night at Zanzibar's." Duncan muttered a curse, and Claire nodded in agreement, then continued, "When he couldn't get the laptop case from us that night, he broke into the car thinking that my duffel bag was the same case. When Annabelle showed up at my house that morning, he followed her back to her hotel and they talked, but then she got away—"

Duncan muttered another curse and tried to breathe, but he kept envisioning Claire alone in her house with a professional killer waiting for her. Claire must have sensed the direction of his thoughts, because she placed a soothing hand on his arm. His muscles tensed under her soft touch before he released a heavy sigh and relaxed into her touch.

"I still don't understand why you can't tell the police all of this," he said, shaking his head.

"Because he threatened to kill me, to kill . . . to kill us both if I went to the police. And I believed him. He doesn't care who has the code. He just wants it by Tuesday at midnight."

Duncan raked a hand down his face and sighed. He shook his head and asked tentatively, "Do you have the code?"

"Before we left the lab, I looked in my laptop bag, but I didn't see anything out of the ordinary. Annabelle visited me at the lab a few days after the first attack. She was alone in my office for a few moments after we returned from getting coffee. She could have taken it out of my bag then."

Duncan sighed again, then asked drolly, "You don't have any other good friends from high school that I should worry about, do you?"

She smiled slightly before her mouth hardened into a tight line and she said, "I should have known that Annabelle was up to something as soon as she called and asked to meet me. I hadn't seen her in fourteen years. What did I expect? She used me. She lied to me."

Fear momentarily dampened Duncan's anger. Not fear for Annabelle but fear for himself. He said hesitantly, "Maybe Annabelle had a good reason for doing what she did."

"A good reason to lie to me?" Claire asked, her eyes wide with disbelief. "I'm supposed to be her friend, someone she loves and cares about. You don't lie to people you care about."

He swiped at the sudden beads of perspiration on his forehead. "Maybe everything happened so quickly that the whole situation got out of control. Maybe she wanted to tell you but couldn't because she was afraid of your reaction."

Claire's expression was unforgiving as she said coldly, "She lied to me, and I can never forgive her for that. My father taught me that. He turned away my mother after she had had enough of her lover and wanted to come back to our family. My father told her that some things are unforgivable, no matter how much you love the person."

"Life isn't that black-and-white," Duncan said desperately.

"Life isn't black-and-white but trusting someone is. My father loved my mother more than life, but he rejected her because he knew that once someone betrays you, you can never trust that person again."

Duncan gulped over the lump in his throat and he mumbled, "I guess you're right."

Claire's voice softened as she said, "If I had never struggled with him over my briefcase, he would have the code and you wouldn't be involved. Now I don't know where the code could possibly be, you've been beat up—"

"I was making a comeback," he interrupted, for what felt like the tenth time since he had known her.

She ignored him and said, "And now you're being threatened, too."

Duncan's anger slowly melted when he saw the distress on her face. He quickly wrapped his arms around her and pressed a kiss at her hairline.

"I'm involved if you're involved," he whispered, tilting her chin until she met his gaze.

Claire gave him that soft smile that sent his senses into overload, and Duncan settled a whisper-soft kiss on her mouth. His blood began to roar through his veins even as he thought of her expression when she had talked about Annabelle lying to her. Claire obviously didn't forgive easily, which didn't look good for Annabelle and looked even worse for him, especially since he was in love with her—hook, line, and sinker.

"If you have the account code, we'll find it. If you don't have it, we'll find Annabelle. Then we'll turn everything over to this Mr. Vittels. It was his to begin with, right? No harm, no foul."

"I should start looking for—"

"We have time," he murmured as he placed another kiss on her waiting lips, not wanting to release her at that moment. Not when she was so soft and lush in his arms. Not when her yielding breasts were smashed against his chest. And definitely not when she was looking at him like that. "We have all the time in the world."

She mumbled something unintelligible before he captured her mouth in a slow, fire-burning kiss that was designed to satisfy them both, but just left him wanting more. One of his hands traveled to her hair and released the satin-soft strands from her ponytail. He dug his hand into her hair, massaging her scalp, while his tongue continued to massage her mouth in long, slow strokes. Claire abruptly stiffened and wrenched free from his grip, her hair drifting around her shoulders, framing her face like a black curtain. Duncan moaned and held on tight, in case she thought about leaving him entirely alone.

Excitement danced in her eyes as she said, "I know where we can find Annabelle."

"I must really be losing my touch," he grumbled, licking his dry, kiss-swollen lips. "I'm trying to seduce you here, if you hadn't noticed."

"And you're doing an excellent job," she assured him in a soothing tone, then said, "Annabelle needs money and a place to stay where the average person couldn't find her. And I think I know where she would go to find both of those."

"Where?"

"Club Sunset," she said with a wide grin. "Last weekend, Annabelle told me that she always goes there when she needs to find a rich man to get her out of the country."

"Great," he murmured, distracted, then turned back to the most pressing matter at hand—satisfying his aching hard-on. He moved aside some hair and nuzzled her soft neck. He inhaled the scent that was undeniably Claire. Yep, it was official. He was in mad, crazy love with this woman.

"But we don't know what night she'll be there, or even what time she'll be there," Claire protested, that big brain of hers still spinning. "For all we know, she could have already found her sugar daddy and be on her way to Ibiza."

"Then we'll ask someone who knows," he replied simply.

"But who—"

"You're the smart one, remember? You'll think of something."

Duncan smiled as he felt Claire relax against him. He kissed her once more on the mouth, taking his time, enjoying the feel and taste of her. Her hands wrapped around his neck and she pulled him closer. Her eagerness made him hotter than he already was. Duncan had had many lovers, maybe not as many as he claimed to his friends, but a man had to keep the boys guessing, right? Yet he could not remember any woman feeling as right in his arms, as delicious in his mouth, as Claire did.

Duncan stood, bringing her to her feet. She stared up at him and licked her lips, exactly as he must have been doing. Duncan grinned, then led her toward the bedroom. He flipped on the overhead light and glanced around the bedroom. She had cleaned up from the night before, because when Duncan had left the room, the sheets had been tangled at the foot of the bed and her clothes had been tossed in different corners. Now the bed was neatly made with fresh sheets, the room was spotless, and there was a hint of jasmine in the air.

Duncan turned to her, his hands already undoing the buttons of her suit jacket. "You expecting company?" he asked, lifting one eyebrow.

Claire smiled in response, then took his hands in hers, leaving her jacket half-buttoned. Duncan gulped, his hope fading like a popped balloon. He was aching all over his body. He needed her tonight, especially after hearing she had been threatened by the Incredible Hulk. He needed her every night.

"I want to touch you tonight," she whispered, breaking the stillness of the bedroom.

The hope came back, and so did Duncan's painful erection. "I was hoping that we'd touch each other."

She shook her head, then caught him by surprise, pushing him in the chest and sending him sprawling onto the bed with a grunt. Duncan watched with wide eyes and an incredibly dry throat as she crawled onto the bed and straddled him, her skirt riding up on those beautiful, thick thighs that Beyonce would wish she had.

Claire smiled down at him, then tugged his sweater off and tossed it onto the ground. Her hands rested on his chest over his T-shirt, but Duncan could practically feel her touch to the tips of his toes. Her weight pressed down on his stomach, her breasts and lips just out of reach. He could have easily reached her, flipped their positions, and taken control, but he didn't. It was the best uncomfortable position he had ever been in in his life.

Her husky voice tore holes in his resolve to lie still as she told him, "When you start touching me, I lose the ability to focus on anything but how you make me feel. I want to focus on you tonight, Duncan. You already know my body better than I do. I want to know yours."

Duncan gulped, then forced a smile as he laced his fingers behind his head and lay back on the bed. "I'm all yours," he said, attempting to sound lighthearted and flirtatious, but somehow it came out sounding like an eternal pledge.

"I know," Claire whispered; then she pulled off his T-shirt.

Duncan dug his fingers into each hand and closed his eyes. This was going to be either heaven or hell, but either way, there was nowhere else he'd rather be.

Claire tucked loose hair behind her ears as she stared in awe at Duncan's bare chest. He was so beautiful. She was a scientist; she knew the human body. She knew more about the human body than the average person would ever care to know. She could explain the functions of the endocrine gland, synapses, nerve endings. She had seen many bodies over the last ten years—nude, clothed, and in various states of undress during various clinical trials—but Claire could have sworn that at that moment, Duncan was the only body she had ever seen in her life.

His rich chocolate brown skin stretched taut over the defined muscles in his arms and stomach. He had a broad, muscled chest, arms that bulged with veins and muscles, and Claire didn't know where to begin. All of that brown, beautiful skin waiting for her. And she wasn't even ready to think about the insistent hardness nudging her in the back of the thigh. Beautiful. She took a deep breath, then placed her hands on his chest. Just a light touch, but that was apparently all Duncan needed. The muscles in his stomach clenched and he hissed as if she had hurt him.

Claire smiled to herself. Perfect. She felt like she was in the lab, judging the reactions and responses of a test subject to different stimuli. Except this wasn't a subject. This was

Duncan, and Claire envisioned having the rest of her life to learn his reactions and responses. She had gone into this thinking she could have a casual affair—right a few high school wrongs. This was the first plan in her life that had gone completely awry, and Claire didn't know who to thank for that.

Claire eyed one of his blackberry-dark nipples, then brushed her hand across the hard pebble. Duncan bit his bottom lip in response, his eyes still tightly closed. Claire suddenly felt giddy. He was going to let her do whatever she wanted to him, and he wasn't going to stop her. She slowly leaned forward, then flicked her tongue over the pebble-hard nipple.

"Claire," Duncan hissed, sounding almost pained. "Whatever you're planning to do, you better do it fast."

"We're just getting started," she said with a laugh, feeling powerful and sexy and smarter than she had ever felt in her life. She pulled the nipple into her mouth and suckled. The muscles in Duncan's arms tensed, as if he was battling himself. Claire moved to the other nipple. She loved the feel of his nipple against her tongue. She loved the feel of his clenching and unclenching muscles under her hands, the silky feel of his skin.

His groans filled the room as she trailed her tongue from bathing that nipple down his stomach. She allowed the tips of her hair to move across his stomach and she was rewarded by a growl. He squirmed under her touch, then released a guttural curse when she dipped her tongue into his navel. She grinned in excitement as he bucked, nearly unseating her from on top of his stomach. She had found a weak spot.

"Baby, I'm warning you," he said, opening his eyes to pin her with a hard look.

Claire was flowing with too much warmth and heat to stop anything. The dark storm in his eyes alone told her that she couldn't stop. He was close, and she hadn't even really touched him.

Claire pretended to ignore his hot look and, instead,

skimmed her hands over his arms. She lingered at his straining biceps, on display due to his hands behind his head, and squeezed. The hardness at her thigh grew longer and heavier.

She looked at the front of his pants and smiled when she saw his length clearly outlined. She placed her hands on the front of his pants and massaged his length. Duncan cursed again, his eyes sliding closed. He felt so hot and heavy in her hands. Claire couldn't wait to have him inside of her, but right now she had other things to take care of.

She unbuttoned his pants, the fit made snug by his bulging erection. The groan deep in his throat filled the room as Claire pulled down his pants and briefs all at once. His erection sprang free, glistening and angry. She scooted down his body with his pants, then pulled them off his feet and threw them on the floor. Her gaze settled on his erection, and she nearly touched herself as her thighs involuntarily clenched. He was so thick and long. He was as perfect there as he was everywhere else on his body.

She wrapped one hand around him. Satin and strength all in one area of his body. A drop of moisture glistened on the tip of his penis, and her own core clenched at the emptiness, as if begging her to hurry.

"Claire," Duncan moaned, his head falling back as he arched into her hand.

Claire tentatively licked the tip of his erection. He went completely still. Too still.

"Are you all right?" she asked, concerned.

"No," he responded in a strangled whisper. "But don't stop."

Claire smiled, then placed her mouth on him. He tasted salty and delicious. It was a struggle, but she closed her mouth around him and pleasured him until he was breathing heavier than an Olympic athlete at the finish line. She abruptly pulled her mouth from him, and he popped free, impossibly larger and harder than before.

"Turn onto your stomach," she ordered hoarsely.

"What?" Duncan cried, opening his eyes to glare at her.

"Turn over," she said, giving him her best Dr. Scott glare.

He mumbled but slowly turned onto his chest, his arms at his sides. Claire instantly climbed onto him again, settling on his thick, muscled thighs. She dug her hands into the perfectly rounded twin globes. He was the perfect male specimen. Not an ounce of fat anywhere on him. She ran her hands from his behind to his broad back, placing soft kisses on the length of his spine, as she stretched over him like a contented cat. She just loved the feel of being so close to him, riding up and down as he took one heavy breath after another.

"Claire," Duncan said in a careful voice that made her smile. "I'm not trying to rush you or anything, darlin', but I'm on the edge here and I don't think you're ready—"

"You're underestimating yourself, Duncan," she told him confidently. "Studies have shown that the average man is able to—"

She didn't get to finish her sentence. She whooped in surprise as Duncan moved quicker than she had known possible. One moment she was lying on top of him, all content and right with the world; the next she was lying flat on the bed, her skirt around her waist and her stockings at her ankles. Duncan's eyes bored into her like black coal as he ripped open a condom packet and put the condom on with jerky movements. Claire knew he was too far gone for her to protest that she wasn't finished examining him—not that she would have protested anyway.

He paused, poised in between her legs, his length inches from her opening and hot enough for her to feel the heat radiating from it. She grabbed his arms in anticipation as his hands clenched her hips, and he suddenly rammed into her. She screamed his name at the feel of him filling her, filling all the empty places. He pulled out of her completely, then plunged into her again. The pace was quick, fast, and almost brutal.

Claire's entire body rocked with each stroke, and she had to hold on to his arms for dear life, but it felt so good that she couldn't be bothered to make any sign of protest. Her brain finally stopped working and her body took over—showing her the wonder of having Duncan inside her, stroking and filling her, taking her to ecstasy. All of the feelings spiraled into a heated pinpoint, and after one more earth-shattering stroke, Claire screamed and went over the edge. Duncan grunted and rammed into her a few more times before he followed her to the stars, her name a cry on his lips.

Chapter Eighteen

"It's your turn to pay for breakfast," Alex informed Duncan as the two men, along with Tavis, walked into Nate's diner to pick up their breakfast order before heading to the Estefan job site.

Duncan murmured noncommittally in response. He had barely heard anything his brothers had said since he met them at their offices earlier that morning. His mind was too busy racing with the full-color, full-sound replay from the past weekend. Every word, every touch, every murmur. He had half a boner just from thinking about Claire's exploration last night. He had never been examined in such detail, with such love. It had almost been embarrassing, except he had been too aroused to care. Not to mention her water work that morning in the shower before she left for work.

Duncan was in big trouble. He was in love with her. Not just love, but he was in lust with her. He desired her. And hell, he liked her. A lot. She made him laugh. She made him want to learn new things. The player had fallen like Rome, and it had only taken a week. Hawk was going to have a field day with this news.

"You jokers are late," Kobie greeted from the counter where he sat with crutches next to him. His left ankle was wrapped in an Ace bandage; otherwise, he looked no worse for wear. "I leave the job for a few days and everything is going to pot, isn't it?"

Alex winked at Kobie and Tavis, then said to Duncan,

"Kobie, Tavis and I decided that you're not getting paid this month."

"OK," Duncan replied as he slid onto a stool at the counter.

He snapped from his daze when he heard their combined laughter. Or cackling, more accurately. He glared at his brothers, who looked entirely too smug and knowing.

"What are you three laughing at?" he demanded.

"You," Alex said simply.

Tavis grinned and said, "Alex told me to expect this behavior this morning, but I didn't believe him."

"I didn't know it was this bad," Kobie said to Alex, shaking his head.

"When a man doesn't return his brothers' calls for three straight days and misses church *and* Mom's Sunday dinner, you've got to figure that it's really bad," Alex informed them.

Duncan became more irritated as the three exchanged knowing glances. "What are you guys talking about?"

"Here's your order," Nate greeted, setting four bulging white paper bags on the counter.

"Duncan is paying," Alex told Nate.

Duncan automatically pulled out his wallet, which prompted Alex, Kobie, and Tavis to collapse into little-boy giggles.

"That's it," Duncan snapped. "What the hell is going on?"

Alex grinned, then looked at Tavis, who looked at Kobie, who turned to Nate. Duncan stared at Nate expectantly. He had that same knowing grin on his face as his younger brothers before he glanced at the few other diners in the restaurant, then leaned closer and said, "You know that Saturday night is date night for Toya and me—"

"What the hell is date night?" Duncan grumbled.

Tavis sighed heavily and said, "It's a device that wives have come up with to torture husbands. At least one night a month we have to take our wives out, leave the kids at home, and pay for a babysitter. It's supposed to be a real date, like the two of you would have gone on before you were married."

"Even though you got married precisely to avoid dating," Alex chimed in with a huff of indignation.

"Anyways," Nate said, pointedly glaring at his brothers for interrupting him. "It was late, around midnight, and Toya and I drove by your house. Newspapers and mail were piled on your porch. We were worried, especially since no one had heard from you. We went inside with the spare key just to make certain that everything was all right, and it looked like you hadn't slept in your bed in at least a couple of days."

Duncan groaned as his brothers all laughed. Nate placed a hand on Duncan's shoulder and said, "I told Alex, Kobie, and Tavis that it looked like you hadn't been home since you were in here with Claire on Friday."

"You spent the whole weekend with one woman?" Tavis asked, disbelief evident in his voice.

Duncan glared at his brothers' expectant stares. He had expected this response from Patrick or Hawk but not his brothers. Then Duncan remembered all the jokes he had made about their lives: how he would call marriage an institution that he wasn't ready to be committed to, how he would laugh until his stomach hurt at the spit-up on clothes that each inevitably came to work with. Duncan guessed he deserved a little hell in return.

Duncan admitted begrudgingly, "She's different."

Alex grinned; Tavis rubbed Duncan's shoulder in sympathy; Kobie shook his head. Nate sighed and said, "I remember saying those exact words to Dad about Toya."

"How does it feel realizing that your life as you know it is over?" Tavis asked seriously, but Duncan heard the hint of laughter.

"I give you a year—then you'll be asking Kobie where he got his swing set in the backyard," Alex said, not bothering to hide his amusement.

"You'll start thinking about the practicalities of a mini-van," Kobie chimed in, then added in explanation, "There's more room for strollers."

"When you read the newspaper, the words *family pack* in

the travel section will become the Holy Grail," Nate said, nodding.

"And don't get me started on diapers," Tavis said, irritated. "I spent more money on diapers last year than I spent on food."

"When you think of summer, you won't salivate over the thought of women in bikinis and sundresses. Your first thought will be swim lessons and soccer leagues," Alex said.

"Restaurants with real tablecloths and menus not covered in plastic will be a distant memory," Nate said with a sigh of longing.

"A night out on the town will be a talent show at the kids' schools, *talent*—of course—being subjective," Tavis said, then added, with a grimace, "all four hours of it."

"You'll convince yourself that the minivan's gas mileage more than makes up for the fact that you're riding around in a bigger, uglier station wagon," Kobie muttered, apparently still focused on the minivan.

"Oh, and you can forget coming home after work, kicking back, and watching the game on television," Alex said. "There will be homework, fighting kids, irritated and stressed-out wife, dog poop piled in the backyard—"

"Permission slips to sign, baths to give, teeth to brush, science fair projects that you have to do because your kid tells you, 'Oh, Daddy, my science fair project is due tomorrow. Can you help me?' and bedtime stories to read," Tavis interrupted, warming to the subject.

"Not to mention the state of the house," Nate sang, laughing in glee as Duncan's eyes grew wider and wider.

Alex abruptly looked at Nate, Kobie, and Tavis and asked, in an almost pleading tone, "Why is there always so much trash? I take out the trash at night and, I swear, by the time we all wake up the next morning, the trash cans are full again."

The three laughed while Duncan stared at them horrified. He occasionally kept one or some of his brothers' children on the weekend, but it had always seemed fun. He hadn't thought about homework or science fair projects or . . . Did Alex say something about shoveling dog shit?

Nate smiled, then said, "And speaking of future joys, one of yours just walked in."

The brothers turned in unison to the front door, and Duncan inwardly groaned as Al Scott walked into the restaurant and headed toward an empty booth, oblivious to their scrutiny. Duncan would never understand how a man that skinny could inspire such fear.

"I guess I should go say hi," Duncan said, then glanced at his brothers to refute him.

"In-laws have their own special category in the joys of family life," Alex muttered sarcastically, shivering at some memories that he obviously would not share with his brothers.

Duncan handed Nate his credit card to pay for the food, then stood. He looked at Al, who had opened a menu. Duncan turned back to his brothers, who looked sufficiently depressed as they probably mentally continued their litany of complaints.

He asked hesitantly, "OK, guys, before I go over there, give me something. Something good about all of this."

Four identical blank expressions stared back at him before Tavis said, "We just did."

Duncan laughed in disbelief. "I said something good. What you guys just described sounds like hell."

Nate smiled and said, "It's just another day in paradise, Duncan."

Duncan frowned, then stared for confirmation at Alex, Kobie, and Tavis, who all nodded. He finally shook his head and muttered, "You're all insane."

He ignored their laughter and forced himself to walk across the restaurant to Al's table.

"Good morning, Al," Duncan said with an awkward half wave.

Al looked at him, and Duncan almost thought that the older man didn't recognize him because he studied him for so long. But then Al nodded and murmured, "Duncan."

The two men shook hands, and Duncan took a step in retreat. Obviously Al was not the talkative type, but before Duncan could make it to safety, Al ordered, "Sit down."

Duncan inwardly cursed, then forced a smile as he sat down on the opposite side of the table. He dared not look at his brothers because he knew they were probably laughing their asses off or giving him smug I-told-you-so looks.

"Have you been watching the Lakers?" Duncan asked, going on the offensive. "With all the trades and rumors of trades, it doesn't look good—"

"Claire is very, very smart," Al said as if Duncan had never spoken, his gaze steady.

Duncan gulped, then said, "I'm aware of that, sir."

"But she hasn't had a lot of experience with men like you."

"Men like me?" Duncan repeated with a confused smile. "I don't understand—"

"Her mother left when Claire was very young. I did the best I could with Joan, but Claire . . . I didn't know what to do with her. Kids like her require so much more and, paradoxically, so much less. I'm a trash collector; I had no business having a kid like her. By the time she reached the fourth grade, she was teaching me stuff." Al paused, as if waiting for Duncan to speak. When he only stared, Al said grimly, "I like your father, Duncan. He's always been a fair man. When my girls were young and I didn't have much money, your father built a family room onto my house and didn't try to cheat me."

"I didn't know that," Duncan said, trying to keep up with Al's random conversation topics.

Al's voice lowered and his eyes narrowed into golden slits as he said, "But if you hurt my daughter, Vincent Hillston will be minus one son."

Duncan stared across the table at the older man and realized that Al was not joking or giving the traditional overprotective speech. He was dead serious. Duncan gulped over the lump in his throat and nodded stiffly.

Al nodded, then looked down at his menu again, the conversation over. Duncan cleared his throat and said, "It was nice talking to you, sir."

Al didn't respond, and Duncan quickly stood and hurried across the restaurant, where, as he predicted, his brothers were behind the counter, grinning like a pack of hyenas.

. . .

"You're humming, Claire," Vino accused as he walked into her office.

Claire flinched in surprise at his sudden appearance. She had been so wrapped up in her frantic search of her office for the account code that she hadn't even heard her office door open or Vino walk inside.

"I don't hum," she protested lamely.

She had been humming all morning. Her body had been humming since last night. Even now, her skin sang as she remembered Duncan running his mouth across each inch. Then when he had discovered the angry bruises on her shoulders from the man's hands, Duncan had cursed, then spent the next hour worshipping that area and the rest of her body to soothe the pain. She stopped the smile that threatened to cross her face when she realized that Vino continued to study her.

"You were humming," he said flatly. "And I just had to hear from Phyllis in Marketing that something happened in the lab this weekend involving you. Something about you bringing in a visitor who should be modeling Calvin Klein boxers on a billboard, and the police. Now, you can guess what I'm picturing here."

Claire laughed, then shook her head. "Believe me, it's not what you're thinking. Someone broke into the lab, and continuing my string of luck, I happened to run into him."

Concern crossed Vino's face and he sat in the chair near her desk. "Are you all right?"

"Fine."

"Is this related to the mugging and the car theft?"

"No," she lied. When Vino continued to stare at her expectantly, Claire averted her gaze and repeated firmly, "No."

"Break-ins, muggings, car thefts . . . this is better than an episode of *Charmed*," he said excitedly.

"Vino, your addiction to women's television is very disturbing. I'm sure if Fiona knew how far it's gone, she wouldn't make you watch those shows anymore."

"I have a little secret, Claire: Fiona didn't start me on watching those shows. I got her to start watching them," he added with a shrug of his hefty shoulders. Claire laughed; then Vino handed her a bound stack of paper. "Everything is ready for the trials next week."

"Good," Claire said excitedly. She grinned at Vino and said, "I can't wait to get started."

"Me neither." He indicated the stack of sealed envelopes on her desk. "You haven't mailed out the draft of your article yet for comments?" he asked, surprised.

"I completely forgot. I'll do it tomorrow." She flipped through the papers he had given her, then felt his stare and looked up to find him looking stunned. "What?"

"You forgot to do something," he said, amazed. "What in the hell is going on with you, Claire Scott?"

Claire wanted to answer, "Duncan," but instead only grinned. Thinking about Duncan always made her smile.

Vino shook his head with an amused laugh. "You really have it bad, don't you?"

"I have no idea what you're talking about, Dr. Ricardo."

"I get that same goofy smile the morning after Fiona tries out a new routine on me," he said, nodding. "I'm assuming that this has something to do with Duncan and that the walking Calvin Klein billboard was the infamous Duncan."

"It was Duncan," she admitted, her grin growing wider just from saying his name.

"And he's the reason you've been humming horribly off-key and making the interns bring up the subject of hazard pay?"

"I don't kiss and tell," she said haughtily, but then grinned when Vino continued to stare at her.

The telephone rang, interrupting his interrogation. Of course, Claire planned to tell Vino everything. She had never had anything to tell Vino about in the men department, so they were operating on untested ground. But weren't girls supposed to dish to their best friends? And since Vino had started watching women's television, he had become much easier to talk to.

"Dr. Scott," Claire greeted into the telephone receiver.

"Claire, it's Joan," her sister greeted, sounding stiff and formal.

Claire inwardly groaned, then motioned to Vino that she had to take the call. Vino suspiciously narrowed his eyes at her but left the office, closing the door behind him. Westfield was a small community, and Claire had always known that she would eventually receive this call from her sister. After all, Joan took her maternal duties very seriously.

"Hi, Joan," Claire said, attempting to sound busy. "You know that we start preclinical trials next week, and I'm right in the middle—"

"I called you four times this weekend, and you didn't return any of my calls," Joan said flatly. "If I hadn't caught you at work this morning, I was going to call the police and report you missing."

Claire thought guiltily about the red light blinking on her answering machine. She hadn't checked her messages all weekend. She had been in a Duncan fog, assuming that the rest of the world had stopped just like her world had. Judging from the annoyance in Joan's tone, the rest of the world had kept going.

"I didn't check my messages this weekend."

"Why not? Because you were busy with Duncan Hillston?"

Claire gripped the telephone and searched for the right response. Telling Duncan that she loved him seemed almost child's play compared to telling Joan that she loved Duncan.

Joan continued over Claire's silence, "Not only did you bring him to the spelling bee, giving Kira all types of ideas about her having an *Uncle Duncan*, but I heard you were practically salivating over him at Nate's Grill Friday night. What is going on, Claire?"

Claire said softly, "I'm in love with him."

Joan's silence worried Claire more than an outburst would have. Joan didn't usually react to surprising news with a silent response. Joan screamed or laughed. She didn't hold her tongue.

"Well," Joan finally said, sounding as if she were choking.

"Is that all you have to say?" Claire demanded, frustrated. Claire told herself that Joan's opinion didn't matter, but—of course—her opinion mattered. Only in the lab was life black-and-white.

"You're a grown woman. It's your life. If you want to date Duncan Hillston, then date him."

Claire released the breath that she hadn't known she had been holding. At least, she knew now. "You don't like him."

"I don't know him . . . besides the rumors, of course."

"Last week, you were encouraging me to go out with him."

"But I never thought you would," she wailed in response. "You don't ever notice men. I didn't think that you'd ever see him again."

"Thanks, Joan," Claire said drily.

"Well, you're so dedicated to your work," Joan protested. "I thought you didn't want anything to interfere with your research until the preclinical trials were over."

"Duncan won't interfere," she said unconvincingly.

"And you've known him—what?—a week?"

"Why does everyone keep saying that? We've known each other since ninth grade."

"No, you haven't, Claire. You were a child in high school, and he was a skirt-chasing teenager. You don't know the adult Duncan. You're in love with a fantasy you created when you were eleven years old."

"That is not true," Claire protested, then admitted begrudgingly, "That may have been true in the beginning, but now I know the adult Duncan. And he's amazing, Joan. Better than I could have ever imagined. Maybe I was more predisposed to like him because I had a cru—because of high school, but I'm going into this with both eyes wide open."

Joan's voice softened as she sighed, then said, "I just don't want you to get hurt."

"I won't," Claire said.

"Fine," Joan said, then added reluctantly, "Invite him over to dinner one night at my house."

Claire grinned because she had known that Joan would

give in. "He really is wonderful, Joan. He makes me feel like a regular person."

"You're not a regular person, Claire, and that's what I'm scared of," her sister said quietly. "I'll talk to you later."

Claire listened to the dial tone for a few seconds, then hung up the telephone, suddenly in no mood to hum anymore.

Chapter Nineteen

Later that evening, Claire stared at the rambling spilt-level home that sat innocently in the middle of Westfield and tried not to shiver in disgust. The Richards home had always looked so innocent—the neatly tended rose garden, the immaculate lawn, and the brightly painted window trim—but Claire could remember many late nights when Annabelle would appear at the Scott front door. Al would always open the door, without a word, and Annabelle would always enter, without a word, and usually spend the night. Claire had never known the reason for those late-night visits until their senior year in high school when she had witnessed what made Annabelle run on those late nights.

Next to Claire, behind the steering wheel of his truck, Duncan noticed her hesitation and placed a hand on her arm. His warmth brought her back to the present.

"Are you all right?" he asked, concerned.

Claire forced a smile at him, then said, "I should talk to Annabelle's parents alone."

"Are you sure?"

"They don't know you. They won't talk in front of you, and I have a feeling that her father knows where she is. Annabelle would never want him to worry about her."

Duncan glanced past her to the dark house as obvious discomfort flashed in his eyes. "I don't know, Claire," he said hesitantly. "It doesn't look like anyone is home. Besides, you said that Annabelle would never come back here. I don't see why we need to bother the Richardses—"

"I'll be fine, Duncan," she said, and she was surprised how convincing she sounded.

"All right," he said begrudgingly, but squeezed her arm—whether for her sake or his, she didn't know.

Claire stood away from the truck, slamming the door. She glanced over her shoulder at Duncan, who watched her. She feigned a reassuring smile; then she started toward the house. She was an adult now. She could handle Mrs. Richards. Claire wiped her sweaty palms on her suit jacket as she climbed the porch steps. Not for the first time, Claire wondered how Annabelle had come home to this every day after school. For a brief moment Claire pushed aside her anger at Annabelle and felt pity.

Claire rang the doorbell, then lightly knocked on the dark brown security screen. A few seconds later, the porch light glowed on, brushing back the early-evening darkness, and Claire heard the sound of locks disengaging. The front door abruptly flew open, and through the heavy screen door Claire saw Greg Richards. She sighed in relief that Annabelle's father had answered the door.

"Mr. Richards," she said, forcing herself to sound cheerful. "I know it's been a while, but it's Claire Scott, Annabelle's friend from high school."

"Claire," he said uncertainly, then more firmly, "Claire."

Greg opened the screen door, and Claire couldn't help the smile that crossed her face at the obvious surprise on his lined vanilla wafer–colored face. Except for her chocolate brown skin, it was obvious that Annabelle had taken after her father. Same nose, eyes, and lips. When Annabelle had been younger, the similarity had been scary, but now, while she seemed to glow with life, Greg Richards looked like a black-and-white version of his former self. His once-black hair had turned gray; his eyes were sunken in; he had lost weight, making his former thin frame look emaciated, and there were wrinkles everywhere. Greg and

Claire's father were the same age, but Al looked ten years younger.

Claire kept smiling even though she noticed that Greg kept the security door half-closed and he did not invite her inside the house. Behind his drooped shoulders she caught sight of the living room. It was still spotless. Too spotless.

"How have you been?" Claire asked the older man.

"Just fine, Claire," he answered in a voice that told her nothing had been fine for him in thirty years. "What about you? If I remember correctly, after high school you were going to Yale."

"Harvard," she corrected gently. "I graduated from Harvard, then I went to MIT, and now I'm working at a pharmaceutical research firm in Santa Monica."

"That's wonderful, Claire," he said, with a half-smile. "I always knew that you would do wonderful things."

There was an awkward pause as the two stared at each other. Claire cleared her throat, because she knew that Greg would not mention Annabelle.

Claire glanced around him into the house once more, then lowered her voice and asked, "I was wondering if you've seen Annabelle lately."

Greg flinched as if he had been shocked; then he quickly glanced over his shoulder before he turned back to Claire and almost pleaded, "You have to go now, Claire."

"I need to find her," Claire said, not moving. "Do you have any idea where she might be?"

"I haven't seen her in years."

Claire believed him. He probably hadn't seen his only child in years, but that didn't mean that he hadn't spoken to her. "Have you talked with her recently?"

Greg stopped sending panicked glances over his shoulder long enough to stare at Claire. "Is Annabelle in trouble?" he asked in a hoarse whisper.

"Yes," Claire answered matter-of-factly. "Her life is in danger."

Greg gasped in horror and gripped Claire's arm tight

enough to make her wince. "If anything happens to her, I'll never—"

"Who are you yammering at, Greg?" came a harsh voice from behind him.

Icy fear seized Claire's heart as Rose Richards, Annabelle's mother and tormentor, came into view. Even though Claire was almost thirty years old, when Rose's intense brown eyes fastened onto her, she felt like she was fifteen years old again, cowering under Mrs. Richards's withering verbal and physical attack because Claire had accidentally dropped orange juice on the highly polished living room floor. Mrs. Richards had flown at Claire with a broom in her hand and had beaten Claire from one end of the room to the next while Annabelle and Greg had watched unmoving and obviously horrified. Claire had tried to protect herself, but it had been hopeless against the superhuman strength of the older woman.

Claire had finally managed to get to the front door and out of the house. She had run the several blocks home, with blood soaking through her shirt from the bruises on her back. She had run straight into her house and into the shower because she hadn't wanted Joan or Al to know what had happened. Even though Claire had known that it wasn't her fault, she had felt embarrassed and ashamed. And she had felt scared for Annabelle. Later that night, Joan had somehow seen Claire's bloodied clothes and had flown into a fit that put Mrs. Richards to shame. Joan had forced the truth from Claire and had left the house, murder on her face, heading for the Richards home.

Claire had never asked Joan what happened at the Richardses', but the next day at school, Annabelle had hugged Claire and laughed more in one lunch hour than she had laughed in the previous three years. Claire never could get the image from that night out of her head. Mrs. Richards had looked like every kid's picture of a monster crawling out from under the bed late at night—eyes flashing, features contorted.

Even though Annabelle never admitted it, Claire knew that Annabelle had been on the receiving end of many of Mrs. Richards's blistering attacks. But when the social workers Al had called later that night, after Joan told him what had happened, interviewed Annabelle, she would only say that her mother had never physically hurt her. Greg Richards had supported his wife, saying that the attack on Claire had only happened because Rose had been under a lot of stress at work. Claire had never gone to Annabelle's house again, but she continued to be the fourth member of the Scott household.

"Now, isn't this a surprise? Child prodigy Claire Scott. All grown-up," Mrs. Richards said in a silky tone as she came to stand next to her husband. If possible, Greg shrank even more in his wife's presence. Claire gulped down the lump of fear in her throat because she was once more on her own with this woman.

Rose Richards did not look like the Hollywood version of the abusive mother and wife. She was not poor, she dressed well, and she didn't have flames shooting from her hair. Her brown hair hung in loose waves around her shoulders, her chocolate brown skin was unlined and shone with health, and she had a trim, petite figure. Standing next to Greg, Mrs. Richards looked like she was standing next to her father. If Claire hadn't known the truth about her, she would have thought Mrs. Richards a beautiful woman.

"Mrs. Richards," Claire greeted stiffly.

"You're slumming tonight, aren't you? Back in the old neighborhood?" Mrs. Richards asked with an obviously fake laugh.

Claire stared at the older woman, then looked at Greg and said, "If you do see her, please have her call me. Immediately. She has until Tuesday and then I can't help her anymore."

"See who?" Mrs. Richards instantly demanded as Greg hung his head and avoided Claire's gaze.

"Annabelle," Claire said, defiantly meeting Mrs. Richards's gaze.

Mrs. Richards laughed, clearly amused. "If that slut shows her face here, I'll call the police. The last time she was here, she stole my mother's favorite brooch. You know what she's been doing the last few years in Europe? She pretends that she's some big fancy model, but really she's been spreading her legs for any man that can meet the price. Why any man would pay to get anything from her is beyond me. I guess the Europeans don't have a lot of taste."

Greg said softly, "Rose, please."

Rose Richards continued, ignoring her husband, "But once a slut, always a slut. She was like that in high school, corrupting you. I tried to tell your father not to let you hang around her, but he wouldn't listen, and now she's done something to get you in trouble, hasn't she? I can tell. You should have done what I did a long time ago—banned the stealing, lying whore from ever entering your house."

Claire flinched as if she had been hit. She was angry with Annabelle, didn't really like her at that moment, but to hear her own mother speak about Annabelle like that made Claire see red. She clenched her hands into fists, then glanced at Greg once more. He still stared at the ground.

Claire shook her head in disbelief. Annabelle had never stood a chance in this house.

"I'm sorry to have bothered you," Claire said through clenched teeth.

She turned to leave, but Mrs. Richards's grating voice stopped her. "You're still friends with my slutty daughter? I thought you were better than that, Claire. You're just as dumb as she is—"

"Annabelle is not dumb," Claire screamed, whirling around to face Mrs. Richards. The older woman's eyes widened in surprise, as they had that night when Claire had unsuccessfully tried to grab the broom from her hands. Apparently, no one had ever fought Mrs. Richards back. "She was never dumb! She was never a slut! She was just scared! You scared her, and you made her scared of everything! If you had been half of a real mother to her, instead of constantly telling her that she was stupid or a whore, maybe her life would have turned out different."

Rage choked Mrs. Richards's features as she shrieked, "Get off my property, you sanctimonious bit—"

"Annabelle was a good person, and you distorted all of

that," Claire continued, through her tears. "Whatever she is now is because of you. How is she supposed to know what love is when she's never been loved?"

"Claire," came Duncan's concerned voice behind her.

She turned to find him standing next to her, no longer in the truck where she had left him. Claire knew that she could handle Mrs. Richards on her own, but she was glad that with Duncan beside her, she didn't have to.

Duncan glanced at Mrs. Richards, who was trying to come down the porch but was being held back by her husband. The two struggled on the porch, but Greg must have been stronger than he looked, because he finally got her into the house and slammed the door.

"What in the world is going on?" Duncan asked, bewildered. "Was that Annabelle's mother screaming like a banshee?"

Claire wiped at the tears on her cheeks. She hadn't even known that she was crying. She said softly, "Let's go."

The two had almost reached the truck when Claire heard running footsteps behind her. She whirled around, expecting to find Mrs. Richards flying toward her to attack, but it was Greg. Duncan stepped in front of Claire, his muscles tensed, and Greg came to an abrupt stop.

Greg looked at Claire imploringly and she nodded at Duncan, who moved aside one step.

"Club Sunset. Tomorrow night," Greg said breathlessly.

Claire's eyes widened in disbelief. "Annabelle will be at Club Sunset tomorrow night?"

He nodded, then pleaded, "You always took better care of her than I did, Claire. Keep her safe." Without another word, he ran back toward the house and slammed the door.

"I'm confused," Duncan said, staring down at her.

Claire stood on her tiptoes and wrapped her arms around his neck. Without question, Duncan pulled her close. She inhaled his clean scent and his warmth, allowing his strength to make her feel strong again.

"I'm hungry," she announced, abruptly pulling away from him.

Duncan studied her, then asked in surprise, "You're really not going to tell me what just happened, are you?"

"Feed me, Duncan."

He shook his head in disbelief, then said, "My mom is probably just setting dinner on the table. Would you be all right with heading over there?"

Claire looked at him, surprised, then smiled when she noticed the surprise on his face. He probably hadn't been expecting to invite her to meet his parents. Were they at that stage yet? Claire made a mental note to head to the university library as soon as possible. She needed to research the evolution of a romantic relationship. Duncan had met her family, but Claire hadn't invited him; he had just shown up. This was an actual invitation to meet his parents.

"Or not," Duncan said with a laugh when Claire still didn't answer.

"I'd love to meet your parents," she said sincerely.

Duncan grinned, then opened the passenger door for her. Claire took one last look at the Richards house, then climbed into the truck.

Vincent Hillston and Dorrie Hillston were just as warmly, all-American apple pie as Claire had expected. Dorrie Hillston, with her warm smile and bright brown eyes, could not have been a further contrast from Rose Richards than if Claire had created the two extremes of motherhood in the lab. And Vincent was as loud and gregarious as Greg Richards had been timid and withdrawn. Claire was glad that Duncan had brought her to his parents' cheerful house after the experience at the Richardses'.

Duncan had been right. When they walked into his parents' house, his mother was just setting food on the table. She used serving dishes and had floral centerpieces on the dining table and generally seemed to take the idea of dinner very seriously. According to Duncan, Dorrie set the table every night with a couple of extra place settings just in case one of her sons or grandchildren stopped by. And usually they did.

It was a slow night in the Hillston household. Around the table there were only Vincent, Dorrie, Duncan, Claire, Duncan's brother Kobie, his wife, Lee, and their two adorable young daughters, who had monopolized the table conversation with the trials and tribulations of life at the summer day camp. This was just a fraction of the Hillston family, and there were more people at the dinner table than in Claire's entire family.

Claire had been nervous when she and Duncan had first walked into the house, but Dorrie and Vincent had welcomed her as if she came to dinner every night at their house. Claire now understood the studies that indicated some people remained with spouses because of fear of hurting the spouse's family. Claire could easily fall in love with the Hillstons.

"That was delicious as usual, Mom," Duncan said after finishing off his second piece of apple pie.

"Thanks, son," Dorrie said as she stood to clear off the table. Everyone else began to help her.

"Dorrie is perfecting her apple pie recipe for the block party," Lee told Claire with a proud smile.

"I can't let Harriet Wilson beat me. She would have to find something else to obsess about if she actually won the best apple pie contest," Dorrie said with a determined twinkle in her eyes.

"This year, the Hillston household is going to sweep all the food categories," Vincent announced, then said to Claire, "Come by Friday and bring your dad. I'm going to have a final taste test on my barbecue sauce."

Claire grinned, noting that Vincent didn't mention anything about Duncan bringing her. He had invited her. Claire had never craved acceptance from anyone, but she craved it from these people.

Everyone walked into the kitchen carrying a pile of dirty dishes. Each person seemed to know exactly where to set his or her pile, even the children. Claire stared around, confused, with the salad bowl and gravy dish in her hands. Duncan patted her hip and indicated an empty spot on the kitchen sink. Claire smiled gratefully and set the dishes down.

"Who wants to see my brand-new grill?" Vincent said cheerfully while edging toward the kitchen door.

"I know what you're doing, Vincent," Dorrie said with a laugh. "You're just trying to get out of your turn to wash the dishes."

He laughed and said, "Damn right—"

"Grandpa!" six-year old Danielle said, shocked, then held out her hand. Vincent winced, then handed two quarters to Danielle and one quarter to four-year-old Yvette, who giggled with glee.

"Go on before you end up owing the girls our life savings," Dorrie said, amused, while shaking her head.

Vincent walked out the house with Kobie limping behind him, hanging on to an exasperated Lee. Duncan didn't move but stared at Claire. She forced a smile at him, suddenly feeling nervous at the idea of being alone with Dorrie. Claire had always felt slightly uncomfortable around other people's mothers, mainly because she had never known how to act around them. Mothers and daughters had always seemed like a secret club that Claire would never have the key to, so she had avoided meeting her friends' mothers—which hadn't been a problem, since the only friends she had were Annabelle, whose mother was insane, and Vino, whose mother still lived in the Philippines.

"Are you going to be all right?" Duncan asked her quietly as Dorrie turned on the kitchen faucet.

"Come on, Uncle Duncan," Danielle urged, pulling Duncan's hand toward the door and drawing his attention.

Claire smiled down at the little girl. Nate had not been exaggerating about Duncan's relationship with his nieces. It was clear that it was a two-way mutual admiration society.

"I'll be fine," Claire told him.

Duncan winked at her, then picked up one little girl with each arm and walked out of the kitchen. Claire smiled at the girls' giggles and felt a little tug in her heart. Another research topic for the library—biological clocks. She felt like hers had gone from zero to red alert. All of this domestic bliss had even almost erased the taste of the Richards home from her mouth.

The kitchen door closed, leaving Claire with Dorrie, who was already washing dishes in the sink. Claire grabbed the towel hanging on the refrigerator door and walked to the sink. Dorrie smiled at Claire in encouragement, and she forced a smile in return.

"Thank you for dinner, Mrs. Hillston," Claire said, breaking the silence. "It was delicious."

"Call me Dorrie. And you're welcome here anytime, whether you have Duncan on your heels or not."

Claire smiled because she had the feeling that Dorrie really meant that. Claire felt a brief pang of regret that in high school she hadn't known Dorrie. Besides Joan, the only mother Claire had known was Mrs. Richards. Claire could have used a Dorrie-type mother.

"Is something wrong?" Dorrie asked, concerned, staring at Claire.

"I just . . ." Claire took a deep breath as she felt the tears coat her eyes. She never should have started thinking about mothers. Claire couldn't cry in front of Duncan's mother, but paradoxically, Claire felt like Dorrie Hillston was the one person whom Claire could cry in front of.

Claire finally shook her head, unable to speak for fear that she would burst into tears. The meeting with Mrs. Richards had obviously affected her more than she'd thought.

Dorrie turned off the faucet and wiped her hands on her skirt before she wrapped her arms around Claire. Claire hiccuped, then turned into the older woman's embrace, ashamed but so relieved to have such strong, loving arms around her after dealing with Rose Richards and dealing with her own memories about her own mother. Claire was an intelligent person. She had psychoanalyzed herself in college and she had put everything about her mother's abandonment behind her, but apparently she hadn't done a good job.

After a few moments when Dorrie patted Claire's back as if she were a baby, Claire reluctantly pulled from her.

"All better?" Dorrie asked with a soft smile. Claire nodded, still unable to speak. "When you went to the bathroom, Duncan told me that you were at the Richards home before dinner," Dorrie continued in a gentle tone.

"Mrs. Richards and I have . . . We have a history," Claire finally managed to say.

Dorrie snorted and said, "That woman has a history with everyone in this neighborhood." Claire looked at her, surprised, and Dorrie nodded. "I know all about Rose Richards. I've known mean people, but there's something more—"

"She's manic-depressive, and maybe borderline schizophrenic," Claire said. She had analyzed Mrs. Richards's symptoms around the same time she'd started looking at herself.

"I don't know all the fancy words for it; I just always thought she was crazy. A long time ago, I tried to get her to see someone, but that was back before average folks went to see psychiatrists. She never spoke to me again after that conversation. Almost twenty years later, and she still refuses to speak to me. Whatever happened to her daughter? The poor thing."

"Annabelle is . . . She's not doing well."

Dorrie shook her head sadly. "We never saw any evidence that Rose hit that child, but sometimes I thought the things Rose said to her were worse than if Rose had beat her every night."

"They were," Claire whispered, nodding.

Dorrie smiled and placed her hands on Claire's shoulders. "God has a way of working things out. Don't worry."

Claire took a deep breath, then nodded. Dorrie smiled, then turned to the sink and resumed washing dishes, as if she had known that Claire needed one private moment to pull herself together.

"Look at you," Dorrie continued. "The whole neighborhood thought once your mother left, she ruined whatever chances you could have, but I wasn't worried because I knew you had Al and Joan. Al is a good man, and I knew with Joan Scott in your corner you would turn out just fine. And I was right."

Claire stared at Dorrie, not really seeing her, because Claire's entire life hadn't become clear until that point. All of her studying and self-analyzing hadn't told her what Dorrie had obviously known for almost three decades. Claire had Joan. Claire had always been grateful that Joan had taken such an active part in her life, but she had never really analyzed how much Joan had given up, how much she had sacrificed, to be Claire's mother.

Joan had been a child herself and had had to raise Claire, and most times Joan had been there for Annabelle, too. Claire had spent most of her life silently bemoaning her motherless fate, wanting to prove to the world that she could do everything that had been predicted for her, even though she hadn't had the traditional household. But the truth was, Claire had had a mother, a damn good one, in Joan.

"You're right," Claire said softly.

"I know," Dorrie said simply, and continued to wash dishes. Claire picked up the towel she had dropped on a chair and started drying. Then she laughed. Because she knew why Duncan loved confident women.

Chapter Twenty

Duncan followed Claire into his house after dinner. He had always considered his home the essential bachelor pad, with the high-on-comfort-and-low-on-style masculine furniture; the large-screen plasma television that dominated the living room; the rarely used kitchen; and the few decorations in other parts of the house. But with Claire in his house, it felt different. Better.

During dinner, Kobie had watched Duncan rush to pour iced tea into Claire's half-empty glass and had shaken with silent laughter. Duncan knew he would be hearing the riot act from his brothers tomorrow morning, but he hadn't regretted one second of the night. Seeing Claire in her usual suit sitting next to his four-year-old niece, making the little girl laugh as she explained about covalent bonds, which Yvette actually listened to and understood, had been worth it. Duncan's family apparently accepted Claire, and that was important to him. And Claire accepted his family, which was even more important.

Duncan closed and locked the front door as Claire shrugged out of her suit jacket and rolled her head from one side to the other.

"My parents really like you," he said lightly, as he walked up behind her to gently massage her shoulders.

The muscles in her back and shoulders were tight with tension. Judging from the confrontation with Mrs. Richards earlier that evening, Duncan was surprised that Claire wasn't more upset. Duncan had been sitting peacefully in his truck, dreaming about getting Claire to his house and getting her long legs around him, and the next moment he had heard someone screaming like her dog had just been murdered.

After that, Duncan had taken one look at Claire's face and had known what she needed—not another marathon session in bed but something that Duncan couldn't give her: home cooking. Taking her to his mom's house had been the only thing he could do, and judging from Claire's laughter during that dinner, had been the right thing.

"I really like your parents, and they obviously love you very much," she murmured, her eyes closed as she accepted his ministrations. She abruptly frowned and opened her eyes to stare at the floor. "I'll never forgive myself if anything happens to you because of me."

Duncan turned her to face him. He guided her chin up until she met his eyes. "Nothing is going to happen to me, baby."

"These are dangerous people we're dealing with, Duncan. I did some research on the Internet at work, and Henri Vittels is a suspected weapons broker. He apparently brings together dangerous groups who want to exchange weapons for money—"

Duncan pressed a kiss on her mouth until she stopped talking and moved into his embrace. His penis twitched eagerly, but Duncan was prepared to be the king of self-restraint tonight. Tonight was about Claire. Well, actually it was about both of them, because they were both going to enjoy every minute. Duncan wasn't worried about Henri Vittels—weapons broker or not, Duncan was a black man who had grown up in Los Angeles—but Claire was worried and he wanted to take her mind off it for a few hours.

"Kissing me doesn't make any of it less true, Duncan," she whispered, her gaze on his mouth.

"Probably not, but it sure does feel good," he replied before he wrapped his arms around her waist to draw her close and kiss her again.

Damn. She tasted even sweeter than he remembered from

the night before. Her lushness filled his arms, imprinting every inch of his body as she subtly moved against him. He had never cared about the worries of anyone else, besides his family. If a woman started talking about bills or ex dramas, Duncan sensed a trap and would head toward the nearest exit. Not with Claire. Her worries were his. Her triumphs were his. The bet was a distant memory that Duncan hoped would eventually fade from his consciousness. He had finally found "the One." And besides the bet, he would never have to lie to her about anything else in his life again.

She tore her mouth from his, but Duncan noticed she kept her arms around his shoulders. "Duncan, we have to talk about what we're going to do tomorrow."

"We're heading to Club Sunset, grabbing Annabelle, and hanging her upside down from a pier until she tells us where the code is."

Claire laughed and playfully punched him in the chest. "That's not funny. What if we give the code to Henri Vittels and he doesn't let us go? He's a criminal. Why should we expect him to be true to his word?"

Duncan reluctantly released her because she obviously was not going to allow the subject to drop, despite what he once considered his very persuasive skills.

"I spoke to Alex earlier tonight. His ex-marine buddies who have that agency will back us up at the meeting. They'll make sure we get out OK."

"Won't they be expensive?"

Duncan rolled his eyes in exasperation, then grabbed her around the waist again. All of her soft curves pressed against him, and his hard-on, which had been withering under the inquisition, instantly returned.

"We're going to be fine, Claire. I promise."

Claire nodded, with a relieved sigh. Then she asked abruptly, "What if they let us go, then find us again—"

"And what if I get hit by a bus crossing the street or I get electrocuted wiring the Estefan addition? We can only take things one day at a time."

"Speaking of electrocution . . . I've been reading some of

the latest manuals about electrical installation, and I think we should discuss your safety standards and protocols to make certain that you're following the latest—"

"Is this what being smart is like? Constantly worrying about everything?" he asked, amused.

Claire frowned at him, but he saw the amusement twinkling in her eyes. "I can't help it."

"You can worry tomorrow, but there's nothing you can do about it tonight. We know where Annabelle is going to be, and we'll find her." He planted a kiss on the tip of Claire's nose, then said, "Now, quit wrecking my evening. I have big plans for us."

Her voice dropped to that husky tone that made Duncan want to clear all obstacles and be buried inside of her as she asked, "What do you have in mind?"

"I've worn you out the last couple of nights—"

"No, you haven't," she said quickly while her hips subtly pressed against his. He briefly closed his eyes at the feel of her heat next to his pulsating hardness. He would never grow accustomed to his body's reaction to her. Quick-fire and powerful.

"It occurred to me while I was watching you licking the whipped cream from your fork during dessert at my parents' house that you've never experienced a real Duncan Hillston seduction," he said smoothly.

"You mean, a night at Nate's Grill doesn't qualify as the patented Duncan Hillston seduction routine?" she asked while blinking with feigned innocence.

Duncan growled and squeezed her behind, causing her to squeal in delight. She tried to squirm out of his grip, but he held her tight, begrudgingly transferring his hands to her hips.

"I was thinking more along the lines of a hot bath with lots of bubbles, candles . . . maybe even a full-body massage if you act right."

"I'll act right," she said eagerly.

Duncan grinned, then forced himself to release her. "My robe is hanging on the door in my bedroom. You change into that, and I'll get everything ready."

Claire smiled at him, then quickly disappeared down the hallway to his bedroom. Duncan watched her hips and behind move like silk under her skirt; then he forced himself to snap out of his daze and get ready.

Twenty minutes later, Duncan realized that his seduction plans had worked before because he could control himself with other women. His brothers had installed a whirlpool tub in his bathroom, and Duncan had used it to create steamy bliss for numerous women over the years. He would make the bathwater just right, add in the lavender-scented bubble bath that he hid under the sink when there was no woman to make a bubble bath for, and pull out his entire candle collection and strategically place them around the bathroom after turning off the lights. Then he would start to bathe the woman with an oversize sponge. It had worked wonders in the past, but Duncan realized that same approach wouldn't work with Claire.

After one touch of her soapy skin, she had moaned and closed her eyes and Duncan had gotten as hard as a rock. His fingers had clenched around the sponge, mangling it, and he had just stared at her. He had tried to wash her back, but that had seemed like too much effort for his suddenly Gibraltar-heavy arms. His body seemed to say that it wouldn't move unless it was to be inside Claire. The water stopped just below her beautiful glistening wet breasts, her hair was piled on top of her head, with cottony soft curls framing her damp face, and Duncan had given up.

Duncan hadn't touched the bottle of champagne near his feet. He had forgotten to turn on the Jaheim mood music that was piped into the bathroom through speakers on the wall. He had only touched Claire once, and this whole seduction routine was a total bust. Duncan should have been ashamed of himself. He was no better than an eighteen-year-old kid, trying to impress an Anne Bancroft–Mrs. Robinson.

Claire opened her eyes and stared at him, a small smile playing on her lips, the original picture of temptation.

"This is all very nice, Duncan, but something is missing," Claire murmured, her gaze never leaving his face.

He tried to speak, but his mouth was too dry, as he noticed droplets of water beading on her extended cranberry-red nipples.

"What?" he finally choked out.

One soapy hand grabbed his shirtfront as she said, "You."

Duncan smiled as he shook his head. "This is supposed to be about you—"

"It is about me, and I want you in the water with me. Now."

He abruptly stood and began tearing off his clothes at lightning speed. "I guess a man can't argue with that."

She giggled as he stepped into the tub, sloshing water over the sides and sending waves to snuff out the candles. So much for suave seduction moves. Duncan managed to sit in the tub without drowning her, and soon his back was on the water-warm tile and her body was plastered to the front of his. His legs stretched out around her, and he felt all of her softness brushing his hairy legs. With the addition of water made silky by the suds, Duncan didn't think life could get much better than this.

Claire sighed in contentment and leaned against his wet chest, causing strands of her hair to cling to him. Duncan laid back his head on the tile and wrapped his arms around her, the undersides of her breasts hanging over his arms. It was just enough touching to make him hungry but also enough to allow him to maintain some form of self-control.

The two lay in comfortable silence for a moment before Duncan whispered against her ear, "I want you to know that it's never been like this for me before, Claire."

She smiled, her eyes still closed, as she said, "That sounded like an accusation."

"It was."

"It's never been like this before for me, either," she finally responded. "I was so busy trying to prove that I was worth all the praise I received when I was a kid that I never even gave men a chance."

"That works out for me," he said, with a self-satisfied

smile, before he added, "but you don't have to prove anything to anyone, Claire. You came from a blue-collar Los Angeles neighborhood to become one of the top scientists in the world, who's months away from discovering a cure for ovarian cancer. No one can say that you haven't lived up to everything that was predicted of you as a kid and more."

"Except me," she reminded him.

"You're your own worst enemy, but that's what I'm here for. To constantly remind you how amazing you are."

Duncan kissed the top of her head, inhaling the sweetness of her shampoo. Everything about her was sweet.

"How do you always manage to say the right thing to make me feel special?" she whispered with a slight smile.

Duncan ignored the brief flash of guilt. A small voice warned him about the bet. He dismissed the voice because Claire would never know. Tomorrow he was telling Hawk that the bet was off. Or, if he wouldn't agree to cancel the bet, then Duncan would take the loss and announce to the neighborhood that he was a loser. Duncan would say it on a loudspeaker throughout Los Angeles County if that was what Hawk wanted. Duncan didn't care anymore about what anyone else thought, not when he had Claire.

"You are special," he murmured, tightening his arms around her; then he grinned and said, "And I guess your theory about smart women and dumb men was shattered."

She laughed, then replied, "Not really. You and I don't fit the parameters. You're not that dumb, and I'm not that smart."

"Flattery will get you everywhere with me," he murmured, then lowered his mouth to her neck, where he sucked on the soft skin. She squirmed and he released the skin, then kissed the slightly red area. He nuzzled his way to the other side of her neck.

"Duncan," she whispered, the longing edging her voice as she turned in his arms.

Duncan stared into her huge eyes as she straddled him. She caught his lips in a possessive kiss that rocked him to the core of his soul. She laid claim to him. She possessed him. Her tongue played in his mouth, rocking him to her gentle rhythm, as her hands ran down his arms, slick from the bathwater.

He felt her move over him and he gripped her hips to steady her. Then he felt something hotter than the water, hotter than his own body, at the tip of his penis. Her. Duncan cursed as she lowered on top of him, sending more bathwater splashing over the tub rim and onto the floor, soaking the rugs.

"We're getting your rugs wet," Claire noted in a strained voice.

"I'll buy new ones," he said through clenched teeth as she pulled the pleasure and love from his body, then dumped it back into him.

"You don't have to buy new rugs. We'll just put these in the dryer," she said logically.

Duncan cursed, then said, "Who gives a damn about the rugs, Claire?"

He threw back his head, straining to keep the pace easy and gentle. A condom briefly flashed across his mind, but then Claire was moving on top of him, drawing the depths of his soul into her body, playing him like a piano. Their groans and moans filled the bathroom, along with the sounds of splashing water.

"This is fun, Duncan," she said in between heavy breaths.

"I'm a fun guy," he managed, then smiled when he heard her soft laughter.

Duncan knew that he would never forget the sight of Claire on top of him. Her wet breasts bobbed excitedly in unison with her undulating hips, her head was thrown back, her eyes closed, and her mouth was open in a silent cry of ecstasy. It was a beautiful image for a man to have. Duncan was trapped, unable to really move beneath her, but holding on to her hips for sanity. And then he closed his eyes as pleasure washed over him like a warm thunderstorm, or maybe it was the splashing bathwater. Whatever it was, it made him explode at the same time that Claire screamed his name, then collapsed against him.

Duncan held her to him, the their chests rapidly rising and falling in unison. They hadn't used a condom. Duncan had never not used a condom in his life. For the life of him, he couldn't find the energy to care at that moment. He lazily kissed Claire's shoulder, and she snuggled deeper into his grip.

Chapter Twenty-One

"Hey, man," Hawk said as he slid across the booth from Duncan in Nate's Grill early the next morning.

Hawk looked official and halfway respectable in his LA city parking enforcement uniform. Duncan could only imagine the glee Hawk must have felt every time he was able to stick one of his tickets under a car's windshield wiper. Hawk liked to pretend that parking enforcement was a temporary job for him, but considering he had been doing it for the last eight years and kept being promoted, Duncan didn't know how temporary it was. Duncan thought it was the perfect job for Hawk. It helped him get out his aggression without anyone getting hurt.

"You want any coffee?"

"Did the sun come up this morning?"

Duncan waved to Bethany, the morning waitress, who was busy taking an order from three police officers in another booth; then he walked behind the counter to grab the coffeepot. He poured himself and Hawk each a cup of coffee and refilled a few other customers' mugs before he returned the coffeepot to the warmer and went back to his seat.

"So, what's going on?" Hawk asked suspiciously as he sipped his coffee. He was momentarily distracted as he stared into his coffee mug. "Did Nate change the coffee?"

"It's a Costa Rican blend," Duncan answered, but didn't mention that it was Claire who had told Nate about it.

"This is the best coffee I've ever tasted," Hawk said,

awed. Before Duncan could respond, Hawk said, "You've been MIA the last few days, ever since Patrick said he ran into you and Claire here. I didn't think it was possible in our lifetime, but Patty has actually stopped talking about Kellie. Now he talks about Claire. You better watch out, or you may have some competition."

"I've lost the bet," Duncan blurted out, causing Hawk's amused smile to slowly turn into a frown.

"What are you talking about? You still have a few days left. And, according to Patrick, your soothing worked, because Claire seems more comfortable around you than he could ever remember her being. So, I guess now you're on to seducing and enticing, or maybe it's vice versa—"

"Listen to me, Hawk," Duncan said, frustrated. "I've lost the bet. At the block party, I'll tell all the guys that I'm a liar, that I never had the freeway woman, or Janette Baxter, or any of the other women I've invented or embellished over the years. Hell, I'll even tell them I'm a virgin, if you want. But the bet is over."

Hawk's mouth dropped open in shock and he gaped at Duncan for a few moments. Bethany took that moment to come over to take their order.

Duncan smiled at her and said, "The usual."

"What about your mute friend?" Bethany asked, indicating Hawk.

Hawk quickly snapped from his daze, then glanced at the menu before he said, "The weekday special with scrambled eggs."

"Coming right up," she said, then left the table.

Hawk immediately turned back to Duncan, still looking shell-shocked. "You've fallen in love with her," Hawk accused in a strangled voice.

Duncan thought about denying it, because he didn't need to get the same treatment from Hawk that he had already gotten from his brothers that morning, who had listened with glee to Kobie's description at dinner the night before, but Duncan was done lying. His need to lie—and he wasn't fooling himself into thinking that he was simply exaggerating—was what had gotten him into this mess in the first place.

"Yes, I'm in love with Claire," Duncan finally responded, meeting Hawk's gaze.

Hawk grinned and said, "It's about damn time."

Duncan coughed in surprise before he asked, amazed, "That's it? That's all you have to say?"

Hawk appeared to be in deep thought for a moment before he shrugged and said, "I'm a pretty uncomplicated guy. Watching you suffer through loving a woman like Med—Claire is all the reward I need, and don't doubt it, brother, but that woman is going to be a handful."

"I know," Duncan said with a satisfied smile.

Hawk shook his head, then muttered, "You're going to be worse than Patty."

Duncan sighed in relief. He should have known that this would be easy. Hawk was and always would be one of his best friends. Who else would have put up with Duncan and his impossible-to-believe stories all of these years?

"And you don't have to say anything at the block party," Hawk added seriously.

"Are you sure? Because I will—"

"Don't push it," his friend warned, scowling at him, but there was a twinkle in Hawk's eyes. Duncan laughed, then nodded in agreement. Hawk studied him for a moment, then mused, "So, Patrick was right. You're really in love."

"Patrick said that? I didn't even know I was in love with Claire when Patrick saw us."

Hawk shrugged, then took another gulp of coffee before he said reluctantly, "I guess I have to meet her, don't I?"

"You'll like her," Duncan said confidently, then hesitated and added, "But maybe we should wait to introduce you until after I tell her about the bet."

Hawk nearly choked on his coffee before he sputtered in disbelief, "You're going to tell her about the bet? Are you insane?"

Duncan had wondered the same thing late last night when he'd come to the decision that he would tell her about the bet. At the time, Claire had been snuggled against him in his bed, her smooth leg entwined between his and her left hand resting on his chest. Duncan had never felt more content in his life than at that moment, and that was precisely when he realized that he had to tell. He couldn't build their lives on a lie, no matter how much he feared Claire's reaction to the news.

"I have to tell her," he said to Hawk. "I can't spend the rest of my life lying to her."

"Why not?" Hawk asked hoarsely. "And it's not like you're lying to her. If she ever asks, 'Hey, Duncan, did you make a bet that you could get me to fall in love with you?' you can tell her the truth then."

"Loving her makes me want to live up to every good thing she thinks about me, that she's thought about me since high school. If I don't tell her the truth about the bet, I'll be a fake. Our relationship will be fake. I can't do that to her, and I can't do that to myself. I'm going to give the truth a chance for a change."

Hawk slowly nodded in agreement; then he said quietly, "It'll be all right. You'll tell her, and if she hates you, then you'll create the three steps on how to get back the woman you love."

Duncan glared at Hawk for a moment; then both men simultaneously burst into laughter.

"We'll never find her in this throng," Claire groaned to Duncan as she glanced through the flashing neon lights and pulsating crowd in Club Sunset. Claire had lived in Los Angeles for most of her life, but she had never gone out on the famous Sunset Strip. Now here she was, in the most famous of the famous clubs in the city, and she just wanted to go home, snuggle next to Duncan, and read a book.

Claire hadn't known what to expect from the club, but she certainly hadn't expected to see this. There were gorgeous men and beautiful women everywhere—black skin, brown skin, white skin, and every shade in between—on display like an ad for designer clothes. They posed against the bar, sauntered across the dance floor, or looked fabulously bored in the plush chairs in the lounge area.

Everyone in the club was beautiful and young, except the gaggle of older men in expensive suits who congregated in the lounge and watched the young men and women. Claire felt like she was in the middle of a Discovery Channel special, watching a pack of lions hunt a herd of gazelles, picking off the weak ones.

Claire often felt insecure in social situations, but there may as well have been an arrow pointing at her head that screamed in neon lights, *This one doesn't belong*. She wasn't a rich old man and she definitely wasn't a young, beautiful person. She hadn't bothered to change clothes after work. She still wore a gray suit with sensible black pumps and her sensible black handbag.

If she had known that this would be a runway model commercial, she would have . . . Claire didn't know what she would have done. She didn't have clothes that could make the cut for a runway model commercial. She didn't think they made clothes like that in her size.

She glanced at Duncan, who looked perfectly comfortable in these surroundings. In fact, he looked too comfortable. Claire swore if one more woman bumped into her to get a chance to get a closer look at Duncan, she was going to start swinging.

"Do you see anyone who even remotely looks like Annabelle?" Claire asked him desperately. She had to get out of this club as quickly as possible before she lost IQ points just from being in the room. Finding Annabelle and getting Henri Vittels off her back suddenly seemed less important than getting out of this casting call for *America's Next Top Model*.

"Mr. Richards said that Annabelle would be here," Duncan protested, screaming over the blaring techno music. "We have to find her."

Claire nodded and forced herself to take a deep breath for calm. They had to find Annabelle and find the account code. She could handle the glares from the women, who looked like they should have been the models in skin care commercials.

"Excuse me," said a hesitant deep voice behind her.

Claire turned to face one of the male model look-alikes, who had all begun to blend together in one mass of prominent cheekbones and chiseled bodies. This one's dark hair was slicked back and his hazel eyes were bright, even in the darkness. Claire stared at him, confused, as he smiled nervously at her. She knew that his nervousness could be a sign of drug usage.

"Would you like to dance?" he blurted out.

Claire stared at him, shocked. He wasn't on drugs. He was nervous because he was asking her to dance. Duncan wrapped an arm around her waist and pulled her against his hard chest as he glared at the male model.

Her potential dance partner's eyes widened and he quickly said to Duncan, "I didn't mean to—"

"Go ahead and dance, if you want to, baby," Duncan whispered in Claire's ear. She stared over her shoulder at him, surprised by his encouragement. He smiled at her and murmured, "You've been moving around like you've been wanting to dance since we walked in, and I don't dance. It's one of the things we Hillstons do only upon the threat of death. This guy can dance with you all he wants, but I'm the only one going home with you."

Claire glanced at the male model again, and he stared at her expectantly. She hesitantly nodded, then followed him onto the dance floor. She looked over her shoulder but lost Duncan in the crush of finely sculpted and emaciated bodies. She turned back around and followed the male model to the middle of the dance floor. He instantly began to move to the beat of the pulsating house music.

He smiled at her as she stood frozen, flinching as she was jostled by the moving bodies on the floor. He took her hands and shouted over the music, "Come on."

"Why did you ask me to dance?" she shouted back.

His smile momentarily faltered as he said uncertainly, "I didn't notice your boyfriend—"

"No, I mean, why did you pick me?" she asked, her brow furrowed.

"No one has ever asked me that question before—"

"I'm a scientist," she explained.

"So, that means you ask weird questions on the dance floor?"

Claire laughed at his bewildered expression; then she said, "No, it means that very few men have asked me to dance."

He shrugged, then said, "I asked you to dance because you looked like you might say yes or, at least, you wouldn't be mean about saying no."

"Women say no to you?" she asked in disbelief.

"Wanna go back to my apartment?" he asked eagerly.

"No," she said, trying to mask her horror.

He grinned with an I-told-you-so look, then began to move again to the music. She smiled at his open grin, because it was that simple, if she would allow it to be. She nodded in response, then slowly began to move, trying to find the beat to the music. She rarely danced—actually, she could only remember dancing once in the last few years, when her lab had gotten that grant from the Kirkwood Foundation. She and Vino had done a happy dance across the lab.

Then Claire realized that while she was so busy thinking, she had begun dancing. She held her arms over her head and laughed out loud, causing the male model to whistle in appreciation and laugh with her.

Duncan smiled as he watched Claire on the dance floor. He had never felt more proud of himself. He had seen the slime-ball staring at Claire from across the bar and Duncan thought he had given the pretty boy the clear hands-off glare that was universal among men—but apparently pretty boys didn't follow that rule, because he had walked over and asked Claire to dance. Duncan had almost pummeled the man until he had seen Claire's reaction.

Her eyes had grown large and she had looked intrigued, almost as if she had never been asked to dance before. Duncan had quickly gone through his high school memories and realized that he hadn't seen her at any school dances. She could have gone dancing in college, but he doubted she would have. She would have been locked in a lab, because as she told him last night, she wanted to be the best, to prove to herself that she really was as gifted as everyone had said she was. So, Duncan gave her this one dance with another man, which had been pretty big of him—if he did say so himself. And when he saw her grin at the pretty boy, Duncan decided it would be her last dance with another man as long as he was alive.

Duncan briefly saw a flash of Claire as she swung her head in wild abandon, sending strands of hair loose from her ponytail to hang in her face. She certainly wouldn't win any *Soul Train* dance-offs, but Duncan couldn't take his eyes off her. His growing hard-on became almost painful as his gaze raked over the silk blouse stretched across her breasts. He smiled to himself. Then the pretty boy wrapped his arms around Claire's waist and pressed her against his body, against his groin.

Duncan's hands clenched into fists. The dance was officially over. He started toward the dance floor and bulldozed into a woman in his haste. He placed his hands on the woman's shoulders to keep her from falling and stared straight into Annabelle's tinted-green eyes. Her eyes widened as recognition glimmered in her eyes before she quickly looked over her shoulder.

"I can't talk right now, Duncan," she said, then attempted to brush past him.

Duncan grabbed her arm and growled, "Claire and I have been looking for you."

"Take a number," she muttered, then wriggled from his arm as fear played across her face again. "I really have to go."

She managed to tear from his grip and pushed through

the crowd like a woman possessed before Duncan could protest. He almost shouted her name just before a man in a dark suit brushed past Duncan, knocking him almost off-balance. Duncan cursed and managed to steady himself just as another man in an identical dark suit rushed past him. Duncan's protests remained on the end of his tongue as he saw exactly who the two men were looking at. Annabelle.

Annabelle flew through a door at the back of the club, and the two men soon followed. Duncan cursed and pushed his way across the dance floor to Claire. The pretty boy's hands were almost resting on top of her behind. Duncan grabbed Claire's arm and debated wasting time to smash in the pretty boy's face, but instead dragged her toward the door Annabelle had used.

"Thanks," Claire called over her shoulder to her dance partner, then asked, confused, "What are you doing?"

"Annabelle is here," he replied without slowing his stride. "And she has company."

Claire began to push him faster through the crowd. The two finally made their way to the exit and pushed the door open. The door led to the small VIP parking lot behind the club. Duncan scanned the parking lot, then spotted Annabelle, kicking and screaming, being dragged toward a waiting van by two men.

"Stay here," he ordered Claire.

He raced across the lot toward the scuffle. His one year of playing high school football kicked in, and Duncan used his momentum to tackle one of the men to the ground. Duncan grunted in pain as he landed hard on the ground, his elbows taking the majority of the blow as the man he took out fell on top of him, fists swinging. Duncan barely avoided a knockout-inducing fist to his face before he managed to drive a knee in the man's chest. The man grunted and Duncan got his feet in the man's chest and pushed him away. The man flew off Duncan and slammed into the nearby chain-link fence.

Duncan scrambled to his feet and quickly glanced over his shoulder to see Claire pulling on the other man's jacket while Annabelle tried to wrench herself free. Duncan cursed. Claire was supposed to be waiting at the door. His anger was forgotten as a fist rammed into his stomach. Apparently, his new friend had not been down and out for the count. Duncan felt the distinct urge to vomit on the man's shoes from the flash of pain, but didn't have time as he ducked a vicious-looking boot-encased foot aimed for his head.

Through sheer luck and quickness Duncan managed to avoid the flurry of fists and feet the man directed at him. This man was obviously a trained professional, à la *The Matrix*, and Duncan admitted that he was no match for him. It was only a matter of time before Duncan didn't duck in time, and then it would be lights-out for about three days.

Duncan spied a discarded piece of lumber next to the fence. He fell to the ground to avoid another vicious kick and smoothly rolled toward the lumber. He grabbed it at the same time that he leaped to his feet. He swung around in time to meet another kick. The wood splintered in two pieces that Duncan barely managed to hang on to with each of his pulsating hands.

Duncan gulped and met the man's beady dark eyes. He smiled at Duncan, as if to say, "Now what you got?" Duncan's anger spiked and as he swung one piece of lumber he actually caught the linebacker off-guard and caught the man in the stomach. He grunted in surprise and instinctively clutched his stomach at the same time that Duncan brought down the other piece of lumber in his other hand on the back of the man's head. He dropped to the ground unconscious.

Duncan tried to control his heavy breathing, then dropped the wood and quickly checked the man's pulse at his neck. Strong and steady. Duncan sighed in relief, then nearly fell on top of the man when he spied the shoulder holster and gun visible in the man's open jacket.

"Duncan," Claire called in a panicked voice.

Duncan looked up to see Annabelle holding a gun on the other man while Claire stood behind her. Duncan quickly ran over to them. He had gone hunting a few times with his father and brothers when he was younger and had a gun at home for protection, but the glint of metal in Annabelle's hands was a frightening sight.

"Get in the back of the van," Annabelle ordered. The man glanced uncomfortably at his unconscious friend, then back at Annabelle. "Now!" she barked, sounding very forceful for a woman in a black leather halter dress and matching towering stilettos.

"Ms. Richards," the man began in a soothing tone. "We just want to help—"

"I mean it," she shouted, releasing the safety on the gun.

The man quickly climbed into the van. Annabelle slammed the back door shut, locked it with the key in her hand, then tossed the key across the parking lot. Then like a professional mercenary, she dismantled the pistol in a series of efficient and skilled moves, then threw the pieces into the front of the van.

She motioned at a shocked Duncan and Claire and shouted, "Come on."

Claire and Duncan watched her run—or, more accurately, hobble, in her stilettos—across the parking lot.

"What should we do?" Claire asked hesitantly, staring at Duncan.

Duncan heard a pained moan from the kickboxing champion on the ground behind him. He definitely did not want to be around when that guy woke up. Duncan grabbed Claire's hand and said, "Let's get the hell out of here."

The two ran after Annabelle, who fortunately hadn't gotten very far in her high heels.

Chapter Twenty-Two

"Should we turn her over to Vittels to do whatever he wants to her before or after she uses all the hot water?" Duncan grumbled from his seat at the dining room table in his house an hour later.

Claire continued to gently dab a damp cloth at the blossoming bruise at the corner of his left eye. It would soon match the fading bruise on his chin from the mugging. Claire felt a wave of tenderness for this man, who had once more gotten involved when he didn't have to. And as soon as Annabelle fell asleep—if she required sleep as most humans did—Claire was going to reward him.

The three had returned to Duncan's house after speeding from Club Sunset in his truck. Duncan had said that he felt safer in Westfield, with neighborhood cops he knew and his brothers' homes around him, so the three had gone to his house.

As soon as the three had walked into his house, Annabelle had walked into the bathroom, and she hadn't come out for the last hour. Claire had heard a mixture of the shower and the bath faucet running at various points.

Claire finished cleaning Duncan's cut and placed a Band-Aid with dancing *Peanuts* characters on it.

"Can't you find anything else?" Duncan muttered in disgust, glaring at her.

The only Band-Aids he had in the house were ones he'd

bought for his nieces and nephews. "Sorry," she said with a shrug, then added, "You're man enough to pull it off."

"Not even The Rock could be man enough to pull this off," Duncan grumbled, then grabbed the hem of her blouse and pulled her into the vee of his legs. "Hurry up and kiss me before I start thinking all girls have cooties."

Claire smiled and wrapped her arms around his neck. She leaned over and kissed him, intending a light, playful peck, but Duncan responded with a hunger that should have scared her. Instead, she opened her mouth under his passionate request. He framed her face with his hands, inhaling her, and Claire felt the tremble in his hands.

"Are you all right?" she asked softly, pulling from his mouth.

"No," he said, staring at her with bottomless eyes. "Claire, if anything happens to you—"

"I thought we had both decided that nothing would happen to either one of us," she lightly reminded him.

He didn't laugh but pulled her into his lap. Claire was a tall woman and probably wouldn't have fit easily in most men's laps, but Duncan's was a perfect fit. She thought he would kiss her again, but he just held her. And Claire felt as special as he said that she was.

"Do I need to throw some cold water on you two?" came Annabelle's cheerful voice.

Claire met Duncan's irritated gaze, then turned to face . . . Well, Claire wasn't exactly certain who she was facing. Belle was gone. In her place was the woman Claire remembered from high school. Here, finally, was the real Annabelle Richards. Underneath Duncan's oversize robe, which Annabelle had wrapped around her body, her breasts had shrunk at least one cup size. Her hair no longer streamed in a blond and brown mass down her shoulders but dangled in wet, dark cotton clumps to her chin. And her eyes were back to their original brown color. In place of her usual stilettos were Duncan's too-large Adidas slippers. No makeup, no bright colors, no va-va-voom—just Annabelle Richards.

"Annabelle," Claire gasped, surprised.

Annabelle looked momentarily shy before she squared her shoulders and said saucily, "If you two need me to get a hotel room, direct me to the nearest Four Seasons and I'm there."

Belle was back. Claire felt Duncan stiffen under her as his expression turned hard. Claire quickly stood from Duncan's lap before he dumped her on her behind as he jumped to his feet.

"You have a lot to answer for," Duncan exploded at Annabelle.

"You sound like my mother," she replied in a bored tone, then headed toward the kitchen. "Do you have anything to eat?"

Duncan gaped after her. He looked at Claire for some explanation, but she shrugged in response. The two hurried into the kitchen, where Annabelle was rooting through the refrigerator while humming. Duncan slammed the refrigerator door closed, causing Annabelle to flinch in surprise and stare at him with wide, innocent eyes.

"Do you have any idea the trouble you've caused?" Duncan snarled at her. "You put Claire's life in danger! She's been mugged, attacked, and threatened! Not to mention that they know where she works and lives and have made habits of hanging out in both locations. All because of you!"

Claire was just as angry as Duncan, maybe more so, but she also had dealt with Rose Richards up-close-and-personal. Screaming and shouting didn't scare Annabelle.

Claire placed a hand on Duncan's arm and shook her head when he glared at her. He threw up his hands in obvious exasperation, then leaned against a counter, crossing his arms over his chest to pout.

"Is that true, Claire?" Annabelle asked, surprised, turning to her. "Were you mugged and—"

"Yes," Claire answered, glaring at her.

Annabelle sighed heavily and said, "I never meant to put you in danger, Claire. I swear." She shrugged, then said lightly, "But what are you going to do?"

Claire thought that Duncan would explode as he nearly shook with anger. "Did you just say, 'What are you going to do?' in response to the news that Claire is being followed by international criminals because of you?" he asked in a low, dangerous voice.

Annabelle blinked at him, and Claire instantly stepped in front of Duncan before he could build up enough steam. Claire could control her emotions. She was used to doing that. Duncan wasn't. She needed to handle Annabelle.

Claire explained patiently, "One of Henri Vittels's men followed you to Zanzibar's last week when the two of us met for drinks."

"I thought someone was following me," Annabelle gasped, as if she had solved one of life's great mysteries.

"He saw you slip the account code that you stole from Mr. Vittels into my briefcase."

"I tried to make it look like I was looking at one of the envelopes in your briefcase, and when I put that envelope back I slipped the envelope containing the code underneath it. I guess my sleight-of-hand tricks need some more work," she said with another shrug, then grabbed a banana from the fruit bowl on the counter. "I'm hungry. What about you guys? Let's order pizza. I haven't had pizza in years—"

"Why did you give me the code, Annabelle?" Claire snapped, her patience reaching its limit. "Why involve me?"

"I didn't know I was involving you," Annabelle said with an exaggerated sigh. "I knew Henri's men would find me, and when they did, I wanted the code to be as far away from me as possible. I thought it would be safe with you. The best-laid plans and all that. And now the FBI is involved—"

"FBI?" Duncan repeated, coming back to life.

"Yeah, in the parking lot at Club Sunset. Those were FBI agents. They want me to rat out Henri. They claim that if I don't cooperate, they'll charge me as an accessory to whatever dirty deeds they get Henri for, or something like that, but I told them—"

Duncan interrupted her with a hoarse cry. "Those men in

the parking lot were FBI agents?! You took an FBI agent's gun?! I hit an FBI agent?! I'm going to jail. I'll be the first Hillston in jail since my uncle Shane. My mother will cry; my father will cry. . . . Hell, I'll cry."

"Duncan, I'll handle this," Claire said calmly.

Duncan stared at Claire speechlessly; then he stalked from the kitchen, mumbling under his breath about never watching *Oz* on HBO again.

"That's a real winner you picked there, Claire," Annabelle said with a snort, then began to peel the banana. "By the way, how is it going with you two? Judging from things in the other room, that affair thing is working out—"

"I don't want you to talk unless it's to answer a specific question that I ask you," Claire said through clenched teeth.

Annabelle froze, then slowly set the banana on the counter, as if prepared to run. Her gulp was audible in the kitchen as she stared at Claire. "You're really angry, aren't you?" she asked hesitantly.

Claire ignored the question and said, "Start from the beginning, Annabelle. How do you know Henri Vittels?"

Annabelle sank into a chair at the kitchen table in the corner of the room before she said, "I wasn't exactly the success in Paris that I told you I was. I did a few runway shows when I first got there, but they told me that I wasn't skinny enough or tall enough for runway and apparently I'm not pretty enough for print work."

"What did you do?"

"When times were tough, I taught English in second-rate schools, but mostly . . ." Annabelle visibly hesitated, then lifted her chin and said, "Mostly, I dated generous men who like a little color in their lives." Claire's gut twisted in sympathy, but she wisely kept silent when she noticed the defensive look on Annabelle's face. She had known Claire too long, though. Annabelle spat out, "Save your pity. I had fun. I've been on trips around the world in private jets and yachts. I've had the finest wine, the most expensive caviar. I have a shoe and dress collection that would make most grown women weep. Life is good."

This time, Claire avoided Annabelle's gaze. Her voice softened as she continued, "Then I started dating Henri Vittels. People tried to warn me that he wasn't like the other wealthy men I had targeted—er, I mean dated. They told me that he was dangerous. I didn't believe them until it was too late. Henri wanted to control me, to own me. He wouldn't let me go anywhere without bodyguards—for my protection, he claimed, but the truth was they were my wardens. Henri doesn't trust anyone. He has spies who spy on his spies. After a few months, I had had enough. I snuck away from the mansion during a big party and I took a few things."

"Like what?" Claire asked warily.

"A few jewels that Henri had given me and . . . and the account code to a Swiss bank account."

"Why?"

"Because Henri owed me more than a few diamonds that he could just have his insurance company replace, and I knew the account code was important. Swiss banks have a lot of precautions. The account code is the sole access to your account—it's your everything. The day before I left, there was a lot of activity in the house. A group of men in dark suits and sunglasses had arrived. I heard Henri tell one of the men that he would transfer the money from that account when he accepted the delivery."

"Delivery of what?" Claire asked.

"I don't know," Annabelle answered with an apathetic shrug. "All I knew was that the money in that account belonged to men in suits who made Henri nervous. When Henri and the others went to join the guests downstairs—which included Henri's wife, coincidentally, even though he told me that she wouldn't set foot in his mansion because she despised him—I went into his office and opened the safe where I saw him place the envelope with the account code and I took it."

"What were you planning to do with the code? You must have known that you could never touch that money or they would trace it back to you."

Annabelle wouldn't meet Claire's eyes as she said defiantly, "I deserved something for all those months of captivity. I gave that asshole four months of my life."

"You were planning to sell the code back to him?" Claire guessed, then shook her head in disbelief and disgust.

"I was," Annabelle begrudgingly admitted, then sighed heavily and leaned against the counter. "Then I got to LA, and I caught wind of someone following me. I dumped the envelope in your briefcase. I was planning to take it back from you, but when I looked in your briefcase at your office, it was gone. Then Henri's men, Felix and Jacques, found me at the Ritz and . . . . I've been running ever since."

"I still have the code?" Claire asked, feeling the panic build.

"You have to," Annabelle said, her eyes intense and a little scared.

Claire dropped into one of the chairs next to her. She shook her head in disbelief. "But I don't know where it is."

"We have to find that code, Claire," Annabelle said desperately, grabbing her hand.

"I know that," Claire shot back, yanking her hand from Annabelle's tight grip. "Duncan and I are planning to hand it over to your boyfriend's goons tonight."

"We don't have to hand over anything," she protested. "We can still salvage this. I don't know how much money is in that account, but the men the money belong to are the bigger problem. Henri will pay us whatever we want—"

Claire glared at her, effectively cutting off her sales pitch. "Annabelle, your plan has failed. Henri is going to kill you, and he's going to kill Duncan and me while he's at it, unless we give him what he wants."

"Listen to Dr. Scott, Annabelle. She's a smart woman," came a deep accented voice from the kitchen doorway.

Annabelle and Claire jumped to their feet as a man walked into the kitchen, a big, deadly gun in his hand pointed directly at Claire. It was the man from the lab, the man who had been following her all over Los Angeles. Claire's heart beat double time and she instantly scanned the kitchen for a weapon. Her eyes landed on the knives neatly settled into the wooden block. Now all she had to do was get across the kitchen and tell the man to stand still while she stabbed him with one.

"Felix," Annabelle spat out, disgusted. "Still doing Henri's dirty work? Don't you ever get tired of being his errand boy?"

Felix nodded in greeting, as if the two had just been introduced at a debutante ball.

"Where's the code, Belle?" Felix asked tonelessly.

"You said we had until midnight," Claire said while wracking her mind for a solution. She could solve any problem if she looked at it long enough. Unfortunately, she had never had to solve the homicidal-maniac-with-gun-in-his-hands problem.

"I lied," Felix said with a casual shrug, then focused on Annabelle once more. "Where is the code?"

Annabelle gritted her jaw in response and crossed her arms over her robe-clad breast. Felix cocked the gun and aimed it at Annabelle's knee, visible through the slit in the robe.

"Such lovely legs," he murmured. "It'll be a shame if one is missing a kneecap."

"Do what you have to do, bastard, but I'll rot in hell before I give Henri anything else," Annabelle screamed angrily. "I gave him four months of my life and that's all he's getting from me."

Felix smiled in admiration, but then Claire saw his finger begin to squeeze the trigger.

"Wait!" Claire screamed, surprising all of them with the volume of her voice. Felix and Annabelle both looked at her, surprised. Claire smiled nervously and held up her hands, as if to calm Felix, the raging wild beast, even though he was the calmest one in the room. "I know where the code is," she blurted out.

Annabelle glared at her and said through clenched teeth, "Don't tell him anything, Claire."

"It's at the lab," Claire instantly told Felix. "I just remembered what Annabelle was talking about . . . the envelopes. That night at Zanzibar's, I was carrying ten envelopes in my bag. I'd been asked to write an article by the *New England Journal of Science* on the controversy around stem cell research, and I had drafts of my article in my briefcase that I planned to mail to several well-respected colleagues for their comments. Stem cell research is actually an interesting topic. I realized that—"

"Get on with it, Doc," Felix ordered, exasperated.

"Right," Claire said, shaking her head. "The day after the attack, I took all the envelopes out of my briefcase and set them on my desk at the lab. With everything going on, I still haven't mailed them. They're sitting on my desk. The account code must still be there, too."

"Then we're going to the lab," Felix said cheerfully.

Annabelle groaned, and Claire sighed in relief that at least no one's kneecaps were getting blown off. Then, for the first time since she'd seen the gun, Claire thought of Duncan. Maybe he had heard the commotion and was planning to rescue her and Annabelle. . . . Then the kitchen door flew open.

Duncan walked into the kitchen, blood flowing from his reopened cut, the Band-Aid gone. He looked angry, but all limbs were accounted for. Another tall, well-built man dressed in all black, holding another big gun, stood behind Duncan. So much for the cavalry.

Duncan held Claire's gaze and she nodded at his silent question. She was fine.

"Jacques, I expected better from you," Annabelle said with a long-suffering sigh. "Felix here has absolutely no imagination, but you could actually do something with yourself besides kiss Henri's ass."

Jacques winked at her, then puckered his lips for a kiss, which made Annabelle narrow her eyes and hiss like a cat. Jacques actually flinched in response.

Felix waved his gun at Jacques and said, "I'm taking the

good doctor to the lab. You take the boyfriend and Belle to Mr. Vittels. He's waiting at the Santa Monica Airport."

"Like hell," Duncan growled, and began to struggle against Jacques's grip. Jacques grunted in exertion but managed to hold on before he dug the nozzle of the gun under Duncan's chin. He immediately stilled.

Tears filled Claire's eyes and she said in a shaky voice, "It'll be all right, Duncan."

Duncan clenched his teeth, then reluctantly nodded. He pinned Jacques with a glare that made the bigger Frenchman release him and take a few steps back.

"At least give me a few minutes to change," Annabelle demanded, sounding almost bored.

Felix smiled and said, "No. I think Mr. Vittels will enjoy seeing you like this. It'll be the first time he's seen you where most of your skin is actually covered."

Annabelle rolled her eyes, then stalked out of the kitchen toward the living room.

Duncan glanced at Claire, and she forced a confident nod because she saw the anger and pain in his expression. He visually caressed her face, then glared at Felix and warned, "If one hair is missing on her head, so help me God . . . I'll hunt you down and tear you limb from limb."

Felix and Duncan engaged in a staring contest before Felix stiffly nodded. Jacques tugged Duncan's arm and pulled him out of the kitchen, the gun in his back.

Claire took a deep breath for courage, then turned to face Felix. He stuffed the gun into the waistband of his pants and said politely, "It looks like it's just you and me, Dr. Scott. We should hurry, since we don't want to keep Mr. Vittels or your friends waiting. Shall we go?"

Claire had no choice but to walk out the kitchen door that led to the driveway.

Chapter Twenty-Three

Duncan screamed in outrage and kicked the locked door in frustration. He had been screaming for the last ten minutes, but he and Annabelle were still locked in the janitor's office in a hangar at the Santa Monica Airport, and Claire was still alone with a murderer. Duncan finally admitted defeat, then slid to the floor while running his hands over his hair.

Jacques had hustled Annabelle and Duncan into a waiting dark Mercedes and made him drive while Annabelle sat in the passenger seat. Duncan had been really careful to take all bumps in the road gently, since Jacques, from the backseat, had kept the gun trained on the backs of their heads. Jacques had directed Duncan into the open doors of the deserted hangar, which was half the size of a football field.

All of Duncan's hastily made plans of overpowering Jacques once they got out of the car were abandoned when the hangar doors were pushed closed by men carrying Uzis, and five or six other men, wearing dark suits or fatigues, milled around the hangar carrying Uzis of their own.

Duncan and Annabelle had been locked inside the office ever since.

"Have you tired yourself out yet?" Annabelle asked dully.

Duncan glared at her. She had immediately taken the only chair in the room and propped her feet on the desk, after commandeering the uniform on the back of the door for her own. Somehow she had even made the uniform look chic, by rolling up the legs and tightly cinching the belt at the waist.

Duncan dropped his hands to his sides and said, half-amazed and half-annoyed, "You are something else, Annabelle. You know that?"

"Somehow, I don't think that's a compliment," she murmured.

"If I didn't know better I would think that you're enjoying yourself."

"I get to see that bastard Henri one last time, which means I have one last time to spit in his face. I'm very much enjoying that thought."

Duncan shook his head in disbelief and said, "It doesn't bother you, even a little bit, that Claire is right now God-knows-where with that homicidal maniac?"

"Who? Felix?" Annabelle asked blankly.

Duncan took several deep breaths for patience, then said, "Yes, Felix."

"Claire is a smart woman, Duncan. As soon as she and Felix walk into the lab, she'll give some sort of signal to the security guards, and Felix will spend the night cuddled up next to some guy named Bubba in prison who has a thing for French accents," she said lightly.

"Claire is very smart—so smart that she knows if Felix doesn't return with her and the code, your boyfriend will kill us. And Claire would not allow that to happen." He laughed bitterly when he saw the comprehension dawn in Annabelle's eyes. "Now you're starting to understand the predicament? Thanks for tuning in, Annabelle."

"Claire wouldn't really come back here for us, would she?" Annabelle asked, sounding uncertain for the first time.

"Of course she will," he said, annoyed. Duncan cursed, then raked a hand down his face tiredly, because he couldn't entirely blame Annabelle. He was responsible for Claire being in danger, too. He muttered, "I never should have approached her that night."

"What night?"

"In Zanzibar's," he said tiredly as he stared at the cement floor. "If I had not been walking her to her car that night, I would not have held Felix off long enough for Claire to call nine-one-one. Felix would have taken the briefcase, gotten the code, and none of this would be happening. She would have been scared for a few moments when it happened, but she would have been safe."

"How were you supposed to know that Felix would try to take her briefcase that night?"

"I didn't, but I shouldn't have been there. . . . That damn bet." He cursed again and had the urge to stand up and punch something, but he was too tired.

"What bet?"

Duncan hadn't realized that he had said the words out loud until Annabelle spoke. He stared across the small office at her. He didn't like the expression on her face—suspicious. Annabelle was the one person Duncan would never be able to lie to. He was no match for her, as she probably told lies on a regular basis.

"What bet, Duncan?" she asked more forcefully, setting her feet on the ground on full alert. "Did you make some kind of bet about Claire?"

Duncan sighed to himself, then muttered, "Yes."

"This bet was with your friends from high school? The two who were with you at Zanzibar's, who watched you talking to us?"

"Yes," he bit out. "I used to brag that I could make any woman fall in love with me. So, they bet me that I couldn't do it with Claire. I had to make her fall in love with me in time for the Westfield block party this weekend."

Annabelle shook her head in disgust. "Whenever I start to have some hope for humanity in this world, I meet someone like you."

"You're no prize, either, Annabelle," he replied, annoyed, then ran a hand over his head because Annabelle was right. He was a first-class ass, a jerk, a species of life lower than . . .

lower than even Annabelle. He was everything he had always tried not to think of himself as being. He used women, he seduced them for sport, and he was a liar. But did that mean he didn't deserve happiness? For the first time in his life, he loved a woman, and now she was going to die because of him. It wasn't fair that Claire should have to pay for his past bad deeds.

"What were you supposed to win for this feat of superior manhood?" Annabelle asked drily.

"Five thousand dollars for a European tour. If I lost, I had to . . . I had to admit to all the guys at the block party that I'm not the player I admit to be, that I . . . that I've lied about my experiences."

Annabelle grimaced in sympathy. "Ouch."

Duncan smiled at her look of empathy, because only Annabelle—another player—could understand how much that would hurt. He said, "The funny thing is . . . after Claire, I didn't have to lie anymore. She loves me for me."

"And you love her," Annabelle guessed.

"And I love her," he admitted. "Before Claire, I didn't believe in love. And I thought the men who bought into it had been hoodwinked by a woman. Imagine my surprise when I found myself falling in love with Claire. This woman, who I thought would fall on her knees and worship me because I took her to dinner, had me on my knees. I just thought she would instantly fall in love with me because . . ." His voice trailed off and shame filled his cheeks.

"Because she's a dorky scientist," Annabelle supplied.

Duncan glared at her, but he realized that he was being a hypocrite again. That was exactly what he had thought.

He continued, "Besides my family, no one has ever thought I was worth anything. I was always the not-very-athletic Hillston brother; then I started high school and girls started falling at my feet. Then people started remembering me because of the girls, and I started inventing girls and women until I had to keep coming up with bigger and bigger stories that not even I could believe.

"I couldn't just go on dates with normal women anymore. If I went out with a bank teller, by the time I told my friends she had become a Brazilian model in town for a swimsuit calendar. I don't know why I kept doing it. I don't think anyone believed me anymore, but it made me unique, y'know." Duncan sighed heavily, then murmured, "I wish I had known Claire in high school. She makes me feel like I matter, and for some reason I've always needed to matter."

Annabelle was quiet for a few moments; then she said, "And Claire doesn't know any of this?"

"No," he said, shaking his head. A burst of anger at himself made him slam the door with the side of his fist. "Do you see how this is as much my fault as it is yours? If I had never taken that stupid bet, if I had never tried to prove to my friends that I was the supreme player, if I had—"

"Oh, please," Annabelle interrupted his pity party with an annoyed sigh. "Do you know how many 'if I had never' thoughts I have in my life? About a million a day. But guess what, Romeo? It doesn't help anything to think that way, and it only gives you frown lines. Right now, we need to think about how we're going to get out of this alive, and then you can beat yourself up later."

Duncan actually smiled at Annabelle, finally understanding what Claire had once seen in her. He abruptly stood and walked to a counter loaded with various clear plastic cartons filled with tools, nails, masking tape, and other maintenance items. There were also nearly empty canisters of engine starter fluid, oil, a bag of fertilizer, and mulch stacked in the corner of the office. He turned to his right and saw two fire extinguishers.

Annabelle joined him at the counter and said, "I can't think on an empty stomach, so you think and I'll find us something to eat." She knelt in front of the mini-refrigerator under the counter and opened the door.

Duncan suddenly froze for a second as a million thoughts

crashed through his head. The one skill that Duncan had learned over the years was being prepared. If a man had to lie, at least he didn't have to get caught on the small details. Before his first date with Claire, Duncan had read some of her published articles and research.

He turned to stare at the doorknob. Metal. He tried to keep his voice even as he asked Annabelle, "Are there ice cubes in there?"

"Yes," she said, then sighed, dejected. "But no food."

Duncan glanced at the bright glow of the lightbulb hanging from the ceiling, then back at the doorknob. He felt the first spark of hope in the last hour. He immediately pulled a long metal tube from behind the counter and peered through its empty column. He smiled, satisfied, then grabbed a sheet of newspaper from the trash can near the desk.

"What are you doing?" Annabelle asked, bewildered.

He ignored her question and poured a thin line of powder fertilizer onto the newspaper. Then he grabbed the can of engine starter fluid. "Tear off a thin strip of that robe," he ordered.

"You want me to tear your robe? Why?"

"I need it for the bomb—"

"Bomb?" Annabelle gaped at him, then said in a Gary Coleman imitation, "What you talkin' about, Willis?"

Duncan ignored her and said, "After you do that, I want you to hold up the ice cubes and the metal tube to the light-bulb. The ice water will fall down the tube and then freeze on the door lock."

Annabelle didn't move but continued to stare at him, dumbfounded. Duncan stopped his frantic movements and turned to Annabelle, unable to control his impatience. "Pretty soon, Claire will be here with the account code. All of us will be in serious shit when that happens. We've got to do something."

"But is now really the time to play black MacGyver?"

"I've learned a lot of things hanging around Claire," he

said, then attempted to sound firm. "This will work. Tear the robe and then start melting the ice cubes. Got it?"

"OK," she said, annoyed. "All you had to do was ask."

Claire frantically searched through the stack of envelopes on her desk at the lab as Felix hovered over her. She ignored her trembling hands and continued scanning address labels. She had tried to think of various ways to tell the BioTech security guards that Felix was not the average visitor, but every scenario in her mind ended up with someone being shot and Duncan and Annabelle being dead. As a result, Claire hadn't said anything when she and Felix signed into the lab with the security guard in the lobby. She could only be grateful that none of her team was in the empty lab. Considering it was almost midnight, she hadn't expected to find anyone, but since they were so close to preclinical trials, Claire wouldn't have been surprised to find any of them there.

Claire's heart skipped a beat when she flipped to an unmarked envelope. She quickly opened it and a small metal cylinder, the same size and shape as an ink pen, fell out. She curiously stared at it, then accidentally pressed a button. A fourteen-digit number shone on the floor, beamed directly from the end.

"Very well done," Felix said with an actual smile.

She quickly placed the code inside the envelope and handed it to Felix. Now what? One of the scenarios she had avoided thinking about involved Felix killing her in the lab since he didn't need her anymore.

"Let's go," Felix said, motioning her out of the office and into the lab.

Claire quickly obeyed and tried to breathe. At least, he had put away the gun when they had reached the doors of BioTech, and he hadn't pulled it out again. As long as the gun was hidden, she could think.

Claire and Felix had just reached the entrance to the lab when Vino and a few of the postdoctoral students walked into the lab, carrying several aromatic pizza boxes. Claire gulped and quickly glanced at Felix, who had pasted a smile on his face, as if the prospect of meeting her team were a joy he could barely contain.

"Claire," Vino said, surprised, stopping in front of them as the two postdocs took the pizzas to the back of the lab. Vino looked at Felix and his smile grew wider. Claire inwardly groaned. She could already see the wheels spinning in Vino's very big, green-haired head. "You must be the infamous Duncan. I've heard a lot about you," Vino said while offering his hand.

Felix shook Vino's hand, then slipped his arm around Claire's waist. He squeezed her waist. Hard. Claire understood his threat. He would kill Vino and the others if she alerted them in any way.

"I've been very curious about you," Vino said to Felix. "It isn't every day that our Claire misses a team meeting. I had to meet the man responsible."

Claire groaned, momentarily forgetting about the danger, as she thought about the nine o'clock meeting that had taken place that night. It was supposed to be their last official meeting before the preclinical started. Around that time, she had been running for her life outside Club Sunset.

"I'm so sorry, Vino. I completely forgot about the rescheduled meeting."

"I took care of it," Vino assured her. "Besides, you deserve some time off."

"What happened in the meeting? Did you come up with protocols for the volunteer testers?" Claire asked curiously, then flinched when she felt another squeeze on her waist. "I mean . . . We have to go. We're meeting some friends for late-night drinks."

Vino nodded but didn't move from her path. Instead, he openly studied Felix. Claire grew more nervous as she felt all of his considerable muscles tense. She said desperately, "Vino, we really have to go."

"Somehow, I pictured you not so . . . WWE," Vino said to Felix.

"It's the jacket," Felix said tonelessly.

Vino sent Felix a strange look, then shrugged. "I'll see you two later."

Claire nodded and hurried out of the lab, with Felix close on her heels, before Vino could say anything else.

"Are you sure this is going to work?" Annabelle asked nervously as Duncan wrapped masking tape around the rolled-up newspaper that held the contents of his makeshift bomb.

"I hope so," he muttered, then grabbed the matches they had found in a desk drawer. He glanced at the metal door-knob that was turning white with frost from the melted ice water that Annabelle continued to hold to the lightbulb from her position on top of the chair.

He anxiously glanced at his watch, then said, "That should be good enough."

Annabelle hopped off the chair and nodded at him. Duncan grabbed one of the fire extinguishers and struck the lock. There was a loud crack, and the lock instantly shattered to the floor and the door opened. He tried not to act too surprised, but he couldn't control his wild grin and turned to Annabelle for a high five, but she just blankly stared at him. He frowned. Claire would have given him a high five.

Annabelle asked suddenly, "Duncan, have you thought about what we're going to do if we actually make it out of this room?"

"When Jacques brought us in here, I noticed a small door at the back of the hangar. You're going to run out that door as fast as you can, find a telephone, and call Detective Hansen at the Santa Monica Police Department—"

"The police," she protested. "I can't call the police. They want to arrest me—"

"Annabelle, they'll kill Claire and me if you don't get the police here as quick as you can," he said seriously.

Annabelle actually hesitated; then she stiffly nodded. She

rolled up the sleeves to the jumpsuit, then asked, "And while I'm condemning myself to life in prison, what are you going to be doing?"

Duncan motioned to the rolled-up newspapers and said gravely, "Getting Claire. I'll distract them with the bombs, then use the fire extinguishers to create a smoke screen. In the confusion, I'll grab Claire and get out before the smoke clears."

Annabelle eyed his bombs, the doubt clear in her expression. "That sounds a little complex. Are you sure it's going to work?"

"Unless the laws of chemistry have changed in the last hour, it should work."

Annabelle caught his small note of insecurity. "Should?"

"You're really a killjoy, you know that?"

She ignored his sarcasm and said, "If I know Henri, he has guards patrolling the perimeter. You'll never get close enough to Claire for your alleged bombs or your supposed smoke screen to work. They'll shoot you on sight."

"It's a chance I'll have to take," he said gravely.

Duncan kicked the door open and jumped out, prepared to take on the whole army, but there was no one around. He couldn't see past a stack of large crates and boxes, but he heard men's voices and the sound of running car engines. The door marked with a neon green exit sign overhead was in the opposite direction of the voices.

Duncan motioned to Annabelle to run out the door. He grabbed her arm before she could move past him. "Claire and I are counting on you, Annabelle."

She nodded, then said softly, "You're not the only one who loves her, Duncan."

Before he could respond, Annabelle ran toward the exit. Duncan didn't release the breath he held until Annabelle disappeared into the night darkness outside. Duncan turned back toward the voices. Using a bomb and a smoke screen to distract seven men with guns while he grabbed Claire had been a good plan inside the safety of a locked room; now it seemed . . . a little crazy.

Then Duncan heard the sound of a car engine, and the excited murmur of the voices grew. It was now or never. Duncan edged toward the voices, heaving under the weight of the fire extinguishers. The most frustrating part was that if it did work, no one would believe one word of this story.

Chapter Twenty-Four

Claire gulped in fear as Felix stopped the car in the middle of the airport hangar. He stood from the car and walked to the group of armed men who stood a few feet in front of the car. Only one man didn't carry a gun. He was short, with a generous belly under an expensive suit jacket, and had slicked-back gray hair that covered the half-bald crown of his head. The other men obviously deferred to him, and Claire decided that he must be the infamous Henri Vittels. She was surprised that a man who looked like a high school principal could inspire such fear. Then his beady green eyes locked on her in the passenger seat and Claire felt a spark of fear. High school principals would have paid to be able to inspire such fear in one look.

Claire slowly stood from the car as Felix handed Henri the envelope. He looked inside, then smiled, satisfied, closing the envelope. He spoke to Felix for a few moments; then Henri started toward her.

"Dr. Scott," he said in a polite French-accented voice, stopping a few feet from her. "Thank you for returning my property."

"I did what you asked. Now bring me Duncan and Annabelle so we can go," she said, sounding more in control than she felt.

He smiled slightly, as if he could see straight through her act, then said, "I'm afraid I can't do that."

Fear and anger gripped Claire's heart, and she barely managed to stand on her trembling legs. "Why not?"

"They're gone," Jacques answered, breaking from the pack to stand next to Henri.

Henri smiled at Claire, a nasty smile that made her suddenly go cold. "It looks like it's just you and me, Dr. Scott. Your boyfriend obviously didn't care enough to stick around to make certain that you got out of this alive. And since he didn't live up to his end of the deal, I think it's only fair that I don't have to live up to my end."

Claire's nostrils flared as she tried to take in more air to make up for her rapidly pounding heart. She didn't know if Duncan had really escaped or if Henri had him imprisoned somewhere, but she knew that Duncan would never leave her willingly.

"What about Annabelle?" Claire managed to ask.

"Ahh, yes, my Belle," Henri said with a goose bump–raising smile. He turned to his men and ordered, "Bring her out."

In response, two men rounded a tall row of boxes while holding a kicking and screaming Annabelle by the sleeves of an ugly, baggy, olive green uniform. Claire sighed in relief at the sight of a live and very angry Annabelle. The other men sighed in admiration at the sight of flashing dark brown skin from gapes at the front of the uniform as she continued to squirm.

Henri spoke to Claire, but his gaze was on Annabelle as he said, "We caught her wandering around outside in a no-doubt half-hatched attempt to escape, which like most of her schemes was poorly planned and even more poorly executed."

The men released her, and Annabelle whirled around on them, as if prepared to strike. Both men flinched in fear, despite their larger size and the nasty-looking weapons they carried.

Annabelle snorted in disgust, as if the men weren't worth her time, then turned to Henri. She stalked toward him, then slapped him, sending a resounding crack through the warehouse at the sound of flesh hitting flesh. Claire winced in sympathetic pain, along with the men behind Henri.

Henri's head had turned from the force of the slap. Claire held her breath, expecting him to attack Annabelle, but instead he slowly looked at her, a small smile on his lips. "You always did like to play rough," he said as he lovingly rubbed his cheek where a red mark was forming.

"Eat shit," Annabelle shot back.

"Such crass language, Belle. Just accept it. The game is over, and you lost," Henri told her. "You never were smart enough to figure out when to stop playing."

Annabelle rolled her eyes, then walked to stand beside Claire. She grabbed Claire's hand and said to Henri, "You got what you wanted. Your precious account code. Now let her go."

"No attempts for pleas of mercy for yourself, Belle?" Henri asked, sounding amused.

"I lived with you for four long months," Annabelle spat out. "I know that you're not letting me go anywhere."

"Annabelle, no," Claire said quietly, so Henri and his men couldn't hear. "I'm not leaving you with this psycho."

"Shut up, and stay close to me," Annabelle whispered back, never taking her eyes off Henri.

"I did have fun with you, Belle. I've never met a woman who could take as much as you," Henri said; then his smile disappeared and a cold hatred entered his eyes. "But you made me look foolish in front of the Ukrainians, and I do have a reputation to maintain. I bet you didn't even know how much money you held in your greedy little hands with that account code."

"How much?" Annabelle asked reluctantly.

"Ninety million dollars," he answered instantly. Claire thought that Annabelle would faint at the number, while Henri smiled knowingly. "A Middle Eastern terrorist group is paying my Ukrainian customers ninety million dollars to take a nuclear weapon off their hands. Once I transfer the money into the Ukrainians' account, they will ship one nuclear weapon to the terrorists and I'll get my twenty percent commission. If you had played your cards right, foolish girl, you could have gotten a cut of that."

"You can't sell nuclear weapons," Claire blurted out, ignoring Annabelle's grip tightening on her hand.

"Of course I can," Henri told Claire matter-of-factly. "And I will as soon as I meet my buyers in another hour across town. But first there is the matter of what to do with you two ladies. Excuse me. One lady and then Belle."

"You could start by kissing my ass," Annabelle snarled, then added, in a louder voice that rang throughout the hangar, "and if I was thinking about executing another stupid plan, now would be the perfect time."

Claire stared at Annabelle, bewildered by her strange statement. Then everything seemed to happen all at once. To her right, there was a fantastic boom followed by a small explosion that caused boxes to fall over onto some of Henri's soldiers. Flames spread to the crates, and something in one of them must have been flammable, because there was an even louder explosion, with more flames. Several of the gunmen dropped to the floor, then scrambled to their feet and began to run from the flames. In the confusion, another small explosion went off behind Henri, who shrieked and dropped to the ground.

In just three seconds, pure mayhem had taken over. Everyone in the hangar seemed surprised, except Annabelle, who yanked Claire to the ground next to the car as fire and secondary explosions rocked around them. She coughed into her hand as thick smoke from the explosions and something else thick and white began to fill the air, making it virtually impossible to see anyone around her, besides Annabelle.

"The exit is one hundred feet straight back," Annabelle screamed at Claire over the noise of exploding crates and screaming, confused men. Another crate blew apart, sending wood pieces flying down, and more flames into the air.

"Where are you going?" Claire demanded, hanging on to her arm when she realized that Annabelle was about to run in the opposite direction.

"I've got to get the code from Henri."

"Annabelle, the money is not important. Haven't you realized that by now—"

"It's a nuclear weapon, Claire. Imagine a terrorist group getting its hands on that. We can't let Henri leave this hangar with that code," Annabelle said desperately. Claire nodded and started to run in the direction in which Annabelle had been heading, but Annabelle yanked her back. "You've got to find the police. Duncan is in the hangar somewhere. He'll find you. Go!"

"Annabelle—"

"Let me do something to make this right," Annabelle said, her voice choked with tears and smoke. "Get the police."

Claire nodded reluctantly, then hugged Annabelle, who squeezed her back. She jumped to her feet and ran toward the exit. She couldn't see anything through the thick smoke, but she blindly ran as fast as she could. She finally reached the outer edges of the thickest smoke and saw a regular door marked EXIT next to the closed hangar doors. She didn't dare look over her shoulder for fear that she would see a gun aimed at her back. In the movies, didn't the professionals always tell the crazy women who got themselves in this type of situation not to look back? Claire wasn't looking back.

Claire finally reached the door and tried to push it open, but a strong hand grabbed her arm. She screamed bloody murder.

"Claire," Duncan said, his mouth next to her ear.

Claire threw herself into his arms, and for a moment the two clung to each other before he pushed her away and said, "Let's get out of here!"

With a he-man yell, he kicked open the door. The two ran into the night just as several police cars, with lights flashing and sirens blaring, screeched to a stop no more than ten feet from them. A black van marked SWAT rammed through the hangar doors, sending metal flying inward, and screaming, uniformed men jumped out of the van and ran inside.

Claire dropped to her knees, coughing from the inhalation of smoke and from adrenaline. She managed to lift her head just as Detective Hansen ran toward her, looking like Combat Barbie in bulletproof gear.

"Are you two all right?" Detective Hansen asked, squatting next to them.

Claire nodded even as she hacked out a lung. "We're fine," Duncan answered. "But how did you find us?"

"Vino Ricardo. When Claire left the lab earlier tonight with a man purporting to be Duncan, Vino called lab security because he said something about the man with her not looking like any Calvin Klein billboard his girlfriend had ever drooled over," she answered with a confused shrug. "BioTech security followed Claire here and alerted us."

"Thank you," Claire said to the detective and to Vino, wherever he was. Duncan wrapped his arms around Claire, and she suddenly could breathe. It was over. It was all over.

Claire sat at the small, round table, deep in the bowels of the FBI headquarters and tried to pretend that Annabelle wasn't sitting across from her. She and Annabelle had been sitting together in a windowless locked room for the last two hours. The only contact they had had with anyone was with a female agent who had brought Annabelle a set of gray sweats that had FBI emblazoned on the pants and a gray sweatshirt. Annabelle had instantly stripped in plain view and slipped into the sweats, even though she complained that gray was not her color. Claire had remained in her seat and tried to concentrate on the fact that she was alive, not on what had just happened. But the scent of smoke radiating off both of them made it hard for her to forget.

Claire had glanced anxiously at the door countless times in the last thirty minutes. Even prisoners got a phone call. Claire hadn't been allowed to talk to anyone but Annabelle and had no idea where Duncan was. Claire needed to see him. She still wasn't done reassuring herself that he was alive and well. For one brief horrible moment in the hangar, she had thought that Duncan was dead. She didn't want to ever feel that magnitude of loss again. She loved the adult

Duncan. Not the teenager who had stolen her heart, but the man who had done anything and everything for her.

"You know, I still haven't eaten," Annabelle said with a heavy sigh.

Claire ignored her and stared at the door. She hadn't spoken to Annabelle since the two had been placed in the room and didn't plan to. Claire blamed their last-minute hug in the hangar on the situation.

"You should have seen me, Claire. You would have been proud. I created bombs out of newspapers and tape and I figured out a way to freeze off the door lock . . . OK, I'll admit that Duncan helped a little, but I surprised myself. Hanging around you must be rubbing off on me . . ." Annabelle's voice trailed off, as Claire continued to stare pointedly at the door. The silence didn't last long before Annabelle abruptly whined, "Claire, talk to me. I'm going crazy in here."

When Claire once more refused to respond, Annabelle said stiffly, "I would think you'd show a little more gratitude. I did save your life . . . and Duncan's life too."

Claire stared at her, outraged. "You're not serious, are you?" she managed over her disbelief and anger.

"Well, I did," Annabelle insisted, with a pout. "If I hadn't distracted Henri's guards when I did, they would have found Duncan, and he never could have set off those bombs. And if he hadn't set off those bombs, you would still be trembling in fear in front of Henri right now."

Claire narrowed her eyes and said, "Do you really want me to talk to you, Annabelle? Fine. You're irresponsible, immature, and totally disregarded the danger you placed me in. Happy? We're talking now."

As if it was possible, Annabelle looked on the verge of tears. "We've been friends for twenty years, Claire. You're probably the only real friend I've ever had. You know that I would never purposely place you in danger—"

"No, I don't know that," Claire spat out. "All I know is that I just spent the last two weeks of my life living in fear and because of you my preclinical trials will have to be postponed for at least another week. I know this may not matter to you because it doesn't affect you, but a week in cancer research is one less week that we can get the product to the hospital. You're not my friend, and you're not an acquaintance. You're nothing to me."

Annabelle narrowed her eyes and said tightly, "Must be nice to be so perfect all the time."

"You're not really trying to make this mess my fault, are you?" Claire asked in disbelief. She shot to her feet, knocking over her chair in the process. "You lied. You stole from a known criminal. You almost got us killed. You've been in town for less than two weeks and managed to almost destroy my life."

Shock and hurt flashed across Annabelle's face before she lashed out, "Destroyed your life? Are you kidding? If I had never come to town, you wouldn't have a life. You would still be hiding behind your beakers and petri dishes, trying to convince yourself that it doesn't matter that life has passed you by." Annabelle snorted in disgust as she looked from Claire's sensible pumps, to her dark gray skirt and cranberry sleeveless silk sweater, to her ponytail. "You haven't changed at all since high school. Still the scared little girl afraid to walk into a room by herself, who always found fault in everyone but herself. At least you had an excuse then. You were young. Now what's your excuse?"

"At least I don't have to convince myself that I'm not just a high-class prostitute," she replied coolly.

Annabelle flinched as if Claire had punched her in the stomach, and Claire instantly regretted her words. If she could have taken them back she would have, but the damage was done. She stuck out her chin and crossed her arms over her chest and met Annabelle's gaze. There was no going back now.

Annabelle slowly stood to her feet, her chest heaving with outrage. "I may be a high-class prostitute, but, at least, I know when a man is using me."

"What is that supposed to mean?"

"You're a bet, Claire," Annabelle said flatly. "That night at Zanzibar's, Duncan bet his friends that he could get you to fall in love with him by the Westfield block party. If he wins, he gets money to go on a European tour. If he loses, he has to announce at the block party that he's a big, fat liar about his supposed numerous conquests. I guess we both know that he's won the bet. You're head over heels in love with him. Anyone can see that."

Claire's vision blurred with tears and she suddenly found it difficult to breathe, as if she were swimming underwater with her mouth wide open. "You're lying," she choked out.

"No, I'm not," Annabelle said, holding Claire's gaze. "Duncan told me when we were locked in the hangar together. You're nothing to him but a bet, Claire."

Claire quickly hunched over as she placed a hand on her throat to keep down the bile. She shook her head silently. Annabelle was lying. Duncan loved her. He had told her; he had made love to her; he had . . . Claire almost threw up again. Was it true? Could Duncan have been lying to her all this time? Was every word, every touch, for a stupid bet? Claire tried not to believe it, but she knew that Annabelle was telling the truth. Not even Annabelle was cruel enough to come up with a lie like that.

"Claire," Annabelle said softly.

The door opened and Agent Sullivan walked into the room. Judging from his stony expression, he still held a few hard feelings from Claire and Annabelle's jumping him in the parking lot of Club Sunset. If he noticed Claire's tears, he didn't comment.

He simply said, "Dr. Scott, you're free to leave. You may retrieve your belongings from the agent at the entrance of the building."

Claire gulped, then asked worriedly, "Do I have to worry about—"

"We rounded up Henri and all of his men, including his buyers and suppliers," Agent Sullivan said with a begrudging amount of respect. "You don't have to worry about Henri Vittels again."

"What about me?" Annabelle demanded. "Can I leave, too?"

"You aren't going anywhere for a while, Ms. Richards. You may as well make yourself comfortable," he replied evenly.

"I had a feeling you would say that," she said with a heavy sigh.

Claire walked toward the door but hesitated and looked at Agent Sullivan. "What about Duncan?" she asked in a shaky voice.

"If you wait a few minutes, I'm on my way to release him."

"I don't want to wait," she said, then walked out of the room. She didn't look back.

Chapter Twenty-Five

Four days later, Duncan sighed in relief when he spotted Claire and Kira walking down the street toward the cordoned-off block party. It was barely noon, and it seemed like the entire community was already there. Hundreds of people were already crammed in to the street, and the games, competitions for prizes, and food contests had already started. A band was playing rousing hits from the 1970s on a makeshift stage at the end of the block, and people were singing along and dancing.

Duncan ignored all of that and stared at Claire. It had been four long days since he had last seen her, reeking of smoke and clinging to him outside the hangar. He had spoken to her on the telephone the few times he could catch her, but her side of the conversation had been stilted and distracted. He knew she was trying to keep the preclinical trials on-track and he tried not to interfere, but Duncan missed her. He missed her a lot. After spending almost every free minute he had with her during the last week and a half, he felt like an addict going through withdrawal when he wasn't able to get his daily Claire fix.

Duncan smiled as he watched her move gracefully through the crowd; then he realized that something was different. It was her. No ponytail, no suit. She wore her hair hanging around her shoulders in soft curls and a feminine, flirty sundress that stopped just above her knees and emphasized the flare of her hips and full breasts. His chest suddenly felt tight, and the arousal that was never too far away when he thought of Claire came crashing back to rock his world. She looked beautiful and, she was right, without the severe suit she looked about five years younger. Duncan felt five years younger around her. Maybe they couldn't go back in time to high school, but they could make up for lost time for the rest of their lives.

Duncan grinned and waved at Claire. She stared at him for a moment, then halfheartedly waved back before she bent to tie her niece's shoelaces. Duncan's smile faltered. Something was wrong. He could feel it. Something cold snaked into his belly as he thought about the bet. He quickly shook off the bad feeling. It was just his imagination. Everything was perfect with Claire, like it always was.

Duncan watched Claire take Kira to a game of jump rope with other little girls, who welcomed the animated Kira with excited waves. Much more excited waves than Claire had given him, Duncan noted. Claire stared at him, then averted her gaze and began to walk toward him. Too slowly, as far as Duncan was concerned.

"Hi," she said softly, making no move to reach for him when she stopped in front of him.

Duncan decided to ignore his paranoia and wrapped his arms around her. She felt so good, so soft. For a brief moment he thought about the danger she had been in with Felix and Henri, and his grip tightened.

"I've missed you," he whispered against her ear, mindful of Kira and her friends pointing at them and giggling, but not caring.

Claire extracted herself from his grip and smiled at him. A real smile. Duncan released the breath he hadn't known that he'd been holding. He definitely had imagined her initial hesitation. She was probably stressed out from work, and considering her past week, he realized she hadn't had much time to relax. He vowed to change all of that tonight. She wasn't getting away tonight. After the block party, he was going to pamper her from head to toe and then make sweet love to her like he should have done on numerous other occasions but had been too eager and hopeless to do.

"I'm sorry that I haven't been in touch, but I've been so busy at the lab," she said apologetically. "We have orientation for the test administrators and new protocols to set up. It's been crazy."

"I understand," he said while framing her face with his hands. "I'm just glad you're here. And you're giving me tonight, right?"

"Anything you want, Duncan," she said with a sweet smile.

Duncan grinned, linking his fingers with hers. "I like hearing those words out of your mouth," he murmured before pressing his mouth over hers.

He sighed at the familiar feel of her thick, petal-soft lips, and her mouth opened under his. He instantly slid his tongue into the dark, moist recesses of her mouth. She tasted like cotton candy. She tasted like his woman. This was what he had been waiting for. This was what had kept him awake for the past four days when he had to mentally restrain himself from driving to her house because he knew she needed her rest.

She quickly pulled away and glanced around at the numerous people milling nearby. Duncan grinned at her downcast expression, then fingered several strands of her hair that the wind lifted.

"New look?" he asked curiously.

"I thought this look would please you," she said in a strangely formal voice.

Duncan frowned, then brushed aside her weird comment and said, "You please me no matter what you're wearing. I thought you knew that by now." He grabbed her hand and said, "Come on; Patrick has been asking about you, and the other guys can't wait to meet you. They still think of you as that kid from high school."

He kept a tight grip on her hand and led her into the thick

of the crowd, where his friends were gathered around a picnic table set up in the middle of the street. For the first time in his life, Duncan felt that everything was exactly as it should be, no exaggeration needed.

After alternately cursing and crying for the past four days, not to mention working fifteen-hour days at the lab, Claire had come to the block party determined to talk to Duncan. She refused to believe Annabelle. Considering the last few weeks, Claire couldn't believe that she had been stupid enough to entertain Annabelle's lies for a second, let alone for four days.

In fact, Claire blamed herself for immediately accepting Annabelle's outlandish lies. It was her own insecurities. A part of her still felt eleven years old and could not believe that Duncan wanted her. But Duncan did want her. The smile on his face when he saw her just now proved it. And if that smile hadn't been enough, there had been the kiss filled with longing that he had greeted her with. No one could fake something like that. The more she thought about the whole ridiculous story, the angrier she became at herself and Annabelle. She had allowed Annabelle and her own insecurities to keep her from Duncan for three days.

"Is that your dad's barbecue station?" Claire asked, relaxing her hand in Duncan's warm, familiar grip as she looked across the street to where Vincent stood with a red and white apron before a smoking grill. "Let's go over there. I never did get to his taste tasting—"

"Later," Duncan said hastily. "I want you to meet the guys first."

Claire stared at him, his anxiousness for her to meet his friends sending a small sliver of doubt through her heart. But she took a deep breath and forced herself to keep pace with his long stride. He wound his way through the crowd and group of picnic tables until they came to a group of men holding beer bottles and looking like the arrogant, obnoxious jerks that they all had been in high school. Claire instantly recognized all of them. The supposed kings of their high school class. The men who had tormented her, Annabelle, and their friends. Even fourteen years later, with potbellies, balding heads, and jowls, the men looked at Claire as if she should be grateful to be in their presence. These men were the reason Claire had avoided previous block parties.

Claire immediately stiffened under their openly appraising looks. She hadn't even felt this disgusted under Henri's reptilian gaze. Then Claire's gaze moved to Patrick. He nodded awkwardly at her before he quickly looked at his beer bottle, almost as if he was too ashamed to look at her. She got the same strange reaction from Hawk, who stood next to Patrick.

Claire's stomach dropped like a lead ball, and the euphoria she had been feeling at being outside on a beautiful day with Duncan disappeared. In that moment, she knew everything that Annabelle told her had been true. Duncan had been using her. She was nothing but a bet.

Her throat clogged as she realized that every man—every jerk from high school whom she had at one time or another insulted with a creativity that would have made Einstein jealous—was now laughing at her. Waiting to see her act like a fool.

Claire squared her shoulders and gritted her teeth. She didn't plan to make the jerks wait any longer. After Duncan introduced her to the men, she decided it was time to help him win his precious bet.

Claire turned to Duncan and said, in a sweet tone that was a cross between that of a porn star and that of a kindergarten teacher, "Have you eaten yet, sweetheart? Would you like for me to fix you a plate?"

Duncan stared at her, surprised, whether because of her offer to get him a plate or her tone, she didn't know. "I'll just go with you," he said, staring at her closely.

"I'd be happy to do it. I want to please you," she said, keeping her eyes wide and blank. Duncan sent her a weird expression, then glanced around at the other men, who were broadly grinning at him.

"I've never had a woman say that to me, man," one man said with a leer in Claire's direction. "How'd you manage to do that?"

Claire remembered him as the boy who had tripped her in the cafeteria on her second day of high school, which had sent her lunch flying and made her land flat on her face. Lionel Edmunds.

"Yeah, man, don't pass up a free thing, especially when it comes in that package," another guy chimed in, the same guy Claire remembered pushing her against a locker and stealing her brown-bag lunch the second week of high school. The man took Claire's stare as some expression of interest and ran his tongue over his top lip in an apparent attempt to be sexy. "Who would have thought that Medusa would turn out like this?"

Claire resisted a sarcastic retort and instead turned back to Duncan, who was looking more and more worried.

"Just tell me what you want, Duncan. Anything. It's yours," she said.

"Thanks, Claire," he said hesitantly. "But I'm good right now."

"Do you want something to drink?" she asked eagerly.

Duncan stared at her for a moment before he said, with his own forced smile, "No, I don't want anything. Why don't we go say hi to my parents? They've been waiting for you—"

She frowned, pretending concern, and moved closer to him. She said in a pleading voice, "You look tired, honey. I bet you've been on your feet all day, helping set up for this block party. How about I give you a nice foot massage? I can kneel down right here and do it."

She ignored the burst of laughter from some of the assembled men while others began to mumble and stare at her like she was some crazed domestic robot. Her gaze remained fixed on Duncan, who suddenly looked annoyed.

"I can think of some other things you can do while you're

on your knees, baby," Lionel said, causing more laughter from everyone but Duncan, Hawk, and Patrick.

His expression murderous, Duncan glared at the offender, and the laughter instantly stopped. "Watch your mouth," Duncan warned in a low, dangerous voice.

Claire pretended that none of that had happened and said, businesslike, "You're being shy in front of your friends, but I know how much you like my foot massages. There's no reason to deprive yourself just because a few of your friends are here."

She began to kneel in front of him on the street. The men began to cackle again, drawing looks from people around them.

"Claire," Patrick said worriedly, stepping toward her.

"Shut up, you morons," Hawk snapped, glaring at the other men, who continued to snicker.

Duncan grabbed Claire's arms before she could get on her knees. Confusion and anger warred in his eyes as he demanded, "What the hell is wrong with you?"

Claire allowed her hatred to shine through as she yanked her hand from Duncan's grip. The entire block suddenly became still as everyone saw the struggle and turned to them. Claire looked at Hawk and Patrick and said tonelessly, "Duncan won the bet. I'm in love with him."

She started to walk away, but then she turned to Lionel Edmonds and said coolly, "I would sit here and insult you with a bunch of big words you wouldn't understand, but I don't have to do that. The knowledge that high school was and forever will be the brightest spot in your pathetic life is all the revenge I need."

He sputtered in reply, but she brushed past him. Duncan called after her, but Claire continued walking, ignoring her sister's concerned gaze from across the street, her father's watchful stare, and Duncan's parents and brothers. They all had seen everything. They all now knew that she was a fool, that she had fallen in love with Duncan Hillston when she had been nothing but a bet to him.

By the time Claire reached the barriers blocking the

street to car traffic, she had broken into a full-out run. Then the tears started. The faces she passed of people walking toward the block party blurred into one blob until eventually she was far from the center of the party and the only one on the street. She sighed in relief when she realized belatedly that she had been running to Joan's house, where she had parked her car earlier.

Claire tried to insert the key in the car door, but her hands were shaking too badly. Suddenly she felt familiar hands on her arms, holding her tight. Claire allowed herself one moment of weakness to sink into his touch before she whirled around to face him. Regret and guilt ravaged his features. Her heart broke a little more.

He began brokenly, "Claire, let me explain—"

"You won your stupid bet. You don't need me anymore," she snarled, then tried to pull her arms from his iron grip, but he held on. "Get your hands off of me."

"You're wrong, Claire. I still need you. I love you—"

"I don't want to hear it," she screeched, horrified that tears continued falling in streams down her face.

He still clung to her, his expression pleading as he said urgently, "Please listen to me. It started as a bet; I won't lie about that. But after getting to know you, I fell in love with you. You are the most amazing person I've ever known—"

"You don't even know what love is," she interrupted. "You're a parasite and a liar. You use women and their emotions to make yourself feel better. You're pathetic, and you make me sick."

"That's all true, Claire," he admitted softly. "I was all of those things before I met you, but I changed. You made me change. Everything between us was real; it is real. I wasn't lying when I kissed you, when I made love to you, when I told you that I had never felt this way before in my life. Please believe me, Claire. You have to."

She rolled her eyes, laughing bitterly. "You deserved to win that bet, Duncan. I didn't suspect anything. All of your compliments and persistence. The 'you're so special, Claire.' The 'you're amazing, Claire.' The 'I love you, Claire.' . . . I told you things that I've never told anyone in my life, not even Joan. I made love to you—" She had to stop talking as a hiccup of tears threatened to overtake her. She tried to pull from his grip once more, but he still refused to release her. His expression was tortured as he searched her face. She turned from him and said in a broken whisper, "I can't stand to look at you."

Duncan stepped closer to her, trapping her in between the car and his muscled body. She defiantly met his gaze, refusing to give in to her body's desire to melt into him. To forgive him.

"Nothing I told you was a lie, Claire," he insisted, his fingers digging into her arms. "I love—"

"Don't even say it," she choked out, squeezing her eyes shut to avoid his tortured expression.

"I do, Claire," he said. "I love you. No one can fake what we have. I did approach you at Zanzibar's because of the bet, and I did ask you out because of the bet, but . . . that's all the bet did. Everything else: dinner at my parents' house, the phone calls, the conversations, making love—" She abruptly began to struggle to get away from him as every memory of their lovemaking rushed back like a bad nightmare . . . his mouth on hers, his tongue snaking into her, sliding across her body. It all flashed in her mind in full color, over and over again. Her uninhibited responses stuck out in her mind. She had never been uninhibited before, not in bed, in the lab, or in life.

And, worst of all, there was nothing special about her. She may have been smart, but just like every other woman, she had fallen for the first pretty face to show her any attention. She had been perfect for his bet. A lonely, repressed scientist. She couldn't have made it any easier for him.

Duncan continued, his voice shaking with an emotion she refused to identify, "I should have told you about the bet, but I knew you wouldn't believe that it meant nothing to me. And I knew I would lose you, and I was so damn scared of losing you. I've been looking for you my whole life, without knowing what I was looking for. Don't give up on us, Claire. Don't throw this away. I want a lifetime with you. I want the mortgage, the kids, and, God help me, even the minivan—"

"Stop it," she whispered, her voice breaking. Her white-hot anger had been replaced by a sadness so dense that she almost couldn't breathe. She had tried to be normal, she had tried to believe that she could lead a normal life, and she had been slapped in the face. She hung her head as the tears silently fell. She shook her head. She said weakly, "I can't take this anymore, Duncan. Please let me go."

Duncan slowly released her but didn't give her any space. Claire turned her back to him and fought through her tears to insert the key into the car door. She swung open the door and stumbled over her heels as she tried to sit in the car.

"You're in no condition to drive," he said softly, his breath an unwanted caress on her cheek. "I'll leave, but don't drive like this. Go inside your sister's house. OK?"

Claire refused to look at him, but she realized that he was right. She wouldn't be able to stop crying long enough to make it down the street without crashing into something. She felt his stare on her back, and she finally nodded in response.

"I am sorry, Claire," Duncan said.

She clenched her teeth in anger and forced herself to look at him. An almost debilitating jab of pain stabbed her in the stomach as she met his eyes, which shone with suspicious moisture, as if he was crying. She refused to believe anything about him anymore.

"You are sorry, Duncan," she agreed, disgusted.

Duncan held her gaze for a moment; then he turned and walked down the street, back toward the block party.

Claire sagged against her car and tried to remember to breathe. She had done just fine on her own, without Duncan, and she would do just fine now. Or she would be just fine once her heart stopped breaking.

Chapter Twenty-Six

Two weeks later

"What do you think of the drywall? Should we subcontract it out or can we handle it?" Alex looked at his brothers around the conference table. Duncan noted that Alex's gaze lingered on him longer than the others'. Duncan ignored Alex and pretended to study the plans taped to the board in front of the one-room office at Hillston Brothers Construction.

Soon the lines on the drawing all melded together, and Duncan gave up. He couldn't concentrate. He hadn't been able to concentrate on anything in the last two weeks. He had left numerous messages for Claire—on her home phone, her cell phone, even her work phone. Not one word from her in return. Not even a sign that she wanted him to stop calling, or a return message to tell him that he was an SOB who deserved to rot in hell. Nothing.

Duncan's brothers, one-by-one, had tried to get him to talk about it. Hawk and Patrick had tried to get him to talk about it. Even his mother had dropped by his house the other day on the pretense of bringing an apple pie, and she had tried to get him to talk about it. But there was nothing Duncan could say. He deserved all of Claire's hatred. Maybe it was punishment for his past sins, for being such an unremorseful jerk to women for so many years. He would be punished for not respecting love all of these years by losing the only woman he had ever loved.

Duncan suddenly realized that no one in the office was speaking, and he looked around the table and saw that all of his brothers were staring at him. The same concern and frustration in their eyes that had been there since Duncan had returned to the block party two weeks ago, his face red and his hands clenched into fists, was now present. At Duncan's glare, they each pretended to be suddenly engrossed in the plans on the board.

"I vote we contract it out," Tavis said to Alex, turning the conversation back to the matter at hand, as if there hadn't been a pause.

"I agree," Kobie said quickly.

"Duncan?" Alex said uncertainly.

"What Tavis said," Duncan mumbled, having no idea what Tavis said.

"We contract it out then," Alex said, nodding. He closed the pad of paper that contained the list of topics for the meeting. Duncan couldn't have told anyone what was on the list if his life depended on it, even though they had spent the last hour going through it.

"How about lunch at Nate's?" Kobie asked with obvious feigned cheerfulness.

"Sounds good," Tavis said, then nudged Duncan in the arm. "Doesn't that sound good? I'll even pay."

"That's so generous of you, Tavis, considering it's your turn to pay," Kobie said drily.

Tavis laughed, but his laugh sounded hollow as he studied Duncan. He abruptly stood and forced himself to look at his brothers before he said, "I'm going to stick around here and finish some of the invoices, so you guys won't be buried while I'm gone. You guys go ahead."

Duncan knew he must have been pathetic because his brothers, Patrick, and Hawk had all chipped in to pay for Duncan to take his European vacation—not using one cent of the Bachelor Party Fund. Duncan had had to feign excitement when Alex presented him with his ticket and itinerary last week. He didn't want to go, but if he had said that, he would have had to explain why.

"Are you sure?" Kobie asked uncertainly. "It's your last chance to eat at Nate's before you leave tonight for London."

"I'm sure," Duncan said as he walked across the room to sit at his desk near the back window.

There was a long silence before Alex said, "You two go ahead. I'm not that hungry, either. You know Kathleen has me on that low-cholesterol diet. I may as well not even eat, considering what I'm allowed to have."

Kobie and Tavis laughed obligingly, then walked out of the office, leaving Duncan alone with his worst fear: Alex. Duncan focused on the computer screen and ignored his brother, who openly stared at him. Duncan knew that Alex could break him down and make him talk, but Duncan didn't want to talk. He couldn't talk. He felt too numb, too cold. He hadn't realized how much warmth Claire had brought into his life until it was gone.

"Are you ready for your trip?" Alex asked casually as he walked across the large room to rest a hip on Duncan's desk.

"Almost," Duncan lied, his gaze still on the computer screen. Duncan left for London on the red-eye that night, and he hadn't even pulled his suitcases from the garage.

"Do you need any help?"

"No, thanks, I have everything under control—"

"You're really starting to piss me off," Alex said abruptly. Duncan stared at his brother, surprised by the anger in Alex's expression. "For the first time in your life, you've run across a bump in a relationship. . . . Hell, for the first time in your life, you had a relationship. . . . And because you've run into this bump in the road, you're ready to throw it all away."

"I think it's considered more than a little bump when the woman you love hates you," Duncan said irritably. "She won't talk to me. She won't return my phone calls. And, to be honest, I don't blame her. I was an asshole."

"You've always been an asshole," Alex said flatly. When Duncan glared at him, he shrugged and added, "That never stopped you before."

"She'll never forgive me." The brief spurt of anger left Duncan tired, and he began to rub his forehead as one of his now-frequent migraines began to pound at his temples. "She thinks that everything I told her was a lie to win the bet. She doesn't believe that I love her. It's over, Alex."

"Don't let it be over."

"What more can I do?" Duncan asked with a frustrated sigh. "I've sent her roses almost every day. I've sent her chocolate. I've sent her diamond earrings—"

"Duncan, you're still doing it," Alex said with a short dry laugh. "You're still playing the role that you think you're supposed to play. Roses and chocolate, Duncan? Come on. Claire doesn't strike me as the roses and chocolate type."

"Well, what else am I supposed to do?" Duncan demanded desperately.

"Go see her. Tell her everything that's in your heart and is so visible on your face every time I look at you."

"It won't work," Duncan said softly.

"I won't say that I understand why you and Hawk would make a bet like that, but you're not a bad person, Duncan. You're just a very stupid one—"

"Thanks, Alex," he muttered sarcastically.

Alex laughed, then said seriously, "I just mean stop punishing yourself. Talk to her. She's a smart girl; she'll see the truth. And before you know it, you and I will be making midnight diaper runs together."

"I can't," he said with a burst of anger. When Alex stared at him for explanation, Duncan sighed, then said quietly, "I want her to have the opportunity to decide for herself, with all the cards laid on the table. Something I didn't give her the chance to do before."

Duncan tried to smile when Alex looked pained, but thankfully his attempt was cut short by the sound of the office door opening. Duncan swiveled his chair around and froze as Al and Kira walked into the office. Duncan instantly got to his feet. He had wondered what would happen upon his first encounter with Al after the block party. The neighborhood was small, and the story about the bet had circulated around the party before Duncan had returned from his confrontation with Claire. He knew Al knew, but so far Duncan hadn't seen Al until that moment.

Duncan forced a smile and waved at Kira, who excitedly waved back. He figured that Al wouldn't kill him in front of his granddaughter. At least, Duncan hoped Al wouldn't.

Since Duncan was frozen in silence, Alex stepped forward and said, "Mr. Scott, how are you?" Al nodded at Alex and shook his offered hand; then Alex smiled at Kira.

A heavy silence followed Alex's cheerful greeting until he said abruptly, "I'll join Kobie and Tavis at Nate's."

Alex sent Duncan an encouraging look, then walked out of the office, leaving him alone with Al. Not entirely alone, since Kira, at least, looked happy to see him.

"Duncan," Kira said excitedly, running toward him.

Duncan stepped around his desk and his smile became genuine as she threw her arms around him. He bent on one knee to hug her in return. His heart squeezed as he stared into her dark gaze, which reminded him so much of Claire. Duncan glanced at Al, then swallowed the thick lump in his throat. This visit was obviously not Al's idea.

"Where have you been, Duncan?" Kira asked, finally releasing her death grip on his neck.

"I've been busy," he said lamely, then asked, "How are you, kiddo?"

"I'm very excited," she replied. She practically danced as she tugged on his shirtsleeve. "Guess what? Ben Osbourne is not going to the regional championship in Glendale tonight. He came down with the chicken pox. The school called and asked if I would be willing to go, even though I haven't had the opportunity to prepare. I said, 'Of course.'"

"Really? That's terrific, Kira!"

"And I would like for you to attend," she said as she handed him a brightly colored flyer with information about the spelling bee on it.

Duncan glanced uncertainly at Al, whose stony expression had not changed since he walked through the door. Duncan returned his gaze to Kira, who stared at him with her huge brown eyes.

"You have to come, Duncan," she pleaded, grabbing his arm. "I don't believe in superstition or other paranormal happenings, but . . . I must have the same people in attendance at the Glendale spelling bee that were at school."

Duncan glanced at the flyer once more. He could squeeze in the spelling bee before his flight if he had his suitcases in the car before he drove to Alex's. But Claire would be there, and she had made it pretty obvious that she wanted nothing to do with him. Not to mention Joan and Elgin, who would have the same reaction as Al. Duncan could tell from Al's narrowed gaze that Duncan was *persona non grata* in the Scott clan. Still, he would dare any one of the Scotts to look at Kira and tell her no.

"I'll try to make it," Duncan finally said, forcing a smile.

Kira didn't budge as she pressed, "You will *try*? Or you will make it?"

Duncan grinned and said, "I'll be there, Kira."

Kira hugged him once more, then ran back to Al, who had remained by the door. Duncan stood to his full height and said stiffly, "How are you, Mr. Scott?"

Al visibly clenched his jaw before he said, "Disappointed."

Duncan held the older man's gaze for a moment before he averted his gaze, unable to look at him.

"What are you disappointed about, Grandpa?" Kira asked, perplexed.

"We should leave Duncan to his work," Al said to Kira, sounding more animated than Duncan had ever heard him. It was obvious that granddaughter and grandfather shared a special bond. Another knife stabbed in Duncan's heart. He would have liked the chance to know the Al Scott Kira knew.

"I'll see you tonight, Duncan," Kira called before she pushed open the door and walked out of the office. Al just left.

Duncan sat back in his chair and stared at the flyer.

Duncan wiped his sweaty palms on his khakis, then pulled open the door and walked into the cool auditorium. He glanced around the large room, surprised by the number of people and the TV cameras in attendance for a spelling bee. Duncan couldn't help but relax. He would never find Claire or her family in this throng. He could sit in the back, watch Kira, and then slip out before anyone noticed. Duncan's best-laid plans were ruined when he headed for one of the few empty seats in the auditorium and walked straight into Elgin's large frame. The two men looked at each other and for a moment Duncan thought that Elgin would hit him.

Then Elgin frowned and muttered, "You may as well sit with us." He didn't give Duncan a chance to protest but stalked off toward the front of the auditorium.

Duncan longingly looked at the empty seat he had been heading for, which was now filled, then followed Elgin to the second row from the front. Joan looked up, smiling at Elgin. He wordlessly pointed to Duncan, and when she saw him, Joan's smile immediately disappeared. Her expression turned to ice. Duncan offered her a smile, but she just glared at him before she nudged Claire. Duncan inwardly cursed, because he could tell immediately from the shocked expression on Claire's face that she hadn't known he was coming.

Duncan knew that he should have felt guilty and walked out of the auditorium, but he hadn't seen her in two weeks and, like an addict, was drinking in the sight of her. She looked tired. Dark circles under her eyes and unyielding lines around her mouth showed him that. He hoped it wasn't because of him, but because the preclinical trials were going as planned.

Even with the hostility directed at him from Joan, Claire, and Elgin, Duncan couldn't think about anything but taking Claire in his arms. Who was he kidding with this stupid trip? He could travel to Mars and back, and he still wouldn't be over her.

"Kira invited him," Al said from his seat next to Claire.

Claire, Joan, and Elgin stared at Al, surprised. He motioned for Duncan to sit in the empty seat next to him, and Duncan complied. His legs brushed against Claire's as he passed her, and she flinched as if she had been shocked. Duncan lowered himself into the chair next to Al and was surprised when Al nodded at him. Duncan would have never thought that Al would be his inside man in the Scott camp.

The spelling bee passed in a blur. Kira survived until the sixth round and then was eliminated. As usual, Elgin was upset, while Kira skipped off the stage to sit on her father's lap. After that, Duncan could only think about Claire. Every time she shifted in the chair, Duncan noticed. When she leaned over to talk to her father, Duncan noticed. He thought he could almost detect a scent of her sweet-smelling soap in the air. Duncan was half-hard, the exact opposite reaction he wanted to have with Al sitting in between them, but it was a reaction he couldn't control around Claire.

An hour later, the proctor gratefully signaled for an intermission before the final rounds. Without one glance in Duncan's direction, Claire jumped to her feet and was outside the auditorium before even the back row had emptied. Elgin and Joan took Kira to the snack bar in the lobby while Duncan tried to think of something to say to the man he had once hoped would be his father-in-law.

"Go talk to her," Al ordered Duncan.

Duncan stared at the older man, surprised, then said, "I've tried, but she doesn't want to—"

Al glared at Duncan, effectively interrupting his excuses. "Claire has loved you since she was eleven years old. I knew you weren't ready then, which was why I never did anything to push you two together, but now . . . now, I thought maybe you were finally worthy of her love. Was I wrong?"

"No, sir," Duncan said instantly.

Al actually smiled as he added, "Besides, you're growing on me. I don't want to have to kill you like I promised, so go make this right."

Duncan didn't need to be told twice. He immediately stood and wove his way through the crowd to exit the auditorium.

He scanned the lobby but didn't see any sign of Claire. He walked outside the stuffy lobby and inhaled the cool night air. He needed to think. If Al still thought that Duncan stood a chance, maybe he did. Then he saw her. She stood apart from the crowd at the bottom of the steps that led from the sidewalk to the front doors, staring at the sky.

For the first time, he noticed that she wasn't wearing a suit. She looked soft and beautiful in worn jeans and a T-shirt, and she looked like she would never be his.

Duncan took a deep breath and walked to her side. "Hi, Claire," he said quietly.

She flinched at the sound of his voice, then turned to face him. Her expression was colder than ice as she said, "Duncan."

"I'm leaving tomorrow for London," he said. "I'm going on a fourteen-day tour of Europe."

"You did win the bet. You deserved the trip," she said with a shrug.

Duncan grimaced and said with a dry laugh, "Direct hit." Her mouth tightened and she continued to stare at him, as if he were just a stranger who had come to bother her. He said quietly, "This trip is not because I won the bet, Claire—"

"You're under the mistaken impression that I care," she said in that same cool tone that was driving him insane. He wanted to take her in his arms and slam his mouth over hers, but she wasn't showing any sign of emotion, any of the anger and tears that she had on the day of the block party. Duncan felt even more hopeless.

He said quietly, "You're not sleeping."

Her voice was sharp as she told him, "That's not your concern."

He moved closer to her, his gaze intent on her frozen face. "You're my concern, baby."

"You can stop the charade, Duncan; you won the bet. No more reason to pretend," she said stiffly.

Duncan refused to be swayed from saying everything he had to say, now that he had her in front of him. He stepped closer to her until she was forced to look at him. "I will be sorry that I hurt you for the rest of my life. I don't ever want to be responsible for the look that was in your eyes that day at the block party."

"The competition is about to start," she said.

Duncan continued before she could walk away, "I never should have taken the bet, but I did. I regret that I didn't tell you the truth, but I don't regret taking that bet. If I had never taken that stupid bet, I never would have spoken to you that night, and I never would have fallen in love with you. You make my life richer, Claire. You make me want to go back to high school to start over.

"I would talk to you then, cherish you, and believe in you as much as you believed in me. We would have gotten married, and I'd have followed you to Harvard and then MIT. And then we'd have moved back to Westfield, and you would have gone to BioTech and I would have gone to work with my brothers. And I'd be just like my brothers, in love with a woman I had known since puberty, with three or four kids and a minivan. And I'd be so happy that I'd know exactly what it means when someone complains about bills, diapers, and minivans and then says, with a genuine smile, 'It's just another day in paradise.' "

The nerve at her right eye twitched slightly, but otherwise she didn't move. She didn't speak, either, but Duncan found some hope in the fact that she didn't leave.

Duncan smiled softly and said, "I'm not giving up on us, Claire. You can ignore me, but I'll be here. You waited for fourteen years for me to see that we were right for each other. Maybe now it's my turn."

Duncan saw the tears in her eyes before she abruptly turned from him and walked up the stairs to the auditorium. Duncan stuffed his hands into his pockets and walked to his car.

Chapter Twenty-Seven

Three days later, Claire flinched as the telephone on the wall of the lab rang. Her heart skipped a small beat as she instantly thought of Duncan. He had sent her an e-mail that morning from London, telling her about London, acting as if she cared that the gold of the crown jewels reminded him of her eyes when she was on the verge of climaxing. His two-page-long e-mail had been a love letter that would have made a lesser woman tear up, but not Dr. Claire Scott.

Claire had immediately deleted it and then allowed herself to move the e-mail from the "trash" icon to the "saved items" icon, where it sat with the other e-mails that he had sent last night telling her about the people on his trip and how he wished that she were there with him. She told herself that she could always delete the e-mails later. What she was going to do with the pound of British coffee that had arrived at her doorstep that morning was another story. A sane woman did not throw out imported coffee.

Claire glanced at the phone and sighed in relief at the green light blinking on the console, indicating that it was an inside call. She looked at the clock hanging above her office door and was surprised that it was almost ten o'clock at night. She had arrived at the lab at six o'clock that morning, as she had done for the past three weeks, and she hadn't looked at the clock since. She hadn't spoken to anyone, either, including Vino, who had learned to give her a wide berth. In fact, no one in her lab spoke to Claire anymore. What was once a collegial and relaxed environment had become tense and claustrophobic, as if everyone was waiting for Claire's next outburst. It was not the atmosphere that Claire wanted when all of the team's hard work was reaching a crucial point, but she couldn't help herself. She wasn't a good actor . . . like some people.

"Dr. Scott," she answered the phone dully.

"Dr. Scott, your sister is here," said the regular security guard, Harry. "Should I escort her to the lab?"

Claire inwardly groaned. She had done a good job of avoiding Joan. Claire always made certain that Kira was nearby or that Joan would be too busy to talk. Now, apparently, Joan refused to be ignored anymore.

"Yes, that's fine," Claire responded, then hung up.

She hurried into her office to attempt to look presentable. Cleanliness had been the first thing to go in her quest to throw herself back into her work. Claire found a brush in a desk drawer and ran the bristles through her tangled hair, which she hadn't bothered to put in a ponytail in days. The brush tangled in her locks, and she managed to yank it out. A trip to the beauty salon had also been pushed to the bottom of her to-do list in the last few days.

She threw the brush back into the drawer, then wiped her face with a damp cleansing tissue before she applied a brief coat of lipstick. She glanced at her reflection in her compact mirror and sighed. Didn't help.

"Claire," Joan called as she walked into the lab.

Claire forced a smile and walked out of her office. Joan held up a casserole dish covered with aluminum foil, and a paper bag.

"Dinner," Claire said with an attempt at enthusiasm. "Over here."

Joan set the items on the empty counter space that Claire indicated, then hugged her. Claire bit her bottom lip, surprised by the rush of tears. But the unbidden thought circled her head that no one had hugged her, besides Kira, since Duncan. Claire had lived most of her life never fully realizing the joys of touching until Duncan. Now she felt like a plant without water, without his caresses and kisses.

"Are you all right?" Joan asked worriedly, finally releasing Claire and staring at her rumpled jeans and wrinkled shirt. Claire had given up on the suits around the same time she gave up on her hair. She blamed it on the preclinical trials, regardless of Vino's dubious looks. But, frankly, Claire didn't think she needed the suits to look older anymore. The haggard, weathered look on her face did that just fine.

"Of course I am," Claire said, forcing herself to sound cheerful. She sniffed the air and then hurried to the casserole dish, mostly to avoid Joan's inquisitive stare. "If I didn't know better, I would think that my most favorite sister in the whole world brought me veal piccata."

"And salad, homemade rolls, and a slice of lemon Bundt cake."

Claire eagerly pulled the items out of the paper bag, along with two plastic plates and plastic silverware. "You are a goddess among women, Joan." Claire began to scoop large portions of veal piccata onto a paper plate and said, "I have two sodas in the mini-refrigerator in my office."

Joan disappeared into Claire's office, then returned with the cans. Claire prepared two plates, then set them on the counter. She pulled up two stools, then greedily dug into the food, barely able to taste it because she was eating so fast, but throwing her all into the attempt to fool Joan that her heart was mending.

"This is delicious, Joan," Claire asked in between mouthfuls of veal piccata.

Joan ignored the compliment and said flatly, "You've been working a lot, Claire."

"I told you that this is a busy time for us—"

"You come into the lab before the sun rises, and you don't leave until eleven or twelve at night."

"I'm setting a good example for the team—"

"Claire, you have to talk to him," Joan said quietly.

"Who?" Claire asked while praying that Joan would not answer.

"Duncan," she replied with a frustrated groan. "You can't just pretend that he doesn't exist."

"Actually, I can," Claire responded stiffly, pushing the half-full plate away from her because her appetite had fled, as it always did when she thought of Duncan. She had probably lost ten pounds in the last three weeks. If she kept getting her heart broken, she would be down to her dream size 6 within the next month. At least that was one benefit. Now if only she could turn her depression into an exercise craze, she could be ready for the next LA Marathon.

Joan whispered, "You love him, Claire. I finally saw that at Kira's spelling bee. You really love him, and he loves you."

"I don't want to have this conversation," she snapped, unable to hold back her anger as she glared at Joan.

Joan pressed, "I'm worried about you."

"Don't. I'm fine."

"No, you're not," Joan protested, an edge in her voice. "I went to your house last night because I was hoping to catch you at home. You weren't there, but I saw the state of your house. You haven't cleaned in there in weeks. It should be condemned."

"I've been busy," Claire said defensively. "I'm trying to find a cure for cancer. Cleaning the house is a little low on the priority list right now."

"Claire, your research could take years, maybe a lifetime, before it's complete. You always tell me that," Joan said, exasperated. "We both know this isn't about your research. You fell in love and you got hurt, but that doesn't have to be the final chapter."

"I have a life, and I'm sick of you interfering in it," Claire exploded, jumping from the chair. "I'm not three years old anymore, Joan. I don't need your help. If I want to have a messy house, not comb my hair, and not change my clothes, that's my business."

Claire's ragged breathing filled the lab as Joan stared at her, a mixture of guilt and anger playing across her face. Then Joan clenched her jaw and began to slowly tidy the

Tupperware, ignoring Claire. She groaned and raked her hands through her hair.

"I'm sorry," Claire said softly, touching Joan's arm.

Joan sat still for a moment, as if gathering her patience, then said stiffly, "You've never seemed to understand this, Claire, but when you hurt, I hurt. If you can't sleep, I can't sleep. If you don't eat, I don't eat. We're a team. You and me."

"I know, Joan. I do know," Claire said sincerely. Joan sent her a gentle smile before she squeezed Claire's hand. Tears filled Claire's eyes, and she instantly moved from Joan's touch, then took several deep breaths to hold back the flood. "Look, I tried, but I belong in a lab. Things make sense in here."

"Nothing in here makes sense, Claire; nothing out there makes sense. We all just do the best we can. If you love him, forget about what makes sense and what doesn't and just love him."

"I can't," she said, shaking her head. "He made a fool of me. He lied—"

"He did lie. He took part in a stupid high school prank, and you should give him hell for it. But I refuse to believe that he lied about loving you. I saw the way he looked at you at Kira's spelling bee. He couldn't fake that, and you know it. Even Dad knows it. Somewhere deep down inside of all that wounded pride and insecurity, you know it."

"Thanks for dinner, Joan, but I should get back to work," Claire said abruptly.

Joan hugged Claire once more, hanging on a second longer as she kissed her cheek. Joan whispered in her ear, "He's not Mom, Claire, and you're not Dad. You've always taken chances inside the lab. If you never had, you wouldn't be this close to a cure for ovarian cancer. Now try taking one of those chances outside the lab this time."

Claire didn't respond but held her sister tighter.

Chapter Twenty-Eight

Five days after Duncan had landed in London, it was official—his European vacation was a bust. When Duncan had first learned about the tour, he had feared that the other twenty people on the tour would be senior citizens. When Duncan first had stepped onto the tour bus at Heathrow Airport, he thought he had accidentally stumbled onto the *Sports Illustrated* swimsuit model bus. Every one of his tour mates had been young, single, and beautiful. The women had come in all shapes, colors, and sizes and were all ready for a good time. Apparently, Duncan had been the last person to snag the spot on the tour with the sisters of Delta Pi Gamma from the University of Arizona. Duncan didn't even tell his brothers or Patrick or Hawk about his "good fortune," because none of the women were Claire, so it didn't matter.

Since Duncan was the only man the sorority sisters saw for hours at a time during their long bus rides across Europe, he had dealt with his fair share of come-ons and more-than-harmless flirtations. But Duncan had inevitably driven each and every one of the women away because he couldn't help but start talking about Claire. Most of the group now avoided him like the plague, while the rest of the women would huddle around him and encourage him to explore his feelings, which Duncan gladly did.

And instead of acting on the curious and bold women he had encountered in London, where African-American men were few and far between, and then during their three-day trip in Ireland, where African-American men were even fewer and farther between, Duncan spent most of his free time scouring the foreign streets for exotic coffees and Internet cafés where he would sit for hours composing e-mails to Claire. He didn't know if she even read his e-mails. She could have blocked all mail from his account and he would never know the difference, but Duncan still sent the e-mails. Long, mushy e-mails that Hawk would laugh at but that Patrick would sympathize with. Sometimes Duncan would just tell her about what the tour group had done that day or about the coffee he had found for her, but mostly he wrote about how much he missed her and how much he loved her.

Everything reminded Duncan of Claire. The lilt of an Irish accent because he thought of Irish coffee, which made him think of Claire. London rain because he thought of umbrellas and he had seen an umbrella stand at Claire's house. . . . Duncan had now become his worst nightmare—Patrick.

Now Duncan stood in front of the massive Eiffel Tower and while tourists around him giggled and laughed and took pictures of one of the enduring symbols of Europe, Duncan just thought of Claire. He was going to spare everyone— himself, Delta Pi Gamma, and the Europeans—any further misery and take the next flight home.

Duncan wiped at the sweat on his brow from the oppressive August heat and stared at the towering iron structure. It was impressive, but he could have been looking at the Watts Tower back home for all he cared.

"Studies have shown that more pictures are taken in front of the Eiffel Tower than any other landmark in Paris," came a familiar sweet voice behind him.

Duncan didn't want to believe it. He had dreamed about her so much, imagined her so much, and talked about her so much, that he could almost believe that he had made her up. Then he felt her. That feel in the air whenever she was around. He couldn't imagine that.

Duncan slowly turned and stared into the most beautiful face he had ever seen in his life. Claire stood in front of him, with a small smile playing at her mouth that left *Mona Lisa* in the dust.

"Claire," he gasped in disbelief.

"*Bonjour,*" she greeted him in French, then smiled. When Duncan continued to just stare at her open mouth, her smile faltered and she said haltingly, "Nate gave me your itinerary, and I took the red-eye last night. A group of women who were waiting at the front desk of your hotel heard me asking the front desk about you and they started yelling my name as if they knew me. They told me that you were here."

Duncan laughed, his first laugh in a long time, then wrapped his arms around her. She felt real. He grabbed a handful of her loose hair and inhaled the soft strands. She smelled real. He released the air trapped in his lungs and hugged her to him. He picked her off the ground and spun around in a circle, not caring that they now looked like some cheesy commercial made by the Parisian tourism bureau.

Duncan finally set her down and framed her warm face with his hands. She tried to speak, but he hugged her to him again and buried his face in the crook of her neck. He inhaled her familiar scent, felt her familiar curves against him, and wondered why he had ever made fun of his brothers for wanting exactly this. And—please let it not be true—but were those tears in his eyes? Her laughter rang in his ears, the most beautiful song he had ever heard.

"I missed you so much," he whispered, finally able to speak.

"I know. You told me that in the twenty-one e-mails you sent me," she said, laughing.

"It's actually twenty-two. I sent the last one three hours ago, when you must have been flying here," he said matter-of-factly, then released her just a fraction so he could look at her. He rapidly blinked back the unmanly tears, and if she noticed, she didn't comment. Another reason he loved this woman more than life. Even though he was a wuss, she still wanted him.

"Thanks for all the coffee," she said, smiling at him. He registered that she was speaking, but he could only smooth her hair from her face before lingering on the satin-soft feel of her cheek.

"You're real," he whispered, his smile fading. "You're really here."

She caressed his cheek before she said, "I'm really here, Duncan, and I don't care about any bet. I don't care why you spoke to me in Zanzibar's or who told you to; I'm just glad that you did. I love you."

His arms grew tighter around her, holding on, as the love she felt for him fused into his muscles and bones, relaxing the tension he had felt since that horrible day at the block party. "I'll never be able to express how sorry I am for making you think that I—"

She gently placed a hand over his mouth, then said softly, "I've been able to logically examine my reaction to this bet over the past few weeks, and I owe you an apology. You were wrong to not tell me the truth sooner, but I should have known that your love for me was not a bet. And I would have, if it wasn't for that insecure eleven-year-old that's still buried deep inside of me, who never truly believed that you would want me—Medusa, the geek. I should have trusted my instincts, instead of giving in to my innermost insecurities—"

"Enough psychoanalyzing for one day," Duncan said with a laugh. She laughed, too, and he felt like everything was right with the world. Now he knew why his brothers walked around with goofy smiles most of the time. A woman could do that to a man. "I don't care why you're here. I don't even care if you're planning to make me your sex toy for the rest of my life—although I should add that I have no aversion to your using me like that—I'm just glad that you're here."

She laughed, then pressed her mouth against his for a chaste, brief kiss that didn't nearly do justice to the fact that they were in one of the most romantic settings in the world. Duncan deepened the kiss, his tongue snaking into her mouth, soothing her tongue, branding her mouth as his because she was his.

"I love you, Claire," he said, finally giving her room to

breathe. "And even if you give me the rest of my life, I'll never be able to prove how much."

"You wanna bet?"

She laughed, her eyes twinkling with amusement and that indefinable emotion that some would have called intelligence, but Duncan just called it Claire. He held her tight and didn't let go for a long time.

Epilogue

Two Years Later

Claire heard the front door slam and stared down at the beautiful brown four-month-old baby in her arms. Joan Annabelle Hillston continued to sleep, obviously not disturbed by the commotion her father made as he clamored through their big old house in the heart of the Westfield neighborhood. Claire and Duncan had gotten married five months after they returned from Paris. Duncan, Patrick, and Hawk had finally had a legitimate reason to use the Bachelor Party Fund. The three had flown themselves, all of Duncan's brothers and his father, Elgin, and Al to Mexico for a four-day deep-sea fishing excursion. Hawk had voted for Las Vegas, but he had been outvoted. After the wedding, Claire and Duncan had settled in Westfield in one of the abandoned Victorian homes that Duncan and his brothers had restored to its original grandeur.

Duncan's loud steps thundered down the hallway, and Claire smiled at her still-sleeping baby. Joanie was probably used to noise, considering the large family that had greeted her birth with enough celebration in the hospital to scare some of the nurses. Claire had loved the idea of moving back to the old neighborhood. A trusted family member was, at the least, a block away—Al Scott—and, at the most, five blocks away—Nate and his family. Even Annabelle would volunteer to babysit when she visited, since she now had a reason to visit—Claire couldn't stay mad at a woman who had saved her life and Duncan's by providing a distraction in the hangar. And with Claire going through the clinical trials at the lab, she had needed all of the family.

In fact, Joan Annabelle had so many potential babysitters that Claire sometimes felt like she was the UN between warring factions, when all of Duncan's brothers, his parents, Big Joan, and Al got involved. Of course, there wasn't any real feuding. Each person just loved Joanie so much that they all wanted to spend time with her. As far as Claire was concerned, there were worse things in life than to have too many people loving her child.

Duncan walked into the nursery on the second floor of the house, and his face instantly transformed when he gazed upon their daughter. Claire fell in love with him a little more each day when she saw how he looked at Joanie, how much he loved her. Duncan's family had been right. He was a terrific dad, and he was already pressuring Claire for more children. Claire couldn't exactly call it pressure. All Duncan had to do was stroke her thigh or nuzzle her neck and she was all for whatever he wanted.

"Hi, beautiful," Duncan said softly while bending over to press a gentle kiss on Joanie's forehead. He looked at Claire and the heat that leaped in his eyes she knew matched her own. "Hi, beautiful," he repeated, but in an entirely different tone, before he kissed her.

Claire murmured in regret when he pulled from her too quickly. He waved a magazine around and said, "Guess what was waiting in the mailbox outside? *Newsweek*."

"The article," Claire said excitedly.

Duncan grinned at her and nodded. She stood and carefully transferred the still-sleeping Joanie into his waiting arms. Claire touched her baby's soft cheek for a moment, then took the magazine from Duncan as he cuddled Joanie close to his chest. He was one of those few men born to hold a child. Claire forced herself to stop staring at her most favorite sight, then stared at the cover of the national magazine.

She giggled, even though she had known for months that she and Vino would be on the cover. Claire and Vino had been photographed in their white lab coats, with their arms